# Crisis

# FELIX FRANCIS

## A DICK FRANCIS NOVEL

# Crisis

SIMON &
SCHUSTER

London · New York · Sydney · Toronto · New Delhi

A CBS COMPANY

First published in Great Britain by Simon & Schuster UK Ltd, 2018
A CBS COMPANY

1 3 5 7 9 10 8 6 4 2

Simon & Schuster UK Ltd
1st Floor
222 Gray's Inn Road
London WC1X 8HB

Simon & Schuster Australia, Sydney
Simon & Schuster India, New Delhi

www.simonandschuster.co.uk
www.simonandschuster.com.au
www.simonandschuster.co.in

A CIP catalogue record for this book
is available from the British Library

Hardback ISBN: 978-1-4711-7311-0
Trade Paperback ISBN: 978-1-4711-7312-7
eBook ISBN: 978-1-4711-7313-4

Typeset in Sabon by M Rules
Printed and bound by CPI Group (UK) Ltd, Croydon, CR0 4YY

MIX
Paper from
responsible sources
FSC® C020471

Simon & Schuster UK Ltd are committed to sourcing paper
that is made from wood grown in sustainable forests and support the Forest
Stewardship Council, the leading international forest certification organisation.
Our books displaying the FSC logo are printed on FSC certified paper.

The *Oxford English Dictionary*
defines a crisis as:

'A time of intense difficulty or danger'

For my granddaughter
Sophie Elizabeth Francis
Born June 2018.

With my grateful thanks to:
Merrick Francis, Chairman, Lambourn Trainers'
Association; Matt Bosworth, solicitor and crisis
manager; and to the trainers and people of
Newmarket who gave me huge help.

And also to my wife, Debbie, with love.

At the 'Guineas Ball' in Newmarket in April 2018, an auction lot was sold to have the successful bidder included as a character in this book. The funds raised were for the Injured Jockeys Fund, in particular for the Peter O'Sullevan House rehabilitation centre to be constructed at the British Racing School in Newmarket.

Mrs Michelle Morris was the successful bidder and hence she and her husband Mike exist as themselves within these pages.

All other characters are fictitious.

# 1

*May 2018*

According to my business card I was one Harrison Foster, Legal Consultant, but I was known universally as Harry and my speciality was crisis management.

And today's crisis involved a murder – not that anyone knew it at the time.

'Newmarket!' I said. 'But I know nothing about horse racing. I hate it and don't even enter the office sweep on the National.'

'No matter,' ASW said. 'You know about business and you're needed.'

ASW was Anthony Simpson-White, founder, chairman, chief executive, owner and driving force behind the Simpson White Consultancy Ltd – my Boss with a capital B – and he was standing in the doorway close to my desk.

'Can't one of the others go?' I asked. 'Rufus loves the horses. He spends most of his salary at the bookies.'

ASW shook his head. 'Rufus is stuck in Italy with the wine people. You're my best available man.'

I looked around at the other desks in what was called the Operatives' Room. Each of them was unoccupied.

Even on a Monday morning, I was his *only* available man.

'And, anyway,' he said, 'the client has asked for you specifically.'

'Oh,' I said, somewhat surprised. 'Who is the client?'

'It will all be in the brief. I'll send it to you by email while you're on your way. Take a fast train from King's Cross to Cambridge.'

'Not Newmarket?' I asked.

'Cambridge is better. You'd have to change there anyway to get a local service. I'll get Georgina to arrange a car and driver to meet you.'

Georgina was his PA: fifty-four years old, divorced with two grown-up sons, she was always smart, bright and happy. She was also ASW's mistress, not that either of them would ever admit to it. But we operatives knew. Of course we knew. As the Boss was always telling us: 'I expect my operatives to know everything about everyone.'

'Whose stables in Newmarket?' I said.

'That'll be in the brief, too. I'll get Georgina to book you a room. Now get going, Harry, there's a good chap.'

In spite of his genial tone, it was an order not a request.

I immediately closed the laptop on my desk, stood up,

put on my jacket and collected my already-packed suitcase from the cupboard in the corner where it sat, permanently on standby, primed for an instant departure to anywhere in the world, hot or cold.

How to pack was one of the first things taught to new operatives at Simpson White.

The main rule was that the suitcase had to be small enough to fit into the overhead lockers on an airliner – standing waiting at baggage reclaim was considered to be time that could be spent more productively with the client.

Two clean shirts, a change of underwear, washbag, hairbrush, razor, phone and laptop chargers were all essentials; chinos, trainers and a polo shirt were optional, while shorts and flip-flops were frowned upon. Operatives were expected to always wear a suit and tie to the office so as to reduce the need to pack them.

My case also contained a small first-aid kit – scissors removed – a pair of swimming trunks and a small rolled-up Union Jack.

One never knew when that might be useful.

Anything else that an operative might need on assignment was expected to be bought 'in theatre', as ASW called it, and he provided us with a company credit card for the purpose, although any purchases were tightly scrutinised to ensure that they were absolutely necessary.

Not that Simpson White was exceptionally mean towards its employees. In fact, quite the reverse. Operatives travelled business class on long-haul flights so as to be rested and ready for work immediately on arrival, and provision of a comfortable car with a driver was the norm, as were four- and five-star hotels.

'I need my staff fresh,' ASW would say, and he would charge his clients accordingly.

Retired colonel, Anthony Simpson-White had established Simpson White Consultancy Ltd in the mid-1990s, partly with his gratuity paid on completion of eighteen years' exem- plary service in the British Army. But ASW had not been a fighting soldier. He was a lawyer.

He had served as a senior officer in the advisory branch of the Army Legal Corps, dispensing advice on military and international law to prime ministers and the High Command, including during British wars in the South Atlantic, Persian Gulf and Bosnia.

'I spent most of my time telling the bigwigs what they really didn't want to hear,' he'd once said by explanation of why he had finally resigned his commission even when tipped to be a future director general of Army Legal Services. 'Not that things have changed much since,' he'd added with a laugh, 'except the bigwigs now pay me more for the privilege.'

He'd started as a one-man operation, giving legal advice and opinions to companies in financial or operational dif- ficulty, using the same authoritative and blunt manner that he'd employed at the Ministry of Defence. The company directors might also have not liked hearing what he had to say but he had an uncanny knack of cutting through the chaff to the meat of a problem before offering a lifeline, pal-atable or otherwise. It was then up to the company to decide whether to accept or reject his recommendations – to survive or go under.

And ASW was never one to stand idly by and say nothing when he believed that his intervention would help. One of his favourite sayings was: *If you live without making a dif-ference, what difference does it make that you have lived.*

Over the years his reputation had grown and so had his business, so much so that he now had ten operatives work-ing under his watchful eye, and there was talk of recruiting numbers eleven and twelve.

Most of us were lawyers but there was also an ex-special-forces sergeant plus two financial whizz-kids enticed from the City not so much by a huge pay cheque but by the promise of a more varied and exciting life.

And varied and exciting it had proved to be.

I was operative number 7 – 007, I liked to think – and I had been with the company for almost seven years having become bored with conveyancing houses, drawing up wills and submitting divorce petitions – the staple diet of a local high-street solicitor in rural Devon.

One particular wet and tedious Wednesday afternoon in Totnes, I had spotted a small, understated advert in the corner of the jobs section of the *Law Society Gazette*.

'*Vis mutare aliquid magis excitando tuum?*' was all it said, with a London telephone number alongside.

*Vis mutare aliquid magis excitando tuum?*

I'd done a year of Latin at school but, clearly, not enough.

I typed the words into an online translator and it spat out: 'You want to change to something more exciting?'

On a whim, I called the number.

'Can you come to our offices for an assessment?' asked a female voice immediately without so much as a 'hello'.

'Certainly,' I replied. 'When?'

'As soon as possible,' said the voice.

'Where?' I asked.

'That is your assessment. Don't call this number again or you will have failed.' She had then hung up, leaving me baffled but intrigued.

I remember having sat staring at the phone in my hand, quite expecting it to ring as the woman called me back. But she didn't. It remained silent. There had been no name offered, not even the name of the firm. The voice hadn't even asked for *my* name.

Was it a scam? Or was someone just playing silly buggers?

Or was it actually for real?

But where did I start? There were over ten thousand law firms in the UK, almost half of them in London alone. Did I go through the Legal Directory looking for a telephone number to match? But this number seemed to be just for the advert, not the one for the firm's switchboard.

I entered it into Google but, predictably, it gave no clue to the number itself ... but it did provide some pointers. By inserting only the first seven digits, the search results showed various entities including a string of foreign embassies, a medical practice and several restaurants. All were in the London SW1 postcode area, and most in subsection SW1X.

I googled SW1X – Knightsbridge and Belgravia – the smartest parts of west London, but both with thousands of addresses.

Hopeless.

I had sat at my desk idly staring out the window at the people hurrying up and down Totnes High Street in the rain rather than getting on with my work, wondering what sort of idiot would place such a stupid advert.

But it made me determined to find out.

So I called the office of the *Law Society Gazette* and asked for the classified-ad department.

Sorry, they said, they were not at liberty to give out the details of who had placed the advert, data protection and all that. Indeed the man I spoke to seemed quite amused by my request, as if it was not the first time someone had asked him the same thing.

Then I searched on my computer for law firms in London SW1X and made a list. There were just eight of them.

Things were looking up.

Next I compared the telephone number in the advert to those of the eight firms. None were identical but three had the same initial seven digits, even if the last four were all significantly different.

Now I felt I was really getting somewhere.

I again called the *Law Society Gazette* and asked to be put through to their finance department.

'How can I help?' asked a female voice.

'I'm chasing an invoice for an advert placed in your jobs section,' I said.

'For which firm?' asked the woman.

'It could be one of three,' I said. 'We act as a recruiting agent for a number of firms.' I gave her the name of one of the firms on my short list.

'Sorry,' she said after a few seconds. 'No record of that one.'

I gave her the name of the second firm.

'Ah, yes,' she said, raising my hopes. 'They advertised with us two years ago for a legal secretary. Is that the one?'

'Is there nothing more recent from them?' I asked, trying to keep the desperation out of my voice.

I could hear her tapping on her keyboard.

'No, nothing,' she said.

I gave her the third name.

'Sorry. Nothing from them either.'

'How odd,' I said. 'I'm sure it was one of our firms in the SW1X postcode. Could you please check again?'

'SW1X, you say?' I could hear her tapping the postcode into her system.

'We only have one other record of an invoice going to an address in SW1X, but that wasn't to a law firm.'

'When was the invoice sent?' I asked quickly.

'Last week. It's for the current edition. But it was sent to an individual rather than a firm.'

'Could you tell me the individual's name?' I asked in my most enticing tone. 'It must have been a mistake.'

'I can't,' she said, sounding almost apologetic. 'Mistake or not, it's against our rules.'

'Could you give me the full postcode then?' I asked. 'I can work out which firm it was from that.'

She hesitated, obviously debating with herself whether that was also against the rules. She decided it wasn't.

'SW1X 8JU.'

'Right, thanks,' I said, jotting it down. 'I'll get on and check.'

I disconnected, smiling. Surely that was it.

But the postcode didn't match any of the eight law firms I had on my list.

Hence, two days later, I had found myself walking up and down Motcomb Street in Belgravia, a road of designer shops, art galleries and fashionable restaurants, wondering which of the unlikely twenty-eight addresses that shared the postcode SW1X 8JU was the one I wanted, assuming that it was one of those addresses anyway.

None of them looked remotely like a legal firm and there were no helpful brass plaques on any of the doors, so I went into each of the shops, galleries and restaurants to ask the staff if they knew of any law offices in the vicinity or anyone who might have placed an advert in the *Law Society Gazette*. None did. But it at least eliminated half of the addresses on my list.

Most of the buildings in the street were fine examples of Georgian architecture, three storeys high with intricate wrought-iron railings surrounding balconies on the upper floors. They had originally been built as single-family homes but each had long since been converted into a self-contained retail space on the ground floor with accommodation above accessed through a narrow front door squeezed alongside the shop and opening directly onto the pavement.

I looked up at the high windows, trying to see someone sitting at a desk or to spot some other clue that would indicate a place of work rather than a residence, but the angle from street level meant that mostly all I could see was the reflection of the sky.

In the end I resorted to simply knocking on the front doors or ringing the doorbells and seeing who was in.

By the time I got to the last one, I was beginning to be disheartened. At eight of the fourteen properties there had been no reply, while at five others the occupants obviously had no idea what I was on about when I told them that I'd arrived for my assessment.

'Get lost,' a man shouted at one property. 'I'm not buying anything.'

At another, the door was opened on a security chain by an elderly woman. 'Are you from the council?' she asked through the crack.

'No,' I replied. 'I'm here for my assessment.'

'I'm the one who needs assessing,' she said. 'Are you sure you're not from the council?'

I explained that I was absolutely certain I wasn't from the council, and she was clearly not pleased at having come all the way down the stairs to open the front door for no good reason – 'not in my condition'.

So, when I pressed the cheap plastic bell on the very last

door, I was thinking more about the times of the trains from Paddington back to Totnes than anything else.

The door was grey with grime. I imagined it had once been white or cream but time had not been kind to the paintwork, which was flaking off badly at the top. The small brass-surround letterbox was corroded green, and the central doorknob had several screws missing such that it hung precariously to the wood.

'Yes?' asked a voice through the tiny speaker situated above the bell push.

'I've come for my assessment,' I said once more, with no hope or expectation.

'Good,' said the voice. 'Come on up.' And a click from within opened the door.

And so I had stepped into the world of Simpson White.

No one ever asked me *how* I found them. Only the fact that I *had* was important, not the means I'd employed. Three hours later, I had an offer of a job, although at the time I'd little or no idea what the job actually involved.

'We are definitely not a law firm,' ASW told me seriously, 'and we're not a PR company either. But we do deal in public relations, and we do need lawyers.' Indeed, he spent more time telling me what they were *not* rather than what they *were*, as if he wasn't entirely sure himself. But I liked him and he clearly liked me too. 'So, do you want the job?'

'How much does it pay?' I asked.

He seemed slightly irritated that I should ask about anything as sordid as money.

11

'How old are you?' he asked, rather than answering my question.

'Thirty,' I replied.

'Married?'

'No,' I said, wondering if that was a suitable question for a job interview.

'Engaged?'

'No.'

'Any relationship at all?'

'Not at present,' I said, although that was surely none of his business.

'Then why are you worried about how much I would pay?'

It was my turn to be slightly irritated.

'I have to live.'

'You'll do that all right,' ASW replied with a laugh, 'and you'll also never feel so tired, so excited or so important, all at the same time.'

'So what would I actually do in the job?' I asked.

'Anything and everything,' he replied somewhat unhelpfully. 'We are basically an advisory service and we give legal and other advice to everyone from presidents and prime ministers to CEOs of major international companies. Anyone, in fact, who is in need of our help and is prepared to pay our fees.'

He drew breath and I sat quietly looking at him, waiting for him to go on.

'We are specialists in crisis management. Crises will always occur, either man-made or from natural disasters, and the perception of how the crisis is managed is almost as important as the relief effort itself. Our job is simply to ensure that, when things are bad, they are not made worse by insensitive or downright stupid words and actions by those who are meant to be making things better.'

'Like Deepwater Horizon,' I said.

'Exactly.'

Deepwater Horizon was a BP oil-drilling rig that exploded in April 2010 causing an environmental catastrophe in the Gulf of Mexico. BP bosses initially claimed it was only a small problem and that it was not their fault. For BP, the public relations disaster was almost as destructive as the physical one.

'We sit on shoulders whispering advice into ears and hope it's listened to – although, thankfully, we weren't involved in that one.'

'Okay,' I said.

'Okay what?' ASW replied.

'Okay, I'll take the job.'

So here I was seven years later, leaving through that same grey, grimy front door on my way to King's Cross and then on to Newmarket.

Horse racing! God help me.

# 2

I didn't need to receive the brief to know what I was going to.

'PRINCE OF TROY DEAD IN STABLE FIRE', read all the headline banners at the newspaper stands in King's Cross.

Even I had heard of Prince of Troy. He was the current wonder racehorse, described by most as the best since Frankel. Some even said he was better.

I picked up the early edition of the *Evening Standard* and scanned the front page with its large 'PRINCE OF TROY DEAD' headline. According to the report, the horse had been a sure thing for the Derby in just over two weeks' time, having swept aside all other contenders with consummate ease in his eight previous races, including in the Two Thousand Guineas, the first Classic of the season, just nine days ago.

But now he was gone, apparently roasted alive while standing in his stall. And, it seemed, he had not perished alone. The paper stated that six other top colts had died alongside him in the huge blaze that had rapidly engulfed a whole stable block overnight, fanned by a strong northerly wind coming straight off the Fens.

'An immeasurable loss to racing,' the paper went on, 'and a personal tragedy for the trainer of the seven horses, Ryan Chadwick, and the whole of the Chadwick family.'

I tucked the newspaper under my arm, bought myself a take-away coffee from Starbucks, and found a seat at a table on the next fast train to Cambridge.

Wireless internet on trains was still pretty variable so Simpson White supplied all operatives with a 'dongle' that effectively turned a laptop computer into a large mobile telephone.

I downloaded my emails, including the one from Georgina with the brief.

Ryan Chadwick was not our client, as I had expected, nor indeed any of the Chadwick family. It was my old friend His Highness Sheikh Ahmed Karim bin Mohamed Al Hamadi, known universally as just Sheikh Karim, and he had been the owner of Prince of Troy.

Ahmed Karim had been a vibrant, carefree Arab crown prince of twenty-two when his father, the ruling emir, had been assassinated by his generals for thwarting their attempts to go to war once again with a neighbouring state. The new young leader had purged the army of his father's murderers, made lasting peace in the region, and had dragged his oil-rich nation out of the Middle Ages and into the twenty-first century. Just thirty years on, it was now one of the leading financial and tourist centres of the Middle East.

But he hadn't done so without the occasional crisis and challenge to his leadership. His rule was fair but firm, with firm being the appropriate word, and there had been a few scandals when overzealous officials in his administration had overstepped their authority, especially in dealing with tourists from more liberal European cultures. Hence, he and I had worked twice together before.

The brief outlined how Sheikh Karim had steadily built up a string of top-rated racehorses and it was his intention to eventually rival other Arab royal owners. He had sent his first two-year-old to the trainer Oliver Chadwick only nine years previously and now had some twenty Thoroughbreds in training in several countries.

His UK operation was still largely based at the Chadwicks' Castleton House Stables on Bury Road in Newmarket and he had been anticipating his first ever Derby success with Prince of Troy.

The brief made it clear that I was to act as Sheikh Karim's representative and to liaise with Oliver Chadwick directly. He'd been told to expect me.

Oliver, it seemed, was Ryan's father and the current head of the Chadwick racing dynasty. Georgina had also added some basic background information on the Chadwicks, including a link to an article in the *Racing Post* written five years previously when Oliver had retired and Ryan had taken over as the trainer.

Oliver Chadwick was himself the son of one Vincent Chadwick, who had bought Castleton House on Bury Road soon after the Second World War. He had built the first stable yard and started training racehorses in 1950.

Oliver's elder brother, James, had initially taken over the training licence when their father was killed in a car crash in the early 1970s, but it had passed to Oliver when James emigrated to South Africa only four years later.

Over the next thirty years, it was Oliver who built the reputation of the business until it was considered that Castleton House Stables was one of the finest racehorse training establishments in the country, with a list of owners that included not just Sheikh Karim but also the great and the good of British racing.

But Oliver had clearly been busy in other ways as well. The brief stated that he'd been married three times and he'd had two children with each of his first two wives – three sons and a daughter in all. Of the four, the three boys were still active participants in the racing industry.

Ryan, the eldest at forty-two, had been a two-time former champion jockey who had ridden many of Oliver Chadwick's greatest training triumphs, including winners of the Derby, Oaks, St Leger and the Breeders' Cup, before retiring from the saddle through injury and taking over Castleton House Stables from his father.

Declan, the second son by two years, had also been a very successful but not quite a champion jockey before following Ryan's move into training. He currently ran a small yard on the outskirts of Newmarket and was just starting to make his mark as a possible star of the future.

Next by age, at thirty-two, was Tony and he was the only one of Oliver Chadwick's offspring who was not married. He was still riding as a jockey, although he had never reached the dizzy heights of either of his older brothers, although, according to my newspaper, he had been widely expected to partner Prince of Troy in the forthcoming Derby.

The youngest, at twenty-nine, was Zoe, the only Chadwick daughter. Even though her married name was Robertson, she apparently sometimes referred to herself as Zoe Chadwick. She had moved away from Newmarket to London aged just eighteen, got married at twenty, and now lived with her husband and two young children close to South Ealing tube station.

Georgina had made a note in the brief that Zoe's husband was called Peter and he was believed to be an estate agent, but lack of time had prevented anything further from our in-house researchers.

I leaned back in my train seat and watched the world rush by at a hundred miles per hour. I actually thought that the research team had done remarkably well in the very short period available, but what the brief failed to tell me was that inter-sibling civil war had broken out big time in the Chadwick family.

I would only find that out when I arrived at Newmarket.

Bury Road was closed in both directions, blocked by three large red fire engines from which snaked big fat hoses full of high-pressure water. In addition there were two television news vans with large satellite dishes open on their roofs. Camera crews and presenters milled around aimlessly, waiting, no doubt, for the next news bulletin and another report.

The driver that Georgina had arranged to collect me from Cambridge Station dropped me as close as he could get to the gates of Castleton House Stables. He jumped out first and opened the rear door of his smart black Mercedes and waited for me to emerge.

'I'll try and wait for you here, sir,' he said. 'If they move me on, I'll park somewhere close by.'

'Right,' I said. 'Thank you. I'll call you when I need you. But I have no idea how long I'll be.'

'I'll be waiting,' said the driver. 'Be as long as you like. I've got a good book to read. You can leave your bag in the boot if you want.'

'Yes, I will,' I said. 'Thanks.'

I picked up the newspaper, checked I had my mobile phone with me, and stepped out of the car.

I was immediately struck by a strong smell of burning – not the sweet aroma of a garden bonfire but the acrid stench of burned flesh that bit painfully into my throat almost causing me to retch.

I'd done fires before and I hated them.

There was something indiscriminate and random about their nature, and so absolute in their destruction. In a flood, one can always dry out precious family photographs or works of art. Damaged they may be, but recognisable nevertheless. But in a fire, they are cruelly gone forever.

And, mostly, fires are accidental or the result of acts of God – a lightning strike, an electrical malfunction or a spitting hearth. No one meant them to happen, yet the urge to blame someone for one's misfortune is inbuilt in the human psyche. *Why didn't someone spot the flames sooner? Why didn't the fire brigade get here quicker? Why did someone build a faulty heater? Why us? Why? Why? Why?*

It is no surprise that anger is the overriding emotion and victims lash out at any form of authority. The need to hold someone to account is very strong. Residents of fire-ravaged Grenfell Tower in west London loudly demanded justice, as if finding a scapegoat would somehow return their friends and relatives to life, restore their belongings and make everything well again.

And I didn't criticise them for doing so. I would have done exactly the same in their position.

It is as if someone has burgled one's house and removed all that one holds dear, except it is worse than that. At least after a burglary there is a focus for one's anger, individuals to blame, and a forlorn hope that lost items may be recovered. After a fire there is nothing but total despair.

Presuming, of course, that the fire *was* an accident.

I walked in through the high gates of Castleton House Stables and was immediately confronted by a young uniformed policeman standing just inside.

'Can I help you, sir?' he asked.

'I'm looking for Oliver Chadwick.'

'Why? Are you press?'

'No,' I replied. 'I'm Harry Foster.' I handed him one of my business cards. 'I am expected.'

'Wait here,' he ordered, and then walked off towards a pair of uniformed senior police officers who were standing near the big house to my left.

Even from this vantage point, it was easy to see from where the smell of burning emanated. Wisps of smoke were still rising from the burned-out remains of what had clearly once been a stable block identical to two others that were still standing, and all around me the ground was covered by a layer of ash like black snowflakes, blowing in the wind.

The three blocks, together with the big house, had formed the four sides of a square around a central quadrangle. There was a wide walkway along the front of each building and an immaculately tended lawn in the middle, bordered by a row of bright spring flowers, their pinks, greens and reds in sharp contrast to the pristine white walls and grey slate roofs of the stable blocks.

Beautiful.

Except that, on the far side of the square from where I was standing, the white walls were now fire-blackened and the tile roof completely gone. One of the stable blocks was nothing more than a shell, a few remaining charred roof timbers pointing heavenwards as if in some form of accusation towards God for allowing such a tragedy to occur.

To my right, sitting on the ground and leaning up against the wall of the nearest untouched block, were five firemen, their yellow helmets off and their heavy fireproof tunics open. I smiled down at them and received nothing but grimaces in reply. They were clearly exhausted, the sweat still standing out in huge droplets on their faces.

'Well done,' I said to them.

'Those poor horses,' one of them replied, shaking his head. 'Nothing we could do.'

'At least you saved the other stables,' I said, pointing at the untouched buildings. 'And the house.'

Indeed, I could see other firemen still hosing down the side of the house to ensure it didn't ignite from the heat even now radiating from the epicentre of the disaster.

The young policeman returned, and, it seemed, he had been given the thumbs-up from his superiors for me to enter the premises.

'They're in the kitchen,' he said. 'That door there.' He pointed.

'Who are *they*?' I asked.

'The whole lot of them. The family, that is.'

His tone implied he was not a fan but at least he kept his tongue civil.

Georgina's brief had indicated that, even though Ryan had taken over the training of the horses in the stables, his father still occupied the house, Ryan and his wife having remained in the modern home on the Fordham Road that they had built in the year he was first champion jockey.

I stepped over the bulging hoses and walked towards the door that the policeman had indicated.

I knocked.

There was no answer, not least because those inside would have had great difficulty in hearing. Not only were there shouts from the firemen manning the hoses and the constant roar of the fire-engine pumps out on the road, but I could also hear raised voices from within.

I stepped through the door to find that I was in an office with wooden desks against two walls, and two upright chairs, both in need of some reupholstery to their seats. On each desk there were computer monitors, switched off, and, above, rows of wooden pegs on which hung a mass of vibrantly coloured racing silks. The window next to the door would give someone sitting at the far desk a clear view out towards the stable yard.

The raised voices were coming from deeper within, so I walked along a short passage from the office towards the kitchen where the door was slightly ajar.

'Why the hell should you care anyway?' I could clearly hear a loud angry male voice. 'You've done your best to put a spanner in my works at every turn.'

'That's not fair,' countered a high-pitched female, emotion causing her voice to tremble somewhat. 'It's not Declan's fault the Sheikh has decided to move the horses. He has always tried to help you.'

'Ha! You call that help? You must be bloody joking. Stupid cow.'

'Don't speak to Bella like that.' It was a second angry male voice. 'If you have a problem with me, let's go outside and sort it man to man.'

'Stop it!' shouted an older male voice. 'We're in enough trouble already without you two behaving like spoilt brats in the playground. Why can't you all just get on?'

I was holding back in the passage, and for two reasons. First, I didn't want to embarrass the family by bursting in when they were in the middle of a slanging match, and secondly, I thought I might just learn something. One never knew when an overheard snippet could be useful.

But there was a lull in the proceedings with just a general background hubbub, so I went up to the kitchen door and knocked loudly.

Everyone inside went immediately silent.

I waited.

A few seconds later, I heard footsteps and the door was pulled wide open by a short elderly man with a full head of wavy grey hair.

'Mr Chadwick?' I asked. 'Oliver Chadwick?'

He nodded. 'That's me.'

'Harrison Foster,' I said. 'From Simpson White. I believe you're expecting me.' I handed him one of my business cards.

'Yes,' he said, not sounding very pleased about it. 'Come on in.'

There were seven of them altogether in the kitchen, four men and three women.

'I'm Ryan Chadwick,' said one of the men, confidently coming forward and offering his hand. 'I'm the trainer here.' He was obviously his father's son, short and wiry with similar features and the same wavy hair, although his was mostly

24

still dark with just a few grey streaks at the temples. 'This is my wife, Susan.'

Susan Chadwick was a petite brunette, and even a catastrophic fire at her husband's workplace had not prevented her from dressing smartly and applying bright red lipstick.

'Declan Chadwick,' said another of the men, stepping forward to shake my hand. 'Ryan's brother. And my wife Arabella.'

Arabella was a good three or four inches taller than her husband, with long blonde straight hair, centre-parted. She too had managed to apply her make-up, complete with mascara-lengthened lashes and rose eyeshadow.

'And I'm Tony,' said the fourth man, coming forward. 'The runt of the Chadwick boys.' He laughed but the others didn't.

Even though I knew that Tony was actually in his thirties, his lack of stature, slight build and fresh face made him look much younger. He wore tight skinny jeans over his tight skinny legs and I wondered if he'd bought them from the children's department.

That left just one other woman and there was an awkward pause before she stepped forward. 'I'm Maria,' she said. 'Oliver's wife.'

She alone of the women gave the impression of having being roused rapidly from her bed by the fire – her long fair hair was straggly and tied back into a ponytail, and she was wearing a loose-fitting grey sweatshirt and joggers.

According to Georgina's brief, Maria was Oliver's third wife, and clearly not the parent of either Ryan or Declan.

For a start, she barely looked any older than them, and there was no acknowledgement from either as I shook her hand. Indeed, they turned the other way as if even looking at her was more than they could bear.

*The wicked stepmother,* I thought. And clearly not in favour.

'Is there somewhere we could speak privately?' I said to Oliver.

He looked at me, somewhat surprised. 'There's nothing you can't say in front of my sons.'

I would have preferred it otherwise but, if he was happy, so be it.

I looked at each of them in turn. 'My name is Harry Foster. I'm a lawyer and I am here as Sheikh Karim's personal representative.' I handed out more of my business cards. 'The Sheikh is very keen to ensure that nothing is said or done that in any way reflects badly on him or his reputation. And that means he also has the wellbeing of you and your stables at heart. It must be clearly understood that nothing should be said by any of you to anyone, and specifically not to the press, without clearing it with me first, and I mean nothing. Not even 'no comment'. That makes it look like you're hiding something. Better to say nothing at all. Do you understand?'

I looked at Oliver and then at Ryan, Declan and Tony.

They didn't like it. I could read it in their faces: *Who is this upstart who is telling us what we can and can't do in our own house?*

'Do you understand?' I repeated.

'Yes,' said Oliver.

I looked at the others and they nodded.

'Good. Now, can you fill me in on what has happened so far this morning? Who knew that Prince of Troy was one of the horses lost? And how did the press find out?' I showed them the front page of the *Evening Standard* with its bold headline.

'I spoke with all the owners I could find,' Ryan said. 'I left a message for the Sheikh.'

I was quite certain that *he* wouldn't have given it to the newspapers.

'Who else?'

'I informed Weatherbys.'

'Weatherbys?' I asked.

'They do all the administration for British racing. I have to tell them immediately if any horse entered in a race has to be scratched. Prince of Troy was one of those entered for the Derby. Weatherbys will have issued an urgent press release so that no more ante-post bets were placed on him.'

'What time did you tell them?' I asked.

'I called their Racing Calendar Office at eight-thirty, when it opened.'

'Did you tell them why Prince of Troy had to be scratched?'

'Of course,' Ryan said. 'I notified them he'd died, and the six others, as I am required to do. And it's hardly a bloody secret we've had a fire. There've been fire engines out on the road since midnight. Doesn't take an effing genius to put those facts together.' He nodded towards the newspaper I was still holding.

He was getting quite agitated, and who could really blame him? Seven of his best horses were dead. His Derby dream had literally gone up in smoke.

We were interrupted by a loud knock on the outside door.

Oliver went to answer it and returned with one of the two senior policemen I had seen earlier. The officer removed his silver-braided peaked cap as he came into the kitchen.

'Mr Ryan Chadwick?' he asked.

'That's me,' said Ryan, stepping forward.

'Superintendent Bennett,' said the policeman, introducing himself. 'Are all your stable staff accounted for?'

'I believe so,' Ryan said. 'Why?'

'Human remains have been found in the fire.'

# 3

The discovery of a dead human along with the dead horses changed everything.

Within minutes the whole place was crawling with more police, many of them in full white forensic overalls, some with hoods and face masks, and blue and white POLICE DO NOT CROSS tape was strung everywhere, including across the door from the office to the stable yard.

Presently, another police officer arrived in the kitchen and asked Ryan for a list of names of all his staff and confirmation that they were accounted for.

The list was apparently no problem, it was in the office, but the whereabouts of the twenty-six individuals was less certain and more difficult to establish.

'They went with the horses,' Ryan explained.

Newmarket, it seemed, had rallied round in time of crisis, and accommodation for the surviving equines had been quickly offered by nearby stables with available space. Great care had been taken to record the location of each of the remaining four-legged residents, but less attention had been apportioned to the two-legged variety.

'How many staff live on site?' asked the policeman.

'Eighteen,' Ryan replied. 'Six in flats built over the old stables and twelve others in a special hostel round the back in the new yard.'

'New yard?'

'Yes,' said Ryan. 'I currently train a hundred and five horses, at least I did before this. It's now ninety-eight. The three old stable blocks in the quad close to the house can each house twelve, that's only thirty-six, and we have four barns each with twenty-four stalls in the new yard, one hundred and thirty-two spaces in total. We call it the new yard but most of it's more than thirty years old now. The last barn was built just before the turn of the millennium.'

'Did anyone live over the stables that burned?'

'No, thank God. We were refurbishing the two flats in that one. Almost finished them too. What a bloody waste of money that was.' His shoulders drooped and he leaned forward on the office desk with a huge sigh as if even standing up straight was too much of an effort.

'Mr Chadwick,' the policeman said quite forcefully, 'there is someone lying dead in your stable block. We need urgently to establish the whereabouts of your staff to eliminate them as the possible victim.'

'Yes, of course. I'll make some calls.'

Ryan spent the next two hours ringing round his staff

and his neighbours. Meanwhile, Declan and Arabella left by the house front door, which opened directly onto Bury Road, to return to their own stable yard; Ryan's wife, Susan, went to collect their children from her mother. Finally, Tony departed for Windsor where he had two rides at the evening race meeting.

Racing, and life, went on, at least for most.

Oliver and I sat at his kitchen table and he talked me through the events of the night.

'I'm in bed by ten most evenings,' he said. 'My bedroom overlooks the old yard and I was woken at midnight by shouts outside from the stable lads. Thought I was having a nightmare. Except it was real. The block was already well alight with flames leaping through the roof. I could feel the heat through the window glass.'

'Was it you or your wife who woke up first?' I asked.

'Me,' he said. 'Maria and I now sleep in separate rooms.' He forced a smile, almost in embarrassment. 'She claims my snoring keeps her awake.'

'Where's her bedroom?'

'Only across the landing,' he said.

'Does it overlook the yard as well?'

'No, the garden. Anyway, I immediately called the fire brigade, and then Ryan. Next I banged on Maria's door to wake her. Then I rushed outside to help try and save the horses. It was pandemonium, pure pandemonium. Horses hate fire. Drives them crazy. We were fighting against them trying to get them out. It was awful.'

He swallowed hard, fighting back tears.

'The heat was so bad we couldn't get close to the block that was alight. All we could hear was the poor horses inside screaming, and that made the others even more frightened. Ryan and I decided they all had to be got away so we took those we could save down the road and tied them to the wooden fences beyond the Severals. We simply left them there while we got the others out. By the time we'd finished, we had almost a hundred top Thoroughbreds tied up in Newmarket town centre. Still had to keep the colts away from the fillies, mind, especially those in season. Even though all were shit-scared by the fire, their natural instincts are pretty strong so it was quite a struggle.' He forced a laugh. 'Funny now, I suppose. But not then, I can tell you.'

'No,' I said sympathetically. 'What are the Severals?'

'Trotting circles. At the town end of Bury Road.' He paused. 'People are pretty good though. When they heard about the fire, and the grapevine works pretty well in these parts, they all came out to help. About half of the horses were taken along to old Widgery's place and the others went to yards all over the town, wherever there was any room.'

'Old Widgery's place?' I asked.

'You must know. Tom Widgery. Used to train on Fordham Road. Big place. Empty now since he died last December.'

I looked blank.

'Don't you know anything about racing?' he asked, making it sound like an accusation.

'No,' I said.

'Tom Widgery was the most famous trainer who ever lived,' Oliver said patiently, as if he was addressing a child. 'Won everything many times over. Still holds the record for number of Classic wins.'

'Sorry,' I said. 'I was always keener on cricket.'

He gave me a stare of disapproval bordering on disgust but then he clearly remembered why I was there and smiled.

'A fine game,' he said, obviously not believing it. 'But it's not really a business.'

*It is for some*, I thought, but it was not worth labouring the point.

'How about Sheikh Karim's horses, other than Prince of Troy? Are they all safe?'

A pained expression came over Oliver's face.

'Sadly not,' he said. 'One of the other six lost was also owned by the Sheikh, a promising two-year-old colt called Conductivity. Cost a minor fortune as a yearling last October. Was due to have his first run this coming weekend up the road. Would have been a future champion, I'm sure. Damned shame.'

'Was it insured?' I asked.

'Not by us,' Oliver said. 'That's the owner's responsibility. You tell me.'

I was pretty sure that Conductivity wouldn't have been insured. Nor Prince of Troy. Sheikh Karim would act as his own underwriter and stand the risk himself.

'How about the stables? Were they insured?'

'You bet they were.'

'And who stands to benefit from that, you or Ryan?'

'I do. I still own everything. Ryan is my tenant. But neither of us are insured for loss of business.'

'But the yard wasn't full,' I said. 'So at least Ryan has the free space to cope with the loss of twelve boxes.' *Particularly with seven fewer horses*, I thought, but decided not to say so.

'I suppose so,' Oliver conceded. 'Not like in my day. Then the yard was full to overflowing with every box taken and a waiting list as long as your arm.'

'Is the business in trouble?' I asked.

'No, nothing like that. It's just ... well, how do I say it? ... He's not me. I suppose a son always finds it difficult taking over a profession from a successful father. I try to keep out of his way as much as possible, but the owners ... you know ... they still want me to guide him.'

It sounded to me like a recipe for complete disaster.

'So are the numbers of horses in the yard still declining or are they on the way back up?'

'Times are difficult,' Oliver said in reply. 'People don't have the spare cash they used to.'

I took that to mean that, yes, numbers were still declining. I thought back to what Arabella Chadwick had said to Ryan while I was outside the kitchen door: *It's not Declan's fault the Sheikh has decided to move the horses.*

I decided it was high time I spoke directly with my client.

\*

By the end of the afternoon several more facts had been established, the most pertinent one being that every one of Ryan's stable staff had been accounted for. So the body in the burned-out stable block remained unidentified.

'Do you have CCTV?' I asked as we sat at the kitchen table.

'Yeah, lots of it,' Ryan replied. 'We have cameras covering every stable block and every exit.'

'So what does it show?'

'Nothing.' He threw his hands up in exasperation. 'The control box with the hard-drive recorder was in the roof space of the block that burned. Whole thing is lost. Unbelievable. I've got lovely pictures of the new yard. Masses of them. That system is housed in the lads' hostel. But for the old yard – nothing.'

'How about sprinklers?' I asked.

'We have them in the new yard,' Ryan said. 'And we were having them retrofitted as part of the refurbishment of the flats in the old. I can't bloody believe it. Another week and those in that block would have been working.'

'Why was Prince of Troy in a building with no sprinkler system?' I asked. 'Surely your most valuable asset should have been in the safest place?'

'I thought it *was* the safest place,' he said quickly. 'It's close to the house. We've had intruders before in the new yard. And I keep all the colts together in the old yard. They're easier to handle there without any fillies around. Before the fire I had twenty-six colts, sixteen three-year-olds and ten aged two.'

'Are all the rest fillies then?' I asked.

Ryan looked at me strangely.

'No. There are also geldings and mares.'

'What's the difference between a filly and a mare?' I asked. Even I knew what a gelding was.

'Age,' he said, with an air of humouring an imbecile. 'In British racing, a filly becomes a mare on her fifth birthday.'

'On the first of January,' I said, rather proud of myself that I knew that all horses have their birthday on the first day of the year, irrespective of when they were actually born.

'In the northern hemisphere, yes,' Ryan said. 'In Australia it's the first of August.'

'August?' I said. 'Why not July? That would be halfway through the year.'

Now it was his turn to be baffled.

'I've no idea. But it's definitely the first of August.'

'So what happens if a horse emigrates from here to Australia or vice versa, does it become half a year older or younger?'

He shrugged his shoulders. His time for humouring me was clearly over.

'Look,' he said. 'Is there anything else? I've got my entries to do and I need to concentrate. They're difficult enough without all this palaver going on.'

He stood up to go.

'Just one more thing,' I said. 'What security arrangements are there at night? Are the gates locked?'

'Of course they're locked,' Ryan said irritably. 'The whole place is locked up tight. My head lad lives in one of the flats and he does a check last thing at night before he goes to bed.'

'Did he do it last night?'

'I'm sure he did. He does it every night.'

'Then how did someone get in and end up dead in the fire?'

'I've no bloody idea,' he said. 'It was probably some homeless bastard. Climbed the gates and broke into the stables, looking for somewhere to bed down for the night. Set the place on fire with a discarded cigarette, I shouldn't wonder. Bloody deserved to die, if you ask me.'

There was a remarkable lack of sympathy all round from the Chadwicks for the person who had just lost his life in their stables. All the compassion was for the horses.

And all afternoon, there was a continuous string of telephone calls from other trainers offering condolences for the lost animals, particularly Prince of Troy. I knew because I listened in on some of them using a second handset, just to be satisfied that the caller was not a member of the press and Ryan was not saying something he shouldn't. But, after a while, I just let him get on with it.

The press were finding out what had happened from other sources.

Both the police and the fire service gave interviews, with senior officers standing on the road outside the gates of Castleton House Stables, and each was carried live on the TV news channels.

I watched on the set in the kitchen with Oliver, Maria and Ryan.

The Suffolk senior fire officer was up first, explaining how fire appliances from as far away as Bury St Edmunds and Ipswich had initially attended the fire along with one from neighbouring Cambridge. He reported that the fire was finally out and he thanked the firemen for their work. In all, five fire engines had been used including the two from Newmarket Fire Station, which would remain on site damping down for the rest of the day. He also stated that, as yet, no cause of the blaze had been established but fire investigators would be moving in just as soon as it was safe for them to do so.

The senior police officer, however, was far more informative.

He confirmed to the waiting press that seven horses had been lost in the fire and also revealed to the eager report-ers that there had also been at least one human victim. Consequently, he said, the stable yard was being treated as a potential crime scene, even though he was at pains to point out that no actual cause of death had yet been established.

But the reporters didn't care about that. Instead, they glee-fully indulged in media speculation over foul play and who might have been responsible.

'That's totally ridiculous,' Ryan shouted loudly at the TV. 'Why would anyone purposely set fire to a stable full of horses?'

I could think of lots of reasons but decided not to mention them.

*

At five o'clock that afternoon, the police were still refusing Ryan access to his stables, not even to the new yard, which was outside the lines of POLICE DO NOT CROSS tape.

'Look here,' he told them with rising irritation. 'In spite of everything, I still have a business to run. None of my horses has had any exercise today other than walking down to the town in the early hours. The stewards allowed me to withdraw my two at Wolverhampton this afternoon but I've got one declared at Beverley tomorrow, and then I have a whole raft of runners later in the week at York, Newbury and here at Newmarket. It's all well and good them being in other people's stables, but their regular bedding is here, as is their food. Horses don't like change. Even without Prince of Troy, I've still got two left in the Dante on Thursday. If I don't get them back here tonight, they'll have no chance.' Then he added, almost as an afterthought, 'Also my staff can't get to their homes. Some of them are still wearing their pyjamas.'

After more heated discussion between Ryan and the senior officers, they finally agreed that he could have access to the new yard, on condition that everyone used the top gate onto the road at the far end, well away from the old yard and house. The lads could also access their hostel, but the old stables and the flats above would still be off-limits.

'What's the Dante?' I asked after the policemen had gone.

'The Dante Stakes. A race at York this coming Thursday over a mile and a quarter. Acts as the last Derby trial, sixteen

39

days before the big one. Prince of Troy was possibly going to run as part of his final preparation.' He sighed deeply. 'Don't have to make that decision now. Still can't believe he's gone. Best horse I've had. Impossible to replace.'

I thought that, if I were he, I'd have been more worried about the human victim than the equine ones.

# 4

One didn't just ring up His Highness Sheikh Ahmed Karim bin Mohamed Al Hamadi for a chat. One had to use email to make an appointment for a call, and mine was set at seven the following morning, UK time.

The previous evening at Castleton House Stables had been relatively quiet compared to the events of earlier in the day.

Soon after six o'clock, the horses temporarily stabled at old Tom Widgery's place were walked back up the road and returned to the new yard via the top gate.

Oliver, Maria and I stepped out through the front door and stood in the evening sunshine, watching the long line of Thoroughbreds snaking past the last remaining fire engine.

So many stable staff from all over Newmarket had volunteered to help that the string was unbroken.

'It's quite a sight,' I said, as the *clip-clop* of the hooves on the tarmac seemed to be never-ending.

'Certainly is,' Maria agreed with a giggle. 'Like watching

41

the circus animals parade through my home town when I was a kid.'

'But no elephants here,' I said.

'No,' Oliver said without any amusement. Then he turned away and went back inside. Maria and I followed him in.

'Fancy a drink?' Oliver asked me. 'I could certainly do with one. A big one.'

He walked over to a cupboard in the corner of the kitchen.

'I have a room booked at somewhere called the Bedford Lodge Hotel,' I said. 'I should leave you two in peace.'

'Gin and tonic?' Oliver said, clinking ice into two glasses.

'I have a driver waiting for me.'

'You don't need a driver to take you to the Bedford Lodge,' Oliver said, cutting up a lemon without turning round. 'It's less than a hundred yards up the road.'

'He has my suitcase in his car.'

'Tell him to take it into the hotel and then piss off.' He handed me a cut-glass tumbler two-thirds full of a clear liquid, which I assumed was not sparkling water. 'I need you here. We have to talk.'

I was surprised not just that he wanted me to stay, but by the intensity with which he said it.

'What about?' I asked.

He downed his drink in two large gulps and then poured himself a generous refill, not skimping on the gin.

He glanced cautiously at Maria but she was already well ahead of him. One empty bottle of Chardonnay sat in front of her on the kitchen table and she was pouring a generous measure into her glass from a second.

'Let's go into the snug,' Oliver said.

He led the way while I called the driver.

'Leave my bag at the Bedford Lodge Hotel reception and go home,' I told him. 'I won't need you again this evening.'

I decided against telling him to piss off as Oliver had suggested.

'What time in the morning?' the driver asked.

'I'll call you if I need you,' I said.

'Okay,' he said. 'I'll be in Newmarket by eight o'clock so five minutes notice will be fine. Unless you need me earlier than that?'

Simpson White never pinched pennies by not having a car and driver ready on standby for operatives on assignment. On this occasion our client could easily afford it.

'Eight will be fine,' I said, although I imagined that Newmarket was wide awake and long at work by then, especially as the sun was up by five in mid-May and horses, like most diurnal mammals, had their body clocks set by the daylight.

Oliver led the way along the corridor and into his snug, a smallish room with a huge television hung on one wall and two deep, black leather armchairs facing it. However, instead of talking he switched on the live racing from Windsor.

'Tony's riding,' he said by way of explanation. 'He's on the favourite in the feature at seven-thirty.'

'For Ryan?' I asked.

'No, for Jonathan Ayers. Also trains here in Newmarket. Tony rides for him quite a lot.'

We both sank down into the folds of the armchairs and watched on the big screen as the ten horses for the 7.30 race circled behind the starting stalls.

'Is there much horse racing in the evenings?' I asked.

'Lots of it,' Oliver said. 'All through the summer months and in the winter too under lights on the all-weather.'

'All-weather?'

'Artificial surfaces. Not turf. There are currently five courses with all-weather tracks in the UK. They race all year round, mostly in the evenings.'

The horses were being loaded into the stalls.

'Six furlongs,' Oliver said, not taking his eyes off the images. 'Listed race for three-year-olds and up.'

I wondered what it was listed on but decided not to ask.

The stalls swung open and all ten jumped out fast and ran like the wind, the multicoloured silks of their jockeys standing out brightly against the green grass.

'Which one is Tony?' I asked.

'Light-blue jacket and orange cap,' Oliver said. 'On the far side, right at the back. He's got a good chance.'

The TV commentator called out the names of the leading horses and the pitch of his voice rose dramatically as the race built towards its finale. But I wasn't really listening. Strangely, I found myself transfixed by the contest, leaning forward in my chair and willing Tony to get a move on, to start overtaking those in front.

Only at the last moment, as the runners were well within the final furlong, did the orange cap make a late surge forward, moving past some of the other runners as if they were standing still, but the winning post came too soon and Tony ended up as a fast-finishing second, beaten half a length at the line.

'Bloody hell,' Oliver said with feeling. 'He should have won that. Left his run far too late.'

I could tell he was angry but I wasn't sure whether it was with the horse or the jockey.

It was with the jockey.

'Tony has never reached his full potential due to his lack of concentration. Not like Ryan. Ryan would have won that easily. Declan would have too.'

'But Tony must surely be pretty good,' I said. 'The newspaper said he was due to ride Prince of Troy in the Derby.'

'Against my better judgement,' Oliver said sharply. 'It was Ryan who decided to stick with Tony, not me. I recommended a change.' He snorted in obvious disapproval that his advice had not been taken. 'I grant you that Tony rode the horse in all its previous races and he did a reasonably good job in the Guineas, but the Derby is a completely different matter. The Guineas is run on a dead-straight flat course here at Newmarket but, at Epsom, there are major undulations and sharp turns. That steep run downhill into Tattenham Corner is the most testing stretch of racetrack on the planet. Needs someone with more bloody nous than Tony. Ryan, now, he was a master at it.'

I felt quite sorry for Tony. Always being compared to his gifted elder brother would have done nothing for his confidence. Nor, I suspected, for the relationship with his father.

'So what is it you want to talk about?' I asked.

'Another drink?' Oliver replied, standing up.

'I'm fine, thank you.'

My glass was still half full and I was taking very cautious sips. The ratio of gin to tonic would have made even Dean Martin wince. Not that it was stopping Oliver knocking it back like water.

He disappeared to get himself a refill from the kitchen while I looked around the room.

To my left was a glass-fronted display cabinet full of small cups and round silver salvers. I stood up to have a closer look.

'The trainer always gets a small trophy,' Oliver said, coming back into the snug with a full glass. 'It's the owner who always walks away with the big one in spite of the fact that *we* do all the bloody work.' It was an obvious cause of resentment. 'Some owners don't even know what their horses look like, other than they have four legs and a tail. It's the trainers who love and nurture them.'

*Yes*, I thought, *but it's the owner who pays the training fees and also puts up the money to buy the horse in the first place.*

Oliver sat down again in one of the armchairs and I joined him in the other.

'Now then . . .' I said in an encouraging manner.

'Not yet,' he said. 'Tony is also riding in the next.'

46

We watched the race but I couldn't raise any excitement this time. Tony's mount was slow coming out of the stalls and, as far as I could tell, became progressively slower as the race unfolded. So much so that it wasn't even in the TV picture as the winner passed the post.

'Useless,' Oliver said, flicking off the television. 'But what do you expect from a Class Six handicap for four-year-olds. The lowest of the low. Just one small step from the dog-food factory.'

At least he didn't seem to blame Tony this time.

'Your drink all right?' he asked.

'It's fine,' I said, and took another small sip.

I was beginning to think he had changed his mind about wanting to talk to me, but I was wrong.

'Harry,' he said finally, laying a hand on my arm, 'what are you going to tell the Sheikh?'

'About what?'

'The fire, of course.'

'What do you want me to tell him?' I asked.

'The truth,' Oliver replied, looking me straight in the eye. 'That it was an accident. That we did everything we could to save his horses.'

'But was it an accident?' I asked pointedly. 'Don't you think we should wait for the police to investigate before I can say that?'

'Are you seriously suggesting that someone set fire to my stables on purpose?'

'I'm not suggesting anything,' I said. 'I just think it would

47

be prudent to await the forensic results. After all, there is a human body to explain.'

Oliver didn't look very happy.

'Tell me about the Sheikh's other horses. How many are there?'

'Nine,' Oliver said, but then corrected himself. 'Only seven now. Five other colts and two fillies.' He laughed. 'I had to talk him into buying the fillies. He prefers male horses. Must be an Arab thing.'

'Where did he buy them?' I asked.

'At the sales, of course,' Oliver said. 'Some over a year ago but he also bought two colts and two fillies from Book One here last October. Conductivity, who died, was one of those.'

'Book One?' I asked.

'The best. The top five hundred or so yearlings of the year.'

'Who decides?'

'The auctioneers. It's their sale. It's determined by the horses' breeding – mostly their sires. There are four books in the October sale. Over two thousand lots altogether. And that's just one yearling sale. There are others in Doncaster, and plenty more in Ireland, France and the US.'

'Big business,' I said.

'Huge. The average price for Book One is about three hundred thousand guineas. The top-priced colt last year went for over four million.'

'That's incredible.'

'Sure is. Especially when you consider the horse is completely untested. Four million simply on a promise and who its mum and dad are. I hope he turns out better than Snaafi Dancer.'

'Snaafi Dancer?'

'Infamous son of Northern Dancer. Sold as a yearling way back in 1983 at Keeneland Sales in Kentucky for an unbelievable ten million dollars and never even made it to a racecourse. Too slow, apparently. And, to add insult to injury, he fired mostly blanks when he went to stud. Sired just four foals in total and they were all useless.'

And most people thought that gambling was only done at the bookmakers.

'Did the Sheikh buy his horses personally?' I asked. 'Was he at the sale?'

'No,' Oliver replied. 'I was there, and Ryan of course. Plus a bloodstock agent, Bill Vandufful. He did the actual bidding.'

'Did the Sheikh know which horses you were going to buy for him?'

'No, but he knew we were planning to buy something. Which particular horses we bought would be determined by the price. We bid on two or three other colts but they went too high. At the sales, you have to be always ready and not miss a bargain.'

'Four million doesn't sound like a bargain to me.'

He laughed. 'Sadly, we're not in that league. Sheikh Karim told me he wanted a couple of good colts but not at any price. Half a million was my limit. Conductivity cost just under that.'

It still seemed like an awful lot of money to me for a young unproven horse.

'How about the two fillies?' I asked.

'Much less,' he said. 'Bargains. Bill and I couldn't believe our luck. Everyone else seemed to have gone off for a coffee after a few really big ones. Too good an opportunity to miss.' He smiled broadly. 'All I needed was to find an owner to pay for them. Sheikh Karim eventually agreed.'

'What would've happened if he hadn't?' I asked.

'I'd have found someone else. It's quite normal for a trainer to buy horses at the sales and confirm the owners later. Buying on spec, it's called. I've done it regularly over the years.'

'But who puts up the money in the meantime?'

'I have an understanding with my bank.'

*Quite an understanding*, I thought, if he could sign cheques for half a million with only untried horses as the guarantee. But who was I to know? There was clearly more value in racehorses than I realised.

Oliver laughed nervously. 'I haven't lost the house and stables yet.'

So the horses weren't the only collateral after all.

'How many did you buy on spec in total at last year's sales?'

'Five, including the Sheikh's,' he said. 'Two colts and three fillies.'

'Who now own them?'

'One of my regular owners bought the other filly.'

'And the colts?' I asked.

'Ah, well,' Oliver replied rather sheepishly. 'We didn't actually find owners for them.'

'I assume you're still trying.'

'That might be a bit difficult now,' he said. 'Both of them died in the fire.'

'So will you personally bear the liability?'

'No, thank God,' he said, holding his hands up in mock prayer. 'I insured them.'

*Did you, indeed?* I thought.

# 5

On Tuesday morning, my phone rang at seven o'clock precisely, but I'd been reading the daily newspapers for over an hour by then.

'Harrison, my friend, how are you?' There was a slight southern twang to the Sheikh's middle-eastern accent, the result of having mostly learned his English from watching old Hollywood movies plus a stint at a US Air Force flight-training facility in Alabama.

'I am well, Your Highness,' I said. 'Thank you.'

'Good. Now tell me what is going on. All I have received is a garbled message from Oliver Chadwick that two of my horses have died in a fire.'

'Yes, sir,' I replied.

I gave him an update of the known facts and the loss of life, both equine and human, including the demise of Prince of Troy.

There was a short pause from the other end of the line,

which may have been due to the distance the signal had to travel.

'Such a noble animal,' said the Sheikh. 'I was in England only last week to watch him win the Two Thousand Guineas.' There was another pause, or was it a sigh? 'I had hoped he would prove to be the foundation of my new breeding operation. I suppose I will just have to go on looking.'

'I'm sorry,' I said.

'Thank you. Who was the person who died?' the Sheikh asked.

'Not yet identified, as far as I'm aware.'

'One of the stable staff?'

'No, sir. All of those are accounted for. Ryan Chadwick thinks it may have been a homeless person seeking out a warm spot to sleep. It was clear but cold here on Sunday night.'

'Please pass my condolences to both Oliver and Ryan Chadwick. Do they know how the fire started?'

'No,' I said. 'The trouble with stables is that there is so much flammable material around. Ryan uses shredded newspaper for his horses' bedding. A careless match or cigarette end would easily set the whole lot alight. The police are still investigating.'

'Try to find out the reason from them.'

'How long do you want me to stay? I don't feel that I'm really required. The press are getting all the information they need from the authorities. There is nothing that should be a concern for you.'

'But I am concerned,' the Sheikh replied in a mildly

rebuking tone. 'Two of my best horses are dead and I don't know why.'

'Of course, sir,' I replied apologetically. 'What I meant was that there has been no press comment concerning you or any other owner. I've checked them all. There is nothing in today's papers that should in any way be a concern for your reputation.'

'That is good.'

'Yes, but I have one question,' I said. 'I overheard a conversation in which it was stated that you intended moving your horses away from Ryan Chadwick.'

He laughed.

'And people ask me why I pay Simpson White's exorbitant fees. That information is highly confidential.'

'Yes,' I said again. 'But is it true?'

His laughter died.

'It is partially true. I am planning to move two horses from Ryan to Declan Chadwick.'

'Which two?' I asked.

'Two fillies that I have purchased.'

'Can I ask why you are moving them?'

There was definitely a pause this time.

'I do not like being told what to do.' He spoke the words very slowly and precisely.

I waited in silence. If he wanted to tell me more, he would.

He did.

'Oliver Chadwick told me I had to buy the two fillies to

save his stables. He was overstretched. Too much in debt and his bank was threatening to take away his house.'

'So you bought the horses to help him out?'

'Yes,' said the Sheikh.

'But now you are moving them?'

'Yes,' he said again. 'I bought the horses only because my bloodstock agent convinced me that they were good value for money.'

'Bill Vandufful?'

'Yes. Do you know him?'

'No,' I said. 'But Oliver Chadwick told me that Mr Vandufful was the individual who did the bidding for him at the sale last year.'

'He had also bought Prince of Troy for me as a yearling. He recognised the potential without having to pay silly money.'

What had Oliver told me the previous evening? *Sheikh Karim told me he wanted good colts but not at any price. Half a million was my limit.*

I was a little surprised that the Sheikh would be bothered about the amount he paid for a champion racehorse. If magazine rich lists could be believed, he was individually worth more than a few billion, to say nothing of the wealth of his nation that he personally controlled. I thought it was the winning that was important, not the price. Maybe I was wrong.

'Moderation in their leader is important for my people,' he said, as if he was reading my mind. 'We have to prepare for the day the oil runs out.'

'But why are you moving the fillies to Declan? Why not to another stable unconnected with the Chadwick family?'

'Vandufful tells me that Oliver has passed Castleton House Stables to the wrong son and that, in time, Declan will prove to be the better trainer of the two.'

'So will you move your other horses to Declan?' I asked.

'I am content to leave those with Ryan,' he replied, but there was something about the tone of his voice that made me think that future purchases might go directly to Declan.

'Are you aware there is bad blood between Ryan and Declan?'

'Bad blood between brothers is nothing new to me. It is commonplace in this part of the world.'

'But your moving the horses from one to the other has exacerbated the hostility between them.'

'There is an old Arab saying that sometimes it is necessary to hit a camel with a stick to see if it has any life left in it.' There was amusement in his voice as if he knew exactly what he'd been doing. It was all a game.

'I just hope your camel didn't turn into a fire-breathing dragon,' I said.

All his amusement evaporated instantly.

'Are you serious?' the Sheikh asked. 'Are you saying that the fire was deliberate?'

'No, I'm not,' I said. 'But I don't know. We will have to wait for the results of the police investigation.'

There was another slight pause.

'I want you to stay in Newmarket,' the Sheikh said. 'I

need you to be my eyes and ears. You will ask questions and determine why my horses died.'

There was now a degree of desperation in his voice as if he was suddenly afraid that his little game had precipitated the disaster.

'Surely the police will do that,' I said.

'I do not control the police in your country. You will report directly to me. I will speak with Colonel White to arrange it.'

'How long do you want me to stay here?' I asked.

'For as long as it takes.'

Just after eight o'clock, I walked from the hotel down Bury Road and in through the top gate into the new yard.

Unlike the old, it was not laid out around a central quad but consisted of three parallel American-style stable barns with a fourth sitting at right angles to the other three at the farthest end from the house. Beyond the barns were an automatic horse-walker and a large covered exercise oval set on the far side of a railed paddock. The stable-staff hostel was tucked into the corner of the paddock close to one end of the cross barn.

I went into the nearest barn.

It had a wide central concrete walkway running the full length between large open sliding doors at the ends. There were twenty-four stalls in total, twelve on each side of the walkway, six at either end, with tack room, bedding and feed stores located between them in the middle.

And everywhere there were large No Smoking signs in

bold black type, threatening instant dismissal for anyone caught doing otherwise.

I expected the place to be a hive of activity but, while there were plenty of horses standing in their stalls, the only human I could find was one small elderly-looking man busily sweeping the walkway with a stiff brush.

'Where is everyone?' I asked.

'Warren Hill,' he replied without stopping his sweeping. 'Second lot went out about half an hour ago now. First lot today was at six.'

'On the gallops?' I said, not completely sure of what he was on about.

'Yeah,' he replied. 'Up the Warren Hill polytrack. They'll be back soon.' He stopped his sweeping, leaned on the broom and looked me up and down. 'And who are you, might I ask?'

'Harry Foster,' I said. 'I'm here to help Mr Chadwick deal with the fire.'

'Dreadful thing, that fire,' he said wistfully. 'Bloody shame.'

I held out my hand and he shook it, the feel of his palm all leathery and dry from a life outside in the elements.

'I'm Fred Piper,' said my newfound friend. 'Been here pretty much all my life. The only one left now from old Mr Chadwick's time. I don't ride the horses these days, mind – hips and knees are bloody crocked.' He grinned briefly, showing me several gaps in his teeth. 'I just keep the place tidy now. Pass me that muck shovel, will you?'

I picked up the metal shovel that was leaning against the

stable wall and handed it to him. He used it to collect what he'd been sweeping and put it in a wheelbarrow.

'All I'm useful for these days is tidying.'

He sighed deeply and I thought there were tears in his eyes.

'I'm sure Mr Chadwick is very pleased you are,' I said.

'Mr Chadwick senior might be,' Fred said with surprising bitterness, 'but young Mr Ryan isn't. Wants me gone at the end of the month. Told me last week he couldn't afford to pay me wages any more. I said I'd do the job for nothing. I'd be lost without it.'

'Where do you live?' I asked.

'In the hostel,' he replied gloomily. 'Losing my home as well as my job. And no one's going to give me another, not at my age. Castleton House Stables is all I know.'

'How old are you?' I asked.

'Fifty-nine.'

He looked much older.

'Where are you going to go?'

'Dunno,' Fred said. 'Had hoped Mr Ryan would change his mind, but that won't happen now. Not with seven less horses to look after. He laid off another two boys this morning. Told them to pack up and go, right there and then when they turned up for work at six o'clock. Bloody disgrace. Back in Mr Chadwick senior's time we had a lad for every two horses. Treated like royalty, they were. Now it's four per lad if you're lucky, maybe five. Same everywhere.'

'Do you have any family?' I asked.

'These are my family,' he said, throwing his arm around. 'These horses and those that went before them.'

At that point our conversation was interrupted by the return of several other horses into the barn, presumably back from Warren Hill, being led by other stable lads.

There was no banter at all. The animals were led silently into their stalls and their tack removed. They were given a brief rub-down and a cursory brush followed by having a rug thrown over their backs. Then the lads trudged off to prepare their next horse for the third lot, hardly lifting their eyes from the floor.

'Not a very happy bunch, are they?' I said to Fred Piper.

'And why would they be?' he said acidly. 'They're worried about their jobs. The yard hasn't had a winner since Prince of Troy won the Guineas.'

'But that's only just over a week ago,' I said.

'A week is an age in racing. Never would have happened in Mr Chadwick senior's days. Last Saturday, we had five runners at Lingfield with three more at Ascot and none of them were even close. Prince of Troy was our only hope and now he's gone. Everyone's wondering who's next for the chop.'

'How many staff have gone already?' I asked.

'Half a dozen or so in the past month.'

'Where are they now?'

'Some have found jobs with other trainers but many of those are cutting back on lad numbers too. More and more work riders are being used – mostly ex-jocks – which means the lads don't actually ride the horses so they can spend more time mucking out. Some yards now have six or seven to a single lad. It's crazy. How can you learn to love them when you've got seven to look after?'

He put out his hand and patted the head of a horse in one of the stalls on my left. The huge creature moved its head up and down as if it were agreeing with him.

'The lads these days don't seem to care as much as we old-timers do.'

The age-old gripe, I thought, of the elder towards the younger.

Was it true?

Maybe, but were things any worse for that? A racehorse was a working beast, bred and trained to run faster than its neighbour. Surely they weren't pets to be loved and mollycoddled like a lapdog.

I personally had never owned an animal of any sort. I'd always had more than enough trouble from the humans in my life without taking on a being that couldn't sit down and have a rational discussion about anything. Not that any members of my immediate family were in that category anyway.

My father always started an argument fairly coherently but quickly reverted to type, shouting down anyone with a view different from his.

If I contradicted him, which I invariably did, he would loudly accuse me of being a 'stupid boy' but without the affection and tolerance of Captain Mainwaring to Private Pike in *Dad's Army*.

My mother was scarcely any better. If forty years of

marriage to my father had taught her anything, it was to keep her own counsel and say nothing. Especially if she wanted a quiet life.

The only thing they appeared to agree on was that a move away from my nice secure job in a solicitors' practice in rural Totnes to the cut-and-thrust, man-eats-man uncertainty of central London was a huge mistake, and very hurtful.

In spite of what ASW had said at our first meeting, I was now earning more than three times as much as I'd done in Totnes, and I loved my work infinitely more, but that was irrelevant as far as my parents were concerned. They only saw that I had forsaken them for the bright lights of the wicked metropolis.

And, if I were being honest, I would have to agree that one of my main motivations for seeking a change from the boredom of Totnes was indeed to put as many miles as possible between me and the family home.

London was far enough away to make a trip home for Sunday lunch very difficult, if not impossible, and I had managed to resist my mother's pleas to come home for any weekend that wasn't near Christmas or her birthday.

But I was not fooling myself. As an only child, I knew that it would come down to me to look after them eventually and, of course, I would then step up to the plate. But, until then, I would keep away as much as possible and hope that, when the Grim Reaper was ready, he would take them both swiftly before they became infirm and incontinent.

At least my parents had one child to care for them in their

dotage. The prospects of me ever becoming a father seemed to be diminishing year on year.

For several years from my late twenties I'd had a regular but neurotic girlfriend and we had even rented a flat together. The romance had been steady rather than deeply exciting or passionate and had come to a dramatic end one night when I'd taken her to a smart restaurant in Torquay.

Having gone down on one knee and removed a very moderately priced solitaire diamond ring from my trouser pocket, I had popped the question only to be given a firm 'Not bloody likely' for an answer.

It seems that she had been planning for some time to end our relationship, as she longed for someone more aspirational than a country solicitor for a future husband. Little did she realise that it was her actions that night which spurred me on to seek out Simpson White less than a year later.

And, if the truth were told, I was more relieved than heartbroken, even at the time. Looking back now, I realise that we weren't at all suited and I had only asked her to marry me because I naively believed it was the next logical step.

It had been a lucky escape and I sometimes still lay awake at night in a cold sweat, thanking my lucky stars that she had turned me down.

I'd moved out of our shared flat that very night and vowed never to ask *the* question of anyone unless I was absolutely certain that I couldn't live without her for a single second longer. As a result, however, I'd since had a string of short-term liaisons with various girls, most of which I had finished almost as fast as they had started because I was in search only of Miss Perfect.

Had I set my sights too high? At the age of thirty-seven was I now in danger of missing out in the matrimonial stakes altogether? Or at least until it was too late to have a family?

Maybe love and marriage would happen one day, or maybe not. I'd long ago stopped worrying about it and had become quite used to living on my own. In many ways it was preferable, not least in being able to please only myself with regard to what I did and when. I suppose it made me selfish, and I did have a few pangs of guilt when my mother spoke of her intense desire to have grandchildren. *She should have had more than one child*, I thought, but then the mental image of my parents procreating together quickly put paid to that.

Perhaps I should be grateful that I existed at all.

The sound of metal horseshoes clattering on the concrete floor brought me back from my daydreaming and I watched as the third lot were ridden out to exercise on the polytrack up Warren Hill.

I went in search of Ryan Chadwick.

# 6

I had to go back onto Bury Road to get down to the house as the old yard was still taped off by the police. Hence I was unable to see into the burned-out shell of the stable block, but some drone shots on the breakfast television news had shown that a square tent had been erected inside, the white of its canvas in sharp contrast to the fire-blackened remains.

I assumed it had been placed over the spot where the human body had been found, about a third of the way along the building from the house.

The fire engines had finally disappeared from outside the main gate but there were several vehicles still parked close by on the verge. One was a white van with 'CRIME SCENE INVESTIGATION UNIT' painted in small black letters down each side, and there were two men in full-cover white plastic overalls standing next to the van's open rear doors, hoods pulled back off their heads and face masks hanging at their throats.

'Find anything?' I asked them as I walked by.

They ignored me completely but I wasn't going to be palmed off that easily.

'I'm Harrison Foster,' I said. 'I represent Sheikh Karim. He owned two of the horses killed in the fire including Prince of Troy.'

They may not have heard of the Sheikh but they certainly had of Prince of Troy. Both of them turned to face me.

'How can we help you, sir?' one said in a tone that implied he had no intention of actually helping me at all.

'The Sheikh wants to know why his horses died,' I said. 'What caused the fire?'

'It's too early to say,' the other man replied. 'We still have tests to carry out in the lab.'

'You must have some idea,' I said. 'Was it an accident?'

'Are you implying it wasn't?' asked the first man.

'You tell me. You're the ones who've been in there. Have you identified the human victim yet?'

'That information will be given out in due course,' the first man said unhelpfully.

'Who's your senior officer?' I asked. 'Is it still Super-intendent Bennett?'

If they were surprised I knew the name, they didn't show it.

'He's in overall charge but our immediate boss is the scene-of-crime officer.' The man glanced over my left shoulder as he spoke.

I turned around and saw a third white-overalled individual coming out of the yard gate and walking towards us.

'I'm the scene-of-crime officer here,' he said, not extending his blue-plastic-clad right hand. 'What do you want?'

'I wondered if you had identified the human remains,' I said.

'And who are you exactly?' He said it in a manner that I thought was more disparaging than intentionally rude, although it was a close-run thing.

'Harrison Foster,' I repeated. 'I am the personal represent-ative of His Highness Sheikh Ahmed Karim bin Mohamed Al Hamadi, owner of two of the horses who died, includ-ing Prince of Troy.' I had used the Sheikh's full name for added gravitas.

I received a look that made me believe that it wouldn't have mattered if I'd been the Sheikh himself, he wasn't going to tell me anything, but I was wrong, at least partially.

'We have yet to establish the victim's identity,' he said. 'Analysis of DNA still has to be carried out.'

'So there was enough of the body left to find some DNA?' I said.

'It is expected so. That will be a job for the pathologist.'

'How about the horses?' I asked.

'What about them?'

'Will you do DNA tests on them too?'

He looked at me as if I were mad.

'To prove they are the horses they are claimed to be,' I said. 'They were very valuable animals and some were insured.'

The 'you are mad' look didn't change but he seemed to comprehend what I was saying.

'Do you know something I don't?' he asked.

'No,' I said. 'It's just the way my mind works.'

ASW always claimed that I'd look for an ulterior motive if my own grandmother asked me over for tea. And he was right.

'I will bear what you have said in mind,' he said. 'Now, sir, please allow us to get on with our jobs.'

'I'm doing my job, too,' I said. 'The Sheikh expects me to find out how and why his horses died.'

'Leave it to the police,' he replied. 'We know what we're doing.'

Perhaps, I thought, but in my experience, the police rarely answered all the questions posed, only those where a crime might have been committed, and then not always those either. It was simply a matter of available resources and priorities.

'Can I get into the house through here?' I asked, pointing at the gate.

'Not until we have finished our examination.'

'But I went in here yesterday.'

'As may be,' he said. 'But not today.'

So I walked along the road and rang the front door bell.

Maria answered the door in a pink dressing gown that hung open at the front revealing a pair of sexy cream silk pyjamas with the top two buttons undone.

'Oh, hello, Harry,' she said with a broad smile and glazed eyes. 'Oliver's out on the gallops. Do you want a drink?'

I looked at my watch. It was twenty past eight in the morning.

'Much too early for me,' I said.

'Nonsense,' she said. 'Come on in.' She threw the front door wide open with an extravagant gesture.

'I'm actually looking for Ryan,' I said, not at all sure that Maria wasn't inviting me in for something more than just liquid refreshment.

'He's with Oliver.'

'On Warren Hill?' I asked.

'No idea. One set of gallops or another. They're all the bloody same to me. But they'll both be back here for breakfast. I know that. Nine o'clock sharp. I'll be in the doghouse if their toast's not ready.' She rolled her eyes and threw her hands up over her head, an action that made the dressing gown swing further open, revealing more cleavage than was good for me at this time of the morning.

'I thought Oliver had retired,' I said, keeping my eyes firmly on hers.

She guffawed loudly.

'If this is his idea of retirement, God help me. He works harder now than he ever did. He didn't want to stop so young but Ryan had to quit riding so Oliver had his hand forced. Now he doesn't trust Ryan not to make a total cock-up of the whole business.'

'And has he?' I asked.

'Has he what?'

'Made a total cock-up of the whole business?'

She suddenly seemed to remember that she was speaking to the representative one of the business's main racehorse owners.

'No, of course not,' she said with a hollow laugh. 'There have just been a few teething problems since Ryan took over. That's all.'

*Five years is a long time for teething problems,* I thought.

A car went by on the road, hooting its horn at her. Maria pulled the dressing gown back round her tightly and waved a two-fingered response in its direction.

'Well?' she said to me, leaning back suggestively on the doorframe, 'are you coming in or not?'

'Not,' I said firmly. 'Which way is it to Warren Hill?'

I walked down Bury Road, past the Severals trotting circles, towards the town centre.

I'd been told in the hotel bar the previous evening that Newmarket was unique in England in having almost as many horse walks as roads, and that it was possible to ride from one side of the town to the other without ever having to walk on the tarmac.

This wasn't quite true as there were intersections where the equine traffic had to cross the mechanical variety, and one of these was at the end of Bury Road, where a line of cars was building up as string after string made their way to and from the training grounds.

'How do I get to Warren Hill?' I shouted to one of the mounted young men as he waited to cross the road. He was wearing a dark-blue puffer jacket and black riding helmet surmounted by a bright yellow cap adorned with a black pom-pom on the top, identical to all the others in the string.

'That way,' he said, pointing behind him. 'Beyond Long Hill. We've just been there.'

'I'm looking for Ryan Chadwick's horses,' I said.

'Poor Ryan,' he said with genuine distress. 'What a damn shame about Prince of Troy.'

'Any idea where I'll find him?'

'At the polytrack. His lads have light-blue caps and red pom-poms.'

The cars stopped and he trotted his horse across and then down the horsewalk on the far side. I waved a thanks at him and looked around me. Sure enough, the strings of horses all had, within them, riders with the same cap colours, and each string was different from the others.

As I walked towards Warren Hill, I seemed to be completely surrounded by horses, some on their way to their exercise and others on the way home again afterwards.

Now the coloured caps and pom-poms made sense.

With reportedly more than sixty racehorse trainers situated in and around Newmarket all using the same gallops, I would have never found Ryan Chadwick's string without them.

Horses have been trained on Newmarket Heath since at least the 1100s but it was the Stuart Kings of England in the seventeenth century that placed the town firmly on the map as the headquarters of the Thoroughbred racing and breeding industry.

I'd looked up Newmarket on the internet.

Exploits on the turf were not the only notable events in

the history of the town. A royal palace once stood on what is now Newmarket High Street and, in March 1642, it was here that Charles I angrily rebuffed a deputation sent from Parliament demanding that he relinquish command of the country's armed forces, an episode that effectively started the English Civil War and ultimately led to the king losing his head.

That palace was torn down during the Cromwell years and, in keeping with the puritanical nature of the period, horse racing was banned as being ungodly.

But, fortunately for the town, Charles II had inherited a love of the horse from his father and, when the monarchy was re-established in 1660, the king built a new palace and made Newmarket his second home, even installing Nell Gwynne, his mistress, in her own cottage that was supposedly connected directly to the King's quarters via a secret underground passage. The cottage still stands on Palace Street although, sadly, the secret passage has long gone.

Indeed, it was Charles II who instituted the first official races on the Heath, and Newmarket racecourse is today called the Rowley Mile in honour of the king's own nickname, Old Rowley, taken from his favourite horse.

However, none of this interesting but useless information made it any easier for me to find Ryan and Oliver Chadwick among the abundance of horseflesh at morning exercise on Warren Hill. Perhaps I should have waited at Castleton House Stables for the horses to come back.

I was also beginning to wish that I'd brought my

wellington boots rather than only my highly polished black leather shoes.

It was while I was scraping another clod of heavy Heath mud from my instep that I noticed half a dozen light-blue caps with red pom-poms going past.

'Ryan Chadwick?' I asked one of them.

'Up there,' he replied, pointing up at Warren Hill where I could see a couple of figures standing to one side, about two-thirds of the way. 'We're just going to do one more canter past them and then we're done. There's another group behind us.'

Sure enough, six more horses topped with light-blue capped and red pom-pommed riders were walking round in a tight circle to my right, waiting for their turn.

One of the two men on the hill waved an arm above his head and the first six started their run up towards them. I followed more slowly, walking on the grass alongside the railed gallop.

By the time I reached Ryan and Oliver, both sets of horses had gone past and the two men were packing away pairs of binoculars into brown leather cases.

'Morning!' I shouted as I approached.

'Hello, Harry,' said Oliver, waving a hand but not really in a welcoming manner. However, he was happier to see me than his son, who just made a reluctant grunt as an acknow-ledgement of my presence.

'I thought the horses would go faster,' I said.

'Just gentle canters today,' said Oliver. 'To maintain

condition. We only do fast gallops twice a week – Wednesdays and Saturdays are the work days, unless they're racing, of course. We aim to get the horses to peak fitness when they arrive on the racecourse. They'd never win a race if we tire them too much on the Heath.'

I realised how little I knew about training athletes of any species and, it seemed, especially horses. I'd imagined they would run flat-out every day to build up their stamina.

'Right,' said Oliver decisively, clapping his hands together. 'Time for breakfast. Are you coming?'

He turned and marched off across the grass towards a Land Rover parked alongside the nearby road.

'I actually wanted to have a private word with Ryan,' I called after him.

He stopped and came back to face me, his angry jutting jaw only about two feet away from mine. Ryan, meanwhile, just stood and stared at me in silence.

'What about?' Oliver demanded.

'I spoke with the Sheikh this morning,' I said.

There was a visible drooping of Ryan's shoulders as if he assumed it was more bad news. Things were clearly far from rosy in Ryan Chadwick's world. And I reckoned it wasn't only because of the fire.

'So tell us what the Sheikh said,' urged Oliver, clearly still agitated and apprehensive.

I had tried once again to speak with Ryan alone but Oliver was having none of it, claiming strongly that he was as much a part of the business as his son and therefore had every right to know what the Sheikh had said.

Hence, the three of us were sitting together round the kitchen table in Oliver's house, drinking coffee and eating our way through a minor mountain of toast that had been left to keep warm on the side of the Aga, presumably by Maria, although there was no sign of her.

I'd had a quick hotel breakfast at seven-thirty but I still managed to scoff down another couple of slices, with lashings of butter and marmalade. I was surprised how a morning on the gallops could give one an appetite. No wonder the Chadwicks ate afterwards rather than before.

'The Sheikh sends his condolences to you both,' I said.

'What else?' asked Ryan impatiently.

'He wants to know why his horses died.'

'We all bloody well want to know that,' Oliver said, clearly irritated. 'What else did he say? What about his other horses?'

'He told me that he was moving two fillies from this yard to Declan's.'

I watched the two men very carefully, hoping to spot some unwary emotion. But they obviously had been expecting me to say this. There was not a flinch from either. They may both have been gritting their teeth internally but, if so, there was no visible external reaction.

'It's a good idea,' Ryan said. 'Declan is much better than me with young fillies. He nurtures them well.'

*You're good*, I thought.

I almost believed that he was being sincere.

Almost, but not quite.

'What about the others?' Oliver pressed urgently. 'Is he going to move those as well?'

'He says he is content to leave them here at Castleton House Stables.'

There was an obvious lessening of tension in Oliver's neck muscles and I realised that the six remaining Karim horses probably made a crucial difference between the stables staying afloat or going under.

Our conversation was suspended by a knock on the kitchen door.

'Come,' shouted Oliver.

The door opened slightly and a head full of tight red curls appeared through the crack.

'Sorry to interrupt, Mr Ryan,' said a soft female voice. 'It's quarter to ten and we haven't yet declared.'

'Good God!' Ryan said, leaping to his feet. 'Well done, Janie. I'll come and do it right now.'

He rushed out towards the yard office.

'Who's Janie?' I asked.

'Yard secretary,' Oliver said. 'Been here for ever.'

'She wasn't here yesterday,' I said.

'She was. She came in early but I sent her home. She was distraught over the loss of the horses. She's been with us since she was a teenager. I don't think we could run the business now without her. Really efficient. She will have prepared the declarations on the computer. Ryan just has to confirm that everything's correct and then send them online to Weatherbys before ten.'

'Declarations for what?' I asked.

'To run a horse. We have to declare all runners by ten o'clock two days ahead of their races. So we are declaring today for those running on Thursday.'

'Is that different from entries? Ryan said he had to do those yesterday.'

Oliver almost managed to smother his irritation that I knew so little.

'To declare a horse to run it must obviously be entered first. Entries close five days before most races but sometimes earlier, in particular for big races. For example, first entries for next month's Derby closed almost eighteen months ago when the horses were still yearlings and hadn't even run.'

'But how do you know at that stage which ones will turn out to be any good?'

'You don't,' Oliver said with a laugh. 'So we entered them all just in case, even those that were still to be named. It's only six hundred pounds a horse at that stage.'

Amazing, I thought. Like paying a few hundred quid to put a newborn baby down for Eton or Harrow in the hope that, thirteen years later, he will be good enough to get in.

Which, of course, was exactly what some people do.

'It must be a disaster if you find you've developed a world-beater that you didn't enter.'

'I arrange with my owners to enter all their colts as a

matter of course,' said Oliver, 'and most of their fillies too. You *can* make a late entry if you need to but it costs much more – eighty-five grand if you want to enter just the week before the race.' He laughed again. 'But worth it, of course, if you win.'

*If you win*, I thought.

Everything about life in Newmarket, it seemed, was about winning, and not just at the races.

# 7

Declan's set-up was much more modest than that at Castleton House Stables. It was also on the other side of the town, on Hamilton Road near the Rowley Mile racecourse, so I arranged for the car to take me there just after eleven o'clock.

Declan wasn't expecting me and I made no effort to fore-warn him of my arrival, instructing the driver to park on the driveway right in front of the house.

However, it was Arabella who answered the front door, her make-up and hair immaculate. Just as yesterday.

'Is Declan in?' I asked her.

'He's in the shower,' she replied. 'Just back from riding out.'

For some reason I was surprised.

'He still rides, then?'

'Of course he still rides. Most days.' She sounded almost affronted that I would even ask. 'He only gave up race-riding two years ago.'

'Only I saw Ryan and Oliver on the gallops and they were in a Land Rover.'

She grimaced as if even the mention of their names in this household was offensive.

'Oliver is too old to ride now and Ryan has a bad knee. That's what forced him to retire as a jockey.' There was no sympathy in her tone, just a clipped statement of facts.

'Why did Declan retire as a jockey?' I asked.

'He always wanted to train horses more than ride them. Most jockeys leave it too late. And, also, he got fed up of having to constantly starve himself to make the weights. Do you want to come in?'

She looked past me to the Mercedes and the driver, raising her eyebrows in question.

'He'll wait there,' I said.

I stepped into the galleried hallway and Arabella shut the door.

'Coffee?' she asked.

'Great.'

She led the way across the parquet flooring of the hall into the kitchen. The house may have been slightly smaller than that of her father-in-law but it was tastefully furnished in pastels, and everything was spotless.

There was a view from the kitchen window straight into the stable yard and, whereas the stable buildings themselves may have seen better days, they looked well cared for with several large pots of red geraniums adding colour at every corner.

'Milk?' Arabella asked.

'Please,' I said.

She poured it in and handed me the steaming cup.

'You have a lovely place here,' I said.

'Thank you. It's not as big as Castleton House but at least it's ours.'

There was clear resentment in her tone. Jealousy towards Ryan was obviously alive and well and living in Hamilton Road.

I decided not to duck the issue.

'Have Ryan and Declan never got on?'

She glanced at me sharply. 'Who says they don't get on?'

I pursed my lips and looked at her. 'Don't take me for a fool,' I said. 'It's pretty obvious. And I overheard him talking to you in Oliver's kitchen yesterday before I came in.'

She sighed. 'That was the first time Ryan had spoken to me in five years. Not that he was very nice.'

'So what were you doing there, then?'

'God knows,' she said. 'Declan thought that we should, you know, after the fire and such, to show some support, but it wasn't a good idea. We have nothing to do with them any more.'

'Did you previously?' I asked.

'A bit, when the brothers were both riding. But not much even then. They are ultra-competitive – everyone is in racing – but Ryan always lorded it over Declan, claiming he was the better jockey simply because he rode more winners.

But he had better horses to ride. Oliver thinks the sun shines out of Ryan's arse, that he can do no wrong.'

*That's not what Maria said,* I thought, but decided not to say so.

'Did Declan ride for Oliver as well?'

'Hardy ever. I don't think Ryan liked it. If he was unavailable or if there were two or more runners in the same race, Ryan told his father to engage other jockeys rather than Declan. Ryan regularly made a joke about it – only it wasn't funny. Not for us, anyway.'

'Was that why the brothers fell out?'

'Not really,' Arabella said, continuing to be wonderfully indiscreet. 'They've apparently been at each other's throats since they were kids. Ryan is the eldest son and he has always insisted on his younger brothers being deferential and submissive. But Declan won't be.'

'How about Tony?' I asked. 'Is he deferential and submissive?'

'He doesn't like it but he fears his riding career might depend on it, and he's probably right. He was absolutely desperate to keep the ride on Prince of Troy in the Derby, not that that matters now. So he bows and scrapes when Ryan can see him then sticks two fingers up as soon as he turns his back. It would be funny if it wasn't so sad.'

'So you think it's sad?'

'Sure it is,' she said. 'Brothers should be best mates, surely, especially living so close.'

'Do you see anything of Susan?'

'Not really. She's too damn preoccupied with her kids.'

'How old are they?' I asked.

'Five and two. A girl first, then a boy.'

'How long have Ryan and Susan been married?'

'Eight years. Same as us. We got married two months after them, even though we'd announced it first. It was as if Ryan couldn't face being second in that race either.'

'Do you and Declan have any children?' I asked, all innocently.

'No,' she said abruptly, and in a manner that made me think that the whole question of children was a sore point. Perhaps that, too, had something to do with the animosity between the brothers.

'Maybe you'll see more of Susan when her kids get a bit older.'

'I doubt it,' she said. 'This has gone too far for that.'

'What's gone too far?' I asked pointedly.

'All this Sheikh Karim stuff. I wish he'd never said he was moving horses from Ryan to us. Ryan is livid. So is Oliver. They accuse us of going behind their backs.'

'And did you?'

'No. Of course not.'

There was something about her voice that didn't ring totally true.

'So you had no contact with the Sheikh at all?' I said. 'I could check with him.'

'Declan and I sat next to him at the Guineas Ball last month.'

'And?' I prompted.

'We asked him to consider sending some horses to us but we didn't expect him to move two fillies already with Ryan. We would never have wanted that.'

'But you agreed to take them.'

'Well, yes. But they're not here yet. We're renovating some old boxes to make room.'

'You could always tell the Sheikh you don't want them.'

She looked at me as if I were mad.

'But why would we? Sheikh Karim is the big catch in racing. Everyone knows that. He's the next Sheikh Mohammed.'

'But Sheikh Mohammed pays millions for his horses.' Even I knew that. 'Sheikh Karim doesn't spend that sort of money.'

'But he might do in time. Sheikh Mohammed's first ever winner was a filly called Hatta, and she cost a mere six thousand as a yearling. And look what that led to. Sheikh Karim told us he intends to greatly increase his involvement in the sport and we want to be part of it. He also wants to start a breeding operation.'

*Yes*, I thought, *with Prince of Troy as his foundation stallion.* I wondered if the fire had put that plan on hold indefinitely.

At this point Declan came downstairs and into the kitchen, his black hair still damp from his shower, and he was clearly not very happy to see me.

'What the hell do you want?' he asked gruffly.

'The Sheikh told me to come round and see if things are ready for his fillies.'

It wasn't true but Declan wasn't to know that.

'Oh, yes, of course,' he said, as if suddenly remembering who I represented. 'Almost ready. Just waiting for the flooring to be done. Should be finished today.'

'Can I see?' I asked.

'Don't see why not.'

We went out the back door and into the yard where his staff were still rushing around with buckets of feed or wheelbarrows full of soiled wood shavings.

'You don't use shredded paper then?' I asked, trying to sound knowledgeable.

'Sometimes,' Declan replied. 'Depends on the price. I've recently switched from shredded paper to wood chippings. It's cheaper at the moment. Also it doesn't blow around as much. Less mess.'

'I always thought that straw was used for horse bedding.'

'Used to be universal but it's so difficult to get good-quality straw these days. It has too much dust in it for my liking, and it can be full of spores. Not good for their respiration.'

Everything, it seemed, was determined by what was good for the horses.

'How many boxes do you have?' I asked.

'Fifty-six, plus the four being renovated.'

'Are you full?'

'Bursting at the seams. The four new boxes are already allocated and I'm thinking of putting up temporary stables round the back as an overflow. I have several owners on a waiting list to increase their strings. Lack of space is my main problem.'

'Did the Sheikh jump the queue?'

'Of course he did,' Declan said with a smile. 'I'd have cleared someone else out completely if I'd needed to. He's what I've been crying out for to finance a move to a bigger yard.'

'So why have you kept his fillies waiting?'

'Only by a few days. They'll be here tomorrow.'

'Your father and brother don't like it,' I said.

He snorted, but with amusement rather than distress. 'Tough.'

In spite of what his wife had said, I wondered if Declan had actively encouraged the Sheikh to move the fillies from Ryan.

We continued to walk past the row of stables, the equine occupants sticking their heads out over the half-doors to inspect us. Declan went over and patted a few, including a big brown horse with a black mane.

'This is Orion's Glory. My best horse by far.' Declan took a carrot out of his pocket and gave it to the great beast. 'Three-year-old colt by Sea The Stars.'

I must have looked blank rather than impressed.

'Sea The Stars won the Two Thousand Guineas, the Epsom Derby and the Prix de l'Arc de Triomphe all in the same year.'

'Oh,' I said. 'Is that unusual?'

'Only horse ever to do it. One of the best there's ever been.'

'Better than Prince of Troy?' I asked.

'We'll never know,' Declan replied, without showing any emotion. 'His death is a huge loss to racing.'

'And to your brother.'

He snorted again. 'He was bloody lucky.'

'Surely you mean unlucky?'

'He was lucky to have had the horse in the first place,' Declan said with passion. 'And lucky not to have then ruined him.'

'In what way?' I asked.

'Ran him too often. Six races as a two-year-old are far too many.'

'But he won them all.'

'Yeah, that was the problem. Ryan was so desperate for winners that he kept going back to the same well time and time again. He was bloody lucky he didn't burn the horse out before he even started in the Guineas. Golden Horn and Galileo, both Derby winners, they ran only once each as two-year-olds, and then not until October. Ryan was just being greedy.'

'How about Orion's Glory?' I asked. 'How many races has he had?'

'Two last season and only one so far this term. His next race is the Derby, isn't it, my boy?' He again patted the taut muscular neck of the horse. 'Should have a damn good chance too, now that Prince of Troy won't be there.'

*How convenient*, I thought.

*

Declan and I made it down to the far end of the yard where two workmen were busy laying a new floor in the last box.

'How's it going?' Declan asked.

'Nearly done,' said one of the men. 'Just sticking the last few mats in place. All finished by this afternoon.'

'Good,' Declan said. 'Well done.' He turned to me. 'I'm trying rubber. It's meant to cause fewer injuries than concrete, and be more thermally efficient. And it had better be at this price.'

'Only the best for the Sheikh's horses,' I agreed.

Declan shook his head. 'His two will be in the main part with the other fillies. These will be for colts. They're the ones that usually do themselves damage by kicking the floor.'

There was no doubt in my mind that Declan knew his business. He was polite but firm to his staff and he showed a genuine affection for his horses, patting each one in turn and dispensing carrots from a seemingly never-ending supply in his coat pockets.

'Here,' he said, offering me a carrot outside one box. 'You give him one.'

I hesitated and Declan must have seen the look on my face.

'Not frightened of him, are you?' he said, with a mixture of amusement and mischief.

'No, of course not,' I replied. It was not so much 'him' that I was frightened of, just his teeth, a row of huge white tombstones that were noisily crunching a carrot into a pulp. I had no desire to look any horse in the mouth, gift or otherwise, but Declan wasn't giving up that easily.

'Hold your hand flat with the carrot resting on it and the horse will take it.' He demonstrated. 'Go on, now. You do it.'

He clearly wasn't going to take no for an answer so I held out a carrot as instructed and forced myself to move my right hand closer to the beast while leaning the rest of my body away from it at the same time.

I could feel the horse's breath on my skin as it placed its muzzle down onto my hand, providing a ticklish sensation. The carrot was swept up into the animal's mouth more by the actions of its lips rather than the tongue as I had expected, leaving my hand dry and empty.

Declan laughed.

'Have you not been with horses before?' he asked, the incredulity thick in his tone.

'Never,' I said, silently counting my fingers to ensure that none had gone the same way as the carrot.

'Not even with a pony as a child?'

'No,' I said.

In truth, I had always been terrified of horses, ever since I was six and had witnessed one go berserk during the annual Totnes town carnival. The rider had been thrown onto the road and then dragged along, his foot still caught in the stirrup. The vivid mental image of the poor man's head bouncing on the tarmac all the way down Fore Street remained with me even now.

'I'm slightly allergic to horses,' I said. 'Asthma.' And I did my best to wheeze a little.

It wasn't true, but it was the white lie I had employed for many years to keep me away from them. It usually worked.

'Sorry,' he said, although for what I wasn't sure.

We continued along the line of stables.

One we passed was empty, the door hanging wide open.

'Jackbarrow,' Declan said, by way of explanation. 'He runs this afternoon at Beverley. Left at dawn this morning.'

'Are you going?' I asked.

'No way,' he said firmly. 'I sent my travelling head lad instead.'

'Is that usual?'

'I go to the local Newmarket tracks and all the big meetings, of course – Ascot, York, Epsom, Chester, Goodwood and so on – but that's mostly for exposure and PR. My job is to train the horses, not sit in a car for three hours each way just to put on a saddle. I'm better employed here.'

'Don't you have to give instructions to the jockey?'

'Did that last night on the telephone. And I'll be watching the race on TV, to make sure he follows them.' He smiled broadly at me and I was certain he'd said the same thing to the jockey in question.

'Another coffee?' he asked.

'Lovely.'

He didn't, however, lead me back to the house but into his yard office, a space clearly converted from the end two stalls of one of the stable blocks.

Outside the door was a large blue plastic barrel half full of carrots.

'Bella's brother is a carrot farmer in Norfolk,' Declan said. 'These are the ones too bent to make it to the supermarkets.'

He leaned down and replenished his coat pockets before going in. I followed.

'Hi, Chrissie,' he said. 'This is ...' He paused. 'Sorry.'

'Harry Foster,' I said.

Chrissie was a large woman of about fifty who was sitting behind one of the three desks. She stood up and we shook hands as Declan put on the kettle and spooned instant coffee into mugs.

'Don't be offended,' Chrissie said. 'He often forgets who I am too. Never forgets a horse's name, mind. I often think he's half horse. Speaks to them in some language or other that they seem to understand.'

She smiled broadly and glanced admiringly at Declan before going back to the task in hand, placing coloured magnetic strips on a plastic-covered metal board. Each coloured strip had a name printed on it in black capital letters.

'What are you doing?' I asked her.

'Tomorrow's lots,' she said. 'Who rides what, where and when. The blue strips are our lads plus the work riders. The reds are the two-year-olds, white are the threes, and the yellows are older horses.'

There were far more red and white strips than yellow ones.

'What happens when the horses get older than three?' I asked.

'I keep a few good ones in training aged four,' Declan said, 'and one or two might go straight to stud, but the rest get sent to the horses-in-training sales. Most are sold to race in

Europe and some go to jump yards. Flat racing here in the UK is mostly about the two- and three-year-olds.'

'So you're always having to find new ones.'

'Absolutely,' he said. 'Nearly half my yard turns over each year. Hence I spend a huge amount of my time at the yearling sales finding the next crop. It's perhaps the most important part of the job.'

I watched as Chrissie continued to position the strips in place. The blue human name labels were down the left-hand side and then there were three distinct vertical groups across the board representing the three lots of equine partners.

'Some trainers now do it on a computer,' Declan said, handing me my coffee. 'But I prefer the old-fashioned method. No horse gets left off by mistake as it's dead easy to see if a strip hasn't been allocated to a rider.'

'Do all the horses go out every day?' I asked.

'Every day except Sunday,' he said. 'If you can't do it in six days, you're not going to do it in seven.' He laughed. 'Our runners for Monday and Tuesday will get a pipe-opener on a Sunday morning but that's it. Day of rest for the remainder.'

'Do the horses ever go out in the afternoons?' I asked.

'I occasionally have horses out later in the day. Often depends if there's someone available to ride them or if I want to avoid the touts.'

'The touts?'

'Newmarket is a Mecca for betting tipsters – the touts. They stand and watch the horses on the gallops – they learn them all by sight – and then they sell tips to gamblers on premium phone lines. The place is crawling with them, especially on Wednesday and Saturday mornings.'

'Work days,' I said.

He looked at me sharply. 'You learn fast.'

'Oliver told me.'

'But I don't hold by that. I work horses most days.'

'To avoid the touts?'

'Not really. I just find it more convenient to spread them out rather than engage a mass of work riders twice a week. If you really want to avoid the bloody touts, work a horse when none of them are watching.'

'At night?' I said.

Declan laughed. 'I'm not that crazy. Galloping fast in the dark is inviting disaster. Best leave that malarkey to Dick Turpin and Black Bess. No. You do what I did ten days ago. Staged my own Derby trial on the Limekilns gallop at exactly three thirty-five in the afternoon. Pitched Orion's Glory against my two best four-year-olds over the full mile-and-a-half. He went away from them near the end as if they were going backwards, and the touts, plus everyone else for that matter, were all at the racecourse admiring Prince of Troy as he was winning the Two Thousand Guineas.' He laughed again at having outwitted the enemy. 'Keep that to yourself, mind.'

'Why was it so important not to be seen?'

He stared at me. 'Because of the price, man.'

I looked at him blankly.

'Look,' he said. 'Suppose I think that Orion's Glory is a very special horse, so special, in fact, that he might well win the Derby. Which I do. He's come on in leaps and bounds since he ran at Doncaster last month. Really filled out behind. The last thing I need is for a bunch of bloody touts to tip him to everybody and bring down the starting price, perhaps even make him favourite now that Prince of Troy is dead.'

I assumed it was because he wanted to bet on it, but it seemed that that wasn't the only reason.

'Other trainers will make plans to foil you if they think your horse has a good chance. I want Orion's Glory to be the surprise package of the race – to sneak up and win when no one's expecting it, when all the favourites are busy covering each other.'

'We're one work rider short for tomorrow,' Chrissie said, interrupting. 'Second lot. Jamie has to go to York. He's riding in the first.'

'Call Bob Cox,' Declan said. 'Ask him.'

'Already have,' Chrissie replied. 'He's laid up with an ankle injury.'

'Have you tried Colin Noble?'

Chrissie picked up her telephone.

'Who are the work riders?' I asked.

'Mainly current or ex-jockeys. Most trainers have their regulars but there's always a group waiting on a Wednesday morning down near the entrance to the Rowley Mile course hoping for a spare ride, and a payday. I use them sometimes if I'm short. May have to do that tomorrow.'

'Couldn't you ride one yourself?'

'I will do if we're desperate – like we were today – but I can't ride them *and* watch them at the same time.'

Arabella came into the yard office.

'I've just had a call from Pete Robertson,' she said. 'It seems that Zoe has gone missing again.'

I happened to be looking at Declan as she said it, and he went completely white as the blood drained out of his face.

# 8

'Was the human victim male or female?' I asked.

'I can't tell you that at the present time,' replied the man sitting in front of me wearing a rather crumpled grey suit.

'Can't or won't?' I said.

'Both.'

I was sitting in an interview room in Newmarket Police Station, where a temporary incident centre had been set up following the events at Castleton House Stables. I had asked to speak to Superintendent Bennett but, according to the man on the other side of the table, he hadn't been available.

'You'll have to make do with me,' he'd said.

'And you are?'

'Detective Chief Inspector Eastwood,' he'd replied. 'I'm now leading the investigation into the fire at Castleton House Stables.'

At least I hadn't been fobbed off with a junior. A DCI would do nicely.

'Now, Mr Foster, what exactly is so important to have had me dragged out of a meeting with my staff?'

'Zoe Robertson has gone missing from her home in Ealing,' I said. 'And she's been missing since Sunday.'

There was a moment of silence while the detective absorbed the information.

'And who is Zoe Robertson?' he asked.

'Robertson is her married name. She's Oliver Chadwick's daughter. Ryan's sister.'

He nodded then sighed, as if there was something he wasn't telling me.

'Are you suggesting that she's the victim of the fire?' he asked.

'I don't know,' I said. 'But I don't like coincidences.'

'Neither do I, but if I overreacted to every coincidence in my career, I'd still be a detective constable. What proof have you got?'

'None. But I thought you should know.'

'Yes, thank you. Has she been reported missing to her local police?'

'I don't know,' I said. 'It seems it's not the first time she has disappeared but her husband claims she's never not phoned home for as long as this before.'

For some reason the policeman's interest was waning fast, as if he didn't really believe what I was telling him.

'How did you come by this knowledge?' he asked.

'I was with Declan Chadwick when Peter Robertson called. Peter is Zoe's husband.'

'Does Mr Chadwick agree with you that his sister may be the victim of the fire?'

'He didn't say so,' I said. 'But, there again, I didn't actually ask him that particular question.'

I hadn't needed to.

Back in his yard office, Declan had taken quite a few minutes to recover from the shock of hearing that his sister was missing, the colour only returning to his face after he'd sat down and drunk a glass of water.

'What on earth is wrong with you?' Arabella had asked as her husband had slumped down on the chair.

'Nothing,' he had mumbled unconvincingly. 'I'm fine.'

'Does she often go missing?' I had asked into the ensuing silence.

'Regularly,' Arabella had said, in a way that suggested that not only was there nothing to worry about but that the whole saga had become a bit of a bore. 'Zoe has mental health problems. Postnatal depression that hasn't gone away.'

But still, I thought, I didn't like coincidences, so here I was an hour later with the police reporting the matter, and hoping to get something in return.

'Have you yet discovered the cause of the fire?' I asked the chief inspector.

He looked up at me from writing something in his notes.

'And who are you exactly, Mr Foster?'

'Harrison Foster,' I said, handing over my business card. 'I represent His Highness Sheikh Ahmed Karim bin Mohamed Al Hamadi. He was the owner of two of the horses killed in the fire, including Prince of Troy. He is keen to understand why his horses died.'

He studied my card.

'Lawyer, are you?' asked the policeman in a tone that implied he didn't much like lawyers.

'Yes,' I said.

'Simpson White,' he read out loud from the card. 'Not a law firm I'm familiar with in these parts.'

'London firm,' I said. 'We specialise in crisis management.'

'Is this really a crisis?' he asked.

'It is if you're Ryan Chadwick. Or Sheikh Karim. The favourite for the Derby has just died in highly suspicious circumstances. I'd call that a crisis.'

'Highly suspicious circumstances ...' The DCI repeated the words slowly. 'Why do you say that?'

'Unknown human body found in a fire started at dead of night,' I said. 'I'd call that highly suspicious, wouldn't you?'

'Unexplained,' he said.

'So you're telling me that you don't know how it started.'

He couldn't resist proving me wrong.

'One of our lines of enquiry concerns the remnants of a cigarette lighter that has been found. The metal parts survived the inferno. We think it may have been used to start the fire, perhaps accidentally.'

*Or perhaps intentionally*, I thought.

'Was it found close to the body?' I asked.

'Yes, right next to it, as if it had been in a pocket.'

I thought back to Ryan's theory of the smoking homeless person.

'Did you find any cigarette ends?'

'No, but the intensity of the fire would have made that impossible, even if they had been present initially.'

'How about a mobile phone?' I asked.

He paused for a moment as if deciding whether to tell me any more.

'None has been found as yet,' he said finally.

'Anything else?'

Another pause. He'd already told me more than I'd expected him to.

'Not at present,' he said. 'Forensic tests still have to be carried out to determine if an accelerant was present – petrol, for example.'

'You wouldn't need petrol to start a fire in those stables, not with all that shredded paper on the floor.'

'No, indeed not. But you are jumping to conclusions, Mr Foster. There is no evidence as yet that the fire was set deliberately.'

'What else could it be?'

'It may have been started accidentally by the victim, or maybe it was the result of an electrical fault, or some other reason. I am confident that our investigation will eventually determine the true cause.'

'Has the post-mortem given you any clues?' I asked.

'I couldn't give you that information even if I had it, which I don't. Not before the coroner has been informed.'

'But a post-mortem is being conducted?'

'Certainly,' said the detective. 'As already reported in the press, the human remains were removed from the stables this morning and taken to Lowestoft Hospital for examination by a Home Office pathologist.'

'One of your scene-of-crime officers told me that he thought there was enough of the body left to get a DNA profile. Will you check that against Zoe Robertson's?'

The DCI pursed his lips as if he didn't like the fact that the scene-of-crime officer had spoken to me. Or maybe it was because he didn't appreciate me telling him his job.

'Of course,' he said.

'And you'll let me know the outcome?'

'If it is found that the remains are indeed those of Zoe Robertson, her next of kin will be informed first, followed by a press release. You will find out the results from that.' He collected his papers together. 'Now,' he said, standing up, 'is there anything else I can help you with?'

'How about the horses?' I asked.

'What about them?'

'Are you carrying out DNA tests on their remains as well?'

'Why would we?'

'To ensure they are the horses they are claimed to be.'

The policeman laughed. 'My, Mr Foster, you do have a suspicious mind.'

'Acquired by experience,' I assured him. 'Well, are you?'

'No, we aren't, and we won't be. It would be a waste of our limited resources. As I understand it, all racehorses are microchipped to confirm their identity. In this case, the microchips are unlikely to have survived the intensity of the heat but that's no matter. If the horses had been switched, it would be to no avail as *their* microchips would prevent them being passed off as others anyway.'

'How about at stud? Prince of Troy would make someone a fine stallion if he'd been spirited away prior to the fire.'

'But not for producing racehorses,' said DCI Eastwood. 'And that's only where any gain would come from. We had a case here a few years ago concerning the alleged mixing up of two valuable foals at the sale ring. One owner accused the other of theft. You get that sort of thing in these parts. But it was easily resolved as all Thoroughbred foals registered since 2001 have had their parentage verified by their DNA. You'd never be able to pass off a foal by Prince of Troy as being by another stallion. Its DNA simply wouldn't fit.'

'Oh,' I said. So that was one wild theory I could disregard. 'So what now happens to the remains?'

'That will be up to Mr Chadwick. Once we have finished our examination of the scene, disposal and clean up of the site will be his problem, not ours, provided he does so in keeping with the law.'

The chief inspector opened the door and stood there waiting for me to go out. He was determined that the interview was over.

'His Highness Sheikh Karim has instructed me to remain in Newmarket for as long as it takes to discover the reason for the death of his horses. He is concerned that his decision to move two fillies from Ryan to Declan Chadwick may have exacerbated the bad feeling between the brothers and that may have had some bearing on the circumstances of the fire.'

'Mr Foster, please leave the detective work to us.'

'But ...'

'No buts,' interrupted the policeman. 'I hear what you are saying. All scenarios will be considered, thank you. But I must now ask you to leave so that I can get back to examining the evidence.'

'Anything to help,' I said, walking out of the door. 'You have my card. Call me if you need anything.'

I thought the chance of the detective ever calling me was slim to non-existent but I didn't want to be accused of obstructing the police, and I had no intention of leaving Newmarket just yet.

'Do whatever the Sheikh tells you. He's paying us, and handsomely. If he wants you to stay in Newmarket, you stay there.' ASW was in full flow down the phone line. 'I'll get Georgina to negotiate a better rate with the hotel for a long-term stay.'

'I need some more information,' I said.

'Shoot.'

'Further depth concerning the whole Chadwick family

and in particular about the daughter, Zoe Robertson, and her husband, Peter.'

ASW didn't ask me why I needed the information. If I'd asked for it, he assumed I must need it. That was enough.

'I'll get the research team on it straight away. Top priority. Something should be with you by the morning.'

The Simpson White Research Team was the rather grandiose name for two young men in the Motcomb Street office, only just old enough to be allowed out of school, who were absolute wizards on the internet and could seemingly discover everything there was to know about anyone. They bounced ideas off each other and could hack into almost anything digital.

No one's secrets were safe from them.

Knowledge was power, ASW claimed, and his operatives were to have more knowledge than anyone else.

All we craved was the wisdom to use it properly.

'Anything else?' ASW asked.

'You could always send Rufus up,' I said. 'He's forgotten more about horses than I'll ever know. He'd enjoy himself here.'

'I'm sure he would, but he's still in Italy. Seems the wine company's complete year's production is contaminated by lactic acid bacteria. The whole lot's off, hundreds of thousands of bottles of the damn stuff already in stores all over Europe. And now they've gone and publicly denied it's their fault. It's another Perrier disaster and Rufus is trying to arrest the meltdown.'

*Rather him than me*, I thought.

The response to the discovery of toxic benzene in Perrier's 'naturally carbonated' sparkling mineral water in the early 1990s remains one of the prime crisis-management examples of how *not* to handle a major problem. There was a lack of a coherent response from the French company, with confusion created by contradictory statements, and then the media was given incorrect information, in particular about the way the so-called 'natural' carbonation of the water was achieved. The resulting drop in public confidence and market share has never been reversed.

Perhaps being stuck in Newmarket with the horses wasn't so bad after all.

'Anything else?' ASW asked again.

'I don't think so,' I said. 'A few tips might be handy. I might go to the races on Thursday for the very first time in my life.'

'My only tip is to keep your money in your pocket,' ASW said with certainty. 'There's no such thing as a poor bookmaker.'

'I thought you liked to gamble,' I said, surprised.

'I do,' he said. 'But not on horses. My whole life's been a gamble but I prefer it when the odds are stacked in my favour, not against them. If I were to gamble seriously, I'd have to be the bookmaker.' He laughed. 'Right, I'll get those research results emailed to you as soon as possible.'

We disconnected.

What I would really like, I thought, was Zoe Robertson's mobile phone records, but not even the Simpson White

Research Team could get those, not without breaking the law, and that would open up a whole new can of worms. Information obtained illegally was not only rightly excluded from any court case, but the fact that it had been gathered in the first place tended to taint everything else, however clean and legitimate the rest might be.

At six o'clock I walked along from my room to the hotel bar and ordered a Newmarket Gin with tonic.

It was difficult to believe that it was still Tuesday and I'd been here for only thirty hours. It felt like so much longer.

After my meeting with DCI Eastwood, I had spent some of the afternoon walking through the town purchasing a few essential articles, like wellington boots, a pair of thick socks and a coat. Even in mid-May, it could be very cold in the mornings.

It was difficult, if not impossible, to get away from horses and horse racing in Newmarket and it was not for nothing that locals referred to it as 'HQ'.

The red-brick Jockey Club headquarters building, with its life-size statue of the horse Hyperion on display outside, dominates the western end of the High Street. Nowadays, it is little more than a private club where one can rent out its grand rooms for weddings, but once this was where the power of British racing was housed and exercised, where the Stewards of the Jockey Club would sit round a horseshoe-shaped table and decide on the future of those suspected of misdemeanours in the sport of kings. Reputations and livelihoods were at stake as the accused were made to stand on a small piece of carpet between the jaws of the table to hear their fate, hence coining the phrase 'to be carpeted'.

Such power had the members of the Jockey Club in the mid-nineteenth century that, with the coming of the railway, they insisted that a tunnel be bored to preserve the lower part of the Warren Hill training grounds. The kilometre-long Warren Hill Tunnel is still in use today and, despite its name, it's probably the only rail tunnel in rural England built under a piece of totally flat land.

Newmarket, for all its racing grandeur, remains a small metropolis, with a human population of only some twenty thousand souls, yet it boasts no fewer than thirteen separate betting shops. But perhaps the most bizarre indication that this is a one-industry – if not a one-horse – town is that the local undertakers have a window display that not only features sober gravestones in black and white marble, but also a blue-painted jockey-sized coffin adorned all over with horse-racing scenes.

I took my drink and wandered round the hotel bar looking at the photographs and artwork hanging on the walls. As expected, nearly all were of sporting scenes but one chronicled the history of the hotel. It had initially been built as a hunting lodge in the eighteenth century, then converted to a racing stables in the nineteenth, before becoming a hotel and spa in the mid-twentieth.

'Mr Foster?' said a soft female voice, bringing me back to the here and now from the history lesson.

'Yes?' I said, looking down at two young women sitting at a corner table, empty champagne flutes in front of them.

'Janie Logan,' one of them said. 'I work for Ryan Chadwick. I saw you at Castleton House Stables this morning.'

'Of course,' I said, remembering the head of tight red curls.

'This is Catherine, my sister. It's her birthday.'

'Happy birthday,' I said. 'Can I get you both another drink?'

The two looked at each other and an unspoken message clearly passed between them.

'Sure,' Janie said. 'We have time. Thank you.'

'Champagne?' I asked, looking at their empty glasses.

The women looked at each other again, then up at me.

'That would be lovely.'

I put my own drink down on the table and took their empties to the bar.

'Two more champagnes, please,' I said to the barman.

'They had Prosecco before,' he replied drily, raising a questioning eyebrow.

In a flash, all my insecurities over women rose to the fore. Did I get them another Prosecco and perhaps be thought of as a cheapskate? Or did I buy the real McCoy and risk being considered too pretentious?

Decisions, decisions. Which way did I jump?

'Champagne,' I said. After all, that was what I'd offered them.

He poured the golden bubbles into two fresh glasses and I carried them over to the table.

'Join us,' Janie said, pulling up another chair.

'Thank you. I will.' I sat down and picked up my gin and tonic. 'Cheers, and happy birthday, Catherine.'

We drank the toast.

'Oh, that's lovely,' Catherine said after taking a sip. 'A real treat. Thank you. And please call me Kate. Only our mum calls me Catherine, and also Janie when she's being bossy.'

'All right, Kate,' I said. 'I will.'

She looked deeply into my eyes and smiled.

It did nothing for my insecurity.

I was flustered. It was not a condition I was familiar with. In my work I was confident, assured and positive, some might even say arrogant, so why did the presence of a pretty girl smiling at me create such a quivering-jelly feeling in my stomach?

'So, are you two off to a birthday party?' I asked, then instantly regretted it, sure that they would think me too forward, as if I was asking myself to go with them.

'Just a small dinner with friends and family,' Kate said. 'I'm too old now for parties.'

She looked about thirty.

'What nonsense,' I said. 'My mother says there's nothing like a good party and she's in her sixties.'

*What am I doing?* I thought, in absolute horror.

Dating rule number one: *Never ever talk about your mother.*

Change the subject, and fast.

'So, Janie,' I said. 'How long have you worked for Ryan Chadwick?'

'Five years now with Mr Ryan,' she said. 'Since he took over. I came with the yard.' She laughed. 'I went to work for Mr Chadwick when I left school. There's nothing I don't know about the place.'

'The fire must have come as a big shock,' I said.

'Massive. Those poor horses.' There were now tears in Janie's eyes. 'I can't bear to think how they suffered. Especially Prince of Troy. He was our great hope. Lovely horse.' She took a tissue from her handbag and blew her nose.

'Janie's mad about horses,' Kate said. 'Always has been.'

'Did you ever ride them?' I asked.

'Sure,' Janie replied. 'I worked there first as a stable lad. Did my two and rode them out every morning. Happy days.'

'What changed?' I asked.

'She had a fall,' Kate said, receiving a stern look from her sister. 'Broke her leg badly.'

'A fall from a horse?'

'Of course from a horse,' Janie said sharply. 'Damn thing dumped me onto the concrete outside its box. Snapped both bones in my shin in multiple places. Three bloody months in plaster and four more in rehab. So I went into the office to help out with the paperwork and I've been in there ever since.' She downed the rest of her drink and stood up. 'Come on, Catherine, we have to go or we'll be late.'

'See what I mean?' Catherine/Kate said with another killer smile in my direction. She stood up and looked at me with a mixture of sorrow and apology. 'Perhaps we'll meet again.'

'You can count on it,' I said.

I stood and watched as the two sisters walked towards the door. Kate turned round and waved.

*Wow!* I thought.

As Tom said in the film *Four Weddings and a Funeral*: 'Thunderbolt City'.

## 9

I spent the evening in the hotel wishing I were elsewhere, thinking about Catherine/Kate Logan. Assuming that she actually was Catherine Logan and not Kate Somebody Else, with a husband and four kids in tow.

I berated myself for not getting her phone number.

I imagined her at the birthday dinner, drinking wine and having fun, and positively ached to be there too.

Instead, I sat alone in the hotel dining room absent-mindedly pushing my uneaten food around the plate, before giving up and going to my room.

My spirits were briefly raised by the red message light flashing on the phone beside the bed. I positively leapt across the room to pick it up but my joy was short-lived as the message wasn't from Kate. It was from Ryan Chadwick inviting me to come out to watch the Sheikh's horses at work on the gallops the following morning.

'Be at the new yard by six o'clock at the latest,' his recorded voice said.

I looked at my watch. Ten past nine. Obviously time for bed.

I'd always been a bit of a night owl and my move to London from rural Devon had opened my eyes to the delights of late nights in the West End. I couldn't remember when I'd last been in bed before eleven o'clock, let alone ten. I would clearly be totally hopeless as a stable lad. Not only would I be frightened of the horses, I wouldn't get up in time to ride them out.

However, on this occasion, I was up, dressed and standing in Ryan's new yard at 5.55 a.m. on Wednesday morning, toasty warm in my new socks, boots and coat.

'Morning, Harry,' Ryan said, all smiles. 'Glad you could make it.' He hurried from one box to another, checking that everything was in order, while I trotted along behind him. 'Still can't get through to here from the old yard,' he moaned. 'We'll have to walk right round the road. It's a bloody nuisance.'

*So is a dead body*, I thought, but I decided not to mention it.

If I'd learned one thing over the past two days, it was that the good folk of Newmarket were grieving far more over the seven equine losses than they were over the human one.

It was a mindset with which I had some difficulty empathising. Did they also grieve for the cow that had died to provide the roast beef for their Sunday lunch? No, of course not. Surely horses were just animals too, weren't they?

Clearly not.

For them, horses were different. They were like family, loved and admired by all, irrespective of their actual owners and trainers, whereas people were just ... people, with all their faults and shortcomings.

'Right,' said Ryan, slapping me jovially on the back. 'Let's get going or we'll miss my slot.'

We hurried down the road to the house and in through the old yard gates, the blue-and-white-police-tape tide having receded a little since yesterday.

'Is Janie in yet?' I asked.

Ryan gave me a look as if he thought it was a strange question to ask, which I suppose it was, to him.

'She doesn't get in until seven-thirty,' he said.

Oliver was already sitting in the Land Rover waiting for us.

'Morning, Harry,' he said, leaning back over the front seats to shake my hand. 'Good of you to join us.'

Both Ryan and Oliver were being uncommonly pleasant towards me, I thought, in spite of the early hour.

I wondered if I was being the subject of a charm offensive. Had they finally worked out that the best way to keep the Sheikh's horses was to be nice to his representative? Or was I just being cynical?

Ryan turned left out of the yard onto Bury Road.

'We're on the Limekilns today,' he said. 'Fast gallops over six or seven furlongs. Some will do eight.'

Was horse racing the only activity left where distances were still measured in eighths of a mile? No metric units here, that was for sure.

'How do you decide which horse does which distance?' I asked, half fearing that the question might further show up my lack of knowledge.

'The two-year-olds will run shorter, the threes longer,' Oliver said, without any obvious irritation at the naivety of the question.

We pulled off the road into a parking area already half full with other vehicles, many with men standing near them by the rail, their binoculars and notebooks at the ready.

'Bloody touts,' Oliver said.

The three of us ducked under the rail and walked across the grass, eventually standing close to a strip of the undulating gallop marked off by pairs of small white discs placed eight yards apart all along its length, at about hundred-yard intervals.

'They move the gallop across a bit every day,' Oliver said. 'So the turf doesn't get too worn.'

'Who's they?' I asked.

'The Jockey Club. They own all the gallops. We pay a fee to use them.'

Ryan stood to one side speaking into his phone.

'We used to have walkie-talkies,' Oliver said to me. 'But the touts would listen in. Phones are better. More private. We've done the lists beforehand. Ryan is just telling them to start.'

We stood and watched as a group of four horses came up towards us, galloping side by side. Ryan and Oliver inspected them closely through their binoculars.

'What are you looking for?' I asked Oliver as the four thundered past us and began to slow down at the end of their run.

'Mostly we are watching to see how they perform relative to the rest of the group. We know how good one or two are and we want to see how the others compare.'

Another four were coming up the gallop towards us. Oliver again lifted his binoculars.

'Two of these are Sheikh Karim's,' he said. 'The one on the far side and second in from this.'

Even to my eye, I could tell that one of the four was struggling to keep up. Thankfully it was not one of the Sheikh's.

'Useless,' Ryan said with feeling as they passed us. 'Meant to be running him next week. No chance now. It would be an embarrassment.'

'So what will you do with him?' I asked.

'More hard work. If that doesn't do the trick he'll have to go to the sales, not that anyone will want him, not after that.'

'How would they know?' I asked.

'That lot,' Ryan said with a disdainful wave towards the men standing by their cars. 'They report everything.'

Another group of four horses was coming along the gallop.

'The one this side is Arab Dancer,' Oliver said. 'He's another of Sheikh Karim's. Two-year-old. Nice colt.'

116

I wondered how he knew which one was which. They just looked the same to me, especially from this head-on angle.

'Do you know them all by sight?' I asked.

'Pretty much,' Oliver said. 'I recognise horses like you recognise people. It's often claimed that Lester Piggott could identify every horse he'd ever ridden when walking away from him in a rainstorm.' He laughed. 'But he was bloody hopeless at knowing the owners. But this one is easy, Tony's riding it.'

As the horses approached I could see Tony on Arab Dancer. Like all the other riders, he was standing on his toes in the stirrups, his knees bent slightly and with his body crouched forward almost horizontally over the horse's neck. In this way, his legs were acting as shock-absorbers, smoothing out the jerky movements of the horse beneath him as it galloped, so that both his head and body appeared to move forward in fluid effortless ease.

The four horses swept past us, the very ground beneath my feet trembling from the impact of their hooves on the turf. Even I had to admit, there was something hugely exciting at being so close to such raw power.

Arab Dancer seemed to gain a thumbs-up from both Ryan and Oliver.

'He's coming on well,' Ryan said. 'He was second on his first outing last month at Newbury. I might send him to Chester next week. Then we're aiming for the Coventry Stakes.' The way he said it made me think that I should know what the Coventry Stakes was. 'It would be nice if Sheikh Karim could be there to see him run.'

'In Coventry?' I asked.

Both Ryan and Oliver laughed loudly. I'd obviously said something totally wrong, and very funny.

'Oh dear,' Oliver said, trying to stop the giggles, and wiping tears from his eyes. 'No. Sorry, Harry. The Coventry Stakes is run on the first day of Royal Ascot. It's the top race at the meeting for two-year-olds.'

They might have been sorry but that didn't stop them continuing to laugh until the next group of four horses finally diverted their attention.

'Right, that's it for the first lot,' Ryan said as the final group passed us. 'Let's go and have a coffee.'

We walked back across the grass to the Land Rover and climbed in, the pair of them still chuckling under their breath.

*Surely it wasn't that funny*, I thought. Anyone could have made such a mistake from the name. Like finding out that a Bombay duck is, in fact, a fish, or that a hot dog has no canine bits in it at all, and a hamburger contains no ham.

'So what makes a good racehorse?' I asked. 'Is it more breeding or training?'

'Both,' Oliver replied. 'Breeding is important. It's almost impossible to turn a poorly bred horse into a top-class winner simply by training, although it's quite possible to do the reverse. And breeding isn't everything. The best horses have to have the right temperament, the right mental attitude.'

'Mental attitude?' I said, surprised.

'Absolutely. They need the will to win. There are lots of good horses that simply can't be bothered to race. Originally, horses were herding prey animals with a strong flight response, like zebras still are. Some are happy to run in the pack while others want to lead it. It's that special mental attitude that can make a good horse into a champion. As the great Italian racehorse breeder, Federico Tesio, once said: *A horse gallops with his lungs, perseveres with his heart, and wins with his character.*'

'And his leg muscles, surely?' I said.

'Those can be produced by training,' Oliver said. 'But without a good heart and a fine pair of lungs you have no chance. A resting horse breathes about twelve times per minute, not unlike a resting human, but at the gallop it breathes with every stride. Its leg action causes the diaphragm to move back and forth like a piston, forcing air into and out of the lungs at high speed. A hundred and forty breaths a minute at full gallop. Sixty litres of air every second. Compare that to Usain Bolt. He takes only one, maybe two breaths during the full length of a hundred-metre race. Hence a horse needs a big heart to pump all that oxygen round the body to its muscles. How big do you think your heart is?'

'I've no idea,' I said, smiling. 'It's not something I worry about, as long as it keeps on pumping.'

'About two hundred and fifty grams,' he said. 'The size of a clenched fist.' He demonstrated by clenching his own. 'How big do you think a racehorse's is?'

'No idea,' I said. 'Bigger, I suppose, because it's a larger animal.'

'Five kilograms on average,' Oliver said. 'Twenty times a

human heart. Larger than a basketball. And it can beat well over two hundred times a minute during a race.'

'Amazing,' I said.

'Secretariat's heart was even bigger, twice the normal size.'

'Secretariat?'

'Fantastic horse. Won the Triple Crown in the United States back in the 1970s. Still holds the record timings for all three races.'

I decided not to ask what the Triple Crown was. I had thought it was something to do with rugby, but I must be wrong.

'And racehorses have another trick too,' Oliver said. 'During exercise they compress their spleens. That dumps another fifteen litres of concentrated red blood cells into their circulation, more than doubling the number of oxygen carriers.'

'Remarkable,' I said.

'They certainly are.'

Ryan drove in through the gates and parked close to the yard office door.

I checked my watch. Quarter past seven. Still fifteen minutes until Janie arrived for work.

We went through the empty office to the kitchen, where Oliver spooned instant coffee into three cups.

'Second lot go out in half an hour,' Ryan said to me. 'You're welcome to come if you like.'

'Are any more of the Sheikh's horses working?'

'Not today,' Ryan said. 'One runs on Friday at Newbury

so is just doing a light canter today. Another of his colts is slightly lame.'

'Lame?' I said, concerned.

'Nothing to worry about. Slight abscess in his rear offside hoof. That's all. The vet's been and given him antibiotics. He'll be right as rain by next week.'

'How about the two fillies?' I asked.

'I'm not bloody working those,' Ryan said with feeling. 'Waste of effort.'

I could imagine that the two fillies had been left to stand idly in their stables ever since the Sheikh had indicated he was moving them. I wondered if they'd been mucked out, or even fed.

'I think I'll give your second lot a miss, then,' I said.

'Right,' Ryan said, downing the rest of his coffee. 'I'm off round the yard. No doubt I'll see you later, Harry. Dad, I'll meet you in the Land Rover.'

He stood up but he didn't get very far.

There was a loud knock from the front door. Ryan and I waited in the kitchen while Oliver went to answer it.

Presently, he returned to the kitchen followed by Detective Chief Inspector Eastwood, who looked across at me and nodded in recognition.

Oliver was ashen-faced.

'What is it?' Ryan asked, grabbing hold of his father's arm.

Oliver didn't speak. He just waved his hand feebly, and sat down heavily onto a chair, his head bent down.

'We've identified the body from the fire,' the detective said to Ryan. 'I'm sorry, Mr Chadwick. It was your sister, Zoe.'

Ryan stood there staring at the policeman.

'That can't be right,' he said. 'There must be some mistake.'

'There's no mistake,' said the chief inspector. 'We have compared the DNA found in the body with your sister's DNA that we had on file. It's a perfect match.'

Ryan stood there as if in a trance.

'On file?' I said. 'How come you had Zoe's DNA on file?'

The detective came over to be closer to me.

'Zoe Robertson was arrested last year,' he said quietly. 'As is customary, her DNA was taken at the time and recorded in the UK National Database.'

'Arrested?' Oliver had heard and he looked up. 'For what?'

'Arson.'

# 10

The knowledge that it was their sister whose body had been discovered in the burned-out stables briefly brought the remaining siblings together again, not that they were united in their grief.

Indeed, they blamed her for the fire.

It was an hour later and we were all again in Oliver's kitchen, together with Arabella and Susan, this time both sans make-up. Only Maria had decided not to join this kangaroo court and I speculated that she might be already too worse for wear through drink, even at eight-thirty in the morning.

I, meanwhile, had simply remained and no one had yet asked me to leave, so I hadn't. If they were foolish enough to discuss private family matters in front of me, I wasn't about to stop them.

'What the bloody hell was Zoe doing here anyway?' Oliver asked no one in particular. 'She hasn't been here for years.'

'She always was a selfish cow,' Declan declared. 'And completely barmy.'

Only Tony, her full brother, stood up for her, and even that seemed a tad half-hearted. 'You lot treated her so badly that it was no wonder she had problems.'

'Problems?' Ryan almost shouted at him. 'I'm the one with the bloody problems and it's all her fault.'

'You can't be sure of that,' Tony said.

'She's been arrested before for arson,' Ryan *was* now shouting at him. 'What more proof do you want? Bloody bitch deserves to be dead.'

'Ryan!' Susan said sharply. 'Don't talk about your sister like that. Think of her poor children now without a mother.'

He pulled a face at her as if he didn't appreciate being chastised by his wife.

'I'll talk about her however I like,' he said. 'Even in death she's ruining my life.'

'As if you didn't ruin hers first,' Tony said.

'You watch out,' Ryan responded angrily, waving a finger into Tony's face. 'Without me, you'd have no future in this business.'

'I'd rather have no future than be beholden to you.'

Tony went to grab Ryan's finger but he pulled it away sharply.

'Stop it, you two,' Oliver shouted at them. 'Have you no sense of decency. Zoe is lying in the morgue and all you can do is bicker between yourselves.'

I personally would have called it more than bickering but I kept silent.

And Declan wasn't to be left out, wading in with his two penn'orth. 'Whatever her problems, there's no excuse for killing those horses.'

'To hell with the bloody horses,' Arabella said, smacking her husband none too gently on the arm. 'This is your flesh and blood we're talking about.' There were tears in her eyes and Arabella, of all of them, was the only one who seemed in the slightest way grief-stricken. 'Has anyone told Yvonne?'

'Oh my God,' Tony said. 'I should be with her.'

Yvonne, it transpired, was an ex Mrs Oliver Chadwick. She was Tony and Zoe's mother, and still lived quite close by, in a village four miles south of Newmarket. Indeed, Tony was still living with her and he had driven from there to Castleton House Stables that morning to ride Arab Dancer.

'Surely the police will have told her,' Oliver said.

'I bet they haven't,' Tony replied. 'She's not her next of kin. That's Peter.'

'She'll hear soon enough,' Ryan said thoughtlessly. 'It'll be on the news before long.'

Tony gave him a look halfway between hate and pity. 'You fucking idiot,' he said. 'I'm going home.' And he went.

There was a brief silence as if the departure of Tony to go to his mother had finally brought home to the rest of them the enormity of the situation. All of them, that was, except Ryan, who seemed totally oblivious to the sombre mood that was descending.

'What shall we do now?' he said jauntily. 'I have horses to train and York Races to go to.'

'Tony was right,' Declan said to him. 'You are a fucking idiot. Come on, Bella, we're going home. And we won't be back.'

He took his wife by the hand and they too departed.

I decided that I had intruded long enough and it was time I made myself scarce. I walked out of the kitchen down the corridor to the yard office. Janie was sitting there with her head in her hands, her elbows resting on the desk. The bad news had obviously permeated through to her.

'Hello,' I said.

She sat up quickly.

'Oh, hello, Harry. Isn't it dreadful?'

'Yes,' I agreed. 'Awful. Did you know her?'

'Yes,' she said. 'I knew her quite well when we were young. I'm a year older than her but we went to the same primary school and then we both moved on to Newmarket College. She was still there when I started working for her father. In fact, it was through her I got the job here in the first place. We used to ride out together on ponies as kids, even though she hated it.'

'Why did she do it then?' I asked.

'I think her father used to make her. Riding was a family tradition.'

'But what was she like as a person?'

'Quiet,' Janie said. 'Rather reserved. Not a very happy girl. She hated it here and couldn't wait to get away. One day she just left. Didn't even say goodbye to anyone. She just vanished. I remember there being a huge hoo-ha about it at the time. Everyone thought she'd been murdered but she turned up alive weeks later in London, living rough.'

No wonder DCI Eastwood had initially been sceptical about my theory that Zoe was the victim of the fire.

'Tony said she had problems.'

'She sure did,' Janie agreed. 'She didn't get on with people easily. Most thought her a bit odd and she was bullied quite a lot by the other kids at secondary school. Nowadays she'd probably be diagnosed as autistic or something, but I don't remember that term being used at the time. She was just thought of as weird. I was probably her only friend, but that wasn't saying much. We were hardly bosom pals, but at least she talked to me. She used to self-harm quite a bit, you know, cut her arms with razor blades and stuff like that. She showed me. Really scary, it was. I thought she was just seeking attention but she claimed she was seriously depressed.'

'How did she get on academically?' I asked.

'Fine, I suppose. Nothing to write home about, bit like me. But we both did reasonably well if I remember, not that either of us went to university or anything. And she disappeared before taking her A levels anyway.'

'Had you seen her since she went to London?' I asked.

'Only once. About five years ago. She just turned up one day demanding to see her father. They had a flaming row. I think it was over him marrying Maria, but I'm not sure. There was lots of shouting, I know that. I could hear it in the office, not that I was trying to listen or anything. But it was so loud, I couldn't help it.'

I had a mental vision of her having had her ear pressed up against the office door, but maybe I was being unkind.

'I remember Oliver bellowing at her that, as far as he was concerned, she was no longer his daughter. It was dreadful. Went on for ages. I tried not to listen. I even put my hands over my ears but Zoe was shouting that she'd now obtained the DNA evidence to prove it. It was awful.'

'Did you ever meet her husband?'

'Yeah, at the same time. He came with her, along with their two children. I didn't even know Zoe was married, let alone a mother. And the kids did nothing but cry all the time. I remember that all right. Poor Oliver. Not the best introduction to his grandchildren.'

'What's the husband like?' I asked.

'Older than Zoe. Quite a bit older, I'd say. And bald. I didn't much take to him. He was very angry and was also involved in the row with Oliver. He was demanding money.'

'Money?'

'Yeah, something about Zoe being entitled to it. Her inheritance or something. Usual problem when an ageing father marries a younger woman. The only thing the kids see is the family fortune going to her instead of to them.'

At this point, Ryan came stomping into the office and clearly didn't like me being there talking to Janie.

Time to change the subject, I thought, preferably to something that was nothing to do with the Chadwicks or racing. But I wondered how much of our conversation he had already heard.

'Did you have a good birthday dinner last night?' I asked.

'Janie,' Ryan said loudly before she could answer me. 'Are all the declarations complete and ready?'

'Yes,' she said. 'All ready. Jockeys too. On your screen. You just need to check them, input your access code and then push the send button.'

He strode over to the computer on another desk and tapped a few keys on the keyboard, seemingly without even glancing at the information on the screen. Then he walked out again without saying another word, not even a 'thank you'.

Janie and I watched him go and sat there in silence until we heard the kitchen door close.

'We had a lovely birthday dinner,' Janie said. 'We had Chinese at The Fountain. Eight of us in all. Great food. I ate and drank far too much. As always. Had real trouble getting up this morning.' She laughed but only briefly.

It was not really a morning for laughter.

'What does your sister do?' I asked.

'I know what she did last night. She wouldn't stop bloody talking about *you*. She wanted to know all about you and what you were doing here.' Janie looked at me. 'And that's actually a very good question.'

She raised her eyebrows at me in a questioning manner.

'I represent Sheikh Karim,' I said. 'He wants me to find out why his horses died.'

'And have you?'

'No, not yet.'

'Is that why you're still snooping around the place?'

129

'I wouldn't call it snooping,' I said in my defence.

'Why not?' she said. 'Because that's exactly what you're doing, asking me all these questions about Zoe.'

I was having some difficulty reading her. Was she actually angry with me? Or being playful?

'Sorry,' I said.

'No need. Snoop away. We all want to know why the horses died, and Zoe too. I'm loyal, but not that loyal. And I don't know for how much longer I'm going to have a job here anyway.'

It was my turn to look quizzically at her. 'Why do you say that?'

'Isn't it obvious? Whole place is going down the tubes if you ask me. The loss of those seven horses will be the last straw, I reckon, unless we get some winners soon. Mr Ryan even cut my pay last month. Said he couldn't afford me.'

*How odd*, I thought. Oliver had told me that the business couldn't run without her and yet his son had cut her wages. Ryan really was an idiot.

Suddenly Janie became very concerned that she'd revealed too much.

'Well, no, it's not that bad,' she said, trying to back-pedal furiously. 'It's really not. I shouldn't be telling you anything anyway, not with you representing one of our owners. I'm just tired, and upset about Zoe. Ignore what I just said.'

*Difficult*, I thought.

'But that's why Prince of Troy is such a huge loss for us,' said Janie, digging herself back into the mire. 'He would have won the Derby, no doubt about it, and that would've eased all our troubles.'

She fell silent and I could see from her facial expression that she regretted saying anything to me at all, let alone her prediction of doom and gloom at Castleton House Stables.

'Did Kate really talk about me last night?' I asked.

'What?' Her mind was elsewhere, and it clearly wasn't a happy place.

'Did your sister really talk about me all through dinner?'

'Yes she bloody did. Yap, yap, yap. Never stopped. Harry Foster this, Harry Foster that. In the end we all had to tell her to shut up.'

I smiled.

'Give her my number, will you?' I wrote it down on a notepad on her desk. 'Ask her to call me.'

Janie tore the piece of paper off the pad and looked at it.

'I might,' she said. 'Or I might not.'

# 11

I was back in the Bedford Lodge Hotel in time to catch the end of breakfast.

Was it still only breakfast time? I felt that I'd been up for at least half a day.

I sat at a table for one and had scrambled eggs on toast with bacon. Living on my own meant that I very rarely had a cooked breakfast, or even any breakfast at all.

A middle-aged couple beat the ten o'clock curfew by a mere second or two and sat down at the table next to me, him with a copy of the *Racing Post*, her with a fashion magazine.

The man's phone went *beep-beep* and he looked down at the screen. 'They've identified the body in that fire at the Chadwick place. Someone called Zoe Robertson.'

*Bad news travels fast*, I thought.

'Who's she?' the woman asked, looking up from her magazine.

'His daughter.'

'Ryan's daughter?'

'No. Oliver's. From a previous marriage.'

'Well, I never did,' she said.

The man was still reading from his phone.

'They're implying she started it.'

'Poor Oliver,' the woman said. 'Bad enough losing your best horses without then discovering it's your own daughter that was the cause.'

'That hasn't been confirmed.'

'But you say they imply it?'

'Yeah, well, sort of. The police haven't said so but, according to this, she'd been convicted before for arson. But they're only going by what's been posted on social media.'

Social media had much to answer for, I thought. It was a rumour-monger's paradise.

The couple went back to their reading material while I finished my scrambled eggs, and then returned to my room.

I flicked on the BBC News Channel and it too was reporting the same social-media 'fact' that Zoe Robertson had started the fire, clearly working on the principle that one couldn't slander the already dead. If Zoe had still been alive, the BBC wouldn't have dared repeat such an allegation without good evidence to back it up.

I checked my emails.

There was one from the Simpson White Research Team with their preliminary findings on the Chadwicks. Someone had clearly been very busy overnight.

The report was broken down member-by-member of the

Chadwick family with Oliver first. Some of the information I already knew, as it had been in Georgina's brief on the day I'd first arrived at Newmarket. But there was plenty of new stuff and some of it was highly detailed. Good job, I thought, and, not for the first time, I wondered how the wizards in the office had found it all out.

Oliver had been born at the now-closed Mill Road Maternity Hospital in Cambridge in early 1950 and educated at the Leys School, also in Cambridge, from where he had failed to win a place at university. Hence he had joined his elder brother, James, in working for their father at the stables in Bury Road. His first marriage had been in May 1975 to Miss Audrey Parker, the daughter of another racehorse trainer in Newmarket, and they'd quickly had two sons – Ryan and Declan. Audrey had died of liver cancer in March 1982 when the boys had been just six and four, and Oliver had remarried to Yvonne Jefferies eighteen months later. Two more children followed – Tony and Zoe. That marriage had lasted almost thirty years but it was said to have been tempestuous and unhappy, and had finally ended in divorce when Oliver admitted his long-term and ongoing adultery with one Maria Webster, a former personal trainer from the local fitness and leisure centre. Oliver had then married Maria when it became known that she was pregnant with his child, but she had miscarried the baby only six days after the wedding ceremony.

No wonder she'd hit the bottle.

By comparison, Ryan and Declan had seemingly led

exemplary lives. Both had left school at sixteen to ride as professional jockeys, and each had been married just the once, to Susan and Arabella respectively. The only visible stain on either of their characters was that Ryan had been officially cautioned by the police for causing a disturbance in a Doncaster hotel, where it was claimed he'd punched a man during an argument, breaking the man's nose. Ryan had been arrested but there had been no ensuing court case, however, as the unnamed victim of the assault had apparently declined to press charges.

There was also a little about Tony but the bulk of the research team's report concentrated, as I'd requested, on Oliver Chadwick's only daughter – Zoe. And there was plenty to know about her.

She'd been born at the Rosie Maternity Hospital in Cambridge in early December 1988. At age four, she had been enrolled at St Louis Roman Catholic Primary, and then, at eleven, she went to Newmarket College, the local second-ary school. She dropped out before taking her A levels and never returned to formal education.

The first time she was reported missing was two days after her eighteenth birthday when her mother had called the police to inform them that her daughter had failed to return home from an evening out with friends.

At the time of her disappearance, the killing of two young girls in nearby Soham was still fresh in local people's minds, and there were some unsolved murders of young women in Ipswich, just forty miles away along the A14. Hence, it was widely believed that Zoe had been another victim of the man being labelled as the 'Suffolk Strangler'. A huge police search had been initiated, with hundreds of volunteers scouring every corner of Newmarket and the surrounding heath looking for Zoe's body.

Nothing had been found, of course, and she had finally been identified by the Metropolitan Police three weeks later on Christmas Eve, living under a railway arch in Croydon, south London, with a number of other homeless young people. Apparently, both her family and the police had been absolutely furious with her but she had claimed she was unaware of the massive publicity generated by her disappearance. She also announced that, as she was now legally an adult, she could do as she pleased, and had refused to go home.

Over the following years, she had not only come to the attention of the police on several occasions, but also to many other agencies, not least the local social services in Ealing who had twice briefly taken her children into care.

Arabella had disclosed to me that Zoe had had mental health problems, and she hadn't been kidding.

The research team had somehow discovered that Zoe had been forcefully admitted to psychiatric hospitals on at least three separate occasions, the most recent being for a two-month stretch earlier in the current year.

Arabella had claimed that post-natal depression was the basis of Zoe's problems but it appeared from the chronology in the report that her first hospital admission had been well before the birth of her eldest child, indeed it had been not long after she'd been found in Croydon.

There was also something about the arson conviction, including two local newspaper reports from the time. Two years previously, Zoe and two other women had set fire to the garden shed of a man who had admitted beating up his wife. The shed in question had been large and had housed the man's treasured model-train layout. The whole lot had been completely consumed in the fire.

The three women had been neighbours of the victim and had seemingly extracted their own revenge after the man had been handed a community service order rather than the jail sentence they all felt he deserved.

The three had pleaded guilty to criminal damage at Ealing Magistrates' Court and had been bound over for a year to keep the peace, with each ordered to pay a hundred pounds in compensation for the loss of the shed. The man, meanwhile, had claimed in vain that thousands of pounds' worth of model railway had also been destroyed, but the lady chairman of the bench had referred to it as simply 'a few toys'.

There was clearly little doubt about whose side she'd been on.

But it was hardly the crime of the year, and surely not worthy of being the reason why the TV news was blaming Zoe for the fire at Castleton House Stables. If the Simpson White research wizards could get the information, then unquestionably the BBC should have been able to do so as well.

However, there was one interesting additional detail at the

bottom of the report that had not been available to the Ealing magistrates at the time the case had come before them: one of the other two women later revealed that it had been Zoe alone who had proposed setting fire to the shed, and that she had also snapped the door padlock shut first, wrongly believing the man to be still inside.

Maybe it could have been the crime of the year after all.

The last part of the Simpson White research report concerned Zoe's husband, Peter Robertson.

As Georgina's original brief had indicated, Peter was an estate agent, but that told only a fraction of his story.

Janie had said she thought Peter was older than Zoe, and he was – almost nine years older. He'd also been married twice before Zoe, and neither of those marriages had ended well. Now his third had gone the same way.

The wizards had attached scanned copies of all three of his marriage certificates, together with the death certificate of his first wife and the High Court judge's divorce certificate that had unshackled him from his second. There were also copies of the official registration of births for his and Zoe's two children.

They all made for interesting reading.

Peter Robertson had married his first wife, Kirsty Wright, at Croydon Register Office when they had each been twenty-one. Both bride and groom had had 'no fixed abode' recorded for their addresses, and 'unemployed' was written in the spaces for their professions.

Kirsty had survived a mere two months after her wedding day and it had clearly not been a happy marriage. The South London Coroner had recorded a verdict of suicide, deciding that Kirsty had killed herself by deliberately stepping off the platform at East Croydon Station, right into the path of the non-stopping Gatwick Express.

Peter had wed for a second time at the same venue two years later, this time to a Lorna Harris. This marriage had lasted longer, three years to be precise, but it too had ended badly with Lorna divorcing him for what was stated in the petition as his 'unreasonable behaviour'.

Neither of these marriages appeared to have produced any children.

He married Zoe Chadwick two years after his divorce, once again at Croydon Register Office, and this time, not only did Peter have a fixed abode but also 'estate agent' was recorded as his profession on the certificate.

The birth of their first child, a daughter called Poppy, was registered at Croydon University Hospital just six weeks after the wedding, with a second daughter, Joanne, following twenty months later, by which time the Robertsons had apparently moved, Ealing Hospital now being recorded as the place of delivery.

Finally, there was a note from the wizards saying that their contact at the Disclosure and Barring Service had confirmed to them that Peter had twice been convicted of the possession of Class A drugs, and they were still searching for further details.

As a solicitor, I wondered just how legal that last enquiry had been. The registers of births, deaths and marriages were all in the public domain, as were the judgements of both the coroner and family courts, but an individual's criminal record was subject to data-protection regulations, or at least it should have been.

But that was why we called them wizards. They were able to use their special magic to find out things that we lesser mortals couldn't.

However, I decided I should keep that last piece of information very much to myself.

I sat for a while reading and rereading all the material until I was sure I had the various relationships understood and committed to memory. Not that any of it gave me any insight as to why Zoe Robertson had ended up alone and dead in her father's burned-out stables, seventy miles away from her home.

I next spent some time thinking about Kate Logan and wondering if Janie had passed on my telephone number. Not that she would have needed my mobile number in order to contact me – she knew I was staying at the Bedford Lodge.

Had it really only been the previous evening that I had met her?

An awful lot seemed to have happened since then.

My phone rang and I grabbed it but, sadly and unexpectedly, it was not Kate but DCI Eastwood on the line.

'Thank you, Mr Foster, for your direction concerning Zoe Robertson.'

'You're very welcome,' I replied.

'Yes,' he said. 'Most helpful, but we would have discovered her identity anyway. It is routine to scan the national DNA database whenever we have an unidentified sample.'

*Then why are you calling me now*, I thought.

I found out quickly enough.

'Perhaps you could further help us with our enquiries?' he asked.

'Anything,' I said.

'You said yesterday that you were with Mr Declan Chadwick when Mr Robertson called to tell him that Zoe was missing.'

'That's right,' I said. 'Peter Robertson actually spoke to Mrs Chadwick. I was with Declan when his wife relayed the message.'

'Did either of them indicate that they had recently been in contact with Zoe Robertson or her husband?'

'Not exactly,' I said slowly, thinking back to the way Declan had gone so pale at the news. 'But ...' There was something else too. Something I'd considered slightly odd at the time. Now, what was it?

'Yes?' prompted the policeman.

'I remember thinking it was slightly strange that Arabella announced that Zoe had gone missing *again*. As if she'd known Zoe had gone missing before.'

'Mr Foster,' replied the chief inspector, his tone full of irony. '*Everyone* in Newmarket knows that Zoe Chadwick had gone missing before. Police officers knocked on every door in the damn town during an intensive two-week search for her almost twelve years ago. What a complete waste of resources that was. I was a detective sergeant on the case at the time.'

So that is what he hadn't been telling me during our meeting yesterday, and he sounded as if he was still angry about it.

'Yes,' I said, 'but Arabella told me Zoe went missing regularly. And she also referred to Peter Robertson as Pete. One doesn't do that unless you've been in fairly regular contact.'

'Thank you, Mr Foster. That is most helpful.'

He was terminating the call.

'Hold on a minute,' I said quickly. 'Don't go. Have you found out anything more about how the fire started? Was it Zoe who started it?'

He hesitated, as if deciding whether to say anything or not.

'After the results of the post-mortem, we now consider it unlikely that Mrs Robertson started the fire.'

There was a distinct pause while the magnitude of what he had just said sank into my brain.

'Because she was already dead,' I said slowly.

There was another pause. A much longer one.

'There are clearly no flies on you, Mr Foster,' the detective chief inspector said eventually. 'I can see that I should have been more guarded. I'll be drummed out of the force if I'm not careful.' He cleared his throat as if emphasising the gravity of what was to follow. 'That is highly confidential information, Mr Foster. You are not to pass it on to any member of the Chadwick family, or anyone else for that matter. That would be construed by me as obstructing a police officer in the course of his duty. Do you understand?'

'Yes,' I said.

I bet he was now wishing he'd said nothing at all. I had simply jumped to home plate from a throwaway comment way out in left field.

'But how do you know?' I asked him, not wanting to lose the opportunity.

He hesitated again but clearly decided that, having already inadvertently given me the treasure, there was no problem in also handing over the map.

'In spite of the intensity of the fire, the core of the body was largely intact, in particular the chest cavity, and, according to the pathologist, no smoke residue or fire damage was detectable in the lungs.'

'So she hadn't been breathing,' I said.

'Exactly. Either she'd already been dead when the fire started or she died suddenly just as it did so, maybe from something like a heart attack. The pathologist is still investigating that remote possibility.'

'So you believe she was murdered.'

It was more of a statement than a question and precipitated another long pause from the detective.

'We cannot say that for sure at present.' Such was his unease at giving me any more information that he almost whispered the response. 'As yet, we have no definitive cause of death. Maybe we never will, such is the extent of fire damage to the head, neck and the other extremities of the body. But murder is definitely one of the possibilities. Perhaps the most likely. Maybe she was strangled or hit over the head or something. Someone then may have set the stables on fire in an attempt to cover up what they'd done.'

But who?

And why?

# 12

About three in the afternoon, having dispensed with the car and driver, I walked from the Bedford Lodge Hotel along Bury Road past Oliver Chadwick's house.

It was almost as much as I could do not to pop into Janie's office and ask if she'd yet given my number to Kate. But best not to be seen to be too eager, I thought, and kept on walking towards the town centre, for I was a man on a mission and I had a difficult decision to make.

I had to decide on just one of the thirteen available.

It was a big question.

Which one?

Which one?

In which one of the thirteen betting shops in Newmarket would I make my bet?

I felt it was time to further my education. I'd never been

in a betting shop before. Indeed, I'd never placed a bet in my life other than buying the occasional lottery ticket, and surely that didn't count.

But that was all about to change.

I'd done a bit of homework on the internet, looking up odds and bet types.

I had naively believed that placing a bet was a straight-forward exercise – you just choose the horse you think will be first in the race and hand over your stake money to the bookmaker, who will pay you out if the horse actually wins, or keep your stake for himself if it doesn't.

Simple.

And, indeed, you *can* bet like that, but I found there are far more things to consider.

For a start, not every bookmaker offers the same odds. You need to search for the best available price, just like in every other type of shopping. There is no sense in making a bet at odds of five-to-one at one shop when another down the road is offering six-to-one.

And then not all bets are 'win only'. In some races, you can back a horse to finish in the first three, or even in the first four. And there are other bets called forecasts, tricasts, exactas and perfectas, where multiple horses in the same race have to come in first and second, or first, second and third in any order, or in the right order.

I discovered that you can also place a single stake on sev-eral horses in separate races, called an accumulator bet, and there are many combinations of accumulators with exotic names such as Trixie, Lucky 15, Goliath, Patent, Canadian and Yankee, to name just a few.

There is even something called a 'Heinz', which consists of 57 separate bets on six horses, each running in a different race: 15 doubles, 20 trebles, 15 fourfold accumulators, 6 fivefold accumulators, and a single sixfold accumulator. Any two horses have to win to start paying out, with greater returns the more of them that triumph, and huge rewards if four, five or six of your selections come in.

However, for all of the glamorous methods of wagering your money, I thought back to what ASW had said to me: *There's no such thing as a poor bookmaker.*

So punters beware.

My first port of call was the BP filling station on Bury Road, where I withdrew some cash from their ATM. Then, empowered by the wedge of banknotes in my pocket, I went in search of the betting shops.

The nearest one was Ladbrokes, opposite the Queen Victoria Jubilee Clock Tower at the top end of the High Street, its bright red and white frontage making it look more like a supermarket than a bookmakers, with special offers displayed on large posters in the window – two bets for the price of one.

I strode purposefully over to the door but found myself looking round furtively before opening it, checking that no one who knew me was watching, as if I were a naughty boy entering a den of iniquity, a hangout of wickedness and immorality.

I'm not sure what I expected to find – maybe a dark, smoke-filled room bustling with dubious individuals, all wearing hats and with their coat collars turned up, silently going about their business, handing over grubby handfuls of cash to a shirt-sleeved croupier behind a metal grill. Perhaps even with Paul Newman and Robert Redford on hand to relieve Robert Shaw of a briefcase full of twenty-dollar bills.

How wrong I was.

It was nothing at all like a scene from *The Sting*.

Instead, it was a sparsely populated, brightly lit airy space, statutorily smoke-free, with a light-oak floor and a scattering of easy chairs and stools upholstered in corporate Ladbroke tomato-red fabric.

On one side there was a glass-fronted booth for placing bets, and on the opposite wall, high up, a line of seven large television sets, some showing live horse and dog races, others displaying the odds of the runners. Under the TVs were pinned the various racecard pages from the *Racing Post*, with a wide shelf beneath for punters to lean on to write down their selections on the slips of paper provided, ready to hand in at the booth with their stake.

In addition, in the quiet corners, there were two electronic fixed-odds betting machines offering casino games such as roulette and blackjack, as well as the regular one-armed bandit spinning wheels.

It was an Aladdin's cave, a whole new world, with new horizons to pursue.

What had I been doing all my life?

I was like a kid in a candy store.

I walked across to the booth.

'Do you have odds for the Derby?' I asked the young woman behind the glass.

'Hold on,' she said. 'I'll get them off the system. They've all changed now that Prince of Troy is confirmed as a non-runner.'

*He's more than a non-runner*, I thought, *he's a non-existent*.

She disappeared into the office behind and shortly reappeared with a printed sheet. She slid it across the counter under the glass.

'They won't all run,' she said confidently. 'Maximum of twenty in the Derby.'

I looked down at the list of horses on the sheet. There were thirty-eight of them in all, the favourite at the top, the outsiders at the bottom.

'Those are ante-post odds,' said the young woman, pointing at the sheet. 'You lose your stake if the horse doesn't run.'

'Or doesn't win?' I replied.

'Yeah, that as well,' she said with a laugh. 'No refunds.'

I scanned the list, looking for Orion's Glory. He was nearly halfway down and quoted at a price of 33–1. Even I knew that was good, but maybe not quite good enough. I would shop around the other companies to see how they compared.

'How often do the odds change?' I asked.

'The next scratch date is this coming Tuesday. The prices will shorten then for all of those left in. Then supplementary entries close on the Monday before the race. It would obviously change things dramatically if any horses are entered at that late stage. And the Dante tomorrow may cause a few fluctuations. Some of those are running in that.' She nodded at the list in my hand.

'But they won't change in the next hour or so?' I asked.

'Not unless another favourite gets killed.' She laughed.

'Good for you, was it?'

'Bloody marvellous. We've taken an absolute shedload on Prince of Troy to win the Derby, much of it since long before the Guineas when his price was really long. All the Chadwick lads came in here like clockwork, every week, to put more on him from their pay packets. They've been doing it for months. We're their nearest shop. We stood to lose a bloody fortune if Prince of Troy won, which he probably would have.'

No wonder Ryan's lads were so gloomy. It wasn't just their pride that had taken a hit.

'Manna from heaven, that fire was.' She laughed again, louder this time.

I didn't join in. I just stared at her.

'I'm sorry,' she said, suddenly, hugely embarrassed. 'It's not right of me to laugh like that. I'm really sorry racing lost such a great horse in that manner.'

*Don't lie to me*, I thought.

I looked down again at the list. 'Is thirty-three-to-one your best price for Orion's Glory?'

'If that's what it says.'

'Not good enough,' I said, shaking my head. 'I'll take my twenty pounds elsewhere. I don't like your attitude to the death of Prince of Troy. In fact, I might call Ladbrokes and complain.'

She was taken aback.

'I'll give you better odds,' she said quickly. 'How about forty-to-one? Just don't say anything to head office. Please. I'll lose my job.'

'Can you change the odds just like that?'

'I have some discretion,' she said, implying she was more important than she actually was.

'Make it fifty-to-one, then,' I said, 'and my lips will be sealed.'

She hesitated.

'I'm sure that Mr Chadwick's lads would also love to know that their nearest betting shop thinks it's manna from heaven that Prince of Troy died in a fire, that it saved Ladbrokes a "bloody fortune".'

'You wouldn't.'

'Try me,' I said, staring at her again.

She was descending into panic.

'All right,' she said finally. 'Twenty quid on Orion's Glory at fifty-to-one.'

'Make that forty quid,' I said, peeling another twenty-note from my bundle. I was unlikely ever to get these odds again, either here or at any of the town's other betting shops.

She hesitated again but I pushed the two banknotes under the glass towards her and she eventually took them.

'Two thousand pounds to forty,' she said slowly while typing it into her computer. She passed over the printed betting slip. 'You'll get me sacked anyway.'

'I don't think so,' I said. 'You've taken a shedload from the Chadwick lads. You said so yourself. And that's all now risk-free.'

I came out of the Ladbrokes betting shop with a real bounce in my step. I was already mentally spending my two thousand pounds. All that had to happen now was for Orion's Glory to win the Derby. All?

I continued down the High Street and, just out of curiosity, I popped into the Paddy Power betting shop and asked for their odds for the Derby. Orion's Glory was again quoted at 33–1.

'Are these your very best odds?' I asked the man behind the counter. 'I got fifty-to-one for Orion's Glory at Ladbrokes.'

'I don't believe you,' he replied matter-of-factly. 'Even thirty-threes is too generous in my view, but it's head office, not me, that sets the prices.' It sounded like he didn't think much of head office. 'I reckon he'll be down in the twenties by tomorrow night, after the Dante. Orion's Glory is a better horse than many people think.'

'But he's not running in the Dante,' I said.

'No, but others are and that will whittle some of them out of the market. I'd take the thirty-threes now if I were you before you miss the boat.'

'Have you backed him yourself?' I asked.

'I take bets, mate, not make them.'

*How pragmatic,* I thought. And less expensive.

My next stop was Marks & Spencer – no, they haven't opened a betting shop – I was also in need of some fresh socks and pants.

It was all well and good having a cabin-sized suitcase always on standby for an immediate departure, but it didn't really contain enough for a whole week's stay away. And I was fed up of having to wash out my socks each night and hang them to dry on the heated towel rail in the bathroom.

True, I could have sent them to the hotel laundry service. Indeed, ASW would have expected me to. But even I baulked at paying more to get a pair of socks washed than it cost to buy new ones, whoever was picking up the tab.

I bought two shirts and a pair of khaki chinos, as well as the new socks and pants. I also acquired a small cheap suitcase from Argos, as I'd need something to put my new clothes into, along with the wellington boots and coat that I'd purchased the day before.

My phone rang as I was paying for the suitcase.

'Hi,' said a voice. 'Kate here.'

My heart went flip-flop.

'Hi,' I replied. 'Where are you?'

'At work.'

'Where's work?' I asked.

'Tatts.'

The way she said it made me think I should know what Tatts was, and where. And I was loath to show my ignorance by asking. I looked at my watch. It was five past four.

'What time do you finish?' I asked.

'Any time from now on,' Kate said. 'It's been a quiet day.'

'Would you like to meet for a drink?' I asked, fearing she'd have a million other things to do.

'It's a bit early for a drink,' she said. 'Even for me. How about tea at Nancy's?'

'Great. Who's Nancy?'

'Nancy's Teashop. On Old Station Road. Say, in about twenty minutes?'

'Lovely,' I said. 'Meet you there.'

'Do you know where it is?'

'I'll find it,' I said.

'I'm sure you will. Bye.' I could hear her laughing as she hung up the call.

'Where's Old Station Road?' I asked the shop assistant in Argos.

'Top of the high street and turn right at the roundabout,' she replied. 'You can't miss it.'

'Thanks,' I said, and scuttled away with my suitcase, stuffing the dark green M&S bag inside it.

If I'd had a bounce in my step earlier, I was now floating on air as I hurried back to the high street and then up to the clock tower roundabout. I turned right into Old Station Road and easily found Nancy's Vintage Teashop about a hundred yards down on the right-hand side.

I was there ahead of Kate and I sat down at a table close to the door so as not to be missed.

There were several groups there, including one of mothers

with toddlers camped out on a big pink sofa in the window. Indeed, pinkness was the overriding perception, with pink napkins on the tables and pink aprons on the staff. But pink wasn't the only colour; there were also pastel blues and yellows among the eclectic furnishings.

Four large cake stands, each covered with a voluminous glass bell-top, stood on the service counter with delicious-looking delights within, and there was a line of old-fashioned teapots on a shelf behind, each decorated with roses and other flowers such that they reminded me of chintz.

I studied the menu in its pink-and-white-striped folder and ordered Nancy's Classic Afternoon Tea for two.

Kate arrived running and slightly out of breath.

'Sorry I'm late,' she said. 'I got held up by a call.'

'You're not late,' I said, standing up. 'Perfect timing.'

*In fact, perfect in every way,* I thought, but decided it was far too cheesy to say so.

We sat down opposite one another with the table between us and I enviously eyed the mothers on the sofa sitting side by side.

'I've ordered the classic afternoon tea for two,' I said.

'I hope you're hungry. Janie and I usually order just one between us, with a second cup, and we can rarely finish everything even then.'

The waitress arrived with what could only be described as a feast fit for Henry VIII himself. A triple-decker plate piled high with finger sandwiches, fresh-baked scones and fancy

155

cakes, plus a huge pot of strawberry jam, and enough clotted cream to feed the biblical five thousand.

'I've given you a few extra scones,' said the young waitress. 'We close at five and we've got plenty left.'

'Thank you,' I said, and watched as she went back out to the kitchen.

I looked at the mountain of food in front of me, and then at Kate, and we both burst out laughing.

'Know of any starving children in the locality?' I said.

We had both just about managed to stop giggling by the time the waitress returned with a silver tray on which sat two teacups, two saucers, a large teapot, milk jug, sugar basin and a strainer with stand, all of them in white china with pink roses on the sides. Just like the ones my grandmother used to own.

'What an amazing place,' I said to Kate. 'Like stepping back fifty years.'

She looked down to the suitcase standing on the floor next to me.

'Not leaving are you?' she said with concern in her voice.

'No.' I laughed. 'Quite the reverse. I've had to buy more clothes as I only arrived with an overnight bag. So I had to get something to put them in.'

'Good,' she said, and smiled broadly. 'Don't go away, ever.'

Wow! Thunderbolt City squared.

# 13

When the teashop closed, we walked up the Bury Road to the Bedford Lodge for a drink and, halfway there, I took her hand in mine. She said nothing, just looked up at my face and smiled.

At Nancy's, we had talked mostly about the food, the weather or the traffic, and certainly nothing about ourselves, but that all changed as we drank champagne in the hotel bar, sitting, this time, side by side on a couch.

'Is that a uniform?' I asked.

She was wearing a dark-blue two-piece suit over an open-necked white shirt, with a burgundy-red scarf tied like a cravat inside the collar. The scarf was decorated with multiple blue bridle bits and numerous strange white logos that looked to me a bit like round-top tables with three legs. The same logo was embroidered in blue on the vees of her shirt collar.

'Certainly is,' she said. 'I came straight from work, remember.'

*At Tatts*, I thought – whatever that was.

'What's the logo?' I asked.

'It's meant to represent the rotunda up at Park Paddocks.'

I was none the wiser and it clearly showed in my face.

'The sales,' she said. 'I work for Tattersalls, the horse auctioneers.'

Tatts – Tattersalls. Of course.

'Doing what?' I asked.

'I'm on the bloodstock sales team. I help prepare the sales catalogues. And I act as a runner at the sales.'

'A runner? In a race?'

She laughed. 'No, silly. When the hammer comes down on a sale, it's my job to run to get the successful bidder to sign the purchase confirmation form. It's quite exciting when the amounts are big – several million guineas.'

'Why are horses still sold in guineas?' I asked, taking another sip of my champagne.

'Tradition, I suppose. Tattersalls have been selling horses in guineas for two hundred and fifty years.'

'Why are they called guineas?'

'Originally a guinea was a coin made from gold found in Guinea, West Africa. I know because we recently had one on display up at Park Paddocks. At first, the value of a guinea used to go up and down but then it was fixed at twenty-one shillings, or a pound and five pence in modern money. The vendor was always paid the pound and we kept the odd shilling for our services. It's pretty much the same these days, but now there's VAT to add, of course.'

'It must really confuse your foreign buyers,' I said.

'There's a big electronic board in the sales ring to help them. It also shows the bid price in dollars, euros and yen.'

'Do the sales go on every day?' I asked.

'Oh no,' she said with another laugh. 'We only sell for thirty-three days in a whole year here. Our next one's not until mid-July. But our Irish division has twenty days or so at Fairyhouse, near Dublin, and they also run a few sale days at Cheltenham and Ascot as well. And that's just Tatts. There are several other sales companies. Racehorses are being sold somewhere in the world on most days. It's a huge global business. We alone sold over thirteen thousand horses last year.'

'Thirteen thousand!' I was astounded. 'That's an awful lot of guineas.'

'How about you?' she said. 'What do you do?'

'I'm a lawyer.'

'I know,' she mocked. 'Janie told me that much. But what do you *do*?'

'I sort out other people's crises, at least I try to, especially their public relations disasters that inevitably follow on from their physical ones. Although, this week, I feel more like a detective than a PR man.'

'A detective?'

'I'm here representing the owner of Prince of Troy. He wants me to find out why his red-hot favourite for the Derby died in a fire.'

'Literally a red-hot favourite,' she said, but then winced at her poor attempt at humour. 'Sorry. That was inappropriate.'

'Very,' I agreed. But I laughed anyway. The way I felt at the moment, I would laugh at anything.

We discussed our backgrounds and our families.

Kate was thirty-five, three years older than Janie, and they had lived all their lives in the Newmarket area.

'Where do you live now?' I asked.

'In Six Mile Bottom.'

I laughed. 'Is there really such a place? It sounds rather rude.'

'Back in the seventeenth century, the original racecourse was eight miles long. There was a dip in the land six miles from the finish and that's how the village got its name.' She smiled and it lit up my life. 'How about you?'

'Nowhere near as exciting,' I said. 'I rent a flat in Neasden, northwest London. I've lived there for seven years, since I first came up from Devon. It's high time I moved somewhere nicer. It really is the most depressing place, noisy and close to the North Circular Road, but there's a good gym just round the corner and it's convenient for the tube, easy for getting to work on the Jubilee Line.'

'Where's work?' she asked.

'Knightsbridge.'

'Harrods,' she said. 'They're in Knightsbridge.'

'I work just round the corner from Harrods but I hardly ever go in.'

'I went once, but all I remember is getting lost looking for the ladies.'

We laughed in unison.

Boy, this felt good.

I ordered another round of fizz from the bar and we sat together on the couch comparing our likes and dislikes, favourite films and music, indeed, anything and everything.

'Best holiday destination?' I asked.

'The Maldives,' she said without hesitation. 'Fabulous villa on stilts set in the turquoise Indian Ocean. Absolute paradise.'

'When did you go there?'

'Twelve years ago,' she said. 'On my honeymoon.'

'Your honeymoon!' I was stunned. 'You didn't say you were married.'

'I'm not. Not any more, anyway. The marriage lasted only a fraction longer than the honeymoon.'

'So why are the Maldives still your best destination?'

'Because I suddenly realised when I was there that I loved the place far more than I loved the man. Woke me up, in fact. I'd have been happier if he'd gone home and left me there on my own. We should have gone on the honeymoon before the marriage ceremony. That would have saved us both a heap of grief. Stupid, really. I married far too young and to the wrong man.'

She looked at me and I wondered what was going through her mind.

'Fortunately the divorce was fairly straightforward,' she said. 'No kids. Realised in time with that one, thank God. Not that I wouldn't like to have some one day, although I'm getting a bit old now. Can you believe it that if a woman has a baby over thirty-five, she's called a geriatric mother?'

She shook her head. 'How about you? Any little Fosters running around?'

'None that I'm aware of,' I said, and decided it was time to change the subject – this one was getting far too heavy much too quickly and I wasn't sure I was ready for a discussion about marriage, let alone children.

'Are you a cat or dog person?' I asked.

'Dog,' she said. 'Definitely.'

'Why not cat?'

'Dogs are more affectionate. Cats don't wag their tails at you when you come home from work.'

'I like that, good answer,' I said. 'Mac or PC?'

'PC at work, Mac at home.'

'But which do you prefer?' I asked.

'Don't mind. I'm used to them both.'

'So you're bilingual?'

'More like ambidextrous,' she said.

'Oh,' I said, mocking her this time. 'I'd give my right hand to be ambidextrous.'

'Oh, do shut up.' She laughed, leaned over and nestled her head on my chest.

I could smell her hair. I stroked it and she remained there in silence, pressing into me. I nearly asked her right then to come with me to my room but I was afraid of being too forward, too impatient.

I glanced at my watch.

'Good God. It's nearly nine o'clock. Do you fancy some dinner?'

'I fancy you more,' she replied seductively.

Now who was being too forward, too impatient?

Did I care?

'So what do you want to do?' I asked.

'Dinner or sex?' she said. 'Decisions, decisions. How about a little dinner first and then lots of sex after?'

'Sounds good to me,' I said. 'Or we could have lots of sex first and then room service after?'

'That's a much better idea,' she said with a giggle, and I wondered if it was just the champagne talking.

Once a lawyer, always a lawyer.

The last thing I wanted was for her to wake up in the morning with a sore head, accusing me of having taken advantage of her, even of raping her, on the grounds that she had been incapable through drink of giving proper consent.

I decided that I'd take my chances with that, but in the end it didn't matter, for we never got to do it anyway.

My phone rang as Kate and I were leaving the bar, hand in hand, en route to my bedroom. I very nearly ignored it, but habits are strong, so I slid my finger across the screen to answer.

'Hello?' I said. 'Harry Foster speaking.'

'It's Arabella Chadwick. Can you come to our house?' There was a degree of desperation in her voice, even panic. 'Please come.'

'What? Now?'

'Yes, now. Straight away. We need you.'

'Why?' I asked.

'The police are here. They're arresting Declan for Zoe's murder.'

Ten minutes later I was climbing out of a taxi in the driveway of Declan and Arabella's house on Hamilton Road, when I'd have so much rather been in bed with Kate.

'Wait for me, will you?' I said to the taxi driver. 'I may need you.'

'You're paying,' he said, reclining his seat and closing his eyes.

There were four other vehicles parked in the driveway, two marked police squad cars, one blue Ford Mondeo and one plain white van with SUFFOLK CONSTABULARY painted on the side.

Arabella was standing outside the front door, as if waiting for me.

'Thank God you're here,' she said.

'Where are they?' I asked, waving at the empty cars.

'Declan is in the dining room with two plain-clothes detectives and a uniformed copper. Four others in white spacesuits are searching the place. I was told to get out.'

'They can't do that.'

'They just did. That's why we need you.'

'What you *need* is a lawyer.'

'But you *are* a lawyer,' Arabella said. 'You told us so on Monday.'

'Yes,' I agreed, 'but Declan needs a solicitor who regularly deals with major criminal cases. Don't you know any other lawyers?'

'No.' She was adamant. 'Declan wants *you*. He says that you can prove his innocence.'

My first, second and every instinct was screaming 'no'. I may be a lawyer by training, and I was certainly accredited by the Law Society, such that I was permitted to practise as a defence solicitor in England and Wales, but I'd done precious little serious criminal work and certainly nothing approaching murder.

My more standard fare in that respect was what I called the five Bs – Bankers, Bonus, Booze, Birds and Barbiturates (although it was nowadays more likely to be cocaine) – bailing over-rich, over-drunk, over-sexed and over-drugged young men out of difficult and often violent situations in nightclubs, while trying to keep a lid on the publicity to protect the reputations of their employers.

I tried explaining all of that to Arabella. But she wouldn't listen.

'Declan needs *you*,' she said. 'Not some other person we don't know.'

'But he only met me two days ago,' I pointed out.

'Better than not at all. Declan trusts you.'

'How can he?' I said. 'He doesn't know me.'

'If Sheikh Karim trusts you, that's good enough for us.'

I stared at her. She was a very determined woman.

'I'll have to make a call,' I said.

I walked away from her and used my mobile to ring ASW.

'I don't see why not,' he said after I'd explained the situation. 'It might help you find out why the horses died. I'm sure the Sheikh would approve. I'll fix it with him in the morning.'

'What about the potential for conflict of interest?' I said. 'If Declan actually did set fire to the stables and killed the Sheikh's horses, then I would then be representing opposing parties.'

'Mmm, I see what you mean. Awkward.'

Ensuring there was no *conflict of interest* should always be a primary concern for any legal entity although, in my experience, some commercial solicitors could evidently barely even spell the words, ploughing on regardless with a case when they should have rightly stepped aside altogether.

'Do you think Declan did it?' ASW asked.

I thought back to how he had gone so pale and faint when he'd initially heard the news that Zoe had gone missing. That had been genuine, I was sure of it. But I was also convinced he knew more than he was telling, otherwise why would the news have produced such a reaction in the first place?

'I don't know,' I said. 'But there's a lot more going on in the Chadwick family than first meets the eye.'

'All the more reason for sticking close to them.'

'If you say so,' I said. 'I'll go along with it for now, but they'll have to find someone else if he's charged.'

At that point the front door of the house was opened and Declan came out escorted by a large uniformed policeman. At least there were no handcuffs. The ex-jockey looked very small and vulnerable next to his burly minder. They were followed out by DCI Eastwood and another man also in plain clothes. His sergeant, I thought.

'I've got to go,' I said to ASW.

I hung up and walked purposefully over to the chief inspector.

'Hello, Mr Foster,' he said. 'What on earth are you doing here?'

'I'm Mr Chadwick's solicitor.'

If he was surprised to see me in the first place, he was now astounded.

'But I thought you represented Sheikh Karim.'

'I do, but I'm also here to represent Mr Chadwick.'

I could tell he didn't like it but he couldn't send me away, that would have contravened Declan's rights, and he knew it.

The uniformed policeman took Declan over to one of the squad cars and placed him in the back seat.

'Where are you taking him?' I asked DCI Eastwood.

'Bury St Edmunds PIC.'

'PIC?'

'Police Investigation Centre. On River Lane.'

I walked over and stood next to the car.

'Declan,' I shouted. He turned and looked out at me through the window. 'Don't say anything to anyone other than confirming your name and address. Do you understand?'

He looked as if he was in a daze.

'Do you understand?' I shouted again.

This time Declan's eyes focused on my face and he nodded.

'Good. Say nothing. I'll be there as soon as I can.'

He nodded again.

I turned back to the chief inspector. 'Mrs Chadwick requires access to her home.'

'No problem,' he said. 'However, my officers will complete their search of the premises. Please advise Mrs Chadwick not to obstruct them in any way or she will be liable for arrest. It would be ideal if she remained in her dining room until my officers have finished. And we reserve the right to seal off any areas of the house we see fit for further examination.'

'She will get a list of any items removed?'

'Of course.'

The DCI climbed into the Mondeo and backed it out onto the road, while the sergeant sat in the squad car next to Declan and was driven away.

I went over to Arabella.

'Why is this happening?' she said desolately. 'Declan would never hurt anyone. It's all a big mistake.'

'Then he will soon be home,' I said, trying to reassure her. 'The police have said you can go back into the house but they are going to finish searching. They have the right to do so. They may also lock some rooms if they think that's necessary. Just stay calm and let them get on with it. Best not to even talk to them. They will give you a list of everything they take away.'

'Take away?'

'Yes,' I said. 'Computers, for example. Or mobile phones. The police are especially keen on seizing people's phones. They can give up all sorts of information.'

'But Declan didn't do it,' she said confidently. 'I know he didn't.'

Was she trying to convince me, or herself?

She started crying, which spoilt the immaculate make-up.

'Is there anyone who can come and be with you tonight?' I asked. 'Or somewhere you can go and stay? Perhaps with friends?'

I didn't suggest she go and stay with Ryan or Oliver. Quite apart from the ongoing feud over the Sheikh's horses, they might not take kindly to the knowledge that Declan was accused of killing another member of the family.

'Maybe I'll call a girlfriend,' Arabella said. But then she looked at me, her black mascara now cascading down her cheeks along with the tears. 'But how can I tell anyone my husband's been arrested for murder?'

*They'll find out soon enough*, I thought.

# 14

I called Kate from the taxi on my way to Bury St Edmunds, to apologise and to tell her that I wouldn't be coming back, not for quite a while anyway. I'd left her in the bar at the Bedford Lodge in the hope that I'd be able to make a quick return, but that wouldn't now happen.

'Who was that woman on the phone?' she asked. 'Was it your wife?'

Ouch!

Kate had obviously been working herself up into a frenzy since I'd left, imagining the worst of me, and who could blame her? It had been the most ill-timed of phone calls.

She had also clearly been topping up with the booze.

'That was not the reason,' I said calmly. 'I don't have a wife.'

'Girlfriend then?'

'No. I don't have a girlfriend either.' *Other than you,* I thought.

'So who was it?'

The breaking news of Declan's arrest would travel round Newmarket at the speed of sound, but it wouldn't be me that leaked it first.

'I'm sorry, I can't tell you that.'

She wasn't happy. And neither was I.

'I've been dumped by men before,' she said acidly, 'but never actually when on my way to bed with them.'

'I'm not dumping you. Quite the reverse. I'm just sorry that something very urgent came up to do with my work.'

'Something you don't trust me enough to tell me about?'

Ouch again!

'It's not about trust,' I said. 'It's just confidential. Legal stuff. I wouldn't even tell my mother.' Oh God, why am I talking about my mother again? 'Can I call you in the morning?'

'I'll be at work.' She made it sound like an excuse for me not to.

'But I can call you there?'

There was a long pause before she answered.

'I'm hurt,' she said slowly. 'I'm drunk, I'm lonely and I'm hurt.'

She was crying, and I felt totally wretched.

'I'm so sorry,' I said. 'I didn't intend to hurt you. But this is something I *have* to do. I'll tell you all about it very soon, but I can't right now.'

She hung up without saying goodbye and I very nearly told the taxi driver to turn round and go back to the hotel, but for what? I couldn't tell her about Declan, so what else would I say? It would only end in an argument and that might result in even more damage than I'd already caused.

I decided that I was better at solving other people's crises than my own.

'I'm telling you, I didn't kill Zoe.'

'Then why are you here?' I asked. 'The police must believe you did, otherwise they wouldn't have arrested you. Why do you think they did that?'

'I have absolutely no idea,' Declan replied.

We were sitting opposite each other across a table in a special room reserved for detainees to meet with their legal representatives at the Police Investigation Centre in Bury St Edmunds.

I'd arrived soon after Declan had been brought in and I'd had to wait while he was processed by the custody officers: photos, fingerprints, DNA sample and clothes removal for forensic examination. All standard procedure. Finally they had collected him from a cell and allowed me to see him.

He was wearing a police-issue tracksuit that was at least two sizes too big for him. If the situation hadn't been so serious, it would have been funny.

The clock on the wall indicated that it was half past ten in the evening. It was an hour and a half since I'd left Kate.

An hour and a half of abject misery.

'What time did you get up this morning?' I asked.

'Ten to five,' Declan replied. 'As usual at this time of the year. First lot goes out at six. Why is that important?'

'Because you've been up for almost eighteen hours. I might be able to argue that you are in need of a night's rest before being questioned.'

'A night's rest? In one of those cells? You must be joking. They're bleak, with only a thin waterproof mattress on a very solid bed. I won't get much rest there. No, let's get on with it. Then I can go home.'

'Declan,' I said, 'have you the slightest idea how much trouble you are in? The police wouldn't have arrested you on suspicion of murder just on the off-chance you might have done it. They must have evidence against you. Now what could that be?'

'I didn't kill Zoe,' he repeated.

'If you say so,' I said. 'But what evidence might they have?'

'I have no idea. Nothing. I didn't kill her.'

'You're not being very helpful.'

I stared at him across the table and, for the first time, I noticed that his nose was slightly crooked. I wondered if that was due to a fall from a horse, or whether Ryan had broken it with a punch in a Doncaster hotel.

There was a knock on the door, which then opened slightly.

'We're ready,' DCI Eastwood said, putting his head through the gap.

'Just a moment,' I said. 'We'll be out in a minute.'

The door closed again.

'Now listen to me, Declan, and listen well,' I said. 'We need to use this session to find out what they have on you,

173

rather than to give them any more ammunition. Do you understand?'

'They can't have anything on me,' he said. 'I didn't do it.'

'When they ask you something, simply say that your solicitor has advised you that you should not answer any questions at this time. Then it's my fault you're not answering, not yours. Remember, you don't have to prove your innocence, they have to prove your guilt. Don't say anything else without referring to me first. This is important. Do you understand?'

'Yes,' he said, but I wasn't sure he meant it.

'Come on, let's go.'

We transferred to a proper police interview room and sat side by side facing DCI Eastwood and the other plain-clothed policeman who had travelled with Declan in the squad car.

The chief inspector pushed a button on the control panel on the wall and a loud, long *beep* was heard.

'For the record,' he said. 'This interview is with Mr Declan Chadwick who has been arrested on suspicion of the murder of Mrs Zoe Robertson. I am Detective Chief Inspector Eastwood and I am accompanied by Detective Sergeant Venables. Mr Chadwick's solicitor, also present, is Mr Harrison Foster.

'Mr Chadwick, may I remind you that you are still under caution, that you do not have to say anything but it may harm your defence if you do not mention when questioned something you later rely on in court. Anything you do say may be given in evidence. Do you understand?'

'Yes,' Declan said.

'I also inform you that this interview is being recorded and that the video and audio recordings may be produced in court as evidence. Do you understand that?'

'Yes,' Declan said again.

'Good,' said the DCI. 'Can you please confirm your full name and address?'

'Declan Vincent Parker Chadwick. Rowley House Stables, Hamilton Road, Newmarket.'

'Thank you. Now, Mr Chadwick,' said the chief inspector, 'when did you last see your sister?'

Declan glanced at me. 'I am advised by my solicitor not to answer any questions at this time.'

*Good boy*, I thought.

The policeman took the lack of an answer in his stride and carried on. 'Is it not true that you saw her last Sunday?'

Last Sunday? Even I would like to hear his answer to that bombshell.

'I am advised by my solicitor not to answer any questions at this time,' Declan repeated.

'Is it also not the case, Mr Chadwick, that you collected Zoe Robertson from Cambridge Station just after midday on Sunday and drove her away in your car, a light-blue Audi A4?'

*What?*

'I am advised by my solicitor not to answer any questions at this time.'

'We have CCTV footage from the forecourt of Cambridge Station that shows her getting into your car. Were you the driver, Mr Chadwick?'

'I am advised by my solicitor not to answer any questions at this time.'

'Where did you take her, Mr Chadwick?'

There was something quite menacing in the way the detective kept adding 'Mr Chadwick' to all his questions. If I was beginning to sense the threat, goodness knows how Declan was feeling. But he appeared to stay calm and unconcerned.

'I am advised by my solicitor not to answer any questions at this time.'

Even I was beginning to be irritated by his response because I, too, would have loved to hear the proper answers to the detective's questions.

There was a brief knock on the door.

'Interview suspended,' said the chief inspector, and he pushed a button to stop the recording before stepping out of the door, leaving Sergeant Venables still in with us.

Declan turned to me as if he was about to say something.

'Don't,' I said. 'Anything you say in here may be used in evidence, whether during the formal interview or not.'

Declan nodded and turned back to face the sergeant.

The three of us waited in silence for DCI Eastwood to return, which he did after a few minutes, carrying a small, transparent plastic bag.

The chief inspector pushed the relevant button and was rewarded with another long *beep* from the recorder. 'Interview restarted,' he said. 'I remind you, Mr Chadwick, that you are still under caution. Are you aware what this is?' He held up the plastic bag. It contained a mobile telephone in a pink case. 'Why was this found hidden under your clothes at the back of your wardrobe?'

Declan looked at me and, for the first time, there was more than a touch of panic in his eyes.

Time for me to step in.

'I would like to speak privately with my client,' I said.

'I want an answer to my questions first,' said the detective, but he hadn't risen to the rank of chief inspector without knowing the law. I knew it too. Declan had a right to speak privately with his legal advisor at any time.

'Interview suspended,' the DCI said reluctantly. He stood up, as did his sidekick. 'In here all right?'

'No,' I said. 'In the previous room.'

He gave me a look but I glanced up at the camera above his head. I wasn't totally confident that the video recording switched off at the same time as the audio.

Declan and I went back into the legal consultation room. I closed the door.

'What the hell's going on?' I said. 'You told me that the police had no evidence against you and then I find out that you collected Zoe from Cambridge Station on the very day she died. And whose phone is that?'

'Zoe's,' he said. 'She left it in my car.'

'So you *did* collect her on Sunday?'

He sat down heavily on a chair next to the table, while I remained standing.

'Yes,' he said. 'I did.' He leaned forward and rested his head on his arms and sighed deeply.

'Why didn't you tell me? I'm here to help you but you have to tell me the truth.'

'I collected her and spent a few hours with her. But I didn't kill her. That *is* the truth.'

'So tell me everything that happened.'

'She called me on Saturday afternoon in a real state. She was shouting down the phone at me. Claimed she needed to talk but not on the phone. She initially wanted me to come to London but I refused. In fact I refused to speak to her anywhere. Then on Sunday morning she called me again when I was in the yard office. Said that she was already on the train from King's Cross and she was coming to see me whether I liked it or not. She sounded completely deranged.'

'What was it that was so important?'

'Family matters,' he said, clearly not wanting to elaborate. 'But the last thing I needed was for her to turn up in that condition at my front door upsetting Bella, so I finally agreed to pick her up from Cambridge.'

'Did Arabella know that?' I asked.

'No way,' he said decisively, glancing up at me.

'Why not?'

'I decided it was best to keep them apart. Zoe had upset Bella enough already.'

'Over what?'

'Money, mostly. Zoe was always in need of money. Used to

say that her need was greater than ours as she had her brats to feed. And that didn't go down too well either.'

I remembered back to Arabella's brusque reaction when I'd asked her whether she and Declan had any kids of their own.

'So you and Arabella can't have children?'

He looked up at me again. 'No.'

'Your fault or hers?' I asked, hopeful that I wasn't prying too deeply.

'Hers,' he said. 'She has something called PCOS. I can't remember what it stands for, but it stops her producing eggs. We've tried every drug there is. IVF too. All bloody hopeless.'

'I'm sorry.'

'Shit happens, or rather it doesn't. Not in our case.'

'Was it money that Zoe wanted to talk to you about on Sunday?' I asked, trying to bring the conversation back to the matter in hand.

'Yeah. Mostly.'

'What happened after you picked her up from the station?'

'I drove around for a bit.'

'Where to?'

'I don't know. Around Cambridge somewhere. We parked for a while outside one of the colleges to talk. Then I drove her to Newmarket.'

'Why?'

'Because she asked me to. She wanted to see if anything had changed since she left. We stopped at a McDonald's for a late lunch on the way.'

'Then what did you do?'

'Drove around the town a bit. Then I dropped her at Newmarket Station to get the train back.'

'At what time was that?'

'About three-thirty.'

'Did you actually see her get on the train?'

'No. It wasn't due for another half an hour. I couldn't wait. I had to get back for evening stables.'

'How was she when you dropped her?' I asked.

'How do you mean?'

'Was she still in a state? Or had she calmed down, back to normal?'

'Normal?' Declan said with a laugh. 'Zoe was never normal. But she was fine, I think.'

'You think?'

'Yeah. She was still angry, but she was always angry.'

'Angry with whom?' I asked.

'Everyone. Me, Ryan, our father, everyone. Psychosis is a very angry disease.'

'Psychosis?'

'She had no grasp of reality. How they ever let her out of a mental hospital I'll never know. She lived in her own little bubble.'

*Yes, as may be*, I thought, *but who burst it?*


'My client would like to read a prepared statement,' I said. 'But he does not intend to answer any questions after it.'

It was half an hour later and we were back in the official police interview room with DCI Eastwood and Sergeant Venables.

And the recorders were running again.

Declan and I had been over everything two more times and, on the second occasion, he had written it all down in chronological order.

'You have to give them something,' I'd explained to him. 'You have to say that you agree with the facts as they have stated them so far – there's no point in denying them when they have the CCTV and Zoe's phone – and then you give your version of what happened last Sunday.'

'My version?' he'd said. 'But I'm telling you the truth.'

'Good. Then the police will be able to verify everything you say. Are you sure there's nothing else you want to tell me?'

'Nothing,' he confirmed.

I was certain, however, that he hadn't told me the whole truth. There were things that he obviously still didn't want to divulge, in particular about why Zoe had wanted to see him in the first place. But this would have to do for now.

Declan read out his statement describing how Zoe had called him from the train and why he had gone to Cambridge to collect her. He then went through the full period between her getting into his car and him dropping her at Newmarket Station at three-thirty, before going home for evening stables.

He finished by saying that he'd found the mobile phone down the side of the passenger seat of his car on Monday afternoon where Zoe must have dropped it. He had panicked and hidden it in his wardrobe so his wife wouldn't find it, but he now realised that he should have handed it straight to the police.

181

When he was finished, Declan laid the paper down on the table.

I could see in the chief inspector's face that he didn't believe a word of it and, to be honest, I wasn't sure I did either.

'Can I go home now?' Declan asked.

# 15

Needless to say, the police did not allow Declan to go home, not on that evening, nor at any time on the next day.

'Who'll look after the horses?' Declan asked me when I saw him just before he was taken off to spend his first night in a cell.

'I'm sure Chrissie will have it all in hand,' I said.

'But she's only the yard secretary.'

'No matter. She seemed very capable to me. And Arabella will surely help too.'

He stared at me in disbelief. 'Arabella is completely useless with the horses. Too bloody busy with her effing make-up.'

I didn't know whether he was joking or not. Probably not, if his tone was anything to go by.

'I'll give her a call anyway. Let her know what's happening.'

He didn't look very happy at the prospect.

'Tell her I'm sorry,' Declan said.

*What for?* I wondered.

'How about you?' he said. 'You can go and sort out what's happening with the horses in the morning.'

'Me?' It was now *my* turn to stare at *him* in disbelief. 'I know nothing about training horses. Don't you have an assistant?'

'He's away in Scotland. His grandmother died. Funeral tomorrow.'

'But I'll be needed here,' I explained. 'To be with you.'

'Not before nine-thirty,' he said. 'You told that detective yourself that I was entitled to proper rest and that I couldn't be questioned again until nine-thirty. You need to be at the yard by six. You can then be here at nine-thirty.'

I looked at my watch. It was already almost midnight. I sighed.

'Isn't there anyone else you could ask?'

'No,' he said decisively. 'Chrissie is good but she needs direction. Tell her to send the whole lot out for a canter. That can't do any harm for one day. Other than tomorrow's runners, of course. And tell Joe to get my two off to York by quarter past seven at the latest otherwise they'll be late, and then I have two more tomorrow evening at Newmarket. But they can be walked over.'

'Who's Joe?'

'My travelling head lad.'

'Right,' I said, resignedly.

'And tell Chrissie to make Saturday's declarations by ten o'clock. I'll have to do the entries later in the day.'

'Declan,' I said. 'You may not be in a position to do anything tomorrow.'

He stared again. 'But they'll have to let me go when they find out I'm telling the truth.' I didn't answer. 'Won't they?'

'They can hold you for twenty-four hours, thirty-six if the superintendent authorises it.' Which he probably would, I thought. 'Then they can apply to a magistrate for extensions to that too. Ninety-six hours altogether. That's four days.'

'Four days?' He suddenly looked despondent, and very vulnerable. 'My whole training business may have gone down the tubes in four days.'

My forty-pound investment on Orion's Glory for the Derby was beginning to look rather too speculative.

I called Arabella from the taxi on my way back to the Bedford Lodge, and to say that she was in a state of severe agitation would have been an understatement.

*Drunk too*, I thought.

She'd obviously been hitting the bottle fairly hard in the three hours since the police had departed with her arrested husband. Declan might have been right about her being useless when it came to helping with the horses, but it wasn't so much the horses' future, or even Declan's, that she was concerned about, it was her own.

'What am I going to do now that Declan's in jail?' she wailed.

'He's not in jail,' I pointed out.

'As good as,' she said. 'How can I face anyone?'

Her earlier cast-iron confidence that Declan was innocent had clearly evaporated.

'The police took away his Audi,' she said. 'Wrapped it all up in white plastic and put it on the back of a lorry.'

'Don't worry,' I said. 'It's normal procedure. They want to do forensic tests, that's all.'

'Forensic tests? For what? A body in the boot?' Now she was openly crying, no doubt aided by the steady intake of alcohol.

'Let's not jump to any conclusions,' I said, trying to sound reassuring. 'He's only being questioned at the moment.'

'About what exactly? What are they saying?'

Discussions between a client and his lawyer are privileged and highly confidential; even the court couldn't force me to disclose what Declan had said to me in the privacy of the legal consultation room. So how much should I tell his wife?

I decided that I could tell her whatever Declan had already told the police. That would be in the public domain sooner or later, especially if used as evidence in a trial.

But first, I had some important questions of my own, and for her.

'Why do you call Peter Robertson "Pete"?'

There was a short but distinct pause from the other end. Perhaps she wasn't as drunk as I'd assumed and she clearly retained some degree of control.

'Why shouldn't I?' she said. 'Zoe always called him Pete.'

'But how do you know that? When did you last speak to her?'

'Oh, I don't know. Some time ago.'

'How long ago exactly?' I asked. 'This is important. Were you in regular contact?'

'Why is it so bloody important?'

'Because Declan collected her off a train at Cambridge Station last Sunday morning.'

'What? Zoe? This Sunday just gone?'

'Yes,' I said. 'The day she died.'

This time there was a much longer pause from her end.

'Is that why he was arrested?'

'Almost certainly,' I said. 'The last person known to have seen the victim alive invariably becomes the chief suspect.'

'Oh God!' she cried. I could clearly hear her sobbing. 'The police also took away our computers and Declan's phone. I thought they were going to take his clothes as well but they simply padlocked shut his dressing room door.'

'Dressing room?'

'We use spare bedrooms as dressing rooms. One each.'

No children, I thought.

'They also found another phone in Declan's room. A pink one. They asked if it was mine.'

'What did you say?'

'I told them I'd never seen it before.' She paused as if not wanting to know the answer to her next question. 'Was it Zoe's?'

'Yes, it was,' I said. 'Declan claims he dropped her off at Newmarket Station on Sunday afternoon, but she left her phone in his car. Didn't he tell you about meeting her?'

'Not a word.'

'Where did you think he'd been all day?'

'He told me he was going to see a yearling. He does it

often on Sundays during the summer in the run-up to the autumn sales.'

'What time was he back?'

'I don't know. I wasn't here. I went to a hotel for the night.'

'On your own?'

I must have sounded surprised.

'Yes. On my own. I went to see a show at Potters Resort near Great Yarmouth. I know the owners. I stay with them. Four or five times a year they have top TV and West End stars performing on Sunday nights. I often go but Declan doesn't want to. He doesn't like live music much.'

'But you were at Oliver's with Declan on Monday when I arrived.'

'Declan called me early to tell me about the fire so I came straight back.'

*But not before you'd put on your make-up*, I thought.

At this point the taxi arrived at the Bedford Lodge.

'I'd better go now,' I said. 'Declan asked me to tell you he was sorry.'

'For what?' she asked acidly. 'For killing his sister or for getting caught?'

I'd only thought it. Arabella had said it.

'You mustn't jump to conclusions,' I said again. 'Declan is totally adamant that he hasn't done anything wrong. There's probably a completely innocent explanation.'

'There is nothing innocent about lying to me about meeting Zoe.'

She was crying again.

'Look,' I said. 'Do you want me to find someone to come and be with you?' Although goodness knows who I would get at this hour. Maybe Susan or Maria? But surely neither would be popular with Arabella.

Or did I dare call Kate? Would she even answer my call?

'No,' Arabella said. 'Thank you. I really couldn't face anyone. It would be too humiliating. I'll be fine on my own.'

'Try and get some sleep. We'll speak more in the morning.'

I disconnected the call and went into the hotel.

Only when I was getting into bed did I realise she hadn't answered my question of why she called Zoe's husband Pete not Peter.

I made a mental note to ask her again when I next saw her.


When my alarm went off just after five, I was convinced that I'd been asleep for only a few minutes. But the clock said otherwise and it was already light outside, the first rays of morning sunshine streaming through a crack in the curtains.

I dragged myself reluctantly out of bed.

I was exhausted.

Was it really only twenty-four hours since I'd got up to go and see Ryan's horses work? It felt more like a week than a day.

*Why aren't I still dead to the world*, I asked myself as I stood under the shower trying to wash the sleep from my eyes. I couldn't comprehend for one second why I'd agreed to go to Declan's yard to see Chrissie. I must be mad.

189

I flicked on the BBC News Channel, more to keep me awake than anything else, and was greatly surprised to see footage of myself walking out of the police investigation centre the previous night and climbing into a taxi.

I hadn't noticed the TV crew at the time, nor the presenter with them who was next seen speaking directly into the camera.

'Police say that a forty-one-year-old man has been arrested on suspicion of murder in connection with the human remains found in Monday's stable fire in Newmarket. The man is being questioned here at Bury St Edmunds.' The shot again showed the building behind the reporter, with POLICE INVESTIGATION CENTRE written in large silver letters on its red-brick exterior wall. 'No details have been officially released concerning the identity of the suspect but the BBC understands that he is being named locally as Declan Chadwick, brother of Ryan Chadwick, the trainer of the dead horses.'

I knew that it wouldn't have taken long for the media to establish who had been arrested but even they had excelled themselves this time.

Maybe my waiting taxi driver of last evening hadn't been asleep after all. One quick phone call, a tweet, or even a post on his Facebook page would have been enough.

And to think I'd put any future relationship with Kate at serious risk by not saying why I'd so abruptly abandoned her, for fear of being the source.

*

My driver and his Mercedes had been reinstated and they were waiting for me outside the hotel at quarter to six on Thursday morning.

There was a copy of a national newspaper lying on the passenger seat with 'FIRE VICTIM'S BROTHER ARRESTED' as its main headline in two-inch-high bold capitals.

I scanned through the front-page story. *So much for the presumption of innocence*, I thought, as paragraph after paragraph implied Declan's guilt. No doubt the lawyers had been through everything with a fine-tooth comb to ensure it wasn't libellous, but it must have been a close-run thing. And, in my view, the reporters had clearly breached Declan's right to privacy – but they were only interested in selling newspapers.

When I arrived in Hamilton Road, there were already two TV news vans parked side by side outside Declan's house, their rooftop satellite dishes facing skywards like a pair of large white hands waiting for a catch.

'Turn into the yard rather than the house,' I said to the driver, but if I thought that meant I would escape the attention of the camera crews, I was much mistaken. They were camped out at every entrance, even if they hadn't actually yet trespassed onto the property itself.

I kept my head down as the Mercedes pulled into the stable yard, where there was considerable confusion around what should be done.

Chrissie was in the yard office and in a bit of a fluster.

'What are we to do?' she asked in desperation. 'Some of the lads haven't even come in to work.'

191

'Keep calm and carry on as best you can,' I said. 'I was with Declan last night and he told me to ask you to send all the horses out for a canter, except for today's runners. He also said to tell Joe to get the two off to York before seven-fifteen.'

'How can we? The place is besieged by the press.'

'Ignore them,' I said. 'The more you carry on as before, the less they'll be interested. That's the best thing you can do for Declan.'

She stared at me.

'Did he do it?' she asked.

'Declan categorically denies having done anything wrong.'

I wasn't convinced she believed it. Did I?

'Has Arabella been out to see you yet?' I asked.

'You're joking,' Chrissie said with a laugh. 'Arabella never appears before eight-thirty even on the best of days. Mostly later. Sometimes not at all.'

I'd have to leave for Bury St Edmunds by eight-thirty, at the very latest, and this clearly wasn't going to be one of the best of days.

'I need to speak to her,' I said, pulling my phone out of my pocket. 'I'll give her a call.'

'I'd wait a bit if I were you,' Chrissie said. 'She has quite a sharp tongue in her head if she's woken too early.'

I knew how she felt, I thought, and yawned.

'Coffee?' Chrissie asked.

'I'll make it,' I said. 'You go and sort out the horses.'

She went out while I put the kettle on.

I yawned again. What was I doing here? I surely could have just called Chrissie on the phone from the comfort of my bed.

I took my coffee out in the yard to see what was going on.

Chrissie was shouting at an unfortunate stable lad who looked barely old enough to be in long trousers let alone in charge of a racehorse. 'Why are you late? You should have been here half an hour ago.'

'Sorry, Miss Chrissie,' he said, cowering away from her. 'My dad told me not to come at all. Not to a murderer's stable.'

'Shut up,' Chrissie retorted angrily. 'Mr Chadwick has done nothing wrong. It's all just a misunderstanding. He'll be back before we know it.' I admired her loyalty. 'Now go and tack up Pepper Mill. Pull out in five minutes.'

The boy went off at a run.

Contrary to Declan's worst fears, Chrissie seemed to have everything pretty much under control as the first lot pulled out and disappeared onto the Heath through a gate at the far end of the yard, pushing the waiting press out of the way.

Chrissie and I watched them go.

'I thought all the yards had coordinated cap colours,' I said, observing that Declan's lads were wearing all sorts.

'Many do,' Chrissie said. 'But it's their choice. There are no hard-and-fast rules. Declan says he doesn't hold with that sort of thing anyway. Tells the lads to wear what they like as long as they've got a helmet on underneath.'

I thought back to Ryan's uniform light-blue caps with red

193

pom-poms and wondered if Declan's decision was simply to be contrary to his elder brother.

Next on the agenda was the departure of the two runners to York. Declan's horsebox was driven into the yard and Joe, the travelling head lad, supervised the loading with a perpetual scowl on his face.

'Right,' he said miserably. 'We'd better get going, although God knows if they'll be allowed to run.'

'Why?' I asked.

'Because the guv'nor's training licence may have been revoked by then.'

He clearly always looked on the dark side of life.

'Surely not,' I said. 'Not before any conviction, and we're a long way off that. He hasn't even been charged.'

'Don't you believe it,' Chrissie said. 'The racing authorities are a law unto themselves. They do what they bloody like.'

*But they're not above the law of the land*, I thought. There may have been a time in the past when decisions of the Jockey Club were untouchable, but not any more. Nowadays, rulings that unfairly restricted someone's ability to lawfully earn their living, in sport or otherwise, could be overturned by a court.

'I am sure Mr Chadwick would want you all to carry on as normal,' I said, and sent the dejected Joe on his way to York, still chuntering under his breath that he'd soon be out of a job, and who would employ him again at his age.

*Just like old Fred Piper at Ryan's place*, I thought.

Getting old was a bugger.

*

I waited until seven-thirty before calling Arabella. I would simply have to take my chances with her sharp tongue.

I tried her mobile but, after six rings, it went to voicemail.

'Try the internal phone,' Chrissie said when I hung up without leaving a message. 'Dial twelve for the kitchen and thirteen for their bedroom.'

I picked up the handset on Declan's desk and dialled 13.

I let it ring about ten times before hanging up.

'She'll still be asleep,' Chrissie said.

'I'll try again in a while.'

But five minutes later there was still no answer and there must have been some concern showing in my face.

'I have a back-door key in here somewhere,' Chrissie said, searching through her desk drawers. 'In case they lock themselves out.' She held it up triumphantly.

But the key wasn't required. The door wasn't locked.

Chrissie hung back nervously outside, so I went in alone.

'Hello?' I called out loudly as I walked through to the front hallway. 'Anyone home?'

In spite of what I'd said to Chrissie earlier, things here would never again carry on as they had before.

Arabella was hanging from the banister of the galleried landing, an upturned chair beneath her dangling legs, and she was stone cold to the touch.

She'd been dead for hours.

# 16

'I need to call the police,' I said to Chrissie when I went back to her.

'And an ambulance?' she asked, deep concern in her face.

'No,' I said. 'Just the police.'

She put her hand up to her mouth. 'Is she . . . ?'

I nodded.

'Oh my God!' She went pale and wobbled at the knees.

'Come on,' I said, taking her elbow. 'Let's get you into the office.'

I steered her across the yard and she slumped down onto her chair. I fetched her a glass of water and some of the colour returned to her cheeks.

Rather than dialling 999, I decided to call DCI Eastwood direct using my mobile, and I went outside so as not to distress Chrissie any further. She did not need to hear the gory details.

'DCI Eastwood,' he said, answering at the second ring.

'Good morning, Chief Inspector,' I said. 'This is Harry Foster. I am at Declan Chadwick's house. I came here to speak to Mrs Chadwick but it would appear that she has committed suicide.'

'Suicide?'

'Yes. I found her myself. She's hanging from the banister in the hallway.'

'Are you sure she's dead?'

'Yes,' I said. I had checked. There had been no pulse in the wrist and there was already a noticeable stiffening of her muscles due to rigor mortis, especially in the face, resulting in what a pathologist friend once told me was known as the death grimace. Even Arabella's immaculate make-up couldn't disguise that. 'There is absolutely no doubt in my mind whatsoever. I reckon she's been dead for several hours.'

'Have you called an ambulance?' the DCI asked.

'No. You are the first person I have spoken to.'

'You should have also called an ambulance. A qualified medic is required to certify death. However, as you are so certain that she is dead, I'll get a police medical examiner there as soon as possible to confirm it. In the meantime, please do not allow anyone to disturb the scene.'

'I won't,' I assured him. 'But be advised that the press are camped outside the property. TV crews included.'

'That's all we need. How do they know?'

'They don't. Not about Mrs Chadwick, anyway, but someone has tipped them off that Declan Chadwick is the man you've arrested. It's been on the TV news since midnight.' I paused. 'I assume you will not now be questioning him as planned at nine-thirty.'

'No. We will postpone that. We're still waiting for some forensic results anyhow. In the meantime, Mr Chadwick can remain in the cells.'

*He won't be happy with that*, I thought, but it was the least of his troubles.

'Will you tell him about his wife?'

'Only after it's been confirmed by the medical examiner.'

He clearly didn't want to take my word for it.

'So should I stay here or come to the investigation centre?' I asked.

'Stay right where you are,' the DCI said decisively. 'I will come there myself.'

The horses returned from first lot and I intercepted one of the older lads and told him that all further lots for the day had been cancelled.

He gave me a questioning look. 'Is that what Miss Chrissie says?'

'Yes,' I replied. 'Miss Chrissie is not feeling too well and she has asked me to pass on the message. Just muck out and feed the horses, then the staff can knock off early.'

He wasn't going to argue with that. 'How about our runners this evening over at the racecourse?'

Decision time.

I decided it would be inappropriate for the horses to run with the trainer under arrest and his wife dead.

'They won't be going,' I said. 'I'll inform the relevant authorities.'

'Right,' he said. 'I'll let the lads know.'

I went back into the office. Chrissie was leaning on the desk with her head in her hands.

'Are you all right?' I asked. Silly question really.

She lifted her head and looked at me with tears in her eyes.

'What are we to do?' she asked desperately.

'I've cancelled the rest of the exercise for today and told the staff to simply feed and muck out, and then go home. And I don't think it's right for any of Declan's horses to run today. Can you call Joe and turn him round? Don't tell him why, just that he's to come back here.' She nodded. 'Then you had better let York Racecourse know they won't be coming. Same for Newmarket this evening. Try not to give a reason other than Declan is indisposed. They will know about that by now from the news.'

She nodded again and reached for her phone. I think she was thankful for something to do.

I picked up the back-door key from her desk. 'I'll lock the house.'

She shuddered at the thought of what was within. So did I a bit.

Somehow it seemed all wrong to leave Arabella still hanging from the banister, but DCI Eastwood had been adamant that I should leave the scene undisturbed.

It would take a good half an hour for him to get to

Newmarket from Bury St Edmunds, especially at this time of the morning, even with blue flashers and his siren on.

I took the key over to the back door but, instead of locking it, I went in.

I wouldn't disturb anything but I thought I might have a quick look around. I'd not get another chance.

Arabella was, unsurprisingly, just where I'd left her, although there was now some pooling of unfortunate fluid on the polished parquet floor beneath her feet. I was thankful it wouldn't be my job to cut her down.

The last time I had seen her alive had been the previous evening when I'd left to follow Declan to the investigation centre. At that time her mascara had streamed down her face with the tears, and she had cried some more when I'd been on the telephone to her at midnight.

Yet her face showed no signs of that now.

The mascara was back in place as if, even in death, her appearance had been important to her.

She had used the belt of a white bathrobe, the remainder of which was laid neatly on the bed in the master bedroom.

Nothing else appeared to be out of place and the bed had not been slept in. I had a quick peep in the bathroom and, in particular, into the medicine cabinet, using a damp flannel from a basin to open it.

One of the other operatives at Simpson White had reliably informed me that one could learn a great deal about people by discovering what pills they took each night.

In this case, all I really learned was that both Declan and

Arabella had lived fairly healthy lives. There were no pills for raised blood pressure or high cholesterol, and nothing that suggested asthma or diabetes. Just a mundane collection of painkillers and indigestion remedies.

I closed the cabinet and returned the flannel to its original position.

Indeed, the only medicine of interest was in the top drawer of Arabella's bedside cabinet. Here I found a half-used bubble strip of fluoxetine together with a box containing three more full strips.

I left them as I'd found them.

I knew about fluoxetine. It was also called Prozac. My former neurotic girlfriend had taken it for anxiety and depression. Living in the Chadwick family and being unable to have children had obviously taken its toll on Arabella.

I went out of the bedroom onto the landing. The door opposite had been secured shut with a crude clasp and padlock. Declan's dressing room, I presumed.

I looked at my watch. It had been twenty minutes since I'd phoned the chief inspector and I didn't want to be still in the house when he arrived.

I went back down the stairs, averting my eyes from the disaster, and had a quick look round the rest of the property. Everything in the kitchen was clean and put away tidily, perhaps obsessively so.

I hadn't been specifically looking for a suicide note but, nevertheless, there was one for me to find, and it would have been difficult to miss. A single sheet of lined white paper was stuck to the fridge door by a small magnetic Eiffel Tower.

It had just two short sentences written on it in neat handwriting.

*It will all come out. I can't stand the shame.*

I didn't touch the note. Instead, I had a quick glance round to ensure I hadn't moved anything, and then let myself out the back door, locking it behind me.

I walked over to the yard office to find Chrissie on the telephone trying to get a word in edgeways.

'But, Mr Reardon, we haven't ...'

I could hear an angry voice on the other end of the line interrupt her.

'Yes, Mr Reardon, but ...'

More inaudible, but clearly irate words, came down the wire.

'Fine, Mr Reardon,' Chrissie said finally. 'As the horse's owner, that's your prerogative. Goodbye.'

She put the phone down firmly and burst into tears.

'That's the third one in the past fifteen minutes. Bloody man is sending someone to collect his horse. They'll all be gone soon.'

The phone rang again.

'Leave it,' I said.

It rang about ten times before stopping. Then I took the receiver off its cradle and laid it down on the desk.

'There,' I said, smiling at her. 'No more problems. Did you call Joe?'

'He's on his way back.'

That wouldn't please him, I thought. He'd be more miserable than ever.

'They hadn't gone too far, anyway,' Chrissie said. 'I also called York. They weren't very happy but ... what the hell.' She sighed. 'I'd better tell the owners that their horses aren't running after all.'

She reached towards the phone again.

'Leave it,' I said again. 'They'll work it out.'

'Yeah, suppose so.' She paused, then looked up at me. 'Where have you been?'

'Checking around the yard,' I said. 'Making sure the lads hurry up and go. We don't really want them all here when the police arrive.'

'But who will help load the horses when the owners arrive to collect them?' she asked gloomily.

'That's their problem. Have they paid all their training fees?'

'Of course not. Owners are always weeks behind with payment.'

'Then we will not release their horses until they do,' I said adamantly.

She smiled wanly up at me. 'Can't you come and work here full-time?'

My mobile rang in my pocket. It was DCI Eastwood.

'I'm outside the front door with the police medical examiner,' he said. 'Where are you?'

'Round the back in the stable yard,' I said. 'Come down the side of the house.'

*

203

It was two more hours before they removed Arabella.

She was zipped into a black plastic body bag and wheeled out on a trolley to a waiting van.

The assembled press had a field day, with the cameramen jostling to push their lenses between the iron railings to get the best shot. A most undignified departure, I thought, for someone who had been so proud of her home.

The event was carried live on the news channels and Chrissie and I watched it together on the TV in the office, where we had been told to wait.

Speculation was rife among the media that the body in the bag was actually that of Declan, but that notion was severely dampened by an interview at the gates with DCI Eastwood, who confirmed nothing other than a 41-year-old man was still in custody and helping police with their enquiries.

Eventually the chief inspector came back to the yard office.

Chrissie and I had already been questioned by Sergeant Venables, who had taken down the details of our movements that morning, not that I'd mentioned my second excursion into the house.

'Did you go anywhere other than into the hallway?' the DCI asked me.

'No,' I replied.

'Not into the kitchen?'

'Not on this occasion,' I said. 'But I've been in there before, on Tuesday morning.'

I wracked my brain to think if I had left any clue this morning.

'Why?' I asked.

'No reason,' he said. He consulted his notebook. 'And can you confirm that the back door was unlocked when you first tried it?'

'That's correct,' Chrissie said. 'I had a key but it wasn't needed.'

'I went and locked the door after I'd spoken to you,' I added. He made another note in his book.

'Thank you,' he said. 'That will be all for now.'

He turned to go and I walked out of the office with him.

'Has Declan Chadwick been informed of his wife's death?' I asked.

'I understand that he was told earlier by the custody sergeant at Bury St Edmunds, once Mrs Chadwick's death had been confirmed by the doctor.'

*Poor Declan*, I thought.

'As his lawyer,' I said, 'I formally request that he be released on compassionate grounds.'

DCI Eastwood pursed his lips. 'I'm afraid that will not happen.'

'Have some sympathy, man,' I said. 'His wife has just killed herself.'

'I agree that this is an unfortunate incident,' he said, 'but I still have a murder investigation to conduct.'

I personally thought it was more than just an 'unfortunate incident'.

And I wasn't giving up that easily. 'I intend applying to a judge to order his immediate release.'

'Mr Foster,' said the DCI intently, 'there have been some further developments of which you are so far unaware.'

'What developments?' I asked angrily.

He paused briefly, as if deciding whether to tell me.

'We have had initial results of the forensic tests on Mr Chadwick's car.'

'And?'

'Zoe Robertson's blood has been found in the vehicle.'

# 17

While the news of Declan's arrest may have swept round Newmarket at the speed of sound, reports of a death at Rowley House Stables moved at that of light, including up to the Tattersalls sales complex.

My phone rang. It was Kate.

'I'm so sorry about last night,' I said before she could say anything.

'It's *me* who should be sorry,' she replied. 'I was inexcusably rude in hanging up on you. And I am more than sorry for what I said. I am totally embarrassed by it.'

'You had every right to be angry,' I said, trying to reassure her. 'It was just not a good moment.'

'No.' She paused. 'I've just seen the news. Was the body in the bag Arabella Chadwick?'

'Yes,' I said. No client/lawyer confidentiality issues this time.

'And was it her on the phone to you last night?'

'Yes,' I said again. 'She called begging me to come to their house straight away. I decided I had to go. But I'd much rather have been with you.'

'I am so sorry,' she said quietly. 'I have no excuse for being so horrible, especially when someone was in greater need. Did you find her dead when you got there?'

'No. She was very much alive then. In fact, I spoke to her on the phone at midnight. It was only this morning I found her dead.'

I explained to her that Declan had been arrested and I had gone to Bury St Edmunds to be with him during questioning.

'I called her on my way back to the hotel.'

'Hold on a minute,' she said. 'Didn't Declan get arrested for killing Arabella?'

'No.' I laughed, although it was hardly a laughing matter. 'He's been arrested on suspicion of murdering Zoe.'

'Blimey,' she said. 'It's like an episode of *CSI*. So who killed Arabella?'

I weighed up in my mind if I was free to tell her and decided that I was.

'It would appear that she killed herself.'

'Oh God! How awful. Poor Arabella.'

'How well did you know her?' I asked.

'Not that well. I met her a few times. Five or six maybe. We all thought she was rather distant and aloof, arrogant even.'

'Who's we?'

'The girls at Tatts. She used to come here sometimes with Declan. You know, for receptions and such.'

'Do you know if she had any problems?' I asked.

'Her husband being arrested for murder was surely one.'

'Yeah,' I agreed. 'But anything else? Something before that?'

'What sort of problems?'

'Anxiety or depression?'

'Not that I'm aware of, but I wouldn't be, would I? People are pretty good at keeping that sort of thing secret. Was that why she did it?'

'I don't know,' I said. 'I was just wondering. I have to go and see Declan and I'm not looking forward to it.'

'Doesn't he know?'

'Yes. He does. He was told by the police this morning.'

'Poor man,' Kate said, but then she changed her tone. 'Unless, of course, he did kill Zoe. In which case he deserves everything he gets.'

'Janie told me she was at school with Zoe. Did you know her too?'

'Vaguely. She was three years below me. She was always known as That Crazy Chadwick Kid. Not very kind, I suppose, but accurate. Then there was all that fuss when she went missing. Let's just say she didn't exactly endear herself to the good people of Newmarket. There was a fair amount of finger-pointing and accusations. All of it unfounded, of course, but the damage was done. Quite a lot of us would have happily murdered her after that.'

'You included?' I asked pointedly.

'You bet,' she said, laughing. 'I was first in line.' She paused again, but then decided to explain. 'All the local men between sixteen and sixty who knew her were questioned and had to account for their whereabouts on the day she went missing. My dad was one of them. He told the police that he was on a business trip to London but his alibi didn't bear out. They threatened him with arrest, so he came clean. He was with another woman, wasn't he? Broke up my parents' marriage, Zoe did.' Only indirectly, I reckoned, but thought better of saying so. 'Look, I must get back to work. I've already taken longer than my coffee break.'

'What are you doing later?' I asked quickly. 'I plan to go to the races this evening. I've never been to a proper race meeting before. Would you like to come with me?'

'Won't you be needed in Bury St Edmunds?'

'Not if I can help it. I'm going there right now but intend being back in time. First race is at quarter past five. What do you say?'

'I'd love to,' she said.

'Great. I'll call you when I know how things lie.'

We disconnected.

My day was definitely on the up. At least, I thought so.

Declan looked smaller and even more vulnerable than ever, his bloodshot eyes having seemingly sunk back deeply into their sockets.

We were once again in the legal consultation room at the investigation centre, and he was slumped down on one of the chairs, his elbows resting on the table with his head in his hands.

'Help me, Harry,' he cried out in despair. 'What am I going to do?'

'First,' I said, 'we need to get you out of here and back to your horses.'

'To hell with the horses.'

That was worrying, I thought. On the previous evening, he had been more concerned about the horses' welfare than his own.

'How can I go on without Bella?'

'You will,' I assured him. After all, he had revealed that Arabella was useless when it came to the horses. *Too bloody busy with her effing make-up* had been his exact words.

And the make-up did worry me a little. Would anyone really redo their mascara if they were about to kill themselves? But, I suppose, just maybe, the 'distant and aloof' Mrs Arabella Chadwick might have done so.

'Is there anything more you need to tell me about your meeting with Zoe?' I asked.

He waved his hand at me as if he considered anything other than the death of his wife was of no importance, but I knew otherwise. He was in a very low emotional state, and that was when he was most in danger of giving up the fight to clear his name.

'Declan,' I said clearly, 'why has Zoe's blood been found in your car?'

That got his attention.

'Where in the car?' he asked.

'I don't know.'

'On the front passenger seat, I bet,' he said. 'I told her to be careful, but you know what she was like.'

'No, I don't know what she was like,' I said. 'Tell me.'

'She picked at her fingers. Always did. At the base of her nails. Made them bleed all the time. Done it since she was a kid and she'd obviously had a particularly heavy session on the train from London. Bleeding all over the place, she was, when I collected her. I told her to keep her hands off the seats, but she clearly didn't. She never did anything she was told, that girl.'

'Is that all?' I asked.

'What do you mean, all? There's no pool of blood in the boot, if that's what you're thinking.' He was getting quite agitated. 'I tell you, I didn't kill her. I dropped her at Newmarket Station just like I said. It's not my fault if she didn't catch the bloody train.'

I suddenly found that I believed him absolutely. My former doubts had been banished. In his current state of mind, and after the death of Arabella, I was certain he would have come clean, here and now, if he really had been responsible for Zoe's demise and the fire.

'What did Zoe want to talk about that was so important she came all the way from London to see you? Why not use the telephone?'

He threw his hands up in frustration. 'You couldn't have a sensible conversation with Zoe face to face, let alone on the phone. She would scream and shout all the time. In the end you'd have to hang up.'

And I knew all too well how annoying that could be.

'But what did she scream and shout about?'

'Money,' he said. 'It was always about money. She was perpetually broke, deep in debt, and always on the scrounge. And then she spent anything she was given on drugs. What a waste of a life.'

'How about her husband, Peter? Doesn't he have a job?'

'Don't make me laugh,' Declan said. 'Calls himself an estate agent but I bet he's never sold a single house in his life. I certainly wouldn't trust him with one. Probably high most of the time. Useless prat.'

'Why did Arabella call him Pete, not Peter?'

The very mention of Arabella's name seemed to spiral him back into deepest misery.

'Oh God!' he shouted loudly, as if seeking divine deliverance from his pain. 'I can't go on.'

'Yes, you can,' I said resolutely. And I wasn't going to stop now. 'So why Pete not Peter? How much contact was there between Zoe and Arabella?'

He sighed. 'They talked a few times on the phone last year and then Bella went to London to see her. Last December, it was. I remember, because she took some Christmas presents for the children.'

*Children again*, I thought.

It was all about children, or the lack of them.

'Zoe always called the prat Pete. So I suppose Bella picked it up from her.'

'Did she actually meet him?'

213

'I don't know. She didn't want to talk about the visit. I didn't even know she was going until after she'd been. And it affected her badly.'

'In what way?' I asked.

'She was nervous afterwards. Anxious and upset. She had difficulty sleeping. She wouldn't tell me why exactly, but I think it was because Bella wanted so much to have children of her own. To love and cherish them. She couldn't bear the fact that Zoe had kids but didn't seem to care, or even to look after them properly. It was like a double torment for her. My poor darling.'

Declan leaned his head back down on his arms and sobbed.

I waited until the worst had passed.

'So Zoe came to ask you for money?' I said finally, trying to move things forward.

'Demanded it, more like,' he said. 'Claimed she was entitled to it as my sister. The stupid girl was delusional.'

'Did you give her any?' I asked.

'Only what I had in my pocket. Fifty quid or so. Anything to shut her up. Maintained she needed it to feed her kids, but I knew she'd use it for her next fix. Either that or for cigarettes.'

'Did she smoke a lot?' I asked.

'All the time. I don't know how she could afford it.'

'Did she smoke when she was with you last Sunday?'

'Like a bloody chimney. Had to buy one of those air freshener things for the car to get rid of the smell.'

'Did she have a lighter?' I asked.

'Eh?' He looked up.

'A lighter? To light her cigarettes? Or did she use matches?'

He paused a moment as if remembering.

'She had a lighter. One of those cheap plastic ones. Red, I think it was.'

Probably the one found next to her remains, although the red plastic had long gone in the fire.

Detective Chief Inspector Eastwood eventually lost his patience and knocked on the door. I went over and opened it.

'We need to question your client,' the DCI said to me. 'Time moves on.'

I looked at my watch. It was already almost three o'clock. My trip to the races was looking increasingly at risk.

'All right,' I said. 'Just a few more minutes.'

We returned to the previous interview room and the DCI again went through the rigmarole of starting the recorders and introducing the same participants, not that Sergeant Venables had said or done anything at all.

'My client wishes to make a further statement,' I said, jumping in before the chief inspector could ask his first question.

Everyone's eyes turned to Declan.

'I reiterate that what I said last night is the truth. I picked up Zoe Robertson from Cambridge Station at noon last Sunday, drove her to Newmarket via the McDonald's drive-thru for lunch, and then I dropped her off at Newmarket Station at about three-thirty before returning home alone for evening stables. I'd like to further add that my sister was in the habit of self-harming, in particular picking at her fingers so hard that they bled. She had done that extensively on the day in question and any of her blood found in my car would be as a result of that activity rather than of anything more suspicious.'

The DCI looked at me with contempt.

The finding of Zoe's blood in Declan's car had clearly been his trump card. But he had shown me his hand, and I'd overtrumped it. If he had wanted me to keep quiet he should have said so, not that I'd have taken any notice.

He seemed dumbstruck, so I took my opportunity.

'My client would like to inquire if you have viewed any CCTV footage from outside Newmarket Station. He maintains that it will show Zoe Robertson after he dropped her there. In addition, my client demands that you study the security CCTV from his stable yard, which will show that he was back at work there by three forty-five.' I paused, but I wasn't finished, not by a long chalk. 'Furthermore, I contend that any evidence you have against my client is none other than circumstantial, coincidental and speculative. Yes, we accept that he was in contact with the victim on the day she died, but that was several hours before her death, and you have nothing that places my client at Castleton House Stables prior to the fire. Therefore I demand that he be released forthwith to attend to the devastating loss of his wife.'

The four of us sat there in silence for a few moments. Declan even patted me on the knee under the table.

216

But the DCI wasn't giving up that easily.

'We do not have a definitive time of death for the victim,' he said slowly. 'Only that she was killed sometime before the fire started. She may have been already dead when Mr Chadwick returned to his stables on Sunday afternoon.'

'So where was the body in the meantime?' I asked.

The DCI clearly didn't like the fact that it was *me* asking *him* questions when he'd intended being the interrogator.

'We are still examining Mr Chadwick's car.'

'Oh, come on,' I said, waving a hand at him. 'If there was blood in the boot, you would know it by now. Or are you seriously suggesting he left a dead body on show for several hours in the front passenger seat of his car while it sat in his stable yard for all to see?'

'He might have stashed the body somewhere else.'

'Where exactly?' I asked. 'Admit it, Chief Inspector, you're just fishing.' I stood up. 'My client will answer no further questions.'

The DCI was beginning to lose his cool. 'But he hasn't answered any questions at all as yet.'

'And he won't,' I confirmed.

The DCI looked up at the clock on the wall.

'Interview terminated at 3.20 p. m.'

# 18

I made it back to Newmarket with twenty-five minutes to spare before the first race, and Kate was waiting for me at the racecourse entrance.

In weather terms, the day had been spectacular with clear blue skies and abundant sunshine. Hence the temperature had risen such that it felt more like midsummer than mid-May. And Kate had taken full advantage, wearing a bright yellow sundress with a wide black leather belt over it, which did everything possible to show off her gorgeous attributes. I was surprised to see that she was also wearing black high-heeled shoes.

*Close call*, I thought.

I'd almost come in my wellingtons, the same as I'd worn on the gallops the previous morning.

In fact, I had misjudged the dress code altogether.

Of course, I knew that one dressed up for Royal

Ascot, but I quite expected a weekday evening meeting at Newmarket to be casual, scruffy even. How wrong I was. The sunshine had brought the ladies out in their finery, albeit without quite the degree of fancy millinery found in East Berkshire in June, and most of the men were in jackets and ties, or suits.

I felt very underdressed in chinos and a sweater.

'I'm sorry,' I said to Kate. 'I should have worn my suit.'

'Don't worry about it,' she said. 'Anything goes these days.'

And she was right. Among the sartorially elegant were a smattering of jeans and T-shirts and even a few pairs of flip-flops, not that they would be allowed in the Premier Enclosure if the notices at the entrance were to be believed.

But it wasn't only the smartness of the people that was a surprise to me.

My only previous experience of attending horse racing had been as a teenager at a wet Saturday afternoon point-to-point at Flete Park in South Devon, where the mud had been ankle deep and a seriously overcrowded beer tent the only shelter from the persistent rain.

Newmarket on this sunny, warm evening could not have been more different.

The public enclosures were pristine, with manicured velvet lawns, neatly trimmed hedges and an abundance of bright yellow and red flowers, seemingly matching the terracotta-red roofs of many of the buildings. Even the track itself would have put many a domestic garden to shame with its lush green grass awaiting the arrival of the horses.

'Drink?' Kate said.

'Absolutely,' I replied. I looked around. 'Where?'

She laughed.

'Tattersalls have a permanent box here. It's not booked by the bigwigs tonight so, after you called, I went and asked my boss if the staff could use it.'

She held up some badges.

'Fantastic. Lead on.'

We went into the grandstand and then up in a lift to the top floor where the thick-pile carpet would not have been out of place in a five-star London hotel.

Definitely not wellington-boot territory.

A party was in full swing in the Tattersalls box with about a dozen people already there. Kate made introductions before getting us drinks from the bar in the corner.

'We've all clubbed together to pay for the drinks,' she said. 'But we'll have to go down if we want any food. The racecourse catering is far too expensive.'

'I don't want anything yet,' I said. 'Later maybe.'

Indeed, I had hopes of partaking of the hotel dinner we'd missed the previous evening, or maybe even the room service.

We took two glasses of Prosecco out onto the box terrace and looked out across the Heath towards the west. It looked fantastic in the late afternoon sunshine. So did Kate. I took her hand in mine and she looked at me and smiled. Last night's troubles were just a fading memory.

'I love evening racing,' she said. 'So easy to come after

work. But this is the only evening meeting of the year held here. All the others are on the July course.'

'The July course?' I said.

She laughed. 'Newmarket has two racecourses, three even, if you count the round course, but that's only used once a year, for the Town Plate. This is the Rowley Mile course.'

'Named after King Charles II,' I said, remembering the history.

'That's right,' Kate said. 'We race here in the spring and autumn. But, in the summer, it's only on the July course down the road over there.' She pointed into the distance.

'In July,' I said, mocking her slightly.

'Yes. In July.' She smiled again. 'But, rather confusingly, also in June and August. We've had some great Friday nights there. They put on a band after racing. Good bands, too. It's always packed.'

'We'll have to go one night,' I said.

'Will you still be here by then?'

'Probably, the way things are going at the moment.'

'How was it in Bury St Edmunds?'

'Fine, I think.' I wondered how much I could tell her. 'They haven't released Declan yet but I don't believe they have enough to charge him.'

'How long can they keep him locked up?'

'Twenty-four hours initially. That's up at nine o'clock this evening. But they can apply for extensions from the courts. Four days is the maximum but I'd be very surprised if they

221

get that long. There simply isn't the evidence, and I'm pretty certain he didn't do it.'

'So who did?' she asked.

'That, my darling, is the million-dollar question.'

The horses came out onto the course for the first race, cantering down to the start far away to our right.

'We must have a bet,' Kate exclaimed. 'Come on!'

She dragged me back inside the box.

'But on what?' I said. 'I don't even know which horses are running.'

She thrust a racecard into my hands. 'Choose one.'

'But I don't know which are any good.'

'Oh, for goodness' sake, just choose one by its name or its colours.'

I glanced down the list of horses in the first race.

'Criminal Lawyer,' I said. 'Number three.'

She grabbed the racecard as if she didn't believe me, but it was true.

'That's got to be a good omen. Let's stake your shirt!'

In the end we decided on something rather smaller, more like a sock. Ten pounds each way, to be precise, and we cheered madly as Criminal Lawyer made a valiant effort, but finished fifth out of the twelve.

'Ah well,' Kate said, ripping up the ticket and tossing the bits away like confetti. 'Better luck in the next.'

She chose one in the second race, a horse called Happy Night, which did not live up to its name, finishing a poor seventh out of the eight runners.

More confetti.

'The bookmakers must love people like us,' I said. 'Selecting horses solely by their names. If I were a bookie, I'd own a horse called "Sure Thing" or "Guaranteed Winner" and then make sure it was useless. I'd rake it in every time it ran.'

'I'll admit it's not the best method,' Kate said. 'We should seriously study the form and go and see the horses to see which one looks the best.'

*But how will I know that?* I thought. They all looked pretty similar to me – four legs, with a head at one end and a tail at the other.

Nevertheless, we went down in the lift and out towards the parade ring to inspect the runners in the third, and ran straight into Ryan Chadwick coming the other way.

And he wasn't at all happy to see me.

'What the bloody hell are you doing here?' he asked angrily, as if spoiling for a fight.

'Just enjoying an evening at the races,' I said light-heartedly, trying to diffuse his anger.

'I thought you'd be with the police and my damn brother.' He thrust his face towards mine. 'I thought you were on *my* side, not his. I'm the bloody victim here.'

I thought that Zoe's husband and children might beg to differ.

'You can tell Declan from me that I'll wring his bloody neck if he ever comes anywhere near me. I hope he rots in jail. The bastard killed my best horse.'

He was working up a real head of steam so I thought it was prudent not to mention that Declan hadn't even been charged, let alone convicted.

But Ryan wasn't finished yet.

'And you're no better,' he hissed, repeatedly poking me in the chest with his right forefinger. 'Worming your way into my father's house then stabbing us in the back. You're nothing but an effing traitor.'

'Shut up, Mr Chadwick,' said Kate, coming to my defence. 'You don't know what you're talking about.'

He turned from me to her with rage in his eyes. He bunched his fists and I was seriously afraid he was going to hit her.

'Who the hell are you to tell me what to do?' he demanded.

'I'm Janie's sister,' Kate said. 'Now go away and leave us in peace.'

Ryan focused on her face and he was still in enough control to realise that punching the lights out of his yard secretary's sister might not be the greatest career move, even if he thought verbally abusing the representative of one of his most important owners had been.

He started to turn away, but I grabbed hold of his jacket sleeve and pulled him back.

'Tell me, Ryan,' I said calmly. 'Why *did* you break Declan's nose in a Doncaster hotel?'

'Is that what he told you? Little shit.'

*No,* I thought, *Declan hadn't told me.* I had guessed. But I wasn't going to say so.

'Is it true?' I asked.

'Yes, it's true, but I was provoked.'

'How?' I asked.

He stared at me for two or three long seconds.

'Never you mind,' he said.

He pulled his sleeve out of my grasp and walked briskly away.

'What was all that about?' Kate asked as we made our way to the parade ring.

'It seems that Ryan is unhappy that I am acting as his brother's solicitor.'

'He's more than unhappy if you ask me. I've never seen a man so angry.'

'It was quite funny though,' I said, laughing.

'What was?'

'Watching a man of only nine stone trying to throw his weight around.'

We giggled, probably more from the release of tension that the encounter had produced. Quite funny, but not really. There had been something rather menacing about Ryan's behaviour, only nine stone or not.

*It will all come out. I can't stand the shame.*

What would come out? What was it that no one was talking about?

We finally had a winner in the fifth race but it was a short-priced favourite and the payout was insufficient to make much of a dent in all our previous losses. But we celebrated nevertheless with another round of Prosecco.

'It isn't the money that's important,' Kate said, 'it's the excitement.'

*Easy for you to say,* I thought, *when it's not your money.*

'Betting on horses is clearly a mug's game,' I said. 'My boss says there's no such thing as a poor bookmaker.'

'Boring!'

Hence I loaded our winnings, and more, on a horse called Love Me Forever in the last race, and then waved goodbye to the cash as the damned nag trailed in at the rear of the ten runners.

But I didn't care.

I'd only chosen that horse so I could scream 'Come on, Love Me Forever' at the top of my voice from the grandstand, and mean every word of it.

'What now?' I said to Kate. 'How about dinner?'

'Lovely. Where?'

'The Bedford Lodge Hotel.'

'I doubt we'll get a table,' Kate said. 'Race nights are always busy.'

'I think we will,' I said.

I'd taken the precaution of booking one earlier, just in case.

We walked out of the racecourse to where my driver was waiting and my phone rang as we were climbing into the car.

*Not again,* I thought.

'Hello?' I said, answering.

'Mr Foster?' said a voice. 'This is the custody sergeant at Bury St Edmunds. I have Mr Declan Chadwick for you.'

'Harry,' he said, coming on the line. 'They're releasing me. Something called RUI.'

'Released under investigation,' I said.

'Yes, that's it. What does it mean?'

'Exactly what it says. You are being released from custody but the investigation of your possible involvement will go on. The police will probably keep your car, phone and computer until they are satisfied there is no further evidence to be obtained from them. Eventually they will either have to charge you or notify you that the investigation is at an end and that no further action will be taken against you.'

There was a pause while he absorbed the information.

'It's a good thing,' I assured him. 'It means you are now free to leave the investigation centre.'

'Can you come and collect me?' he asked.

'No, I can't,' I said adamantly. I was not having him ruin another dinner with Kate. 'But I'll send a car and driver for you. He'll be with you in about half an hour.'

'But where shall I go?' he said miserably. 'I can't go home. Not without Arabella there.'

That was his problem, not mine, but I did feel extremely sorry for him.

'Isn't there someone you could go and stay with?' I asked. Not Ryan, I thought. 'How about your dad? Or Tony?'

From his silence I inferred that neither was a popular choice.

'How about Chrissie, then?' I said.

'But she's just my secretary.'

'As may be,' I said, 'but she's very loyal and I'm sure she will help if she can. Call her and see if she's got a spare room, or even a sofa, you can borrow. I'll speak to you in the morning. I'll call the yard office.'

'But . . .'

'No buts, Declan. You need the horses as much as they need you.'

The Mercedes dropped Kate and me at the Bedford Lodge Hotel and then set off to collect Declan from Bury St Edmunds.

'No problem,' the driver had said when I asked him. 'I get paid by the hour and the mile. The more the merrier. I'll take him to wherever he wants to go. I hear it's very nice in John o'Groats at this time of year.'

He was still laughing to himself as he drove off.

'So they've released Declan?' Kate said, when we had settled at our table in the hotel's Squires Restaurant.

'So it would appear. They obviously didn't get an extension beyond the initial twenty-four hours.'

'Does that mean he's innocent?'

'Not necessarily, but they probably wouldn't have let him go so easily if they really thought he was guilty. Perhaps they've looked at the CCTV from Newmarket Station.'

'What would it show?' Kate asked.

I decided that Declan making a statement to the police

was as good as putting its contents into the public domain, so I explained to her about him having picked up Zoe from Cambridge the previous Sunday, and how her blood had subsequently been found in his car.

Her eyebrows almost disappeared into her hairline.

'No wonder the police arrested him.'

'Yes, but Declan maintains he dropped her off, alive and well, at the station in Newmarket on Sunday afternoon for her to catch a train back to London.'

'But she didn't actually catch it?'

'No. Instead she turned up dead in Oliver Chadwick's stable yard.'

'In the fire?'

'Yes, but the post-mortem shows that she was dead before the fire started.'

The eyebrows went up again, maybe even further this time.

'Wow! No wonder you went off so fast last night. Eat your heart out, Sherlock Holmes!'

I smiled across the table at her.

'But what about Zoe's blood in the car?' she asked. 'How did that get there?'

'Elementary, my dear Watson,' I said. 'Zoe had a habit of self-harming. She regularly picked so hard at her fingers that they were red-raw and bleeding. The blood in the car came from that.'

'She used to do that at school,' Kate said wistfully. 'How dreadful that she was still doing it all these years later.'

'Yes,' I agreed. 'Zoe was clearly a very troubled individual.'

'Obviously Arabella was too,' Kate said. 'And now that Declan has been released, it all seems such a waste. You'd think she would have waited to find out if he'd really done it before she killed herself.'

But I wasn't sure that Arabella's suicide had anything to do with Zoe's murder.

# 19

Sadly, Kate went home later in a taxi.

'I need to get my Tatts uniform for work tomorrow,' was her excuse and, to be honest, I could do with the sleep. By eleven o'clock, I was out on my feet, and an excellent bottle of Saint-Émilion Grand Cru over dinner hadn't exactly helped.

'Maybe we can see each other again tomorrow night,' she said as I walked her out to the taxi. 'I don't have to work on Saturdays.'

'That would be great,' I said. 'I'll call you.'

I went to give her a peck on the cheek, but she turned it into a passionate kiss on the lips.

*Bugger her Tatts uniform*, I thought, as her taxi pulled away and I went reluctantly alone to my room.

The red message light was flashing on the bedside telephone.

Now what? Not Declan again with more bad news?

However, it was not Declan but Oliver Chadwick, and he was apologising on behalf of his eldest son.

'I'm sure Ryan didn't mean to be rude and I trust you didn't take his words in that manner,' he said. 'It's just that it has been rather a stressful time here recently.'

I could imagine the scenario.

Ryan would have worked out that his actions at the racecourse had been somewhat less than prudent, and he had gone to his father to confess that he'd spoken sharply to Sheikh Karim's personal representative.

Oliver would have been furious with him and demanded that Ryan call me immediately to apologise. But Ryan would have refused because (a) he was embarrassed, and (b) he didn't want to lose face, primarily the latter.

So Oliver had had to do it himself, but he'd called the hotel number, rather than my mobile, so that he wouldn't actually have to speak to me. He could safely leave a voicemail. I'd have probably done the same in his position.

There was no reference to Ryan also repeatedly poking me in the chest with his forefinger, so he'd probably kept that little gem from his father.

I listened to Oliver's message again.

'I'm sure Ryan didn't mean to be rude and I trust you didn't take his words in that manner.'

*A bit difficult not to*, I thought, *when he'd called me an effing traitor.*

*

232

I slept the sleep of the just, eight full hours of deep, uninterrupted slumber, and woke on Friday morning refreshed and ready for action.

The first thing on my agenda after breakfast was to call ASW.

'How are things going?' he asked.

I filled him in on the events of the past couple of days, while deciding to leave out any mention of Kate. There are some things the boss doesn't need to know.

'I saw some reports on the news,' he said. 'Seems like a complete mess. Did Declan cause the fire?'

'I don't believe so. I think he's telling the truth but not necessarily the whole truth. There's something else going on in this family and, in spite of the animosity between them and the death of two of their number, no one is mentioning it.'

'So what do you do next?' ASW said. 'I had a conversation with the Sheikh early this morning and he's quite happy for you to stay there a while longer if it's going to be productive. Georgina has provisionally booked your hotel room until the end of next week.'

*If it's going to be productive*, I thought. Easy to say.

'Can we get hold of any bank records?' I asked. 'Money seems to be an important issue here.'

'When is it not?' he said with a laugh. 'Whose money in particular?'

'Zoe and Peter Robertson's for a start. And I'd quite like to speak to Peter Robertson, although he seems to be rather an oddball if what everyone says is anything to go by.'

'And his wife has just been murdered.'

'Yes,' I agreed. 'But the police must have interviewed him by now, if only to eliminate him from their enquiries. In my limited experience, the cops always suspect the spouse first.'

'Can't you ask them what he said?'

'I fear my relationship with the DCI in charge of the case has soured somewhat, but I could try. Or else I could come down to London and go and see him over the weekend.'

'When is his wife's funeral?' ASW asked.

'I haven't heard but it's unlikely to be soon. Zoe's body, or what's left of it, is a major piece of evidence and any future defence team would want their own post-mortem carried out. I should think a funeral is several months away, at best.'

'Poor man. Not only is his wife dead, but he can't even lay her to rest.'

'I think I'll go and see him tomorrow if that's all right.'

'Fine by me,' ASW said crisply. 'I'll send you his address. Keep me posted, and I'll get on to the research boys to see what they can do about the bank records.'

'Thanks. And tell Rufus I'm learning fast about the gee-gees.'

'He's absolutely furious that you're in Newmarket while he's stuck in Florence.'

'Ask him if he needs any tips.'

We disconnected with ASW still laughing.

Next I called Kate at work.

'Hello, Sherlock,' she said cheerily. 'Unearthed any more clues?'

'Do you know,' I said seriously, 'I found Moriarty this morning hiding in my wardrobe.'

'Ha, ha! Very funny.' But she didn't actually laugh. 'So what plans have you got for today?'

'I thought I might go back to the races this afternoon. Get a better idea of what really goes on. For some reason I wasn't properly concentrating yesterday. Then I might go out for dinner. What do you think?'

'Sounds pretty good to me, although the dinner bit seems rather spurious. I thought you were having room service.'

I smiled. 'It could be arranged,' I said.

'Excellent. Now what are you doing this morning?'

'Nothing. Why?'

'Well, I happened to mention to my boss that I was with the personal representative of Sheikh Karim at the races last night and he was dead keen that you should be given a tour of the sales complex.'

'Would you be conducting this tour?' I asked.

'It could be arranged,' she said, mimicking what I'd said. 'But we might have my boss with us. He's very eager for the Sheikh to spend more money on buying horses. That's more money buying horses from us, of course.'

'Of course. How long will this tour take? First race today is at one-forty.'

'Come to the main reception at eleven. That would give us plenty of time.'

'Great. See you then.'

She hung up and I found myself grinning like the Cheshire

235

Cat that had also got the cream. Calm down, I told myself, you've been here before and it didn't work out. But I was determined that neither Declan, nor any other member of the Chadwick family for that matter, was going to ruin my night this time.

I decided that I'd switch off my phone good and early.

But not yet. I had calls to make, and first on the list was Declan.

I called the Rowley House Stables yard office and Chrissie answered. She had clearly put the receiver back on the hook.

'Hi, Chrissie,' I said. 'How are things?'

'Fine,' she said, 'now Mr Declan is back.'

'How many owners turned up?'

'Just one in the end. That bloody Mr Reardon. Arrived with a trailer towed behind a Range Rover, I ask you. Not even a proper horse trailer, neither. More like one of those for moving cows or sheep. Demanded his horse. Stupid bully. I told him to help himself but I swear he didn't even know its name, let alone what it looked like.' She was laughing at the memory. 'He insisted that someone should load his horse for him, so I told him that would only happen if he settled his outstanding invoices first.'

'Good girl,' I said. 'Then what happened?'

'He got back into his flashy Range Rover and drove away. But he had to turn it round. Silly man should have unhooked the trailer first. He was all over the place. Took him a good ten minutes of toing and froing to get it round. It was the funniest thing I've seen in years. The tears were streaming down my face. And the more I laughed the angrier he got. Didn't help his driving, neither.'

'He won't have liked being humiliated,' I said. 'He'll take his horse away anyway.'

'Good riddance,' Chrissie said. 'We'll be better off without him.'

Things had obviously looked up since the same time yesterday.

'Is Declan around?' I asked.

'He was but he's stepped out. Do you need him?'

'Not really. I'm just checking he's all right.'

'I think so. He slept in my spare room last night and was keen as mustard to get here this morning. He hasn't been into the house yet though. Says he can't face it.'

'I can understand that,' I said. 'But how are things in the stable yard?'

'Fine, I think,' she said. 'Declan got cross that I hadn't done the declarations for tomorrow's racing at Newbury. Things must be back to normal if he's complaining about me.' She laughed again.

Next I called Oliver. He should be at home having his breakfast between lots. I had no intention of giving him an easy time.

'Oh, hello, Harry,' he said nervously. 'Did you get my message?'

'Yes, Oliver, I did. You would do very well to tell that bloody son of yours to control his tongue. Remember the Sheikh has horses with Declan too.'

I think Oliver was slightly taken aback by the forcefulness of my reply. I was a bit, as well.

'I'm sorry,' he said. 'Ryan had just had a bad day. He'd come straight back from York where his runners didn't do very well in the Dante. I'm sure he didn't intend to be disrespectful.'

*That's exactly what he had intended*, I thought, but there would be little to gain by persisting further in making his father squirm.

I imagined it must be difficult being a racehorse trainer when it came to dealing with the owners. A bit like the headmaster of an expensive private school dealing with parents who had little idea of the true conduct or ability of their idle, stupid child, while believing absolutely that he or she was both an angel and a genius. A subtle blend of grovelling and realism was required to maintain the cash flow, yet manage future expectations.

And, coincidentally, the cost of keeping a son at Eton or Harrow was almost exactly the same as having a racehorse with a top trainer. Funny that.

'Have you spoken to the Sheikh?' Oliver asked, the worry thick in his voice.

'Relax, Oliver,' I said. 'Rest assured, I will not be reporting the incident to His Highness.' I could hear his audible sigh of relief. 'But I will not expect it to ever be repeated.'

'No, absolutely not. Thank you, Harry, thank you.'

Was his guard down?

'Oliver,' I said. 'Tell me about Zoe.'

'What about her?'

'Everything. What was she like?'

'Strange girl,' Oliver said. 'Always was. Perhaps I was more used to boys. I was one of two boys myself, and I had three sons before Zoe came along. She became quite odd from an early age, you know, surly and badly behaved.'

'How early an age?'

'Three or four. I remember thinking that school would sort her out but, if anything, it made her worse. She was always in trouble with the staff. She used to make things up all the time and then swear they were true. Didn't know the difference if you ask me. We even had the child welfare people round here once because she'd claimed to a teacher that she was beaten and tied to her bed all the time at weekends. It was all nonsense, of course, but it caused us all sorts of trouble at the time, I can tell you.'

'What sort of trouble?' I asked tactlessly.

'Her mother and I argued a lot. Yvonne always took Zoe's side. Made excuses all the time.'

I could imagine Oliver being a bit of a black-or-white father, and not being overly sympathetic to his daughter's strange ways. And it would have undoubtedly made things worse – much worse.

'Tell me about the time she went missing.'

'Oh, you've heard about that, have you? Stupid girl. Her mother was in pieces, thinking she was dead. Then they found her drugged-up under a railway line in south London, and that was dreadfully upsetting. It might have been better for us all if she had died.'

What a dreadful state of affairs, I thought, that a father would have wished his daughter dead. But she was dead now.

'So you don't grieve much for her?' I asked.

'I don't know what to think. It was a terrible shock when the police told me it was her they'd found in the fire. Like she'd come home to die after all.'

But, of course, he hadn't known then that she'd been murdered.

'So who do *you* think killed her?' I asked.

'I have no idea,' he said. 'But that husband of hers would be my bet. He's another strange one.'

'How often have you met him?'

'Twice,' he said. 'And that's twice too often if you ask me.'

I said nothing but silently waited for him to continue.

'The first time was the morning after they found Zoe in London. Yvonne and I went to a police station in Croydon to collect her.' He forced a single laugh. 'What a joke that was. Christmas Day, and Zoe refused point-blank even to see us. Instead, this lout of a young man comes out and tells us that Zoe doesn't need us any more and he will look after her in future. I nearly decked him there and then, I was that angry. But the police said that, as Zoe was now legally an adult, she could live with whomever she liked, even if it was on the streets with a drug dealer. Unbelievable. As far as I'm concerned, she ceased to be my daughter on that day.'

'So you didn't go to their wedding?'

'No chance. We weren't even invited. In fact, I didn't know

they were married at all until they turned up here out of the blue about five years ago, along with their children.'

'What did they want?' I asked.

'What do you think they wanted? Money, of course. Started off with some nonsense about her being entitled to her inheritance early because I'd divorced her mother and was marrying another woman. I told her she could sing for that because I wasn't planning to leave her anything in my will anyway, so they then tried to blackmail me instead.'

He suddenly shut up. I waited but there was nothing more.

'Blackmail over what?' I asked finally into the silence.

'Nothing,' he said. 'Just another one of her crazy made-up stories. So I gave them a bit of an earful and sent them both packing. Look, I must go now, Ryan's ready for third lot.'

He hung up quickly. Rather too quickly.

Had he just let something slip that he hadn't meant to?

# 20

I presented myself at the Tattersalls' main reception at eleven o'clock precisely, having walked down from the Bedford Lodge Hotel.

There was much activity at Castleton House Stables as I passed, and I stood in the gateway for a few moments watching the proceedings.

The police had obviously completed their physical examination of the scene and there was now a collection of bulldozers, diggers and lorries taking away the remains of the burned-out stable block, and its dead equine residents. At Oliver's expense, no doubt, or that of his insurer.

I walked on down the High Street and past the Jockey Club buildings before turning left onto The Avenue and then in through the entrance to the sales complex.

Today, being a non-sale day, the car park was almost empty but, as on every day, it was dominated by a massive limestone classical arch with huge pillars topped by a pediment, complete with moulded frieze. It would not have looked out of place as the ceremonial entrance to a royal palace. How odd, I thought, to have built it here.

'Welcome to Tattersalls, Mr Foster,' said the receptionist. 'We have been expecting you. Please take a seat for a moment.' She indicated towards some comfy upholstered upright chairs. 'I'll just inform the chairman that you're here.'

I don't know what Kate had told them but they did everything for me short of actually rolling out a red carpet.

I was thankful that I'd worn my suit.

Presently a tall lean man appeared, also in a suit, and walked purposefully over towards me.

'Mr Foster?' he said, outstretching his hand. 'Welcome to Tattersalls. I'm Geoffrey Atherton, chairman and chief auctioneer.'

I shook his hand warmly.

'Thank you for inviting me,' I said. 'I had no idea that buying horses was such a grand affair. That's quite a structure you have in the car park.'

'The Tattersall Arch,' he said, nodding. 'It used to be the entrance to the auction house when we were situated in London during the late nineteenth and early twentieth centuries. We moved it here in the 1960s.'

'Quite a feat,' I said.

'Indeed, the original building was earmarked for demolition so it was a way of preserving what had been a symbol of Tattersalls for almost a century.'

'The company goes back a long way, then,' I said.

'Since 1766. It was started by Richard Tattersall selling dogs on Hyde Park Corner.'

'Dogs?'

'Hounds, to be precise. For hunting. But at the end of each day's hound sale, Richard would also sell a few horses, hacks and hunters mostly. However, it wasn't long before he realised there was more profit in selling the horses than the dogs, although we went on selling foxhounds right up to the outbreak of the First World War, and we sold horses for hunting until well after that. But, nowadays, we are exclusively a Thoroughbred sales organisation. Racehorses.'

As he'd been talking he had led the way back outside and we walked together across the perfectly tended grass lawns to a point where we could see clearly into one of the stable yards.

'We have eight separate yards here, with over eight hundred boxes,' Geoffrey said. 'Horses have to be available for inspection before the auction starts. The sales catalogue tells prospective buyers where to find each lot and gives a full listing of its pedigree back at least three generations.'

'How many do you sell in a day?' I asked.

'Up to two hundred and fifty. Some days less, especially on the big days like the October Book One sale. Then we might only sell a hundred and twenty on each of the three days.'

'But they're the most expensive?'

'We think they're going to be, but quite a few in Books Two and Three always outsell some of those in Book One. The price depends solely on what people will pay for them at the auction. The deal is done only when the hammer drops.'

We walked on towards the sales paddock.

'This is where the lots parade just before going into the sales ring.'

*Like the waiting room at the dentist,* I thought. But in this case it wouldn't be the horse that was nervous, more likely the seller, intensely hoping their lot will fetch a good price, and more than the cost of producing it in the first place.

At this point Kate came trotting across the grass to join us.

'Ah, there you are, Mrs Williams.' Geoffrey turned to me. 'I believe you met Mrs Williams at the races last evening.'

'Yes,' I said, trying hard not to laugh. 'Mrs Williams was most accommodating. She invited me into your private box for a drink.'

'Excellent,' he said.

Mrs Williams, indeed. Good job I hadn't had to ask for her by name.

I smiled at her. She was wearing her Tattersalls uniform with its embroidered rotunda logos.

'There's the rotunda I told you about,' Kate said, as if reading my mind. She pointed at a twenty-foot-high round domed structure with pillars, standing nearby. It had a human bust on the very top and a fox standing on a pedestal at its centre.

'In the 1700s it was situated at the corner of Hyde Park,' Geoffrey said. 'It was used by Richard Tattersall as his auctioneer's podium. The bust on the top is George IV.'

'Why the fox?' I asked.

'Foxes are part of our heritage, through our connection

with selling foxhounds. Huntsmen have always been very fond of foxes.'

But clearly not fond enough of them to stop chasing them to death across the countryside. It was a strange world. I wonder if the Pied Piper liked rats?

We walked on through to the sales-ring building itself, an octagonal amphitheatre with steeply raked seating and high-up lantern-style windows, all of it dedicated to the promotion of Thoroughbred horseflesh as the greatest saleable commodity on earth.

'It looks a bit bland now,' Kate said as we walked in, 'but it's really exciting on sale days, especially for Book One, when there's not a spare seat to be found. Latecomers have to sit in the gangways.'

The ring itself at the centre was not round but an oval and the whole place was a lot smarter than I had imagined. But I suppose, if you're going to pay four million guineas for an untested racehorse, you'd want a comfortable seat to sit in as you do it.

'Never mind that yellow shiny stuff you dig out of the ground,' Geoffrey said, 'Frankel was the highest-rated racehorse that has ever been and he was valued at a hundred million pounds, some fourteen times his own weight in gold, when he was retired to stud after an unbeaten fourteen-race career.'

'Did you sell him here as a yearling?' I asked.

'Sadly not. He was bred by his owner, but we have sold some of his progeny.'

And, I thought, prospective buyers would flock to this place to bid on Frankel's offspring in the hope that lightning would strike the same place twice and they, too, might buy a world-beater that would repay their investment many, many times over in the future. And, in bloodstock terms, the future was never too far away, with champion racehorses usually retiring to stud aged just three or four.

'The horses come in from the sales paddock and are then walked around while the bidding takes place above them,' Geoffrey explained. 'Then, when the auctioneer's hammer falls, they are led out the other side and back to their box. It then becomes the new owner's responsibility to collect them from there.'

'After they've paid,' I said.

'Oh yes,' Geoffrey said with a laugh. 'But they can't even bid unless they have good credit. We see to that first.'

'Very wise.'

'But I can assure you that we consider Sheikh Karim's credit to be excellent.'

It was a reminder that I wasn't being shown round by the chairman just for my entertainment. Little did he realise that I didn't represent the Sheikh's racing concerns, only his media reputation. But I wasn't going to say so if Kate hadn't.

'Now, will you excuse me, Mr Foster?' he said. 'Mrs Williams will complete the tour. I'm afraid I have some meetings I need to attend to.'

'Of course, Geoffrey,' I said. 'Thank you so much for your time.'

We shook hands.

'I look forward to seeing you at one of our sales,' he said.

'Yes, indeed.'

He turned and walked out of the sales ring, no doubt back to his office and his meetings, leaving Kate and me standing there alone.

'Mrs Williams?' I said. 'What's all that about?'

'I am Mrs Williams,' she said. 'I never reverted to my maiden name when I got divorced.'

'Why not?' I asked.

'Laziness, I suppose. Having gone to all the trouble to convert everything to Williams in the first place, I couldn't be bothered to turn it all back. And I was never that keen on Logan anyway. I was always being told by people to run, after the film, and they called me Loganberry at school. I hated it.' She paused. 'Also, it makes getting rid of unwanted men easier if I'm a Mrs.'

'Does that happen often?' I asked.

'Quite often.'

'You didn't tell *me* that you were a Mrs.'

'That's because you're not unwanted.'

I smiled at her. 'Good. Now, what's left of the tour?'

'Nothing much, this is it really. Everything of interest happens in this space. This is where the big bucks get spent. During the sale I stand behind the rostrum over there.'

She pointed at a raised box on the edge of the ring.

'When the hammer drops, the auctioneer hands me the purchase confirmation form and it's my job to get the successful bidder's signature on it before he or she leaves the building. I keep the white top copy and give the yellow one to the buyer as a receipt. But I have to keep my wits about me as some of them seem to bid without moving more than an eyelid, and others hide in the stairways up the back there so no one else can see them.'

'Why?'

'God knows. Perhaps they think the price will go higher if someone sees them bidding. And they might be right if it was Sheikh Karim.'

'Don't you start,' I said. 'I'm embarrassed enough already. Fancy getting the chairman to show me round.'

She laughed. 'It was his idea, not mine.'

'But you could have stopped it.'

She looked at me. 'Now why would I want to do that?'

Kate and I went inside the main administration building to visit the 'girls at Tatts', her work colleagues, some of whom I had met in the box at the races.

As we moved from desk to desk, I realised that she was showing me off as her own personal VIP, one who the chairman himself had taken the time to show round. All the girls knew about that, sure enough. *And why not,* I thought. If Kate had visited Simpson White, I'd have shown *her* off too.

'You must come again on a sale day,' Kate said. 'The whole place comes alive. Chauffeurs fight for a spot in the car park, the restaurant is booked out for weeks in advance, and the thrill of seeing rich men bidding against each other is electric.

249

I have friends who come every day just to watch. It's the best theatre in town, and with no admission charge. But what makes it really exciting is that it's not a game, it's deadly serious. Fortunes and reputations are made and lost here.'

'You should be on the marketing team,' I said with a laugh.

'I am.'

# 21

Racing on Friday afternoon at the Rowley Mile course was somehow more methodical and less glamorous than it had been on the previous evening. The weather was not as kind for a start, with threatening dark clouds having replaced the warm sunshine. Hence there were fewer people in the crowd, although today's gathering gave the air more of being here strictly for the serious business of racing and betting, rather than for drinking and having a good time.

I also thought it was less fun, but that may have had something to do with the fact that Kate wasn't with me. I had decided that asking her to accompany me today would have been inappropriate, even if she'd been able to get the time off work. I had business of my own to complete, and it might get nasty.

Over breakfast, I'd looked at the hotel copy of the *Racing Post*. According to the paper, both Ryan and Declan had runners declared here today and Tony was also riding one. Plus I thought it highly likely that Oliver would be here as well. And I had every intention of letting them know that I was here too, and that I was watching them.

As it turned out, however, the first person I saw as I walked towards the entrance was not a Chadwick but Joe, Declan's travelling head lad.

'Hi, Joe,' I said. 'Nice short journey for you today.'

'Yes,' he said, without any amusement. 'I was meant to be at Newbury but the guv'nor decided he'd go there instead, so I'm now here. Suppose you can't blame him. This is too bloody close to home.' We could almost see Declan's yard from where we were standing. 'Too many wagging tongues.'

I couldn't think that it would be much better for him at Newbury but I was just glad that he hadn't hidden himself away altogether.

'Thank God Trevor's back tomorrow.'

'Trevor?' I said.

'The guv'nor's assistant. Been at his grandmother's funeral in some godforsaken spot in the Scottish Highlands. Not that we've got any runners tomorrow, anyway. Chrissie never made the declarations.'

That had been my fault, I thought, but decided not to say so.

'Do you have runners every day?' I asked.

'Not every day,' he said, 'but we usually do on a Saturday during the season. Many owners like their horses running on Saturdays. Makes it easier for them to be there.'

Joe said it in a way that made me think that he didn't really like the owners getting in the way. I wondered if Mr Reardon's horse had been one of those due to run. That wouldn't have done anything to placate him either.

So, with Declan out of the equation, that just left the three remaining Chadwick men for me to hassle. There was something they were all hiding. I was sure of it.

*It will all come out. I can't stand the shame.*

I decided it was time to confront that directly.

I'd arrived at the racecourse well before the first race so I paid my entrance fee and then wandered around the enclosures getting my bearings.

On the previous evening, for obvious reasons, I hadn't been properly concentrating on the racing. I hadn't appreciated, for example, how the horses for each race are brought from the stables to the pre-parade ring before being taken to be saddled in one of the nearby line of saddling boxes. Then they are led into the parade ring proper for the punters to gawp at like contestants in a beauty pageant.

Except these beauties had to run fast rather than simply look good, although Kate had told me that a fit horse was also an attractive horse.

Attractive?

I would have to take her word for it.

As the time for the first race approached, I bought a racecard and checked that I'd remembered correctly that Ryan had a runner. He did. A horse called Momentum, number

8, and, to my surprise, it was also listed to be ridden by Tony Chadwick.

Several horses were already being led around the pre-parade ring by their grooms but I had no way of knowing which one, if any, was Momentum as they were not yet wearing their numbers and I was clearly no tout, nor Lester Piggott. So I hung around outside the saddling boxes waiting for the trainer to arrive.

However, it was not Ryan but Oliver I saw first, walking towards me with what appeared to be a minuscule saddle over his arm. There was a fractional hesitation in his stride when he spotted me but then he came on over.

'Hello, Harry,' he said quite amicably. 'Having a good time?'

'Yes, thank you, Oliver,' I replied. 'Are you?'

'Fine,' he said. 'It feels good to be back on a racecourse after the week we've had. What with the fire, then Zoe and now Arabella. Never mind *annus horribilis*, this has definitely been a week to forget.'

I, on the other hand, would remember it fondly, but for a different reason.

'Where's Ryan?' I asked.

'He's bringing Momentum over from the stables with the stable lad. This particular horse can be a little skittish so we're leaving it as late as possible.'

I held up my racecard. 'I see Tony is down to ride it.' My voice gave away the surprise I felt.

'Yes,' Oliver said slowly. 'Ryan had declared the jockey before.'

He didn't have to explain that it was *before* Tony had told his brother he was a fucking idiot. And I remembered how Ryan had come into the yard office on Wednesday morning when I'd been talking to Janie. He had sent the declarations off without checking the information first, trusting Janie to have got it right. And she would have put Tony down as the rider.

'Couldn't Ryan have changed the jockey?' I asked.

'He could have done easily up to one o'clock Wednesday afternoon, but he obviously forgot. After that you have to get permission from the stewards, and a family tiff is unlikely to be a good enough reason in their eyes. Anyway, they're both over it now.'

I wondered if that was true, or was it just Oliver's wishful thinking. It would be interesting to watch the body language when Ryan had to give his younger brother a leg-up.

Oliver and I stood side by side waiting for Ryan and the horse to arrive and it seemed to me to be too good an opportunity to miss.

'Why did Ryan break Declan's nose at Doncaster?' I asked.

Oliver jumped as if I'd stabbed him with an electric cattle prod.

'Where did you hear that nonsense?' he said, trying to force a laugh.

'Ryan told me.' I paused while that bit of news sank in, before I hit him with my next question. 'And, if they hate each other so much, why didn't Declan press charges?'

Oliver was silent for a moment as he clearly thought what to say.

'Because it was an accident,' he stated finally.

'It didn't sound like an accident to me,' I retorted. 'According to the police report, Ryan punched Declan square in the face. Laid him out proper.'

'Yes,' said Oliver, back-pedalling madly. 'But it was nothing more than a misunderstanding.'

'Over what?' I asked.

'Nothing important,' Oliver said.

'So tell me,' I said.

'Ah, here they are.' The relief in Oliver at seeing Momentum and Ryan arriving was palpable and he rushed forward towards them.

Ryan, however, was not so keen to see me, and well might he not be.

'Hello, Ryan,' I said. 'Have you insulted anyone else today? Or maybe you punched them in the face instead.'

Oliver looked at me with horror.

'Harry,' he said sharply. 'That was not called for.'

*No,* I thought, *it probably wasn't,* but I had to do something to get them riled up, to get them to say something they'd regret, to reveal their big secret.

Ryan, however, was calmness personified. He appeared to completely ignore what I'd just said and went about the task of readying Momentum for his race, a task he performed with the speed and ease of someone well practised in the art.

First, off came the horse's rug, then a thin chamois leather was placed on the horse's bare back. 'To prevent slippage,' Oliver explained. That was followed by a saddle pad, weight cloth, number cloth and then, finally, the tiny saddle, all held in place by a wide girth pulled tight around the horse's belly and connected to the saddle on each side by substantial buckles.

All the while this was going on further back, Momentum's head was being held firmly by his stable lad, not that it stopped him trying to tear himself free, and only quick reactions by the lad prevented huge chunks of the poor boy's hands and arms being bitten off.

Momentum had a small white star in the middle of its forehead and it somehow gave the horse an even more manic look, as if it had three eyes.

Skittish, Oliver had said. I thought that was a rather mild description. In my eyes, the animal was completely off its rocker and I kept well out of reach of both the chomping teeth and the flailing hooves.

Satisfied that all was finally in order, Ryan gave the horse an encouraging slap on its hindquarters and almost got a kick on the knee in return. Ryan then told the unfortunate stable lad to lead him out of the saddling box and into the parade ring, not that the horse was making that an easy task as it constantly tried to pull itself free while, at the same time, kicking out wildly at anything remotely within reach.

Oliver and Ryan followed the horse at a safe distance and, much to Ryan's obvious annoyance, I tagged along with them.

There were a couple waiting for us on the pristine grass of the parade ring.

'Hello, you two,' Oliver called out as we approached. 'Lovely to see you.' He kissed the woman on each cheek and shook hands warmly with the man.

'We couldn't find you in the pre-parade ring so we came through here,' the woman said.

'We brought the horse over late from the stables,' Oliver explained. 'I thought it best to keep him away from the others for as long as possible.' He laughed nervously, clearly hoping that they agreed with him.

The two of them looked at me.

'Sorry,' Oliver said. 'This is Harry Foster. Michelle and Mike Morris.'

The three of us shook hands. Michelle was an attractive blonde with sparkling blue eyes and she was elegantly attired in a figure-hugging double-breasted black coat plus calf-length suede boots. Mike wore a sober suit with a blue tie and had neat short dark hair that was going slightly grey at the temples.

'They own Momentum,' Oliver said to me.

'We don't just own him,' Michelle said with a certain degree of pride. 'We bred him too.'

'So do you have your own stud farm?' I asked.

'Nothing that grand,' Mike said with a laugh. 'My business is construction but, as a hobby, Michelle and I keep a few brood mares at the National Stud here in Newmarket. Momentum was one of our foals. We just kept him to race.'

We all watched as the animal in question continued to twist and turn his head in an attempt to break free.

'Lively, isn't he?' Michelle said.

'Dangerous more like,' I replied.

'Oh, no,' she said with a smile. 'He's only playing.'

*It didn't look much like playing to me*, I thought, as the horse tried once again to take a chunk out of his hapless groom's arm.

'He's an entire colt,' Mike said to me. 'But Oliver thinks we should geld him. Reckons it might calm him down a bit. Michelle is dead against it. His breeding is excellent and she thinks he still might have a future at stud.'

Oliver gave me a sideways look that said *no chance*, but he was much too diplomatic to say that out loud.

'We can't cut our poor baby's balls off,' Michelle said in horror. 'How would you like it?'

*Good point*, I thought, *but I wasn't trying to bite the hand that fed me.*

'I think we should have a good chance today,' Oliver said. 'I believe Momentum is well handicapped in this company.'

My face must have given away the fact that I didn't understand what he meant.

'This race is a handicap,' Oliver explained. 'So the horses carry different weights according to their ability.'

'Who decides which is the most able?' I asked.

'The official handicapper. Every Thoroughbred racehorse in the world is rated each Tuesday.'

'What, every horse?' I asked.

'Just about. Other than a few young ones that haven't run enough times.'

'But that's amazing.'

'It certainly is,' Oliver agreed. 'There are fourteen thousand racehorses in training in this country alone, never mind the rest of the world. The official rating determines how much weight the horse will carry in a handicap. Take this race, for example. It's a Class Five handicap over a mile for three-year-old horses with an official rating of less than seventy-five. The top weight has an official rating of seventy-two but Momentum's is only sixty-three. That's nine less, hence he carries nine pounds less weight on his back.'

'And you think that will make a difference?'

'Certainly should,' he said. 'About a length per pound over a mile. It's like Momentum having a nine-length start over the highest-rated horse. And I tend to think that he's better than the official handicapper does.'

It sounded simple but it was, in fact, far more complicated than I'd imagined. No wonder Ryan had needed to concentrate to do his entries – choosing the right horse with an appropriate rating to enter into a given class of race over a suitable distance at the most advantageous racecourse on a specific day, and all to give it the best chance of finishing in front.

The five of us stood and watched as the nine runners circled around us and, presently, we were joined by Tony wearing racing silks with a green body, light-blue arms and a matching light-blue cap. The Morris's colours, I assumed.

Tony touched the peak of his cap in deferential greeting to the owners but without acknowledging his brother one iota. The atmosphere between them was cool, to say the least.

'Hold him in the pack until the two-furlong pole and then let him go,' Ryan ordered. Tony nodded. 'And don't get boxed in on the rail.' Tony nodded again and grunted something I didn't catch.

At least the two were communicating, even if the exchange lacked any social niceties.

An official rang a bell and Oliver, Tony and Ryan walked over towards Momentum. The horse was still doing its best to pull itself free from the lad but, eventually, Tony managed to collect the reins in his hands, and Ryan tossed him up onto the saddle.

'It's so exciting to have a runner,' Michelle said to me as we stood some way off, out of range of both snapping teeth and thrashing feet.

'Yes,' I said. And it must be, I thought, with all the years of effort she and Mike must have put in to get their 'baby' to the racecourse, balls and all. But I wasn't sure that the horse's jockey was finding the prospect of the contest quite as thrilling as its owner.

*Rather you than me*, I thought, as Tony tried to control half a ton of crazy racehorse with nothing more than a few small pieces of leather, and with no seat belt.

'Don't mess it up,' Ryan said to his brother as a farewell comment.

I watched as Tony mouthed an obscenity back along the lines that Ryan should go forth and multiply. The two might be communicating but it was clearly not the happiest of working relationships.

At least Momentum seemed to have calmed down a bit now that he had someone on his back, although he still gave a couple of token bucks as he left the paddock.

'Do you think we'll win?' Michelle eagerly asked Oliver.

'I hope so,' he said, although without much enthusiasm. 'Some of our results recently have been rather a disappointment.'

And the result of this race was a bit of a disappointment too.

Surprisingly, both owners and trainer remained in the parade ring to watch the race unfold on a large-screen television set up nearby, so, I stayed with them. Ryan didn't like it one bit and he had a scowl on his face as if he'd swallowed a wasp.

Oliver and Ryan were very unalike, I thought. Oliver had charm and charisma whereas Ryan was coarse and uncouth. Ryan was also a bit of a thug, used to getting his own way and to hell with everyone else.

But I presented them with a major problem. I was the personal representative of one of, if not *the* most important of their owners. I had a direct line to Sheikh Karim, who they could hardly afford to lose at any time, and certainly not in their present circumstances.

Oliver was playing the game, swallowing his pride and being polite, explaining things to me when he'd probably prefer me to get lost. For Ryan, however, the situation was more of a challenge and, as he had so clearly demonstrated the previous evening, his natural aggression readily prevailed over logic and reason.

And, on top of everything else, Ryan was failing to measure up to his father's reputation as one of the great Newmarket trainers. And both of them knew it.

Momentum jumped out of the stalls in line with the other runners and then Tony positioned him towards the rear of the pack.

'Come on, baby,' Michelle shouted at the screen, hardly able to resist jumping up and down. Mike just smiled and held her hand.

'He's too far back,' Ryan hissed. '*In* the pack, I said, not at the back of it.'

The horses were running on the straight mile directly towards the grandstand, the camera angle tending to foreshorten the distance from first to last. Nevertheless, even I could see that the lead horse was getting away from the others.

'Hopeless,' Oliver said, seemingly unaware that Mike and Michelle Morris were hanging on his every word.

We watched as Tony pulled Momentum out from behind the horse immediately in front of him and started to make some headway. As they passed the two-furlong pole, Tony went for his whip and gave his mount a couple of reminders to get going faster. But sadly for him, and despite all his considerable efforts, the horse just plodded on at the same steady pace, passing the winning post a frustrating sixth of the nine.

The official handicapper had been right all the time.

Ryan was apoplectic with rage. 'That wretched Tony. Why didn't he do as he was bloody told?'

I personally thought he had done so but, on this occasion, I decided not to say something provocative. I rather valued the straightness of my nose.

Oliver, meanwhile, just sighed heavily and kicked the turf in frustration.

'I'm sorry,' he said. 'Better luck next time.'

*If there is a next time*, I thought. The owners were obviously unhappy. Their earlier optimism had been crushed, leaving nothing but frustration and anger, much of it clearly directed towards the trainer and his father.

The five of us went, not to the winner's enclosure as hoped, but to the place reserved for the unsaddling of the also-rans and waited for the horse and jockey to return. Ryan was working himself up into a real state again, just like on the previous evening. Thankfully, this time, it wasn't me in his sights.

I didn't fancy being in Tony's stirrups.

'You were far too far back,' Ryan complained loudly when Tony slid down off the horse. 'You never gave him a chance.'

'I gave him every chance,' Tony replied icily, removing his saddle. 'When I asked him for an effort at the two-pole there was nothing left. Tank empty.'

'Nonsense,' Oliver said. 'You just didn't ride him well enough.'

The three of them seemed oblivious to the presence of me and the Morrises, who stood there in shocked silence listening to the Chadwick family confrontation.

Tony faced his brother and father. 'I won't ride for you ever

264

again. In your opinion, every horse you run these days seems to be underperforming. I suggest you both look in the mirror before you start blaming everyone else.' And, with that still ringing in their ears, he turned away and disappeared into the weighing room.

I wondered if now might be a good time to ask him if he knew why Ryan had broken Declan's nose.

# 22

Michelle and Mike Morris went off to drown their sorrows in the owners' bar while I hung around outside the weighing room waiting for Tony.

According to the racecard, he had no further rides that afternoon, but it still wasn't until after the fourth race that he finally appeared.

In the meantime, one of Declan's horses won the second, which would probably do nothing for Ryan's demeanour. I watched as Joe led the horse into the space reserved for the winner and he even had a bit of a smile on his face. Miracles will never cease.

Tony came out of the weighing room wearing a green polo shirt and light-coloured chinos and made a beeline for the exit and the jockeys' car park. If I hadn't been on my toes, I'd have missed him completely.

'Tony,' I called loudly after him.

He slowed and turned but I could tell he wasn't keen to stop and talk so I hurried along beside him.

'Shame about Momentum,' I said. 'Your father is very upset.'

'My father is always upset these days,' he said. 'He should never have retired so soon. Harry Wragg was almost eighty before he passed his stable over to his son. Dad should have done the same.'

'But he still seems to be very involved,' I said.

'Too involved, if you ask me. He should just let Ryan get on with it, let him sink or swim on his own. Sink, probably, the way things are going at the moment. Prince of Troy was his only hope, and now he's gone.'

'It must be very difficult for your father to let go when he lives on site and still owns the stables.'

'That was his big mistake. He should have sold it. Caused all sorts of resentment when he just seemed to hand it all to Ryan.'

'Resentment from whom?' I asked.

'Declan, for a start.'

'And you?'

He suddenly stopped and looked at me.

'Why are you asking me all these questions?'

'I'm trying to find out why Prince of Troy died.'

'And what has that to do with my father passing his stable to Ryan?'

*Everything*, I thought.

'I'm just trying to understand the Chadwick family dynamic.'

267

'Snoop, more like. I have to go.'

He turned on his heel and walked away.

'I have one more question,' I said, but he just waved a dismissive hand over his shoulder and kept on walking. So I shouted after him, 'Why did Ryan break Declan's nose at Doncaster?'

He stopped and walked back towards me.

'Be careful,' he said menacingly. 'For your own good, there are some things you shouldn't ask.'

'Are you threatening me, Tony?'

'No, I'm just warning you. Don't ask that again.'

'I won't,' I assured him. 'That is, I won't if you tell me the answer now.'

He simply stared at me.

'What is it that no one is talking about?'

'None of your business.'

He turned again and jogged away out of the race-course exit.

*It will all come out. I can't stand the shame.*

It must be something big, I thought, to unite this family together when everything else was tearing them apart.

I was waiting at reception when Mrs Williams arrived at the Bedford Lodge Hotel just before six o'clock, still wearing her Tattersalls uniform but carrying an overnight bag.

'I brought it with me this morning,' she said with a smile. 'Saves me having to go home to change. Everyone asked me at work where I was going.'

'What did you say?'

'I told them I was going away for the weekend to stay with a friend. But I think they all knew it was you.'

'Was it that obvious?'

'I think it was last night at the races,' she said. 'And you were a huge hit with the girls up at Park Paddocks this morning.'

She was pleased, and so was I, for her benefit.

'Would you like a drink at the bar?' I asked.

'I think I'll change first,' she said. 'We're not really supposed to drink in public wearing our uniforms.'

'You did the other night,' I said.

'I know, but that was last-minute and unexpected. Also, there might be people staying here tonight for the races who are our customers.'

So we went to my room, hand in hand, with me carrying her suitcase.

'Do you want me to go?' I asked, conscious that she might not want an audience while she changed.

'No, it's fine. I'll change in the bathroom.'

She went in and closed the door and, while I waited, I flicked on the TV to watch the six o'clock news. However, as I thought was so often the case, the 'news' was largely BBC opinion served up as fact. I turned it off again.

'How are you doing?' I called out to Kate.

'Just coming,' she shouted back.

The bathroom door opened and she emerged, but she was clearly not yet properly dressed for a drink at the bar.

She was wearing only a hotel bathrobe, and it hung open at the front revealing all the splendours within.

'Wow!' I said.

About an hour and a half later we walked along to the hotel bar for that drink.

Sex between us had been a combination of a journey of discovery and primal human eagerness. We puffed and panted a lot, but we also laughed and, when it was over, we lay entwined together, sweaty and naked on the bed in happy satisfaction.

'God, I needed that,' Kate said. 'It's been a long time.'

'For me too,' I agreed.

Neither of us asked the other how long exactly. It wasn't important.

'I should have ordered champagne and strawberries,' I said.

'Why strawberries?'

'Well, according to Richard Gere in *Pretty Woman*, it brings out the flavour of the champagne.'

'I absolutely adore that film,' Kate said, rolling over onto her elbows. 'Especially that bit when Julia Roberts goes back into the shop where the two bitches have been so nasty to her and then holds up all her shopping bags: "You work on commission, right? Mistake. Big mistake. Huge!"'

We spent a while arguing over which bit of the film was the best and agreed, in the end, that we both loved the scene at the end when the knight (Edward) arrives on his white horse (standing up through the sunroof of a white stretch limo) with his drawn sword (umbrella) to climb up a rope (fire escape) to rescue the princess (Vivian) from the wicked queen's tower (apartment block).

What a pair of right softies, we were. And we loved it.

'Champagne?' asked the barman. He was the same one as had been on duty on Wednesday evening.

'Yes, please,' I said. 'And some strawberries.'

Kate started giggling and that set me off too.

We sat in the bar and consumed a bottle of champagne and a whole punnet of strawberries, and then decided against having room service after all, opting for dinner *à deux* in Squires Restaurant.

We took our time, enjoying each other's company and the wine, in the sure knowledge of what we would be having for dessert.

'What did you do at the races today?' Kate asked over the main course.

I told her about the mad Momentum's race and my various interactions with Oliver, Ryan and Tony.

'Poor Janie,' Kate said. 'She hasn't had the best of times there since Ryan took over. And I know both the fire and Zoe's death have hit her badly.'

'Does she have a theory of who started it?' I asked.

'I think she's trying to blot it out of her thinking completely. She was so upset about the poor horses dying and then to learn that Zoe was in there as well has just about finished her off.'

I remembered back how my just mentioning the fire to her had caused the tears to flow.

'She knew Zoe quite well then?'

'I wouldn't say well, not in recent years, anyway. She knew her a bit better at school. Janie was like a big sister to her at one point. I think Janie was sorry for her, but she also upset her.'

'How?'

'Zoe was quite disturbed. She made things up about people. She also used to cut herself, you know, on the arms and such with a razor blade. She used to tell Janie that her brothers did it but once she told a teacher that it had been Janie's doing. We had the child-protection lot around to our house fast as lightning. I think that caused the end of their friendship.'

'I'm going to see Zoe's husband tomorrow,' I said.

'Are you indeed. What about?'

'I'm not really sure. I just feel he must know *something*. I want to see how he reacts when I get there.'

'Where's there?'

'Ealing,' I said.

'Does he know you're coming?'

'No.' I smiled. 'I'm going to just try my luck and see if he's in.'

'And what if he isn't?'

'Then I will have wasted my journey,' I said. 'But I want to go to my flat anyway to collect a few things, more clothes, for example. I also thought I might stay over Saturday night just to let the neighbours realise that I haven't scarpered altogether.'

'Can I come with you?' she asked eagerly.

My first instinct was to say no, and for two reasons. First, I didn't really want to involve her directly in what I was doing as I feared it might all result in some damaging fallout. And secondly, I wasn't sure in what state I'd left my flat. Usually, it was not good, especially on a Monday morning, which is when I'd last been there.

'I could look after his kids while you talk to Peter Robertson.'

'Haven't you got plans for the weekend?'

'Nothing that can't be changed. And I'd love a night in London. Perhaps we could see a show.'

She was so excited. How could I say no?

'All right, you can come,' I said. 'Which show do you fancy?'

'A musical. Absolutely love them.'

There followed a lengthy discussion on which was the best musical we had ever seen, and we finally left the dining room with her singing 'Don't Cry for Me Argentina' to try to prove to me that it was the best song ever written.

I tried hard to ignore her.

That was, until we arrived at my bedroom, then the opposite was true.


Lovemaking the second time around was more relaxed, slower, and more passionate. The need was still there but the hunger was less desperate.

I ran my fingertips over her bare skin, making her shiver with excitement and anticipation, and then I hugged her close to me, wanting to feel as one with another human being like I had never felt before.

The emotion was so powerful, and that, as much as the physical exertion, left me drained and exhausted.

'That was wonderful,' Kate said.

It certainly was.

We lay together on our backs, holding hands in the darkness. Eventually I drifted off to sleep, at ease, happy and fulfilled.

On Saturday morning, Kate and I caught the 10.47 train from Cambridge to London.

I checked out of the hotel in spite of the receptionist informing me that my booking had been made until the end of the following week, and those were the terms on which the room-rate discount had been agreed.

*Good old Georgina*, I thought.

'I might be back again tomorrow,' I told the receptionist, 'but I have to go away tonight and it seems an unnecessary extravagance to keep my room when no one is sleeping in it.'

I paid the hotel bill, discount applied, with the Simpson White credit card, and promised to let them know as soon as possible if I were returning.

'I can't guarantee that you'll have the same room,' the receptionist said.

*Shame*, I thought. I'd suddenly become quite attached to it.

My driver followed in his Mercedes as Kate drove us in her Mini convertible to Six Mile Bottom. She turned into the driveway of a Victorian red-brick property set back from the main road.

'It used to be a gamekeeper's cottage,' she said. 'It was converted into two separate homes sometime in the 1970s. And I love it.'

I had a quick look round Kate's half while she exchanged the Tatts uniform in her suitcase for what she called her glad rags.

'I can't go to the theatre looking like some country bumpkin, now can I?' she said.

She looked anything but a country bumpkin to me, I thought, in a tight-fitting navy-blue roll-neck sweater and white trousers.

The driver dropped us both at Cambridge Station and, on the train, I logged on to the internet using my dongle. There was an email from ASW with Peter Robertson's latest known address and another from the research team with what they had discovered about the Robertsons' bank account, which was precious little. Indeed, the only thing of interest they had managed to unearth was a memo from a credit reference agency that had given them a rating of 'adequate' when they had recently applied to Ealing Council housing department to move into a larger property.

The wizards didn't say how they came by this information, which was just as well as it was probably illegal.

'Adequate' was a credit rating that indicated that the Robertsons had no significant debt problems and mostly paid their bills on time. I wondered how that was for someone who Oliver described as a drug addict and the worst estate agent in the world.

There was also a note from the wizards about that, too. They had asked round some estate-agent connections in west London and had learned that Peter Robertson was seemingly not connected to a mainstream agency but acted alone. They had been unable to find any details of properties that he had sold. Remarkably, it appears that no professional qualifications are needed to call oneself an estate agent.

I also used the dongle to log on to a West End ticket agency.

'They've got two returned house seats for *Phantom of the Opera*,' I said. 'Row F in the middle of the stalls. Any good?'

'I've seen it before,' Kate said.

'So have I. But not for a while. What do you say?'

'Yes,' she said decisively. 'I love a good love story. Especially at the moment.'

I booked the seats and decided not to bring up the fact that the Phantom's love for Christine was unrequited.

The train pulled into King's Cross Station at half past eleven and we took the Tube to Neasden, walking the last couple of hundred yards to my flat in a nondescript four-storey block on Bermans Way.

'I ought to warn you,' I said as I put the key in the lock. 'It's not very tidy.'

'Don't be silly,' Kate said. 'I'm sure it's fine.'

But nevertheless, she tut-tutted slightly over the stack of dirty plates in the kitchen sink, some of which were developing a fine coating of green mould.

'Take-away vindaloo from last Sunday night,' I explained. 'I hadn't expected to be away for the rest of the week.'

'Always expect the unexpected,' she said, sounding far too like ASW for my liking.

I washed the dishes while Kate went on a tour of inspection of the flat, something that took her precisely thirty seconds. Then she came back to the kitchen, which was really nothing more than an alcove off the sitting room.

'Nice,' she said. 'Do you own it?'

'No. Rent. But I'm thinking of finding somewhere of my own. Getting on the property ladder at last. Should have done it years ago. When I first moved in here seven years ago, I thought it would be temporary, but I've just stayed. Lazy, I suppose.'

'But it's fine for a single man.'

'That's why I should move. I don't want to remain a single man.'

She looked at me. 'Good.'

# 23

It wasn't Peter Robertson who opened his front door when I rang the bell at three-thirty on Saturday afternoon. Instead, it was a grey-haired woman I took to be in her late fifties or early sixties.

Kate and I had some difficulty finding 43 Queen Anne Court, South Ealing, but a friendly taxi driver finally pointed us in the right direction.

Queen Anne Court was a 1950s six-storey concrete tenement block with outside walkways, like many that were built after the Second World War to provide emergency social housing after the Blitz. Most have now been demolished in favour of low-rise tidy estates with lots of greenery, but a few of these monstrosities remained, and this was one of them.

Number 43 was on the fourth floor, accessed by graffiti-daubed concrete open stairways at each end of the building.

'Is Peter Robertson in?' I asked the woman.

'He's gone to the local shop,' she said. 'He shouldn't be

long.' She looked both ways down the walkway but there was no sign of anyone. 'Are you from the local authority?'

'No,' I said. 'I'm a lawyer.'

It was clearly the wrong thing to say.

'We don't want any more lawyers,' the woman said aggressively. 'We've had nothing but the likes of you around here, pestering us ever since it was first in the papers.'

'What was in the papers?' I asked.

'Zoe's death, of course,' she said. 'All offering to get us compensation, as if money for the children could somehow make up for the loss of their mother.'

'I'm not offering compensation,' I said. 'I represent Declan Chadwick.'

That got her attention, sure enough.

'Come here to buy us off again, have you?' she said with even more venom than she'd had for the compensation lawyers.

'No,' I said. 'I've come here to find out the truth.'

'The Chadwick family wouldn't recognise the truth if it slapped them in the face.'

'How would you know that?' I asked.

'Because I'm one of them,' she said. 'I'm Yvonne Chadwick, Zoe's mother.'

Yvonne didn't ask us in, but she agreed we could wait outside for Peter to return from the shop, not that she could have really stopped us.

'What a depressing place,' Kate said as we waited. 'All

279

that graffiti everywhere, and did you notice in the stairwells? Ugh!'

I presumed she meant the piles of rubbish and the overpoweringly sweet smell of rat urine.

'But better than under a railway arch in Croydon,' I replied. 'Which is where they lived before.'

Peter Robertson arrived wearing a New York Yankees baseball cap and carrying a plastic supermarket shopping bag. For a second, I thought he was going to drop the bag and run, but he held his nerve and came slowly along the walkway towards us.

'What do you want?' he asked gruffly as a greeting.

'Hello, Pete,' I said in a jovial tone. 'My name is Harry Foster. I'm a lawyer and I represent Declan Chadwick.'

'And I'm Catherine Logan,' Kate said, using her maiden name. 'I was at school with Zoe. We've come to help.'

'Help?' he said. 'How?'

'Shall we go in?' I asked. 'It's easier to talk inside.'

He fetched a key from his pocket and put it in the lock.

We went inside, the front door leading straight into the living room, and Peter was immediately mobbed by his daughters.

'Daddy, Daddy, what did you buy us?' they screamed in unison.

Peter delved into the shopping bag, triumphantly producing two iced lollies wrapped up in newspaper to keep them frozen.

'And don't drip them down your dresses,' he said, handing

them over. 'Now, girls, stay in here with Grannie while I talk to this man.'

He nodded his head for me to follow him into the kitchen. Kate stayed with Yvonne and the girls.

'Lovely daughters,' I said. 'What are their names?'

I already knew but I didn't want it to look like I had been researching his family.

'Poppy and Joanne,' he said, unloading the rest of the bag's contents onto the kitchen table and then putting it away in the fridge and cupboards. 'Poppy's nine and Joanne seven. My little angels.'

'It must be nice having their grandmother here to help you look after them.'

Peter gave me a look that every husband has made about his mother-in-law at one time or another. I almost laughed.

'She came yesterday,' he said. 'But I've told her I don't want her here and she must go home tomorrow. I can look after the girls perfectly well on my own. I've done it most of their lives anyway. Zoe was hopeless. When she wasn't actually in hospital, she'd often go off on her own. Sometimes for just one night, occasionally for two. But, even when she was here, she couldn't really cope.'

He removed the baseball cap and hung it on a peg by the door. I'd forgotten that Janie had said he was bald, and he was too, with just a ring of dark hair running round the back of his head from temple to temple.

'Now what exactly do you want?' he asked. 'The police told me they'd arrested Declan Chadwick for murdering my wife, so why aren't you in Newmarket making him confess, instead of worrying me and my kids?'

'Because he didn't do it,' I replied.

'Are you sure?'

'Yes,' I said. 'Perfectly sure.'

'Then why haven't the police let him go?'

'They have,' I said.

'But not completely. He's still under investigation.'

'If the police really thought he'd done it, they would have charged him by now.'

'So who did kill her?' he asked.

'I don't know. That's why I'm here. Was it you?'

'The police asked me that.'

'I thought they would have. What did you tell them?'

'The truth,' he said. 'I was here looking after the girls last Sunday. My neighbour, Jerry, brought his girl over to play with mine while he and I watched the final day of the football season together on the TV. We're both Palace supporters. He took his girl home about seven-thirty. After that I was here alone with mine.'

'What time did Zoe leave?'

'The police asked me that too.'

'And?'

'I told them she wasn't here at all on Sunday morning. Nor Saturday. She left sometime during Friday evening. I'd dozed off in front of the telly and, when I woke up, she'd gone.'

'Weren't you worried?' I asked.

'Not unduly. She did it all the time.'

'Where did she go?'

'All sorts of places. The police brought her home a few times. Once they found her asleep in a bus shelter. Another time she was spotted in A&E at Ealing Hospital. She wasn't ill or injured or anything, she'd just gone in and sat in the waiting room to sleep. She did that quite a lot until they worked out what she was doing and stopped it.'

He was far more talkative than I had expected. Relaxed too.

'But she always came home in the end?' I said.

'Yeah. It would be as if her being away somehow cleaned the demons from her system, at least for a while. She always came home happy. They were the best times.'

There were tears in his eyes.

'Was she taking drugs?' I asked.

'All the time,' he said. 'Antidepressants and anti-anxiety pills by the bloody handful. Not that they did her much good.'

'I meant did she take any other drugs when she disappeared? You know, illegal drugs?'

'I reckon she must have,' he said. 'But she always denied it and I wanted to believe her. We used to do stuff a lot, coke mostly, so she'd know where to get some.'

'Used to?' I said.

'Yeah. Used to,' he said vehemently. 'I'm clean now and I hoped that Zoe was too. I haven't had a snort of coke in more than five years.' He laughed. 'Mind you, I've felt like having a bit this past week, I can tell you.'

'But Zoe didn't come home as usual this time?'

'No.' He swallowed hard, clearly trying not to cry. 'I got a bit anxious when she hadn't turned up by Monday. She liked to see the girls off to school at the start of the week. By Tuesday morning I was proper worried. She'd never been gone for four nights at once before.'

'Did you call the police and report her missing?' I asked.

'No,' he said bluntly. 'The police and I haven't always seen eye to eye. Anyway, I thought she'd come back. Always had done before.'

'But you did call Arabella Chadwick,' I said. 'I was there.'

He looked at me. 'I hear that she's dead now as well.'

'Yes,' I said. 'She is. But why did you call her?'

He sighed. 'I don't know. I was that worried, I had to call someone. Arabella, she came here. Just before Christmas. Turned up one Sunday. She loved the girls and said that she wanted to get to know us better. Some guff about the family having to stick together. But it wasn't a good day. Zoe was very agitated and she told her a few home truths about being a member of the Chadwick family.'

'What sort of home truths?' I asked.

Peter suddenly became very defensive. Was he going to keep the big secret as well?

'Nothing much,' he said. 'Mostly things about her growing up in Newmarket.'

I decided that the time for niceties was over.

'Was it the same things you're blackmailing Oliver Chadwick over?'

He stared at me.

'Come on, Peter,' I said. 'Look at this place. Nice furnishings, big-screen TV with satellite sports channels, no debts, girls in nice clothes. Where's the money coming from, Peter? Not from your job, that's for sure. How many houses have you sold recently?'

'I think it's time you went now,' he said.

'I'm not the police, you know. I don't like the Chadwicks any more than you do. Talk to me. Was that why Zoe died? Did she go and ask for more blackmail money and got herself killed for her trouble?'

'I said it was time for you to go.'

'What is it, Peter?' I asked him forcefully. 'What is so awful that a family, who individually hate each other so much, will still stand shoulder to shoulder to keep secret?'

'Get out,' he shouted at me.

Both his girls came running into the kitchen with troubled faces.

'Daddy, don't shout,' Poppy said. 'It frightens us.'

'Will you please leave,' Peter said to me quietly but firmly. 'Now.'

'Fine,' I said. 'I'm going.' I took one of my business cards from my pocket and placed it on the kitchen worktop. 'Call me if you want to talk again.'

I went back into the living room. Kate was sitting on the sofa next to Yvonne. 'Come on, Catherine,' I said. 'We're leaving.'

She stood up.

'It's been so lovely to see you again,' Kate said.

'And you too, Catherine, my dear,' replied Yvonne. 'Such a shame it's in these dreadfully sad circumstances. Please do give my best wishes to your sister.'

'Thank you. I will.'

Kate and I went out onto the open walkway and Peter Robertson shut the door firmly behind us.

'What was all that about?' I asked as we walked away.

'Yvonne reminded me that she once came to our house to collect Zoe. I was there and met her. She remembers Janie well and seems so grateful that Zoe had at least one friend in her life. Sad, really.'

'Did she say anything else?' I asked.

'She said that being in hospital had done no good for Zoe, in spite of the Chadwicks' best endeavours to keep her there. According to Yvonne, it was Oliver who arranged to have Zoe sectioned the first time, and she also claims that he did it without telling her. Seems Oliver found a psychiatrist friend of his prepared to diagnose Zoe with schizophrenia simply based on her behaviour. He didn't even see her or speak to her.'

'That's dreadful,' I said.

'It's worse,' Kate replied. 'The shrink also claimed Zoe was a danger to herself and had to be restrained in a psychiatric hospital.'

'When was this?'

'Just after she was found in Croydon.'

Perhaps Oliver had been doing what he thought best for his daughter. Being in hospital at least kept her away from the cocaine.

'Yvonne said she only found out about it years later, after her divorce.'

'How did she find out?' I asked.

'Zoe accused her of being party to it. Apparently Zoe found out from her medical records and confronted her mother.'

'Did Yvonne tell you who she thought had killed her daughter?'

'No, but she did say one thing that I thought was odd. She told me that she believed that the Chadwick men had killed Zoe a long time ago. What did she mean by that?'

'Maybe she thought that one of them had killed her when she went missing and there was that police search.'

'I don't think so,' Kate said slowly. 'It wasn't quite right for that. More brutal.'

'Can you remember her exact words?'

She thought for a moment.

'Yes. She said the Chadwick men had killed Zoe from a very young age. It was only a matter of time before her lifeless corpse turned up.'

# 24

*Phantom of the Opera* was all I remembered it to be – all I hoped it could be.

From the cymbal-clapping monkey automaton at the beginning to the dramatic denouement in the Phantom's subterranean labyrinth at the end, Kate and I were spellbound, and when Raoul and Christine together sang 'All I Ask of You', I felt as if they were singing it just for us:

> *Say you'll share with me one love,*
> *one lifetime;*
> *say the word and I will follow you.*
> *Share each day with me,*
> *each night, each morning.*
> *Say you love me!*
> *You know I do.*
> *Love me, that's all I ask of you.*

Get a grip, I told myself. Everyone knows you're in deep trouble when you start believing the lyrics of love songs!

We went to dinner afterwards at The Ivy in Covent Garden, sitting at a corner table, still humming the show tunes and basking in the warmth of having just seen a great performance.

'That was fabulous,' Kate said. 'So much better than I remembered. Difficult to believe it's been on at that same theatre since I was only three.'

'It's timeless,' I agreed.

Kate ordered the steamed sea bass, while I opted for the tiger prawn curry.

'Did you know,' Kate said, 'you can tell a lot about someone by what they choose from a menu.'

'What nonsense,' I said.

'It's true, I tell you. I read it in a health magazine. It was proper research, done by a doctor.'

'And you reckon that makes it true?' I said with irony.

She ignored me. 'As we all know, you are what you eat, right? Well, surely then *what* you are must also determine *what* you eat.'

'So what am I?' I asked.

'You obviously like spicy food. You've gone for the prawn curry here and you had a take-away Indian last Sunday.'

'At least that bit's true. I love a hot curry.'

'Well, according to the research, people who prefer spicy foods are known to be risk-takers and thrill-seekers.'

*I'll take that*, I thought.

'How about you, then?' I asked. 'What does choosing sea bass mean?'

'It means I'm bloody hungry and I adore sea bass.'

We both laughed, but she wasn't finished.

'Your personality also affects the *way* you eat. Slow and methodical eating means you're stubborn, while fast and furious indicates you don't have any balance when it comes to life's priorities.'

'What a load of baloney,' I said.

But when our food did arrive, I was very careful not to eat it either too slowly or too quickly and, when we later took a minicab back to my flat in Neasden, I was definitely seeking a thrill.

We took the train back to Cambridge on Sunday evening.

'You can come and stay with me, if you like?' Kate said hesitantly as the Hertfordshire fields sped past the windows.

'I would like,' I said. 'Very much. But I'm working. My boss wouldn't think I was concentrating on the job if I was staying at your place, and he'd be right. I need to be on the scene in Newmarket, so I *will* go back to the hotel, but perhaps you could come and join me there for a night or two.'

'Every night, if you'll have me,' she said, taking my hand in hers. 'I'm terrified that you'll go away and forget me.'

'I won't go away,' I said. 'And I won't forget you.' But I could see in her face that she wasn't convinced.

The driver and Mercedes picked us up from Cambridge Station at eight-fifty, just as the sun was going down.

'I actually think I'd better stay at home tonight,' Kate said. 'I have some washing to do, and some ironing.' She pulled a face. 'My uniform is creased.'

So the driver took us first to Six Mile Bottom, before continuing on with me alone to the Bedford Lodge.

I was surprised how much I hated leaving her, and I was sorely tempted to ask the driver to take me back, but I also had things to do, not least catching up with my report-writing for Simpson White. And I had phoned the hotel from the train to tell them I was returning tonight.

'Welcome back, Mr Foster,' said the same receptionist when I checked in. 'Fortunately we still have the same room available for you.'

'Thank you,' I said.

'And you have a message waiting.' She handed me an envelope. 'It's only just come in. I told the person who called that you'd be back soon.'

I took my luggage, and the envelope, along to my room and opened it there. The message consisted of just a couple of typed lines on a single sheet of the hotel's headed notepaper.

*Harry, Please come along to the old yard as soon as you get in. I have something important I want to show you. Oliver.*

I looked at my watch. It was already ten o'clock. I was tired. Couldn't it wait until tomorrow? But I thought about how much fun I was having with Kate, much of it at Simpson White's expense, and decided that another late-night excursion was the least I could pay, especially as Kate wasn't even here this evening.

I walked out of the hotel, along the Bury Road, and in through the gates I had first used on my arrival last Monday. On that occasion the ground had been covered with fire hoses, but they had long gone, together with the remains of the burned-out stable block. I could see the lights of the new yard through the space it once occupied.

The remaining two stable blocks of the old yard were in darkness, save for one stable at the far end where the door was slightly open, and the light from within spilled out across the concrete.

'Oliver?' I called as I walked towards the light. 'It's Harry. What do you want?'

I reached the stable door and looked in.

I wasn't really expecting some great revelation from Oliver concerning their family secret but, there again, I also wasn't expecting to be struck heavily across my shoulders from behind, and pushed headlong through the doorway.

I was sent sprawling onto the floor as the door behind me was slammed shut. I could hear as the bolts were slid across on the outside, locking me in.

*Damn it,* I thought. That was bloody careless.

And I was not alone in the stable.

The other occupant had four legs, a tail and a mane, and I'm not sure which one of us was the more scared.

Me probably, especially when I realised I had seen this horse before. It had a small white star in the middle of its forehead, such that it fleetingly appeared to have three eyes.

Momentum. The crazy horse that Oliver called just skittish. The horse he wanted to calm down by gelding but the owner wouldn't hear of it. Damn Michelle Morris. Give me a knife and I'd happily do the job right now.

Momentum curled his upper lip, baring a large row of off-white tombstone teeth. Then he pawed at the ground with one of his front hooves, and opened his two real eyes very wide, clearly exposing the whites around the huge pupils.

He obviously didn't take kindly to having his space invaded, and there was little doubt about his intentions, all the more so when he kicked backwards violently against the wall, leaving a deep scar in the wooden cladding.

'There's a good boy,' I said, trying unsuccessfully to keep the terror out of my voice. Where had I read that a horse can smell human fear? I could almost smell it myself.

Momentum began to circle towards me so, like a dance, I circled away from him.

'Oliver!' I shouted. 'Let me out.'

There was no reply, nor any reassuring sliding open of the door bolts. Instead, my raised voice seemed to make the horse even more agitated, so I kept quiet.

I reached into my pocket for my phone but I knew it

293

wasn't there. I'd put it on charge as soon as I'd gone into my hotel room.

Damn, and double damn. How could I have been so stupid?

Then the overhead light went out.

If I had hoped that the darkness would pacify Momentum, I was out of luck. And he could obviously see me better in the dark than I could him.

What had Oliver told me? Horses were originally prey animals. Millions of years of evolution had clearly given them excellent night vision, no doubt to keep them one step ahead of their predators.

Twice Momentum bit me before I even realised he was close, first on the shoulder and then on the left forearm. And both of them bloody hurt.

The second time, I slapped him hard on the side of the head, making him neigh loudly in fright, the sound reverberating noisily off the walls of the enclosed space.

*Would anyone hear that?* I wondered. And would they then take any notice in a town packed full of horses?

What was going on here?

Was Oliver really trying to kill me, or just to frighten me? If it was the latter, he was succeeding admirably.

Surely, another dead body turning up in a Chadwick stable would raise more than a few eyebrows, especially with the door bolted from the outside.

Or did Oliver intend setting this block on fire as well?

That thought made me very scared. At least Zoe had been already dead when the flames consumed her. Would I be so lucky?

Maybe I would, if Momentum got his way.

The horse and I continued our circulating ballet for what seemed like an age, but it was probably for only about ten minutes. Sadly, he seemed not to lose interest in trying to bite me, but even the bites were preferable to the threat from his flailing hooves further back. And I felt it was only a matter of time before he hit me with one of those.

I have a friend who often defined a horse as something that is dangerous at both ends and uncomfortable in the middle.

*Perhaps I should try the middle*, I thought. After all, Momentum had calmed down a lot when Tony got up onto him at the racecourse.

But that was easier said than done.

I'd never been on a horse before in my life and, if it hadn't been for these strange and exceptional circumstances, I'd have been quite happy for it to have remained that way.

I planned my moment of approach.

The stable had a small window. Although I had already discovered that it was heavily barred on the inside and gave no hope of escape, there was just enough outside night-time illumination to make the window appear slightly lighter than the blackness of the surrounding walls.

Hence, as the horse and I circled, there was one point in the revolution when I could see his bulk as he moved past the window.

My first attempt was an abject failure. It was also nearly my last.

As Momentum moved across the window, I ran at the horse and threw myself up with my right leg leading, trying to straddle the animal in the manner I had seen done by Indian braves in many an old Western movie.

However, it didn't work.

I had totally misjudged in the dark how tall the horse was. I simply didn't jump high enough, bouncing off his flank and falling hopelessly to the floor. I found myself being trampled under-hoof, so I curled up tight to make myself as small a target as possible. Nevertheless, Momentum let fly with a murderous kick that just clipped me on the right ear as it thudded into the wall right next to my head.

My ear hurt like hell and I could feel the warmth of blood as it ran down my neck. But I was alive. Just.

*Too close,* I thought. Much too close.

I was quickly on my feet and received another nip on the hand from the tombstones as I again circled round in front of the beast. More blood.

My second try was wholly more successful although, this time, having slightly overcompensated from my previous effort, I nearly jumped clean across the horse and only the wall on the far side stopped me falling off.

I clung on tight, grasping hold of his mane with my fingers.

Not that that stopped him from turning his head and trying to bite my legs. I leaned myself forwards, so that my upper body was almost lying flat, and I stretched my legs out further back so he couldn't reach them.

Initially, he tried to throw me off by tossing his head up and down, but I wrapped my arms round his neck and hung on as if my life depended on it, which it probably did. Slowly, as I'd hoped, he began to calm down.

Momentum eventually stopped pacing round and round, and stood still in the darkness. He was now calm and his breathing was even and slow. I'd read somewhere that horses could sleep standing up and I wondered if Momentum had done just that.

I almost went to sleep myself at one point, and I woke up with a start when I felt myself slipping.

*How long could I stay like this?* I wondered. The stable lads wouldn't be back until six in the morning. Could I stay awake that long so I didn't fall off?

I'd have to.

So I started playing mind games to keep me awake. I tried mental arithmetic, reciting in my head the seventeen times table. One seventeen is seventeen, two seventeens are thirty-four, three seventeens are fifty-one ... and so on, right up to seventeen seventeens are ... the cogs moved slowly ... two hundred and eighty-nine.

Next I tried the twenty-three times table, but I found that it was sending me to sleep more than keeping me awake.

Do something different.

So I started going over in my head everything that had happened over the past week, starting with Zoe being collected by Declan from Cambridge Station last Sunday morning, right up until the moment I found myself in this current predicament.

Had I missed something?

Had someone said something that, at the time, had seemed quite innocent but now was more incriminating?

I'd got as far as Wednesday night, to the point where Declan had been arrested for murder, when, unbelievably, I heard talking close by outside.

'This is all a complete waste of time,' said a man's voice crossly. 'I can assure you, there's no one here.'

'Yes, there is,' I shouted. 'In here. Help! Help!'

But my shouting did nothing for the calmness of Momentum. If he had been asleep before, he certainly wasn't any longer, and he returned to trying to dislodge me from his back, bashing my right leg repeatedly against the wall.

The light went on, blinding me for a moment, and further irritating my mount, which started tossing his head up and down violently. I was beginning to lose my grip round his neck.

I heard the bolts being slid across and then the stable door opened.

Still sitting on the horse, I looked across at the doorway.

Oliver stood there, his mouth hanging open in surprise, and just behind him was Kate.

'There,' she said to Oliver with satisfaction. 'I told you he'd be here somewhere.'

# 25

'It wasn't my doing,' Oliver protested. 'I had no idea you were in there.'

I thought back to his look of surprise on opening the stable door. That had appeared genuine, but it might have been because he was surprised I was still alive and actually riding the horse, both of which were surprises to me too.

I was sitting at the kitchen table in Oliver's house as Kate tended to the cut on my ear.

'This really needs a stitch or two,' she said, washing away the dried blood. 'How did you do it?'

I explained to her that Momentum had kicked me and it didn't take her long to realise how close I had come to having something far more serious than a cut ear.

'Why did you get on him?' Oliver asked.

'Self-preservation,' I said. 'It was the only place he couldn't kick or bite me.'

I recounted the entire saga to them from the time I'd

received the message in the hotel until the moment they had found me.

Kate's eyes grew wider and wider as I described my attempts to get up on Momentum's back.

'But I didn't send you any message,' Oliver moaned.

'Somebody did,' Kate said.

I smiled at her. 'So what brought you here?'

'I tried to call you to say goodnight but you weren't answering your phone, in spite of the fact that I knew it was ringing because it didn't go straight to voicemail. So I called you on the hotel landline but you didn't answer that either.'

She smiled. 'I was worried, so I badgered the hotel's night receptionist into going to your room to check you were still alive. I had visions of you having slipped in the shower and lying injured on the bathroom floor desperate for help.'

I squeezed her hand.

'Anyway, the receptionist called me back from your room to say you weren't there but your phone was. And there was also a message lying on the bed from someone called Oliver asking you to go immediately to the old yard. So I called Mr Chadwick.'

'I told her I had no idea what she was talking about,' Oliver said, looking rather sheepish. 'In fact, I may have been a bit rude to her. Sorry about that. But it was well past my bed-time. I told her to stop fussing and go to sleep.'

'Which, of course, I didn't,' Kate said proudly. 'In the end I drove over here and banged on Oliver's door until he answered. Then I insisted we take a look.'

I checked my watch.

It was past midnight. I'd been in that stable with the mad horse for almost two hours.

'Thank you,' I said, meaning it. 'You probably saved my life.'

'Nonsense,' said Oliver with a laugh. 'Momentum's an old softy, really.'

I stared at him.

Had he really done it after all? Just to frighten me?

At Kate's insistence, we spent the next couple of hours in the Casualty department of Addenbrooke's Hospital in Cambridge for me to have my right ear stitched.

'I'm sure it doesn't need it,' I'd said to her but, as Oliver had discovered earlier, there were times when Kate wouldn't take no for an answer.

She drove me to the hospital in her Mini.

'Aren't you going to call the police?' she said on the way. 'This must constitute assault at the very least.'

'Probably attempted murder.'

'Well then. Shouldn't you tell someone?'

I'd already thought about that.

It wasn't as if I'd been badly hurt, so how much effort would the police actually take in trying to find out who had done it? I'd also have to admit to them that I'd been foolish enough to walk straight into a trap.

But it did clearly show one thing.

Someone thought that I was getting a bit too close to the truth for comfort.

'How did this happen?' the doctor at the hospital asked as he picked and prodded at my ear, making it even more sore than it had been before.

'I was kicked by a horse,' I said, although I don't think he really believed me.

'What were you doing?' he asked. 'Lying down?'

'Something like that,' I said, without going into details.

In the end, he put four small stitches in my ear lobe, an anti-tetanus jab in my arm, a couple of painkiller tablets in my stomach, and told me to be more careful in future around horses.

I assured him that I would.

Next Kate drove us to Six Mile Bottom and I stayed with her after all, getting to bed just before three in the morning. But, unlike my host, I didn't go straight to sleep.

For a start, my ear throbbed badly in spite of the painkillers, but mostly it was because I carried on with the mental exercise that I had been engaged in when on the horse in the stable, which had been interrupted by my rescue.

I went through the rest of the week piece by piece, trying to find the elusive missing clue to what the hell was going on.

It had to be there somewhere.

Kate dropped me at the Bedford Lodge at eight-thirty on her way into work.

'Now be careful,' she said as I climbed out of the Mini. 'No more visiting lonely stables at night.'

I laughed and promised to be more vigilant. 'Yes, ma'am.'

She drove away and I watched her go with what was becoming an all too familiar ache in my heart.

*Pull yourself together*, I said to myself. *You'll be seeing her again later.*

As I walked into the hotel, the receptionist gave me a very strange look before rushing towards me from behind her desk.

'Ah, Mr Foster,' she said almost breathlessly. 'There you are. We've been so worried about you. Very worried indeed.'

'Have you?' I said. 'Why?'

'Because you didn't return last night. Someone called us last evening and was very insistent that something terrible must have happened to you.'

That would have been Kate.

Perhaps we should have rung the hotel to let them know that all was well.

'The night staff were most concerned. When you hadn't come back by six o'clock this morning, I'm afraid they called the police,' she said. 'In fact, a detective is in your room right now. He arrived here about ten minutes ago.' She suddenly looked troubled. 'I hope it's all right that I let him in.'

'Perfectly fine,' I said, smiling at her. If Kate hadn't been so determined, even to the point of driving over at midnight and banging on Oliver's front door, I might have still been in the stable with Momentum. It was good to know that there was someone else looking out for me as well.

To my surprise, the detective searching my room was DCI Eastwood.

He seemed quite surprised to see me too, or maybe he

was just cross at having had his limited resources wasted, yet again.

'I didn't realise that chief inspectors investigated missing persons,' I said.

'Where have you been?' he asked accusingly, sounding awfully like my father.

'Six Mile Bottom.' I said it with a smile. I still found the name funny.

'But you were checked in here.'

'So,' I said. 'Is there a law that says you have to sleep in a hotel room just because you're paying for it?'

'Don't play silly games with me, Mr Foster,' he said. 'Where have you been?'

'I told you. I was in Six Mile Bottom.'

'You check in to this hotel at 10 p. m. Then, five minutes later, you walk out alone – no phone, no coat, no bag. A hysterical female then calls here saying you have gone missing and she is so seriously concerned for your welfare that she convinces the hotel to mount an unsuccessful search not only of your bedroom but also of the rest of the building. You do not return all night and the staff are so worried that they finally call the police. And now, you claim you spent the night safe and well in Six Mile Bottom with no washbag, no change of clothes, nothing?'

'Yes,' I said. Although safe and well was a relative term – my ear was still throbbing rather badly.

'So how did you get there?' he asked.

'You wouldn't believe me if I told you.'

'Try me,' he said.

'Have you ever ridden a horse, Chief Inspector?' I asked.

The DCI shook his head.

'Neither had I until last night.'

'Don't tell me you rode a bloody horse all the way to Six Mile Bottom.'

'No,' I said, laughing. 'But I rode one nevertheless.'

In the end I told him everything. Perhaps I should have done so right from the start.

'Why didn't you call the police last night?' he asked.

'For what?' I said. 'To report a cut ear?'

'Imprisonment is a serious offence.'

'So is attempted murder,' I said. 'But you know as well as I do that Suffolk Constabulary would have been unlikely to come hotfoot at midnight to Castleton House Stables after the event. I would simply have been told to report it in the morning, as I am now doing.'

He didn't deny it.

'Do you believe someone was really trying to kill you?'

'Probably not,' I said. 'They couldn't know I'd leave my mobile in the hotel. That was just their good luck.' *And my bad*, I thought. 'If whoever it was had truly wanted me dead, he could have easily hit me over the head instead of on the shoulders. A couple of good clouts with a metal muck shovel would have done the trick. Why leave it to chance that the horse would do the deed for him? After all, no one could think I'd wandered in there by accident, especially with the door bolted from the outside.'

'So why?' he asked.

'Maybe just to frighten me enough to scare me off.'

'Scare you off from what?'

'Ah, Detective Chief Inspector, that is *the* question,' I said. 'If only I knew the answer.'

I stared at him, and he back at me, in silence.

'Do you fancy some breakfast?' I said. 'I'm starving and I want to ask you a favour.'

We sat in the hotel dining room and I had a full English, while the chief inspector ordered just a coffee.

'I'm buying,' I said. Or, rather, Simpson White was.

'I had my breakfast earlier,' said the DCI, but he still ate a slice of my toast when it came, together with some thickly spread butter and orange marmalade. 'Now, what's this favour you want?' he asked with his mouth full.

'It's actually two favours,' I said. 'I want the Robertsons' bank statements and Zoe Robertson's medical records.'

'What for?' he asked in true police style.

'My client has been arrested for murder and, even though released from custody, he is still under investigation. Hence I continue to work on his defence.'

'So you don't think he did it?' the DCI asked.

'As you know, what I think is irrelevant. But, since you ask, no, I don't think he did it. Neither do you, otherwise you'd have charged him by now.'

He didn't rise to my bait, so I went on.

'I need Zoe's medical records to determine the state of her

health at the time of death, so I can assess whether she might have died of natural causes prior to the fire starting.'

At least, that was my excuse.

He looked at me cynically. 'Grasping at straws, are we?'

'I know it's a long shot but I need to cover every eventuality, however remote.'

'And the bank statements?' he said.

'My client claims that his sister came to see him demanding money. Hence I would like to establish the state of her finances.'

I could tell he didn't like it. Not one bit. The police were always reticent to give away any information, even when they were required to do so by the law.

'Call it disclosure of evidence to the defence,' I said. 'You will have to give them to me eventually if Declan is charged. Having them now might just save you some embarrassment in the long run.'

It was a tenuous argument, but it seemed to work.

'Okay,' he said reluctantly. 'I'll see what I can do with the medical records. That shouldn't be a problem – we've already got those from her doctor. The bank statements, however, will be a bit more difficult, especially if the Robertsons had a joint account. Peter Robertson is still living and data protection would still apply. I wouldn't count your chickens on that score.'

He said it in a tone that implied he didn't think much of the data protection laws.

'Please do your best,' I said. 'And send over the medical records as soon as possible.'

I took another mouthful of my bacon and eggs while the DCI wrote a note in his ever-present notebook.

'How are you getting on, anyway?' I asked. 'Any more suspects?'

'Not as yet,' he said.

'No dodgy alibis overturned by new evidence?'

'None of the Chadwick family seem to have an alibi for last Sunday night anyway, other than Arabella Chadwick, who we know was with friends in Great Yarmouth. And she's now dead.'

'Anything further on that?' I asked, without mentioning the suicide note I'd seen on the fridge.

'Nothing,' he said. 'The initial post-mortem results are consistent with death by hanging.'

'So you're treating it as suicide?'

'Absolutely,' he said. 'There is nothing to indicate otherwise.'

'The back door wasn't locked,' I said. 'Don't you think that could be suspicious?'

'We are satisfied that Arabella Chadwick's death was a suicide,' the DCI said with certainty, clearly wanting to end discussion on that matter. I wondered why he didn't just tell me that she'd left a note. But, in my limited experience with the police, they always loved to keep something back. Perhaps the DCI, like ASW, imagined that greater knowledge somehow gave him greater power. Or maybe the chief inspector just enjoyed believing he knew something I didn't.

But I *did* know it, and I quite enjoyed that too.

My boss would be proud of me.

'Did you say just now that Ryan Chadwick also doesn't have an alibi for Sunday night?' I asked. 'Wasn't he with his wife?'

'His wife was in Ely. She took their children over to see her mother for Sunday lunch and then stayed over with her. So Mr Ryan Chadwick was home alone on Sunday night. As was Mr Tony Chadwick, as his mother was visiting her sister in Ipswich.'

'So Susan Chadwick, then, has an alibi,' I said.

'Ah, well, no. Not exactly,' the DCI replied. 'She claims that, with her mother acting as babysitter, she took the opportunity to go to the cinema.'

'Alone?'

'She says so, but I'm not convinced. I'm not even sure she went to the cinema at all.' He left his suspicions hanging in the air.

'Another man?' I asked.

'Quite possibly. But I'm not pushing her too hard on that at present. Unlike in Saudi Arabia and Pakistan, or even in half of the United States, cheating on your husband is no longer a criminal offence in this country, and there's nothing to suggest that she was involved in the fire.'

'She was certainly at Castleton House Stables with her husband and the others when I arrived there at lunchtime on Monday,' I said. I remembered back to the smart clothes and the bright red lipstick.

'Mr Ryan Chadwick says he telephoned his wife early on Monday morning to tell her of the fire.'

'How early?'

Before the DCI had a chance to answer, my phone rang and I recognised the number on the screen. It was Kate.

'Hello, my love,' I said.

'Oh, Harry, it's so awful.' She was sobbing uncontrollably. 'What a bastard.'

'What's awful?' I asked with trepidation. 'Who's a bastard?'

'Ryan Chadwick,' she said. 'He's just fired Janie.'

# 26

It wasn't just Kate who was crying. Janie had tears too, but hers were more in anger than in sorrow.

DCI Eastwood had kindly given me a lift down through the town to Park Paddocks and I was now sitting in one of Tattersalls' meeting rooms with Kate and Janie.

'I've been working at Castleton House Stables since I was sixteen,' Janie said angrily. 'Half my bloody life. And I always worked far more hours than I was paid for, especially since Ryan cut my wages last month. In fact, if you count all the hours I actually work, I've probably been getting less than the minimum wage.'

'Then report him to an employment tribunal,' Kate said. 'And also take him to the cleaners for unfair dismissal.'

'Hold on a minute,' I said. 'Let's not be too hasty. What reasons did Ryan give for letting you go?'

'The bastard didn't *let her go*,' Kate said angrily. 'He

sacked her. He shouted at her and told her to collect her things and go immediately, and not to come back.'

'He said he couldn't afford me any longer,' Janie said. 'And also that he didn't like me passing on personal information about his business to other people.'

'Did he say which other people?' I asked.

'His exact words were "to your sister and her effing boyfriend".'

*Charming,* I thought.

'He's a fool,' Kate said.

'He's more than that,' Janie said. 'I don't think he has the slightest idea how much I do to make that place run smoothly. I complete all the declarations and engage all the jockeys, to say nothing of the collection of the training fees, vets' bills, transport costs and so on and so on. I do all the statutory HR stuff and the payroll for the stable lads. It's even me that orders the horse feed and the bedding. Most yards have a whole team of people doing what I do. All Mr Ryan does is the entries. I reckon the whole place will grind to a halt now that I've gone.'

'Does Oliver know?' I asked. 'He told me only last week that the place couldn't operate without you.'

As if on cue, my phone rang and it was Oliver. I put him on speaker so the girls could hear.

'Ah, hello, Harry,' he said hesitantly. 'We have a bit of a problem here and I was wondering if you could help?'

'I'll try,' I said.

'I'm trying to contact Janie Logan,' he said. 'I thought you might know where she is.'

'Why do you want her?' I asked.

'Well, it seems that Ryan may have acted rather hastily.'

'What, in sacking her?'

There was a slight pause from the other end.

'Ah, I see that you already know.'

'Yes,' I said. 'In fact, I'm with Janie Logan right now. She is very upset. We are discussing making a claim for wrongful dismissal.'

'Wrongful dismissal?' he said sharply, repeating the words.

'Yes,' I said. 'I believe Janie has worked at Castleton House Stables for sixteen years. That means she was entitled to a minimum of twelve weeks' paid notice. In addition she will also be filing a case with an employment tribunal for unfair dismissal, which I am quite sure she will win.'

'But it's all a mistake,' Oliver said. 'We want Janie to come back. Ryan should never have said what he did. She is *not* sacked.'

'Oliver,' I said. 'I think if your employer shouts at you and tells you to get out immediately and not to come back, then you *are* sacked.'

'But, as I said, it was all a big mistake. Heat of the moment stuff. We desperately want Janie back.'

'Is that also what Ryan thinks?' I asked.

'Yes, of course.'

I could imagine Oliver and Ryan having had another one of their difficult discussions when Ryan had told his father that he'd fired the only person who really knew what was going on in their business.

Oliver was once again on a damage-limitation exercise for his eldest son.

'I will consult with Janie and let you know,' I said. 'But, whatever happens, I assure you that she shall not be returning on the same terms as before. For a start, she would want last month's cut in her pay reversed and she would also require a sizeable raise on top of that, as well as substantial compensation for her distress over this matter.'

'Cut in her pay?' Oliver said. 'What cut in her pay?'

'Ask Ryan,' I said, and hung up.

I could foresee yet another difficult conversation between father and son.

'Harry,' Kate said, clapping her hands together. 'You were brilliant.'

Indeed, the exchange seemed to have cheered them both up.

'But the big question,' I said to Janie, 'is do you really want to go back to work there, even with a significant raise?'

'More to the point,' she said, 'is there going to be a job to go back to anyway? Two of the owners called this morning to say that they were transferring their horses to other trainers. Sorry, they said, but Mr Ryan has been having too many recent losers.'

Owners of racehorses, it seemed, were only as loyal to their trainers as the owners of football clubs were to their team managers, i.e. not at all, not unless they were winning.

In racing or football, or in any professional sport these days, winning wasn't just everything, it was the *only* thing.

'Where are the horses going instead?' I asked.

'One I don't know, the owner wouldn't say, but the other is sending his horse to Declan. At least he'll be keeping the horse in the Chadwick family, he said, as if that was a good thing! Mr Ryan went ballistic when I told him. That's when he fired me.'

'One should never shoot the messenger just because the news is bad,' I said. 'If you do, then no one will tell you what you don't want to hear for fear of being killed. Hence you end up not being forewarned of approaching danger even when everyone else knows about it.'

'That's very profound,' Kate said.

'But true. Hitler got so angry when he was told things were going badly that his generals simply stopped passing on the bad news. He still believed he was winning the war right up to the point where the Russian army was fighting in the streets of Berlin. And, in England years ago, it was considered treason to attack a town crier because you didn't like the news he was shouting.'

'Perhaps we could get Ryan hung, drawn and quartered,' Kate said with a laugh.

'Too good for him,' Janie said, which I thought just about answered the question about her going back to work at Castleton House Stables.

Leaving both Kate and Janie in far better humour than I'd found them, I walked back to the Bedford Lodge and checked in with the Simpson White office.

'ASW is out to lunch,' Georgina said. 'But he left you a

315

message.' I could hear her rustling papers. 'Here it is. He says you only have until the end of this week as he needs you back here because other projects are looming on the horizon. He's fixed it all with the Sheikh, who is happy with the arrangement.'

'Is that all?' I asked. I'd rather hoped that the research wizards might have discovered a smoking gun by now, preferably one nestling in a Chadwick hand.

'No, it's not all,' Georgina replied. 'He also said to tell you to get an effing move on, stop pissing around, and put a thunderflash up their arses ... there's a good chap.'

I laughed at her impression. I could almost hear ASW saying it.

ASW loved his thunderflashes, metaphorically speaking that was. A real thunderflash was a pyrotechnic used for training in the army. It was like a firework 'banger' only bigger and louder. But an ASW thunderflash was anything that produced an explosive reaction.

'Right,' I said. 'I'll do all three.'

I was still laughing when I checked my emails.

And there were two of interest. Big interest.

The first was from DCI Eastwood with Zoe Robertson's medical records as an attachment.

Declan had said that Zoe suffered from psychosis, and Yvonne had told Kate that she had been initially hospitalised for schizophrenia, but her latest diagnosis, from the time of her most recent in-patient stay, was for BPD – borderline personality disorder. It was contained in a scanned letter from a Dr Alan Cazalet, consultant in psychiatry at University College Hospital, London.

I looked up BPD on the internet. In spite of its name, there was absolutely nothing borderline about it. It was a most serious condition characterised by long-term patterns of abnormal behaviour including difficult relationships with other people, inadequate sense of self, and unstable emotions. Sufferers frequently self-harmed and also regularly acted without any apparent concern for their own welfare.

Zoe had indeed been a troubled soul.

I searched back through the file for any triggers for her condition but, whereas the recent ten years of her medical history were covered in some detail, the older records were brief only to the point of providing just an illness title and a date, such as 'Pertussis – May 1992'.

Whereas it was of some mild interest that Zoe had contracted whooping cough at age three and a half, there were no details of the severity of the infection or what treatment had been given.

Equally, her first admittance to a psychiatric hospital in February 2007 was recorded as just that, without clarification that she'd been sectioned, and certainly without any indication that it had been her father's doing, as Yvonne had claimed. It made me think that only the bare facts of the pre-computer era had been transcribed onto the digital record, and maybe there were greater details to be found elsewhere.

I read through it all for a second time to ensure I hadn't

missed something, but there was nothing important that I didn't already know.

However, the second email, the one from the Simpson White research team, was far more sensational.

Even though they had been unable to break into the online banking system, the wizards had somehow acquired a loan request from Peter to a finance company to buy a car. Attached to the application form were copies of three of the Robertsons' joint-account bank statements from the previous autumn.

They weren't so much the single smoking gun I'd been hoping for, more like a whole firing squad of them.

For all his lack of gainful employment, Peter Robertson was clearly no mug. He seemed to be making a good living from blackmailing his in-laws, all of them.

No wonder he hadn't wanted to talk to me, even after the death of his wife. He probably had every intention of continuing the blackmail, and maybe upping the ante to cover murder.

But how was he doing it?

What was the hold he seemed to have over them all?

The bank statements clearly showed regular payments into his account not only from Oliver Chadwick but also from Ryan, Declan and Tony.

Not too much, of course. Just enough so that they would pay without squealing.

It was definitely time to put a thunderflash up their arses.

\*

I went to see Oliver first but he was out.

'Come on in,' Maria said, opening the front door wide. 'Oliver's gone to see some foal or other at a stud farm out near Cheveley. He went some time ago. Probably won't be much longer. Do you fancy a drink?'

She was already holding a glass of what I assumed was white wine.

'Coffee would be nice,' I said, stepping through the doorway.

She wrinkled her nose in distaste but led the way into the kitchen.

'Help yourself,' she said, waving at the kettle, and then poured herself a top-up from an open bottle of Chardonnay on the kitchen table.

I put the kettle on the Aga.

'How about Ryan?' I asked. 'Is he about?'

'No idea,' she said. 'I'm not his bloody keeper.'

There was clearly no love lost between them.

'Why didn't Ryan move in here when he took over the stables?' I asked, spooning instant coffee into a cup.

'Don't be bloody stupid,' Maria said. 'Oliver didn't want to give up his stables. He wasn't about to hand over his house as well.'

'Then why *did* he give up the stables?' I asked. 'Ryan could surely have started up somewhere else. Like Declan did.'

'Apparently, it was always accepted that Ryan would eventually take over the yard from Oliver. But no one expected it to be quite so soon. Ryan broke his knee badly in a fall at

Newbury and was forced to stop riding when he was only thirty-six. Most flat jockeys go on much longer than that, some well into their fifties.'

I poured boiling water over the coffee, and took some milk from the fridge.

'Surely Oliver could still have said no.'

'He should have done,' Maria said with feeling. 'Ryan taking over has been a disaster. If we're not careful we'll lose the whole bloody lot.'

I marvelled at her ability to be so indiscreet. Probably something to do with the wine. But I wasn't about to stop her just to spare her blushes.

'How well did you know Zoe?' I asked.

'Not at all,' she said. 'I knew *of* her, of course. Everyone round here knows *of* Zoe Chadwick. Silly little bitch. Given us nothing but grief even in death.'

'It was hardly her fault she was murdered,' I said.

'No? Whose fault is it, then? She should have stayed in London.'

'What were *you* doing on Sunday afternoon and evening?'

'What's this,' Maria said with a hollow laugh. 'The bloody Spanish Inquisition? You can't think I had anything to do with it?'

*Did I?*

'In that case you won't mind telling me where you were.'

'The police have already asked me that.'

'So what did you tell them?'

'The truth,' she said. 'I woke on Sunday morning with a

migraine so I took some strong painkillers and stayed in bed all day with a cold compress on my head.'

I unkindly wondered if it had been a hangover rather than a migraine.

'Didn't you eat anything?' I asked.

'I can't really remember. I know I was zonked out for most of the day. Those painkillers are pretty strong, especially when you wash them down with Chardonnay.' She laughed and raised her glass towards me.

'Didn't Oliver come and see you at all?'

'He brought me up some tomato soup for lunch.'

'Anything else?' I asked.

'Anything else what?' she asked belligerently. 'Don't you believe me?'

'I didn't say that,' I said. 'I just wondered if Oliver had spent any of the afternoon with you.'

'Not that I can remember,' she said. 'I think he was catching up with *EastEnders* in the snug. He often does on Sunday afternoons. I could hear it coming up through the floorboards. He probably thought that, with me in bed, it was a good opportunity. I hate the damn programme. There are enough arguments and misery in my life already without having to watch more of it in a bloody soap opera.'

I looked at her. *How sad,* I thought.

'How about during the evening?' I asked.

'More painkillers,' she said. 'First thing I knew Oliver was banging on the door shouting at me to get up because the stables were on fire.'

321

'Was Oliver at home all evening?'

'How the hell would I know? I was out of it.' She smiled at me. 'But you can't possibly think that he'd burn down his own stables? Not with Prince of bloody Troy in there?'

'Didn't you like the horse?' I asked, surprised at her outburst.

'I had nothing against the horse, *per se*. I just wished I'd received half as much love and attention as it did. Bloody mollycoddled, it was.'

'But the future of Ryan's training business may have depended on it,' I said.

'Yeah, well, the horse has gone now so we'll never know, will we?'

She didn't sound especially sorry.

'Did Oliver ever mention Zoe?'

'Not recently, that's for sure,' Maria said. 'A long time ago he told me that he no longer considered Zoe his daughter. He said she was not a part of his life and never would be again.'

'Then why was he giving her five hundred pounds every month?'

# 27

Oliver returned from seeing the foal at the stud farm near Cheveley to be met by stony silence from his wife in the kitchen. I was there too.

'What's up?' he asked, sensing the cool atmosphere.

Maria remained silent so I jumped right in to insert my first thunderflash. 'Maria is wondering why you've been paying five hundred pounds a month to Zoe and Peter Robertson.'

If I thought he'd flinched when I'd asked him why Ryan had broken Declan's nose, it was nothing compared to how he reacted now.

The blood drained out of his face and he stumbled slightly, grabbing hold of a chair to lean on.

But his mind was clearly still working.

'For my grandchildren, of course,' he said, recovering some of his composure. 'I can't penalise them just because their mother was a tramp.'

But Maria was not placated in the least.

'You bastard,' she shouted. 'You've been telling me we're so hard up that I can't afford even to have my hair done, and all the while you've been giving away our cash. Are you saying those bloody children are more important than me?'

Oliver turned to me and, for the very first time, his veneer of politeness cracked.

'Get out of my house,' he said angrily.

I made what ASW would call a 'tactical withdrawal' back to the Bedford Lodge to take stock and determine my next move.

First I called DCI Eastwood.

'Thank you for the medical records,' I said. 'But is there any more? They seem incomplete.'

'That's what we got from her doctor,' he said.

'Could you check if there's anything else? What you sent doesn't detail anything more than ten years old. There must be some records from before that.'

I could hear him sigh. 'I have other things to do, you know. I thought you wanted to determine if there was any remote chance that she'd dropped down dead of natural causes. Surely you have enough for that?'

'It would be negligent on my part if I didn't check everything that was available.' I said it in my best courtroom lawyer voice.

'I'll ask my sergeant,' he said with resignation. 'It was he who got them in the first place.'

'Good,' I said. 'I'll wait.'

I don't think he was expecting to have to ask his sergeant straight away but I gave him little choice.

'Right,' he said again, with more resignation. 'I'll go and ask him now and call you straight back.'

Reluctantly, I hung up but, true to his word, the chief inspector called back within ten minutes.

'It appears we do have some paper records as well,' he said.

'Can they be scanned and sent over?' I asked.

'It would seem there are rather a lot. Could you not just come over and see them here? It would save a lot of time and effort, and we are short of both.'

*Limited resources again*, I thought.

'All right,' I said. 'Where is *here*?'

'The Bury St Edmunds investigation centre. We've closed the temporary incident room at Newmarket.'

'I'll come right away.'

Better to do it now before he changed his mind.

'Ask for DS Venables. He'll be expecting you.'

I rustled up my driver and his Mercedes and we were soon on our way to Bury St Edmunds.

I don't know why I thought that Zoe's medical records were important. Perhaps it was because Yvonne had told Kate about Oliver having arranged for Zoe to be sectioned under the Mental Health Act, and that it was shown in her notes.

Had Oliver lied to get Zoe put away in a mental hospital? Was that what he was being blackmailed over? But would he really pay five hundred pounds a month to keep that a secret? Surely not, not after all the years that had passed since.

DS Venables took me down a windowless corridor and into a room with a round table and four chairs. On the table was a cardboard box containing a number of special envelopes standing up side by side with open tops.

'Apparently they're called Lloyd George envelopes,' the DS said flatly. 'After the politician that introduced them. According to the doctor that sent them to me, they've now been superseded by computers.'

He stood to one side, leaning on the wall with his hands in his pockets, while I sat down at the table and reached for the box.

'I don't approve,' the sergeant said.

'You don't approve of what?' I asked.

'My boss letting you see these records.'

'Why not?'

'Stands to reason,' he said. 'Why should we be helping the defence?'

'I thought we were both interested in justice.'

He sniffed his disagreement. He was clearly only interested in a conviction.

'What are you looking for?'

'I don't know,' I said. 'Not unless I find it.'

The box contained four of the Lloyd George envelopes, each one stuffed full of folded papers. They were marked 1 to 4 and were in date order. I started with envelope 1, emptying the contents onto the table.

'There's no need to stay,' I said to DS Venables. 'I'm not going to take anything. I just want to read it all.' I took my mobile phone out of my pocket and put it down on the table. 'I'll just take photos of anything I want to look at again later.'

The detective reluctantly pushed himself off the wall by his elbows.

'I'll come back in half an hour.'

'Make it an hour,' I said. 'There's a lot here. I promise I won't wander off.'

He left the room and closed the door.

I was surprised how much information was logged in our medical records, and how they obviously follow us around from one surgery to another as we move. There were even allocated spaces on the front of the first envelope to record any such changes and, for Zoe, three different addresses were listed along with five separate doctors, together with the date of each change.

I started reading from the beginning.

Zoe Chadwick had been fifty-one centimetres long and had weighed 3.8 kilograms at birth. Every visit she made to a doctor was logged, along with such things as dates of immunisations and her weight at each postnatal clinic visit.

In all, Zoe had been taken to see a doctor thirteen times in her first year of life and ten times in her second. I wondered if that was common or if she was a particularly sickly child. However, at no point had her doctor indicated in the plethora of his notes that it was unusual.

Her whooping cough infection aged three and a half was

well documented as having been quite severe. There was even a record of the antibiotic drugs given to her at the time to prevent any secondary complications such as pneumonia.

Also in envelope 1 was a letter from a minor injuries unit in Cromer that had treated Zoe for a cut left foot during a holiday stay in the town when she'd been four. It stated that the wound had needed two stitches but no further treatment as Zoe's mother had confirmed that the child's tetanus vaccinations were up to date.

All very mundane, and rather boring.

I decided that, at this rate, going through every envelope from start to finish, every doctor's note, every hospital letter, was going to take me far too long.

I skimmed through the other three envelopes, looking for the notes relating to Zoe's first psychiatric hospital admission in early 2007.

They were in envelope 4, obviously shortly before the records became computerised, and there were lots of them, including several letters from both psychiatrists and psychotherapists.

Yvonne hadn't been quite right.

The initial letter had not been from a psychiatrist, as she had said to Kate, but from a professor of psychology at York University who stated that, at the request of her father, he had studied Zoe Chadwick's behaviour patterns and had concluded that she was suffering from schizophrenia and should be considered at risk of harming both herself and others.

That letter had set in motion a chain of events that

ended with Zoe being detained for assessment at Maudsley Psychiatric Hospital in Camberwell under Section 2 of the Mental Health Act 1983.

Not that the assessment had been clear and undisputed.

The letters flying back and forth between the hospital psychiatrists had been copied to her medical notes and I read through them all in chronological order.

The only thing the medics all seemed to agree on was that Zoe was suffering from some form of mental illness, whether it be schizophrenia or another type of dissociative disorder. What they had disagreed about was whether she had represented a significant danger to herself or others.

However, it was a single-sheet letter from one of the psychotherapists that was the real eye-opener.

Whereas the doctors were arguing about *what* was wrong with her, the therapists were clearly concentrating more on *why* she was ill, and one of them had reported that, in one counselling session, Zoe had claimed that she had been sexually abused throughout her childhood by both her father and her brothers.

*What?*

I read it through again twice more to ensure I hadn't misunderstood, but there it was in black and white. No mistake.

However, it seems that it was not the first time such an accusation had been made.

'As before' was written in pen across the top of the letter, presumably by her then GP, followed by a dash and a single word – 'fantasist'.

As before.

It looked like I would have to read through every one of the envelopes after all.

The detective sergeant returned as I was using my phone to photograph the psychotherapist's letter.

'How's it going?' he asked.

'Fine,' I replied. 'But still lots to do yet. I'll be here for another hour or so at least.'

'I'll leave you to it, then,' he said.

'Any chance of a coffee?' I asked.

I could almost see the mental process of whether he, too, should be complicit in helping the defence, even if it was just to fetch me a cup of coffee.

'I'll see what I can manage. Milk and sugar?'

'Just milk, thanks.'

He disappeared and, as I reached for envelope 2, Kate called.

'Hi,' she said. 'Where are you?'

'At the police station in Bury St Edmunds. Going through Zoe Chadwick's medical records.'

'Oh,' she said. 'Are you going to be long?'

I looked at my watch. It was already half past four. Where had the day gone? But, to be fair, I'd done a lot since being dropped at the hotel this morning.

'Another hour, at least,' I said. 'Why?'

'I just wondered if you'd like to meet later for a drink?'

'How about dinner?' I said. 'And why don't you ask Janie to join us?'

330

'Janie?' Kate sounded unsure.

'Yes,' I said. 'She might need cheering up. Let's go to that Chinese. I've had no lunch and I'm hungry.'

'The Fountain?'

'That's the one,' I said. 'How about seven-thirty?'

'I'll book a table,' she said, still sounding slightly tentative.

I hung up and DS Venables returned with a mug of steaming brown liquid that tasted vaguely of coffee.

'Thanks,' I said.

'I knock off at six so you'll have to be finished by then.'

'Should be fine,' I said. 'Come back just before you go.'

The sergeant hesitated for a moment but then shrugged his shoulders and left me alone again. He was clearly fighting his natural instinct to be obstructive.

I went through everything in the notes, but found no great revelations about abuse. The only possible reference was a letter to Zoe's doctor from an educational psychologist expressing concern that the outcome of the recent investigation by the Children's Welfare Department had done little to improve Zoe's state of mind or her ability to concentrate on her learning in school.

The letter was dated June 2004 when Zoe would have been fifteen.

It was in the same envelope as numerous medical reports detailing the extent of Zoe's self-harming, specifically cutting her arms and legs with razor blades or scissors. Three times the injuries had been serious enough for her parents to take her to hospital and, it seemed, there were several other occasions when a visit to the doctor was required.

I felt so sad for her.

How dreadfully disturbed she must have been to believe she had no alternative but to slice open her own skin.

What had she been seeking? Attention? Understanding? Love?

Or was it something totally different?

I remembered back to my time as a solicitor in Totnes. The daughter of a divorce client had regularly cut her arms as a way of punishing herself, believing wrongly that it was all her fault that her parents were ending their marriage.

Was Zoe also trying to punish herself?

If so, for what?

Her medical records gave no clues.

Overall, I was surprised that, considering the number of instances of self-harming, there hadn't been more referrals to specialist psychiatric care during her early teenage years.

In fact, the remainder of the notes mostly detailed only a diet of routine everyday non-emergency medical consultations, dealing with such unexciting problems as an outbreak of acne and a recurring sinus infection.

Indeed, the only other item of any interest I found was a letter signed by a Dr Andrews, director of somewhere called the Healthy Woman Centre in Bell Street, Cambridge, dated 8 August 2002. It was addressed to Dr Benaud, Zoe's then GP, and it reported that the gynaecological intervention, previously discussed on the telephone, had been successfully completed that morning and the sample sent for analysis. Strangely, there was no further indication of the problem or the outcome.

I had just finished taking photographs of anything I thought might be relevant when DS Venables returned to say it was time for me to go.

'Find anything?' he asked sardonically as we walked back along the windowless corridor.

'No,' I said.

'Could have told you that before you even started.' He laughed. 'I wasted my time doing the same thing last week.'

'But it's best to be sure,' I said, and thought about asking him about the letter from the psychotherapist. 'Did you follow anything up?'

'I did try to contact one of her past doctors about her cutting her arms and stuff, but he died three years ago.'

He didn't sound particularly bothered.

'Nothing else?' I asked.

'Nope.'

He let me out and the driver took me back to Newmarket.

The food at The Fountain was all that Janie had claimed it was, with the crispy-duck pancakes going down a real treat.

'Any news?' Kate asked. 'Did you find anything?'

'Not really,' I replied, giving her a quick 'don't go there' glance.

I didn't want to mention anything with Janie listening. I knew she was currently pretty pissed off with Ryan, but I thought she might still be loyal to Oliver. Not that that was going to stop me asking *her* some questions. That's why I'd suggested that Kate should invite her in the first place.

'Tell me more about Zoe,' I said, rolling another pancake.

'What about her?' Janie asked.

'Did she ever have a boyfriend?'

'Not that I remember. All the boys at school tended to steer well clear of her. So did most of the girls.'

'Did she ever talk to you about sex?'

She giggled. 'What about sex?'

'I thought teenage girls talk about sex all the time, just like teenage boys.'

'Of course they do. But I don't remember Zoe doing so. She was never "one of the girls" in that respect. Not in any respect, in fact. She was always so serious and anxious. I don't think I ever heard her laugh.'

'Did she talk at all about her life at home?'

'She didn't talk much about anything.'

'Do you know if she got on well with her brothers?' I asked.

'I don't recall her getting on well with anyone. She used to make things up about them all the time.'

'What sorts of things?' I asked.

'Oh, I don't know. Half the time she would praise them for being so brilliant and then she'd accuse them of being cruel towards her or the horses.'

'Did the social services ever get involved?'

'I know they did at least once,' Janie said. 'Two women turned up at school. But Zoe wouldn't help them. In fact, she accused them both of lying and trying to put her into care. That was typical of her. Just when you tried to help her, she'd go and blame you for something you hadn't done.'

'Like cutting her arms?' I said. 'Kate told me.'

'Exactly,' Janie said. 'She told a teacher I'd done it. All complete twaddle, of course, she did it to herself, but nevertheless it caused me all sorts of problems at the time. Stupid girl.'

'I'm surprised the teacher believed her,' I said.

'I don't think she really did but, you know how it is, everyone covers their own back, just in case. So the teacher simply passed on the accusation to her boss and it just spiralled out of control.'

'But it was all right in the end?'

'Yeah,' Janie said. 'Eventually. But not before I'd been given the third degree. I never trusted her again. No one did – not the kids, nor the teachers.'

'Or believed her?'

'Yeah, especially that. She used to invent stuff about people that was more and more weird. She'd accuse everyone of bullying her, which they probably did, but she'd make up awful things about them and then swear blind they were true. Mind you, she'd been doing that since primary school.'

'St Louis Roman Catholic Primary School?' I asked.

She looked at me strangely as if wondering how I knew.

'It was in the medical records,' I said, even though that was a lie. It had been in the Simpson White report. 'Was Zoe a Catholic?'

'I don't think so,' Janie said. 'But I'm not one either. Only

335

about half the kids at St Louis were, even though we all had
to go to the Catholic church for school services.'

'So was Zoe odd right from the start?'

'I can't really remember,' Janie said. 'I think so. She always
seemed to live in her own fantasy world.'

*Fantasist.*

And no one would have believed her even if some of what
she'd said had been true.


Our main courses arrived and the three of us talked about
other things for a while but, eventually, I couldn't resist
returning the conversation to the Chadwicks.

'Do you happen to know how old Ryan was when he left
home?' I asked.

'Left home?' Janie said. 'Do you mean Castleton House?'

I nodded, popping a piece of beef in black bean sauce
into my mouth.

'He was still there when I arrived,' said Janie. 'But by then
he was living in one of the flats above the old yard. The one
that burned down, in fact. He only finally moved out when
he got married.'

Eight years ago. He'd been thirty-four.

'How about Declan?' I asked.

'He'd gone before I started. But only just, I think.'

Odd, I thought, for Declan not to have flown the nest
sooner, considering the animosity between him and his
elder brother.

'Oliver's very keen to keep his boys close around him.

He's always saying that he is head of the Chadwick dynasty, one that will dictate the direction taken by horse racing for decades to come.'

'Has he been in touch with you again since this morning?' I asked.

'I've had a couple of missed calls on my mobile from the stable office number,' Janie said. 'I didn't answer them on purpose. Let them stew for a while.' She smiled at me but it wasn't the real McCoy. It didn't make it all the way to her eyes.

'You'll go back, then?' I said.

'Yeah. Probably.' She sighed. 'What else can I do?'

'I'm sure there are other stables that would love to take you on.'

'Better the devil you know,' she said.

'But make sure you ask for that raise,' Kate said.

'And compensation for hurt feelings,' I added.

We completed our dinner in happy companionship.

'Are you going home tonight?' I asked Kate as we stood up to go.

'Not unless you force me to,' she said. 'My bag's in the Mini.'

I smiled at her and she smiled back at me.

'Oh my God!' Janie said with a laugh. 'You two lovebirds. It's enough to make me vomit.'

The three of us walked out of the restaurant door onto Newmarket High Street.

'Have either of you two ever heard of a place in Cambridge called the Healthy Woman Centre?'

Both of them laughed.

'What's so funny?' I asked.

'The name,' Kate said. 'It's so misleading.'

'Why?'

'Because everyone knows that the Healthy Woman Centre is just an abortion clinic.'

# 28

I didn't sleep very well and woke on Tuesday morning with the rising of the sun at five o'clock.

My mind was simply too busy whirling facts round and round like clothes in a spin dryer. And the threads were getting just as tangled.

Newmarket in May comes alive well before six and I lay awake listening to the sounds of the morning. Kate was still sleeping soundly beside me and, being careful not to wake her, I got up and dressed.

I used a sheet of the hotel notepad to leave her a note on my pillow.

*Gone out to the gallops. Back for breakfast at 7.30.*

I walked up the Warren Hill training grounds to the very top where the tree plantation grows on the crown of the hill. I sat down on a stump and looked down on the town with the

339

huge cantilever roof of the racecourse grandstand standing out white above the houses in the far distance.

I didn't usually like early mornings but there was something rather special about being up here at this hour, before the ever-strengthening sunshine had driven away the last of the mist from the hollows.

Was it really only a week since I had first walked this same turf, getting mud all over my polished black city shoes?

So much had happened in that time but, here I was, still searching for the key to the mystery of why the seven horses had died in a stable fire.

Had it been just an attempt to cover the murder of Zoe?

Or was there another reason as well?

And why had Zoe been there in the first place?

What did Arabella know that she was afraid would all come out?

Was it to do with sexual abuse?

Had Zoe really had an abortion at age thirteen?

And, if so, who had been the father?

So many questions but precious few answers.

And there was something troubling me about what Janie had said.

I took out my smartphone and sent a text message to the research team containing a couple of requests. One was easy and the other much more difficult.

I knew that the wizards were renowned for getting into work early and leaving late, but I didn't expect the confirmation of reception reply that I received back almost immediately.

It was only five forty-five in the morning.

*They need to get a life*, I thought.

At six o'clock, I watched as the strings of horses started to appear and, each in turn, cantered up the polytrack towards me, the sound of their hooves on the ground growing louder as they approached.

And, talking about hooves, whose stupid idea had it been to lock me in a stable with the mad horse Momentum?

I considered that a real affront to my dignity. I had walked straight into a potentially disastrous situation when I was the very person that others came to in order to get them out of theirs.

I didn't particularly want that on my CV.

As ASW was always telling his operatives, we were in business to protect the reputations of our clients, but the most important reputation we needed to protect was our own and that of our company. Without that we were nothing.

I watched as a Land Rover drove up Moulton Road and parked.

*Ryan and Oliver*, I thought, but only Ryan emerged. Oliver was probably still at home trying to mollify his wife after my exposé yesterday concerning the monthly payments.

I smiled at the memory and decided it was time to insert another thunderflash.

I remained hidden by the cover of the tree line and watched as three strings of light-blue caps and red pom-poms came up the polytrack, Ryan watching them intently through his binoculars.

341

The horses made two runs each up the track and then Ryan walked back to his Land Rover and drove away. Back to Oliver's house for his coffee before second lot.

I stood up, went down the hill and back to the Bedford Lodge Hotel.

'Thought you'd deserted me again,' Kate said when I walked in.

'Never,' I replied. 'I just needed some space to think.'

'Did it help?'

'Not really.'

'You should have stayed here with me then,' she said in mild rebuke.

'Sorry,' I said. 'Fancy some breakfast?'

'To be honest,' Kate said, 'I'm still pretty full from last night's Chinese. But I could murder a coffee.'

*Murder,* I thought.

I needed to remind myself that I was dealing with someone capable of the most heinous of crimes. And he or she would probably do anything not to get caught.

In the end I skipped the coffee as well, opting instead to take a thunderflash along the Fordham Road.

Susan Chadwick opened her front door in jeans and a sweat-shirt, and with no red lipstick in evidence.

'Ryan's up at the yard,' she said.

'I know. I've come to see *you*.'

I could tell she didn't like it.

'I've got the kids here.'

'That's fine,' I said. 'Can I come in?'

'What for?' she said, standing her ground in the doorway.

Just because DCI Eastwood hadn't felt the need to push her too hard didn't preclude me from doing so.

'I want to talk to you about the film you saw on the night of the fire.'

She blushed, her neck and face swept by a crimson tide rising from below.

'What about it?' she asked, the nervousness clear in her voice.

'Good, was it?'

'Excellent.'

'Remind me of the title,' I said. 'I've already looked up to see what was playing that night.'

She stared at me in silence. She knew she was in trouble. She should have done the same research I had. She'd have made a poor spy.

'You'd better come in,' she said.

She led the way down the hall into the kitchen. Her two children were having their breakfast, the two-year-old boy in a high chair with a plate of toast in front of him, and the five-year-old girl sitting cross-legged on the floor watching the TV in the far corner, a bowl of cereal balanced on her knees.

'I'll have to take Faith to school soon,' Susan said.

'What time?'

'She has to be there by eight-fifty, at the latest.'

I looked at my watch. It was eight o'clock. As I'd planned,

it was right in the middle of second lot at the training yard. Ryan, I hoped, would again be on Warren Hill, watching his horses canter up the polytrack.

'Which school?'

'St Louis Primary. It's just down the road. We walk.'

'So we have time,' I said.

'For what?' she asked with trepidation.

'For you to tell me where you really were when the fire broke out.'

'I was at my mother's house,' she said with conviction. 'I stayed there that night.'

'But you weren't there all evening, were you?'

'I told that policeman I went to the cinema.'

'But you didn't, did you?'

'No,' she said sheepishly. 'I spent the evening with a friend.'

'Which friend?'

She blushed again, slightly darker this time but there were also tears of distress in her eyes.

'It doesn't matter which friend,' she said in annoyance. 'It has nothing to do with the fire.'

'So why did you lie to the police about the cinema?'

'Because that's what I'd told my mother. I was afraid they would check with her.'

'Didn't your mother ask which film you'd seen?'

She laughed. 'My mother wouldn't even know where the cinema is in Ely let alone what's on. She was only too happy for me to go out as she then had her grandchildren all to herself. That's what she lives for.'

'Why didn't you tell her the truth?'

'Don't be stupid.'

'Does Ryan know?'

She glanced down at her daughter but the little girl was deeply engrossed in an episode of *Peppa Pig*.

'No, of course he doesn't,' Susan said quietly. 'So don't you go and bloody tell him.'

'Then answer some more of my questions.'

She had no choice and I wondered if I, too, was being guilty of a little blackmail. But, before I had a chance to ask another question, she unburdened some of her anger.

'Do you have the slightest idea what it's like to live in the Chadwick family? Talk about controlling. Ha! The Kennedys have nothing on us. Oliver decides everything. All their lives, he's set the boys at each other's throats so that they won't gang up against *him*. He likes people to think that he's doing his best to make them all get along but, underneath, he's stirring things up as fast as he can.'

'But they do all stick together,' I said. 'They keep the family secrets.'

'Only because that's what they have been taught to do. Drilled into them from the cradle that the Chadwicks are the best, and no one should be allowed to do anything to damage the family. Family first, second and third.'

'But somebody *has* damaged the family,' I said. 'One of your number has been murdered and another has killed herself.'

'Don't be bloody daft,' she said, throwing her hands up in

frustration. 'We women don't matter. It's only the Chadwick boys that count.'

'Are you saying that Oliver is behind the fire?'

'No, I don't think so. He's been losing his grip recently. Poor Ryan is struggling with the training and Oliver is finding that difficult to cope with. And, the more Oliver interferes, the worse the situation gets.'

She glanced at the kitchen clock.

'Come on, Faith,' she said. 'Go upstairs, darling, and clean your teeth. It's almost time to go.'

Faith didn't move an inch from in front of the TV.

'Why didn't Faith go to school last Monday?'

'Because of the fire,' Susan said.

'But you didn't know about the fire when you decided to stay Sunday night at your mother's.'

'I was planning to leave Ely early enough to get back in time but, in the end, after Ryan phoned me with the news, I left both of the children with Mummy. It seemed easier.' She looked at the clock again. 'Come on, Faith.'

Again, Faith didn't move, but went on watching her programme.

'So why did Arabella kill herself?' I asked.

'She was always so bitter, mostly because she couldn't have any kids. I know she hated me just for that. Perhaps it all got too much for her.'

*It will all come out. I can't stand the shame.*

'I don't think it was that,' I said. 'There's something else. What is the big family secret that no one talks about?'

346

'Faith,' Susan shouted, ignoring me. 'Now.'

This time, reluctantly, the little girl dragged herself to her feet and, still watching the TV screen, she moved slowly towards the kitchen door. Susan, meanwhile, picked up the remote from the worktop and turned off the set. She was rewarded with a very surly look from her daughter as she departed up the stairs.

'So, what is the big family secret?' I asked again.

'There isn't one,' Susan said jokily, but I wasn't sure she believed it, even if she didn't know what it was.

'Was it to do with Zoe?' I asked.

'I didn't know Zoe at all. Never even met her. Helped search for her, mind, when she went walkabout all those years ago.'

'Why was that?' I said.

'Why was what?'

'Why *did* Zoe go missing so dramatically as soon as she was eighteen?'

'Because she was crazy,' Susan said with a smile.

Thunderflash time.

'Was it not because she was trying to get away from the ongoing sexual abuse perpetrated by her father and brothers?'

The smile on Susan's face disappeared faster than a magician's rabbit.

'Don't talk nonsense,' she said.

'Nonsense, is it?' I asked sarcastically. 'Then why don't you ask Ryan why he's been paying blackmail money to Zoe and her husband?'

Susan stared at me. 'You're making it up.'

'Am I?'

Faith came back into the kitchen and stood next to us.

'Another innocent little Chadwick girl,' I said, glancing down at her. Then I looked up at her mother. 'Don't let it happen again.'

# 29

My phone rang as I was walking back to the hotel.

'It seems your boy may be off the hook,' DCI Eastwood said when I answered. 'At least for now.'

'How come?'

'The CCTV cameras at Newmarket Station weren't operational on that day so we have no pictures from them, but we have now received some footage from an on-train camera. It shows Zoe Robertson boarding a train at Newmarket bound for Cambridge on the day she died.'

'But ...'

'I know,' he said. 'It doesn't make sense. How come she turns up dead in Newmarket when she'd already taken the train home?'

'Well, she obviously didn't get home,' I said. 'Did any cameras spot her at Cambridge?'

'The ones outside definitely didn't, but we're still searching through the tapes from those inside the station and we've extended the search to later in the day because it seems she caught the train after the one that Declan Chadwick said she did. We're also checking the CCTV from the London-bound trains, although I can't think why she would go all the way down there and then come back again.'

'Zoe Robertson did a lot stranger things than that in her life.'

'She certainly seemed to vanish. The on-board camera had quite a narrow field of view. It only showed her getting on the train, not where she sat in the carriage, or her getting off. But we'll keep looking.'

'Thanks for letting me know,' I said. 'I'll pass on the good news to Declan.'

'Did you find anything in the medical records?' the chief inspector asked.

'Your sergeant didn't agree with you letting me see them,' I said, neatly sidestepping the question. 'He thinks it's a mistake to help the defence.'

'He's very old-school,' said the DCI. 'He doesn't approve of the police graduate-entry fast-track scheme either. I may be different from most coppers but I prefer to work *with* people rather than *against* them. That way, I tend to get more help in return.'

I wondered if he was purposefully making me feel bad.

But I could hardly apprise him of my half-baked theories just yet. I would be no worse than those on social media or in the tabloid press who scatter accusations around at the slightest hint of wrongdoing, without a care in the world for the reputations they are destroying in the process.

I was in the 'reputation keeping' business, not the other way round.

Would he even believe me anyway? DS Venables must have seen the letter from the psychotherapist about abuse and he had obviously dismissed it, just as Zoe's GP had done at the time – *fantasist*.

Now, *that* was one reputation it was difficult to lose.

And I certainly wasn't going to reveal what I knew about any blackmail money because I doubted that the wizards had been acting within the law when they'd obtained copies of Peter's bank statements from the finance company.

No, the DCI would have to wait for some reaction to my thunderflashes in order to confirm my suspicions before I'd mention anything to him.

The answer to my easy request from the research team was waiting for me in my email inbox when I got back to the hotel. They reported that they were still working on the difficult one.

I called up the driver and his Mercedes, and then went into the hotel dining room to have a quick breakfast while I waited for them to arrive. I even found myself glancing through the hotel's copy of the *Racing Post*.

I wanted to check where the racing was today and whether Ryan or Declan had any runners, or Tony any rides.

Ayr, Nottingham and Chepstow were the meetings for racing on the flat, with two additional steeplechase fixtures at Hexham and Huntingdon.

I skimmed through the races looking for the name

Chadwick and found it only once. Trainer D. Chadwick had a runner in the three o'clock race at Nottingham. If he were true to form, Declan would have sent Joe, his travelling head lad, with the horse. So all the Chadwicks were likely to be at home.

I was just closing the paper when a headline on the opposite page caught my eye: 'DERBY WIDE OPEN AFTER LOSS OF PRINCE OF TROY'.

With my forty-pound wager in mind, I read the article beneath from start to finish but Orion's Glory wasn't mentioned once as being among the favourites.

Ah well, I thought, perhaps I could sneak the forty pounds through with my expenses – a necessary outlay in order to get acquainted with the system.

Or maybe not.

However, it was the last paragraph of the article that was the real interest.

Ensuring that none of the waiters were watching, I tore the piece out of the paper, folded it up and put it in my trouser pocket.

'Dullingham, please,' I said to the driver as he held the door open for me.

'The village or the station?' he replied.

'Aren't they at the same place?' I asked.

'Oh no,' he said with a smile. 'That catches lots of people out. The station is almost a mile outside the village. I know it well. My in-laws live there.'

'Well, I want Eagle Lane, number three.'

'Right you are,' he said, and off we went.

Number 3, Eagle Lane, was a small, neat, modern detached house that looked somewhat out of place, sitting as it did alongside a chocolate-box-pretty thatched cottage.

I rang the doorbell, hoping I'd been given the right address. I had.

Yvonne Chadwick opened the front door in her bedroom slippers, and she instantly recognised me.

'What do you want?' she asked gruffly.

'Is Tony in?' I asked.

'No. He's riding out in town.'

I'd hoped he was. That's why I'd chosen this time.

'Good,' I said. 'Because it's you I've come to see. I want to ask you some questions about Zoe.'

'I'm not interested,' she said, and she started to close the door again.

'Don't you want to know why your daughter died?' I said quickly.

'She died a long time ago.'

The door was almost shut and, short of putting my foot in it, I was almost out of options.

'Why did Zoe have an abortion?' I shouted through the last few inches.

The door stopped closing, and then opened a fraction.

'Who told you?' she demanded through the gap.

'Then it's true,' I said. 'You made your thirteen-year-old daughter have an abortion and yet you never reported the matter to the police. Why was that, Yvonne?'

She opened the door wide and looked nervously past me both sides to check that no one else was listening.

'You'd better come in.'

I followed her down the hallway into the kitchen. Why was it always the kitchen?

'I didn't *make* Zoe have an abortion,' Yvonne said. 'She arranged it on her own.'

'I find that difficult to believe.'

'Well, it's true. She skipped off school and went on her own to a clinic in Cambridge. And, it appears, they were under no obligation to tell either her parents or the police.'

'But she was only a child herself.'

'It doesn't matter. The stupid law says that doctors don't have to tell if a thirteen-year-old doesn't want them to. And Zoe didn't. Some guff or other to do with medical confidentiality.'

'So how *did* you find out?'

'She told me, but not till about a year later. We were having a huge row about something else and she just blurted it out. Of course, I didn't believe her, but she had some paperwork hidden in her room. She showed me. As you can imagine, I was horrified.'

'But who paid for it?' I asked.

'The taxpayer,' Yvonne said. 'Seems it was done on the NHS.'

'Did you ask her who the father was?'

'Of course I did, over and over again, but she wouldn't say. She was furious with herself for revealing anything to

354

me in the first place. She claimed that she never meant to tell anyone, ever. I expect the father was some bloody boy from school taking advantage of her.'

I looked at Yvonne closely and wondered if she really believed that, or she was just saying it for my benefit.

'Why did you say that she died a long time ago?' I asked.

'Might as well have done. I grieved for her when she first went missing. Prepared myself over those dreadful weeks for her to be found raped, strangled and dumped naked in a hedge. Then, when they found her alive in London, she refused to see or even speak to me. So I just went on thinking of her as being dead. It was easier somehow.'

'But you've seen her since?'

'Only once. She came here about five years ago with that damn husband of hers. They brought their children with them too. But I think she only did it to make me feel bad. To goad me. That and to accuse me of having had her sectioned. I told her it wasn't true but I don't think she believed me. They didn't even come in. They just drove off again.'

'But you knew where to go last week,' I said. 'I saw you at their home.'

'Tony got the address for me. From Oliver. So I went. I don't know why. It wasn't a good idea. I had to sleep on the sofa. He didn't want me there and the children didn't even know who I was.'

There were tears in her eyes.

'But why did you tell Catherine Logan that the Chadwick men had killed Zoe from a very young age?'

355

'Did I really say that?' She said it in a most unconvincing manner.

'You know you did.'

'Just that it wasn't easy for Zoe growing up with three highly competitive older brothers, plus a domineering father. Particularly as she didn't like horses.'

*There's nothing wrong with that*, I thought.

I waited for Yvonne to go on.

'Ryan was eleven when Zoe was born, Declan was nine, and I think they were jealous of their baby sister.'

'Jealous?'

'She was the apple of my eye. I'd always wanted a daughter. Perhaps I spoilt her too much. And I wasn't the older two's real mother, something they've never let me forget. They always called me Yvonne, not Mum. They still do. It's as if they somehow blame me for their own mother's death, which is nonsense, of course. She died of cancer before I even met Oliver.'

'So they transferred their resentment of you onto Zoe?'

'Yes,' she said with realisation, as if it was perhaps the first time she'd appreciated it in that way. 'That is exactly what happened.'

'How about Tony?' I said. 'Didn't he stick up for his sister?'

'I think he was influenced by his brothers. It was difficult for him.'

Another thunderflash time.

'So when did you first realise that the boys were sexually abusing her?'

A look of shock came over Yvonne's face, but it didn't quite wash. There was something about her eyes that gave her away.

'Sexual abuse?' She spat out the words as if they were somehow unclean and contaminated. 'Don't be ridiculous.'

'And Oliver was doing it too, wasn't he?'

Now the shock did reach her eyes.

'No, of course not.'

Perhaps that bit wasn't true, or maybe she just didn't know.

'But Oliver definitely knew what was happening and kept quiet about it, which is almost as bad. And you did too. Why was that, Yvonne?'

'It was our family,' she said, almost crying.

'And family always came first?'

'Of course.'

'How about Zoe?' I said. 'She was your family too and you betrayed her. What must she have thought when her parents did nothing to protect her?'

'We didn't do *nothing*,' she said indignantly. 'We spoke to them all.'

'Was that before or after you found out about the abortion?'

'Before. Long before. And Zoe was as much to blame as the boys. She would always be climbing into their beds. She'd done it ever since she was able to walk. She was simply trying to make them like her.'

Yet all they were doing was using and abusing her, taking advantage, and damaging her for life in the process.

357

'Oh no,' I said to Yvonne. 'I'll not let you absolve yourself of guilt by blaming the victim. You and Oliver were Zoe's parents. You could and should have stopped it. And Ryan is eleven years older than her. He, at least, must have known that it was wrong.'

Yvonne was visibly upset and, at this point, our discussion was interrupted by the arrival of Tony, back from riding out. He came in through the front door, slamming it shut behind him with a bang.

'Whose is that black Mercedes outside?' he called out as he walked down to the kitchen. Then he saw me. 'What the bloody hell do you want?' he asked with a high degree of aggression in his tone.

In spite of me being a good six inches taller than him, the last thing I wanted was a fight.

I knew jockeys were small but they were also strong and wiry. I was no pushover myself. I was a regular at the Neasden gym and prided myself on keeping fairly fit. Perhaps we'd be evenly matched, but I still didn't fancy putting it to the test.

'Your mother and I have been having a little chat.' I said it with a smile but it didn't seem to help, mostly because Yvonne was still clearly very distressed.

'Have you been upsetting my mother?' he asked angrily.

I felt like saying that it wasn't my doing – facing the truth had been the cause – but I thought better of it.

'So it would appear,' I said.

'What have you been saying to her?' he asked.

'You'd better ask her that.'

Yvonne now really did burst into full-blown tears.

'Get out!' Tony shouted at me, taking a step forward.

'Okay, okay,' I said, taking one back. 'I'm going.'

I edged past him without ever taking my eyes off his hands, then I walked down the hall and out of the front door, closing it behind me.

I sighed.

I had inserted all my thunderflashes.

I'd now just have to wait for any fallout from the explosions.

# 30

ASW called me as I was getting into the Mercedes.

'The research team have had only limited success with your request,' he said.

'In what way?' I asked.

'After much persuasion, the director has finally agreed to speak with you but won't promise to give you any information.'

'Well, that's a start,' I said. 'It could have been a point-blank refusal. I'll go there right now.'

'Ask for Dr Sylvester.'

'Will do. Anything else?'

'Not at present,' he said. 'How about at your end?'

'Several fuses lit,' I said.

He laughed. 'Good. Keep your tin hat on.'

We disconnected.

'Where to?' asked the driver.

'Cambridge,' I said. 'Bell Street in Cambridge.'

'Okey-dokey,' he said, and we set off.

A mile down the road we had to wait at a level crossing as the gates were closed manually in front of us by a man on foot.

'This is Dullingham Station,' said the driver. He pointed to our left. The station was, in fact, just a platform and a signal box from which the man had obviously emerged to close the gates.

'I thought all level-crossing gates were now automatic,' I said.

The driver laughed. 'Not in these parts, clearly.'

A two-carriage train passed in front of us and stopped at the platform. No one appeared to get off or on.

'Which line is this?' I asked.

'Ipswich to Cambridge,' he said. 'Runs every hour.'

The man opened the gates and we continued on our way.

Next I called Kate at work.

'Can you do me a favour if you have a minute?' I asked her.

'Of course.'

'I'd like you to ask Janie something. Better if you do it. I'm not sure she really trusts me.'

'What is it?' she asked.

I explained what I needed.

'I'll do it straight away.'

'I'd rather she didn't mention anything about it to Ryan or Oliver.'

'Not much chance of that,' Kate said. 'Ryan sent her a text this morning asking her to go back but at the same reduced rate as before. Fair to say that Janie wasn't very impressed.'

The Healthy Woman Centre in Bell Street, Cambridge, did not look like an abortion clinic, but what does one of those actually look like?

I suppose I had expected a modern, single-storey building with large windows, perhaps discreetly frosted for privacy. Instead it was a Victorian red-brick mid-terrace house with five steps up to the front door.

There was no brass plaque, nor any name at all, just a modern doorbell incorporated into a plastic intercom box that also contained a small camera, its lens staring out at me like an unblinking eye.

I pushed the bell.

'Yes?' said a tinny voice through the speaker. 'Can I help you?'

'I'm expected,' I said, facing the camera. 'My name is Harrison Foster. From Simpson White. I was told to ask for Dr Sylvester.'

'Please wait,' said the voice.

Presently, I heard a bolt being drawn back and the door was opened by a smart woman in a suit who I took to be in her late forties or early fifties.

'I'm Dr Sylvester,' she said. 'Director of the Centre. Sorry about the security measures, but there are some strange people

362

about and what we do here can be somewhat controversial. We've had the occasional protest in the past.'

She stepped to one side and allowed me in. Then she closed and rebolted the door. 'We can't be too careful. We used to have one of those remote openers but someone forced it, so now we use the bolt.'

She led me into a small meeting room and we sat down at the table.

'Now, how can I help you, Mr Foster?' she said.

'How long have you been here?' I asked.

'Me or the clinic?'

'Both.'

'I joined the team here six years ago. I was appointed as director. I'd previously worked at clinics in Liverpool and Manchester. But the centre has been here much longer. In fact, this was the first such specialist clinic outside London. The Abortion Act came into effect in April 1968 and we opened about a year after that. And a damn good thing, too. Took abortion away from the unregistered and illegal back-street abortionists, who were little more than quacks and butchers, killing women by the score.' Dr Sylvester was clearly very passionate about her work but I felt it was a speech she'd made often before.

'I'm here about Zoe Robertson, Zoe Chadwick as she was then. She had an abortion here in August 2002.'

'What about her?' the doctor asked.

'She's dead,' I said. 'You may have heard recently of a fire in some stables in Newmarket that killed several horses.'

She nodded.

'Zoe was the human victim of that fire. She'd been murdered.'

'Oh dear,' Dr Sylvester said. 'But what has that to do with us?'

'I think that having had an abortion may have a bearing on her death.'

'Are you from the police?'

She made it sound like a concern.

'No,' I replied. I gave her one of my business cards. 'I'm a solicitor and I represent Mr Declan Chadwick. He's been arrested on suspicion of killing his sister but he categorically denies any knowledge of the crime. I am trying to establish his innocence.'

'And why do you think that her former treatment here is relevant?'

'I consider that the victim's previous sexual abuse is germane to who might have committed this crime. Zoe Chadwick was just thirteen when she had the abortion, and I believe the pregnancy was a result of that abuse.'

'Are you quite sure she was treated here?'

I removed my smartphone from my pocket and showed her the photo I had taken of the letter to Dr Benaud from Dr Andrews. 'I found this in her medical records.'

Dr Sylvester took a close look at the letter.

She nodded. 'Gavin Andrews was my predecessor here as director.'

'Do you still have Zoe's notes?' I asked.

'Oh yes,' she said. 'I'm sure we do. We are required by law

to keep records of all our procedures. They will be in our storage area in the basement.'

'Can I see them?' I asked.

'The 1967 Abortion Act specifically prohibits, without the patient's express permission, the notification of a termination to anyone other than the Chief Medical Officer of the Department of Health. I take it that's not you.'

'No,' I said. 'But why, then, did Dr Andrews write to Zoe's GP informing *him*?'

She looked again at the letter.

'It does not inform him that an abortion has occurred, merely a *gynaecological intervention*.'

'But all you do here is abortions. It therefore doesn't take a rocket scientist to work out what the intervention was.'

'Maybe Miss Chadwick had given her permission for her doctor to be contacted, or maybe she had been referred here by him in the first place. I don't know. Either way, unless a patient specifically forbids it, we are customarily in touch with her GP to ensure there are no underlying medical conditions that might put the patient at risk. I tend to use email but I know that Dr Andrews liked to telephone, and clearly he must have done so in this case.'

She paused briefly and folded her arms. 'I'm sorry, Mr Foster, but you can't see the records without the patient's permission and that's final. I have to adhere to the absolute requirements of the Act, otherwise I would be putting our very existence in jeopardy.'

'But the patient is dead,' I said.

'I'm afraid that her being dead makes no difference. I am still unable to give you notification of a termination.'

'But I'm not asking you to give me notification. I already know that the termination occurred. I'm asking for any other aspects of the circumstances that might have a bearing on her murder. Surely you would want to see her killer brought to justice?'

'Of course.'

'Then will *you* look through her records and tell me if there is anything contained within them that might be useful. For example, the letter refers to a sample being sent for analysis. Is that common? What sort of analysis would that be? And do you still have the results?'

She hesitated.

'I could ask the detective chief inspector who is investigating the murder,' I said. 'I'm sure he could get a search warrant.'

Mention of potential police involvement seemed to sway the argument. Visits by the police were clearly not good for business.

'All right,' she said. 'I'll go and look through the records for you. Please wait here.'

While I was waiting for her to return, I wasted some time using my phone to look up the trains between Ipswich and Cambridge. As the driver had said, one ran every hour with alternate trains stopping at Dullingham.

Then Kate called me.

'You were right,' she said. 'Julie confirmed it. Ryan asked

her to sort it on the Friday before the fire and she made the call. But it seems that nothing was set in stone and, by Monday, it didn't matter any more.'

'Thanks,' I said.

Dr Sylvester returned with a buff folder in her hand.

'You're not the first person to ask to see these,' she said. 'There's a note on the front to say that photocopies of all the enclosed papers were made and sent out at the request of the patient.'

'When?' I asked.

She looked again at the note.

'Six years ago. Just before I arrived.'

She opened the folder and studied the top couple of sheets, being careful to hold them up so I couldn't read them too.

'All perfectly standard,' she said, closing the folder again and placing it down flat on the table. 'Nothing out of the ordinary at all. Sorry, Mr Foster, I can't help you.'

'How about the sample sent for analysis?' I asked. 'Are there any results from that?'

She reopened the folder and briefly shuffled through the papers.

'As I said, there's nothing in here that's out of the ordinary.' She was clearly determined that there shouldn't be.

I thought back to what Janie had told me about the flaming row she'd overheard between Zoe and Oliver:

*Zoe was shouting that she'd now obtained the DNA evidence to prove it.*

Was that the evidence to prove that she actually *was* his daughter or to prove something else entirely?

'Is there anything to indicate who the father was? And, in particular, was a DNA profile made of the aborted child?'

'That wouldn't be standard practice,' the doctor said. 'Blood and urine samples from the patient maybe, and only then to determine if there were any sexually transmitted infections present.'

'Can you please check again?' I said. 'This is most important and I will apply to the police to obtain a search warrant if necessary.'

She wasn't to know that I'd probably not get one.

Reluctantly, she opened the folder for a third time and studied the papers, this time taking much longer to go through absolutely everything.

'How very strange,' she said eventually, holding up one piece of paper.

'What's strange?' I asked.

'It seems there was indeed a sample taken from the foetus. That is highly irregular. Highly irregular indeed.' She shook her head. 'Maybe not even legal.'

'Who took it?' I asked.

'It must have been Dr Andrews. No one else would have had the authority.'

'What happened to the sample?' I asked.

She looked again at the paper.

'It was sent to a lab in London.'

'Which lab?' I asked.

I could tell that she didn't want to tell me but I just waited, resisting a temptation to tap my fingers impatiently on the table.

'Somewhere called the Chancery Lane Medical Laboratory,' she said eventually, reading from the paper.

'Do you use them often?' I asked.

'No,' she said. 'I've never heard of them before.'

I typed their name into my smartphone and pulled up their website.

'Specialising in forensic testing for the legal profession' was their strapline.

'Do you have the results?'

'There is nothing in here,' Dr Sylvester said holding up the folder. 'I've been through it all.'

'Would the analysis have been paid for by the health service?' I asked.

'No chance,' said the doctor. 'Lab work hardly ever is. Even nowadays, when about half of the terminations here are done on the NHS, the clients still have to pay for lab tests. And anyway, back then, *all* our procedures would have been private.'

'But Zoe Chadwick's mother told me that Zoe had organised everything herself and it was done for free under the NHS.'

'Not here.' The doctor shook her head with certainty. 'Not then.'

'So how much would it have cost?'

'In 2002? Between two and three hundred pounds.'

'So who paid for it?' I asked. 'And for the lab testing on top? Zoe wouldn't have had access to that sort of money. Is there a receipt in the folder?'

'That information wouldn't be kept in here,' she said. 'These are the medical notes only.'

'So where would it be kept?'

'In our finance department. But I doubt they'll still have the records from so long ago.'

'Let's have a look, shall we?'

I stood up to encourage her.

We walked along a corridor to an office at the rear of the building where a large middle-aged woman in a blue cardigan was sitting in front of a computer screen, tapping away on a keyboard.

'Hello, Barbara,' Dr Sylvester said. 'This gentleman would like to see some financial information from 2002. Is that possible?'

She said it in a manner that expected, and probably hoped, that the answer would be no.

Barbara drew in a breath through her teeth.

'What sort of financial information?' she asked. 'We don't normally keep any paper records beyond seven years. We don't have the space. And 2002 was before we switched over to the computers.'

'I'd like to know who paid for a certain procedure,' I said.

'How did they pay?' Barbara asked.

'I've no idea.'

She noisily sucked in air again. 'In 2002, you say?'

I nodded. 'August.'

'The only record we'd have left would be the receipt book. That's if a receipt was issued. Dr Andrews didn't always bother.'

'Perhaps I could ask him if he remembers,' I said.

'That wouldn't be possible,' Barbara said. 'Not unless you have a direct line to the hereafter. Dr Andrews died in post. Literally. Had a heart attack while sitting at his desk in the next room. He'd been here for twenty-five years but he was still only sixty-two. It was a dreadful shock for us all.'

Barbara was obviously still upset by it.

'I'm sorry,' I said. 'Shall we look in the receipt book?'

The receipt book actually turned out to be a cardboard box full of lots of receipt books stored in a cupboard behind Barbara's desk.

'What date did you say?' Barbara asked.

'August 2002.'

She shuffled through the box and lifted out one of the books. It had about fifty pages with four receipts on each. The top copy of the receipt had clearly been torn out and handed to the customer while the carbonless duplicate beneath remained.

'Name?'

'Chadwick. Zoe Chadwick.'

She scanned through the pages.

'Ah, here we are,' she said triumphantly. 'Chadwick. Two hundred and sixty pounds, received on 4th August 2002. But that's a bit odd.'

371

'What's odd,' I asked.

'Dr Andrews wrote "Do NOT inform the patient" across the bottom in bold black ink and he underlined it twice. I recognise his handwriting.'

'So who was the receipt issued to if it wasn't to the patient?' I asked.

'Mr Chadwick,' Barbara said. 'Mr Oliver Chadwick.'

# 31

Yvonne had stated that she wasn't aware until a year after the event that Zoe had had an abortion. But Oliver had known, all right. Indeed, he had paid for the procedure four days *before* it had been carried out.

*Do NOT inform the patient.*

Perhaps Zoe really had thought the termination had been carried out for free on the NHS. Maybe she also believed that it was her secret. That's what she'd implied to her mother: *She never meant to tell anyone, ever.*

Did that suggest that someone other than Zoe had told Oliver?

If so, I reckoned there were only two names in the frame – the two doctors, Andrews and Benaud.

I was once more in the Mercedes, on my way back to Newmarket.

I called Kate again.

'Hiya,' she said with happiness in her voice. 'I was just thinking of you.'

'Good,' I replied with a laugh. 'Could you do me another favour? Call Janie again and ask if she knows if Oliver knew either Dr Benaud, who was a GP in Newmarket seventeen years ago, or Dr Andrews, who used to run a clinic in Cambridge.'

'The Healthy Woman clinic?'

'Yes, but try not to tell Janie that.'

'Dr Benaud or Dr Andrews?'

'Yes. Gavin Andrews died about six years ago. And Benaud is spelt like Richie Benaud, the cricketer, with a silent "d" at the end. I don't know if he's still practising medicine or even if he's still alive.'

'I'll call Janie right now.'

'Thanks.'

Next I called ASW to bring him up to speed with what I'd found out.

He waited until I was finished before he said anything. 'So you think you know why the horses died.' He said it more as a statement than a question.

The horses, after all, were why we were retained by the Sheikh.

'Yes,' I said. 'I do.'

'And who killed them?'

'Yes. But I probably don't have the legally required evidence to prove it.'

'How about the dead girl?' he said. 'Did the same person kill her?'

'I believe so, yes.'

'So what are you going to do?'

'I'm still working on that.'

'How about the police?' ASW asked.

'They will obviously need to be involved,' I said. 'I haven't yet decided how or when. I have to get some hard evidence first. Everything is circumstantial.'

'Be careful,' he warned.

'I will,' I said ... but just how careful? I required confirmation and perhaps the only way of getting that was to make the perpetrator show a hand.

'Anything we can do this end?' ASW asked.

'Yes. Two things. First, get on to the Chancery Lane Medical Laboratory. See what you can find out about a sample sent to them from the Healthy Woman Centre in Cambridge on 8th August 2002. Specifically, did the lab do a DNA test on the sample and, if so, do they still have the results? And also did they do any other tests associated with it?'

'Other tests?' ASW asked.

'For comparison.'

'Yes, of course. Right. I'll get on to it myself straight away. What's the second thing?'

I hesitated, wondering if my other request would be a good idea after all.

'Is Denzel in the office?' I asked.

Denzel was of West Indian descent and was number 9 of the Simpson White operatives. He was our ex-special-forces man, our former Royal Marine commando, our fixer.

Denzel wasn't his real name but a nickname he'd been given in the military due to his uncanny resemblance to the actor, Denzel Washington. But our Denzel was not just a pretty face. He was six foot four inches tall with big muscles, and he knew how to use them. Hence he got results.

'Ask no questions, get told no lies' was Denzel's favourite catchphrase.

So we asked no questions.

'He certainly is,' ASW replied. 'He's kicking his heels around the office like a bear with a sore head. He's desperate to be doing something.'

'Good,' I said. 'I can use him. I don't think the laboratory is likely to play ball even if they've still got any results, so can you send Denzel off to Ealing to put the thumbscrews on Peter Robertson. I'd like to know how much he knows and, in particular, if he's aware who was the father of Zoe's aborted foetus.'

There was a slight pause from the other end as if ASW was mentally evaluating whether the possible gain of information outweighed the potential for any future legal complications.

I was not averse to attempting a touch of blackmail of my own.

'Tell Denzel to convey most fervently to Mr Robertson that I have proof of his extortion activities and, unless he gives us what we want, I will present all the evidence not

376

only to the police but also to the benefit authorities and the child-protection people. Then he'll lose both his house and his kids, as well as his liberty. However, if he helps us, I will keep it all to myself.'

'Is that possible?' ASW asked.

'I don't know,' I said. 'But I would try my best. Either way, Peter's little earner is about to come to a sudden and complete halt as the lever he is using will become public knowledge, one way or another. Either he tells us or he'll have to explain his swollen bank balance to the cops.'

'Right,' ASW said, making a firm decision. 'I'll brief Denzel and send him over there immediately, but I must stipulate that he is to refrain from using any violence, especially if there are young children about.'

*That's fine*, I thought. I knew that Denzel avoided violence unless it was absolutely necessary, say in self-defence. The threat of it was usually sufficient and anyway, in this case, there were more potent dangers to Peter's welfare than just a few bruises.

'What I'm really interested in is knowing who the father was.'

'Got it,' he said. 'I'll get back to you as soon as we have anything.'

We disconnected but my phone rang again almost immediately. I thought it was ASW calling back but it was Kate.

'Janie didn't know anything about Dr Benaud,' she said. 'But Gavin Andrews was an owner with Oliver for many years. They also used to play poker together every Tuesday evening. Janie says she remembers Oliver being quite upset when the doctor died so suddenly.'

So Oliver Chadwick and Dr Andrews had been card-playing chums.

I could just imagine the good doctor phoning up his friend to say that his thirteen-year-old daughter had turned up at the clinic asking for an abortion. And to hell with medical confidentiality. His friendship was more important.

And Oliver would have known the likely cause of the pregnancy, so he'd done what any good father would have in the circumstances: he'd paid for the termination and kept quiet about it, even from his own wife and daughter.

But he'd done more than that.

He'd asked his friend to extract a sample of the foetus and send it to a lab, almost certainly to determine the identity of the father.

What had been the outcome?

I could hazard a guess, but that was hardly hard evidence either.

I spent most of the afternoon typing up more of my report and waiting eagerly for news from Denzel in Ealing.

ASW called first to report that, as I had feared, the Chancery Lane laboratory weren't prepared to release the results of any tests except to the patient or the patient's doctor, not without a court order, and that was final.

'They wouldn't even confirm whether they still had them or not,' ASW said. 'I told them that the patient was now dead but it made no difference. In fact, if anything, that made things worse. In that case, they said, they would need an order from the coroner to release anything to anyone.'

Hopeless.

'Well, thanks for trying,' I said. 'Let's hope Denzel has more luck.'

But it wasn't until after five o'clock that he finally called me.

'Hello, Harrison, my boy,' he said in his rich deep Caribbean voice. 'Howya doing?'

He was the only one in the office who called me Harrison. It made me smile.

'Fine, Denzel, thank you,' I said. 'Tell me your news.'

'I went to see your man Peter Robertson.' He chuckled. 'He wasn't too pleased to see me, I can tell you. Tried to close the door in my face.' He sounded affronted. 'Good job I had me boots on.' He chuckled again. 'But I eventually persuaded him to allow me in.'

I didn't ask him how. Hence I got told no lies.

'And?' I asked in encouragement. 'What happened then?'

'He didn't say many nice things about you,' Denzel said with another laugh. 'That's for sure. Not when I told him what you'd said about child protection and such. Spitting, he was.' He laughed once more. 'Says he wished he'd thrown you off the walkway last Saturday afternoon. So I gently suggests that I might throw him off it instead if he doesn't answer my questions pronto.'

'And did he?' I asked.

'Not straight away, no.' He laughed again. 'So then I asks him if he knows what a mess his nice large-screen TV would make if I dropped it from four floors up, followed by the rest of his stuff. And you'll never guess what.' Another laugh, longer this time. 'He threatens to call the Old Bill. So I says, go ahead, call them. I'm sure they'll be dead keen to speak to a blackmailer.'

'Where were his kids when all this was happening?'

'In the room with us. We was talking real quiet, real low-key. The kids were engrossed watching something on TV.'

'So you didn't drop it, then?'

He laughed louder this time. 'Naah, course not. But I would have if he hadn't finally coughed up some answers.'

'What answers did he give?'

'Everything. Once he started there was no stopping him. Crying, he was, too. Sobbing. Said he missed his wife some-thing rotten. Devoted to her, he said, in spite of her problems. Wished they'd never ever discovered about the bloody DNA test. Zoe was getting better until then, he said. Afterwards things went downhill again, and badly.'

'How did they discover about the test?'

'Seems she registered with a new doctor and he said something to her about the medical records having arrived safely from her former surgery. So she asked to see them, apparently on a whim. No proper reason. Just because she could. But she found something in them that led her to apply for more notes from that clinic you went to. And that led to the testing lab.'

Simple as that. Exactly the same route as me.

Be careful what you wish for.

Except she had obviously managed to get her results from the Chancery Lane Medical Laboratory, whereas I hadn't.

'So the lab did do a DNA test on the sample sent from Cambridge?'

'Yes. Indeed they did,' Denzel said. 'And they sent the profile to Zoe as the patient.'

And now for the million-dollar question.

'So who *was* the father?'

'That's the strangest thing,' Denzel said. 'Peter says he still doesn't know, and I believe him.'

'What? Why not?'

'Because, even though he has the profile for the foetus, he has nothing to compare it with.'

Hence, I thought, he was blackmailing all the Chadwick sons, because they didn't know either.

But Oliver knew. Of that I was certain.

There would have been no point in him going to all that trouble to obtain the DNA of the aborted foetus unless he had also acquired samples from the boys for comparison. Maybe he'd simply taken hair from their hairbrushes, or some saliva from a glass.

He'd have known all about how and where to obtain a DNA profile from his work with horses.

'Is there anything else?' I asked Denzel.

'Nope,' he said. 'Other than the fact that Peter says that

one of the Chadwick wives knew what had gone on in the past. Seems she'd been here last year and Zoe had told her.'

*Arabella*, I thought.

And she had killed herself, not because she believed her husband was guilty of murder, but because he was guilty of incest – something she had been told by Zoe but chose not to report. And she had remained married to him in spite of that knowledge, and everyone would now know it. That was the shame she couldn't bear. Plus the fact that, due to her keeping quiet, Zoe had ended up dead.

Kate came to the hotel after her work as I was busy looking up some things on the internet.

We sat at one of the garden tables in the warm late-afternoon sunshine, having first a cup of tea, quickly followed by a glass each of chilled white wine.

'So, have you solved the mystery?' she asked.

'I may have,' I said.

She rubbed her hands together excitedly. 'Do tell.'

I looked around us. There were people at some of the other garden tables.

'Not here,' I said. 'Later. In private.'

She seemed disappointed and leaned closer towards me.

'Just speak quietly. No one else will hear.'

But before I could say anything, my phone rang. It was Declan and he was in something of a panic.

'Harry,' he said. 'We've had a bit of a disaster. One of the Sheikh's fillies has got cast in her box.'

'Cast?'

'Stuck down with its legs under it and jammed into the base of the wall. It's rare but it happens sometimes. Just one of those things.'

'So what's the disaster?' I asked.

'Horses tend to panic and they lash out with any leg they can still move. The filly has done this and I fear she's broken her fetlock.'

'How bad is that?'

'It could be terminal,' he said. 'I've sent for the vet and put the knacker on standby.'

Just what the Sheikh didn't need after two deaths already.

'Could you come and see?' Declan said.

'Do I have to?' I asked.

'I think so, yes,' he said. 'It will have to be your decision to put her down or not.'

'Won't the vet decide?'

'Maybe, but I'd prefer it if you were here to listen to what he has to say. He may be able to set the fetlock and put it in plaster. Even if she couldn't race, she could still be a brood mare in time. Her breeding's not bad.'

'All right,' I said reluctantly. 'I'll be there shortly.'

'Thanks.'

He hung up.

'Problems?' Kate said.

'One of the Sheikh's horses has got cast in its box and has apparently broken a fetlock.'

383

I wasn't quite sure what a fetlock was but it had to be somewhere on its leg.

'Oh dear,' Kate said. 'That's awful. It happened to a young colt in one of our boxes a couple of years ago.'

'What happened to it?' I asked.

'It had to be euthanised. We were all very upset in the office.'

'I'd better get on over to Declan's. Will you wait for me here?'

'Can't I come with you?'

'No.' I said it rather more sharply than I had meant to.

'Why not?' she sounded pained.

'I don't want it to upset you again if the horse has to be put down.'

'Well, at least let me drive you there,' she said. 'I'll wait outside in the car.'

I smiled at her. 'That would be great. I'll just get my jacket. I'd better be smart if I'm representing Sheikh Karim.'

Kate drove me round to Hamilton Road in her Mini.

'It'll soon be warm enough to have the top down,' Kate said. 'I love the summer.'

'Park on the road,' I said.

Kate looked at me.

'I'll walk through to the yard.'

Kate pulled up near the yard entrance and I climbed out of the Mini but leaned down to talk to her through the open window.

'Stay here,' I said. 'Lock the car doors and don't come in

under any circumstances. If I'm not back in thirty minutes, call the police.'

She suddenly looked very frightened. 'Why?'

I smiled at her. 'Just a precaution,' I said. 'Last time I went into a Chadwick yard I ended up being shut in a stable with a mad horse. I'm not keen on repeating the performance.'

'Then don't go in,' she said with a degree of panic in her voice.

'I'm sure it'll be fine,' I said.

She wasn't much reassured.

'Please let me come with you.' She was pleading now.

'No,' I said resolutely. 'Promise me you will stay right here.'

She said nothing.

'Promise me,' I said again, quite sternly.

'All right,' she replied. 'I promise, but I don't like it.'

'I won't be long. Back before you know it.' I smiled at her again but she was far too worried to smile back.

I walked in through the yard entrance but, as another precaution, I dialled DCI Eastwood's mobile number. He answered at the second ring.

'Hello, Chief Inspector,' I said. 'I may have some information that might be helpful to you in the case.'

'What sort of information?' he asked.

'I'd rather not talk about it at the moment. I'm just arriving at Declan Chadwick's stable yard. He tells me that one of Sheikh Karim's horses has been injured and might need to be put down.'

'I'm sorry,' he said.

'But if you hold on I could speak to you later.'

I explained what I wanted.

'Fine,' he said. 'I'll be here.'

I put my phone carefully into the breast pocket of my jacket and walked into the yard.

Declan was waiting for me.

'Ah, there you are, Harry,' he said. 'This way.'

He walked off and I followed.

'Is the vet here?' I asked.

'Not yet. He's on his way. I've left one of the lads with the horse.'

I looked around. Everywhere was quiet.

'Have evening stables finished?' I asked.

'Always done by six o'clock. Impossible to get staff to stay any later these days. But I go around again after, just to check.'

'To make sure none are down and cast?' I asked.

He glanced at me. 'Exactly.'

We walked on.

'Oh, by the way,' I said. 'I have some good news for you. The police tell me that they have CCTV footage of Zoe catching the train at Newmarket on Sunday afternoon.'

'That *is* good news,' Declan said. 'I told you so.'

We came to one of the stables where the door was wide open.

'In here,' Declan said, standing to one side to allow me to go in first.

There was no mad horse waiting for me inside. Indeed, there was no horse at all, nor any of the stable lads.

Only the Chadwick men, en masse.

Oliver, Ryan and Tony, with Declan coming in behind me and pulling the door shut.

'What's this?' I said with a laugh. 'Gunfight at the OK Corral?'

None of the four laughed back.

# 32

They all seemed quite pleased with themselves that I had walked so tamely into their little trap.

'I was brought here by a friend,' I said. 'She's waiting for me. The police are also aware that I'm here. It might be difficult to explain away another dead body found in a Chadwick stable. Even if you do set it on fire.'

'Dead body?' Oliver said. 'But we're not here to kill you.'

'Then why are you here?' I asked crossly, going on the offensive. 'I've been lied to. Again. Why is that, Declan? Why did you string me some cock-and-bull story about a horse breaking a fetlock? You, of all people.'

'We didn't think you'd come otherwise.'

'All right,' I said. 'So I'm here now. What the hell do you want?'

There was a slight pause as if they hadn't expected me to be so forthright.

It was Oliver who broke the silence. 'We want you to leave Newmarket tonight and never come back.'

I stared at him.

'Well, that isn't going to happen.'

'I told you talking to him would be no good,' Ryan said.

'So what *did* you say, Ryan?' I asked. 'Perhaps you thought it would be better to break my nose, like you did to Declan.'

'Shut up,' Ryan said, taking a stride towards me. And, for the first time, I noticed he was holding something, a riding whip that he now pointed straight at me. Perhaps it wasn't my nose that he was after, but he was wrong if he thought that the threat of being whipped would stop me.

'No, I won't shut up,' I said. 'All four of you spend far too much of your time shutting up about everything. Not one of you ever mentions or confronts the big Chadwick family secret, so I'll do it for you.'

I paused and looked around at them. What a complete mess.

'Where shall I start?' I said. 'The sexual abuse of Zoe or her abortion?'

They said nothing. They just looked at each other, and then at me with hate in their eyes.

'Come now, gentlemen,' I said. 'Let's not try and fool me that you don't know anything about it. Why then have you all been paying Zoe blackmail money?'

It was Ryan who broke their silence first.

He took two more steps towards me. 'I don't have to listen to this claptrap any longer.'

'Truth hurts, does it, Ryan?' I said. 'Then show me your bank statements to prove you've not been paying.'

He knew he couldn't. He lifted the whip high as if to strike.

'Go on,' I said to him. 'I'm sure the police can add assault to your charge list.'

'How much do you want?' It was Oliver's voice that cut through the tension of the moment.

Ryan lowered his arm and relaxed.

So did I.

'What do you mean?' I said.

'How much do you want?' Oliver repeated. 'It must be money you're after.'

I almost laughed. 'No,' I said. 'No money. It's justice I want. Justice for your daughter. And for Sheikh Karim.'

*But mostly for Zoe*, I thought. I'd never known her but, over the last week, I had developed a degree of empathy towards her. She'd never had a chance to grow up as a normal, carefree child. These four men had used and abused her, damaged and rejected her. And then one of them had killed her.

'Everyone has their price,' Oliver said confidently. 'What's yours?'

'You couldn't afford it,' I said.

'Try me,' he said.

He was serious. He still thought he could buy his way out of trouble.

'Don't pay him anything,' Tony said. 'He knows nothing. He's only bluffing.'

I turned to face him.

'Am I, Tony?' I said. 'Bluffing about what? What is it I don't know?'

'You know nothing,' he said.

'I know that you were paying Zoe blackmail money too, as was Declan and your father.'

'It wasn't blackmail money,' Tony said. 'I was just helping to support my sister and her kids. There's no law against that.'

The others nodded their agreement. They were beginning to regain their confidence. Together they were strong. What I needed to do was to get them arguing among themselves.

It was Ryan who was most volatile. He was the one I had to needle.

'So tell me, Ryan,' I said, 'why *did* you break Declan's nose in a Doncaster hotel? What were you arguing about? Did it concern Zoe? Was Declan telling you that, as the eldest, you should have known better?'

'Shut up,' he shouted at me again, this time with perhaps more anxiety.

I turned towards Declan. 'What was it you said to him? What was so bad that your own brother punched you full in the face and broke your nose?'

'None of your business,' he said.

'Ah, but it is my business. By luring me here today, you've made it my business, to say nothing of shutting me in a stable with a mad horse.'

'I didn't do that,' Declan said vehemently.

'Someone did.'

'Shame the bloody horse didn't kill you,' Ryan said.

Something about the way he said it, with arrogance, even pride at the idea, made me realise that it had been Ryan, not Oliver, who'd been responsible for that little episode. Instinctively, my hand went up to the stitches in my right ear. I owed him for that.

'Did you expect it to frighten me off?' I asked.

'No,' Ryan said with a laugh. 'I expected you to die.'

'So we can add attempted murder to the list. You're going away for a long time, Ryan.'

He laughed again and shook his head. 'You don't know when to give up, do you? You're nothing more than a buzzing mosquito that needs swatting. Admit it, you have nothing on any of us.' He looked around at his father and brothers. 'So crawl away into a hole, you subordinate little worm, and let us get on with our lives.'

His self-assurance was clearly growing by the second. It was time for me to try and deflate it.

'You seem to be forgetting that I represent Sheikh Karim.'

'I don't care if you represent the Queen of Sheba,' Ryan said angrily.

I was seriously losing the initiative here. I needed some sibling conflict.

It was time for me to play my own trump card.

I looked around at the three sons.

'Didn't your father ever tell you who was the father of Zoe's unborn child?'

'Is this more of your nonsense?' Tony said.

'It's not nonsense, is it, Oliver?'

'I don't know what you're talking about,' he said, but there was a nervous quiver in his voice that all of us heard, and the skin on his face had gone rather sweaty and pale.

'Does the Chancery Lane Medical Laboratory mean anything to you?' I asked him.

If anything, his face went a shade paler.

The three boys were now looking at their father rather than me.

'Didn't he tell you?' I said. 'Your father arranged with his friend Dr Gavin Andrews to have a biopsy taken from the aborted foetus and sent to a laboratory for analysis. For a DNA profile to be obtained. Then he compared it to each of your DNA. He's known for sixteen years which one of you impregnated Zoe.'

The sons went on staring at Oliver.

'Zoe herself didn't know,' I went on. 'Six years ago she found out about the biopsy and she managed to obtain the DNA profile of the foetus, but she still didn't know which of you was responsible. So she blackmailed you all, threatening to reveal the profile to the press unless you paid up. You knew that if the profile became public it would lead to irresistible pressure for your own DNA to be analysed and compared. So you paid. Regularly, every month. So did your father, to keep the Chadwick name away from a scandal.'

The four of them were now all looking at me.

'But your father knew the culprit all along. Not that the actual sire of the foetus was any worse than either of the

393

other two. The fact that each of you didn't know for certain that it couldn't be you is indication enough of what had been going on.'

I paused briefly for that to sink in.

'Zoe was just thirteen,' I said. 'Ryan, you were twenty-six. Declan, you were twenty-four. You two, at least, should have known it was wrong? You even fought over the affections of your young half-sister.'

'That wasn't the reason,' Declan said.

'Shut up,' Ryan shouted at him.

'What was it then?' I asked. 'What was so shameful that your wife would rather kill herself than live with the stigma of it becoming known?'

'But wasn't that because Declan had been arrested for murder?' Oliver said.

'No, it wasn't, was it Declan?' I said. 'Murder she could cope with. Arabella killed herself because she knew that all of this would come out, and she couldn't stand the shame of being married to a man who had made his own sister pregnant when he couldn't do the same to her.'

'But it wasn't me,' Declan said resolutely. 'It couldn't have been. I was riding for a year in America when I was twenty-four.'

'Did Arabella know that?' I asked.

From Declan's demeanour it was clear that she hadn't. But, I suppose, a husband's former incest is not the most obvious topic of discussion with his wife over the breakfast table.

'So, if you knew it couldn't be you, why did you pay?'

Declan remained silent but we all knew the answer anyway – it was because he believed he was just as guilty of incest as the others, whether he'd fathered the foetus or not. And he was right.

'Hence, in that Doncaster hotel, you accused Ryan of being the father,' I said. 'And he broke your nose for your trouble. And you didn't press assault charges because you were afraid that a court would demand to know what you'd been arguing about in the first place.'

Declan stood with his head bent down, his body language screaming that it was true, but Ryan was having none of that.

'That's a damned lie,' he shouted.

'So why *did* you hit him?' I asked.

He stared at me. He had no answer.

'But Ryan wasn't the father,' Oliver said quietly into the silence.

Ryan, the wonder boy who could do no wrong in Oliver's eyes.

No, of course it wasn't him.

We all looked at Chadwick senior but he said nothing more.

So the eyes slowly turned towards Tony.

'Oh no,' he said defensively, taking a pace backwards. 'You're not pinning this on me.'

'Why not?' I said. 'The police have the profiles of Declan and Ryan. They're on the UK national DNA database because they've both been subject to arrest. The profile from the lab doesn't match either of them, so it has to be you.'

Now I really was bluffing, but he didn't know that.

'How about I take a DNA sample from you now for comparison?' I said. 'A hair from your head will do.'

I reached out towards him but he cowered away from me.

'Come on, Tony,' I said. 'Give me a hair. Your DNA could exonerate you.'

'It won't,' Oliver said drily.

We all resumed our staring at him.

He had kept that knowledge secret for almost sixteen years, refusing to reveal the truth while it slowly ate a hole through his brain like the hungry caterpillar. And now it was out.

Not that it was a surprise to me.

I'd reckoned for some time that it *had* to be Tony.

The one of Oliver's three sons that he spent the whole time criticising.

I remembered back to the times Oliver had spoken to me about him.

For example, when we'd watched the race at Windsor on my first night in Newmarket: *Tony has never reached his full potential due to his lack of concentration. Not like Ryan. Ryan would have won that easily. Declan would have too.*

Or at Newmarket races last Friday when Tony had reported that Momentum had nothing left in the tank: *Nonsense. You just didn't ride him well enough.*

Tony, the jockey that Oliver had wanted taken off Prince of Troy in the Derby: *That steep run downhill into Tattenham Corner is the most testing stretch of racetrack on the planet. Needs someone with more bloody nous than Tony. Ryan, now, he was a master at it.*

396

Tony, the son that Oliver had continuously belittled for sixteen years because he'd known all along that he had impregnated his own sister.

But Oliver hadn't reported it to the authorities.

Oh no. Instead, he'd covered it up and kept his sons close to him, controlling them, but, in doing so, he'd sacrificed his daughter, consigning her to a life of drugs and depression, hospitals and hopelessness.

However, I wasn't finished yet.

We knew now who had fathered the foetus, but who had killed its mother?

'What were you doing on the Sunday before the fire?' I asked Oliver. 'Specifically between half past three and six o'clock on Sunday afternoon.'

'I can't remember,' he replied immediately.

'Come now, Oliver,' I said to him. 'You can do better than that. The police must have asked you the same thing.'

'I was at home,' he said.

'Doing what?'

'I don't know,' he said with irritation. 'Sunday is my day of rest. Probably slumped in front of the TV.'

'What were you watching?'

He was getting quite agitated. 'What does it matter what I was watching?'

'Because I contend that you were not watching anything. You were arguing with Zoe in your snug.'

'Don't be ridiculous,' he said.

'That's why you were so shocked when she turned out to

be the body in the stable. You were afraid the police would find out she'd been here and accuse you of killing her.'

'But I was with Maria,' he stated authoritatively.

'No you weren't. Maria was upstairs in bed with a migraine, doped up to the eyeballs with a combination of hefty painkillers and white wine. She heard arguing from below and mistakenly thought it was you watching *EastEnders* on the television. But it wasn't that, was it, Oliver? It was you and Zoe.'

'But I dropped her at the station,' Declan said. 'You told me yourself that she caught the train.'

'Yes,' I said. 'She did, but not the four o'clock train, as you thought she would. She caught the next one. And, in the meantime, she walked up to Castleton House Stables to see your father, to demand to know which of her brothers had actually made her pregnant. And you told her, didn't you, Oliver?'

'But I didn't kill her,' Oliver said with a touch of panic in his voice.

'I know that,' I said. 'Because Tony did.'

# 33

There was a shocked silence.

'What rubbish,' Tony said eventually. 'What evidence have you got for such a wild accusation?'

*None,* I thought. At least, none that would stand up in court. But that wasn't going to stop me.

'Zoe came to see you on that Sunday afternoon, didn't she?' I said.

Tony said nothing.

'Maybe she was looking for her mother, but Yvonne was staying with her sister in Ipswich, so it was you who answered the door.'

'But she caught the train to Cambridge,' Declan said.

'Indeed, she did. But she didn't get there, did she, Tony? The CCTV at Cambridge Station showed no sign of her and that's because she got off at Dullingham, the only stop between Newmarket and Cambridge. From there she walked to Yvonne's house. Isn't that right, Tony?'

Tony was beginning to sweat.

'What happened then, Tony?' I asked. 'Did she tell you that you were the father of her aborted child? Is that why you killed her? To keep it quiet?'

He sweated some more.

'And then you took Zoe's body to Castleton House Stables and set the place on fire to try to hide what you'd done.'

'It's not true,' Tony shouted. 'I don't have to listen to this.'

He started to walk towards the door but Ryan stepped across in front of him.

'Not so fast,' he said. 'I want to hear what you have to say.'

But Tony said nothing.

'Did you kill the horses?' Oliver asked.

'Of course not,' Tony protested. 'Why would I do that when I was due to ride Prince of Troy in the Derby?'

'But you weren't,' I said.

I put my hand into my trouser pocket and pulled out the piece I had torn out of the newspaper at breakfast, the piece with its 'DERBY WIDE OPEN . . .' headline.

'Have you seen today's *Racing Post*?'

I held it up so I could read, out loud, the last paragraph.

'Champion jockey, Simon Varney, says he is still looking for a Derby ride after being previously engaged by Ryan Chadwick to ride Prince of Troy in the big race.'

'Is that true, Ryan?' Oliver asked. 'Why the hell didn't you tell me?'

Ryan waved a dismissive hand as if to indicate that he'd been exercising *his* authority as the holder of the trainer's licence, rather than referring every decision to his domineering father.

'It *is* true, isn't it, Ryan?' I said. 'Oliver kept going on to you about how Tony wasn't up to riding the horse on the undulating track at Epsom, and you finally succumbed to the pressure to remove him. Janie Logan has confirmed it. You asked her to call Simon Varney on the Friday before the fire to confidentially offer him the ride on Prince of Troy in the Derby. And he accepted.'

I paused.

'Ryan never told you, did he, Tony? He was probably worried about your reaction. And by the Monday it didn't matter anymore – no one was going to ride Prince of Troy ever again. But you knew anyway, didn't you, Tony? Because you and Simon Varney were riding together on the Saturday afternoon, sharing the same jockeys' changing room at Ascot. I checked on the internet.'

I paused again.

'Did Simon Varney ask you for advice on how to ride the horse? Or did he just gloat?'

Tony said nothing.

'So you decided to get rid of Zoe's body, and to take your revenge on your brother and father at the same time, by setting fire to Prince of Troy's stable.'

*Now who was the fucking idiot*, I thought.

'You bastard,' Ryan said with feeling. 'How *could* you have come into the house on the morning after the fire expressing your sorrow when, all along, it had been you that had started it?'

401

Tony just hung his head in shame.

'Why did you kill Zoe?' I asked.

He lifted his head a fraction and looked at me.

'I didn't mean to. She wouldn't shut up. Kept going on and on at me about having to pay more or she'd go to the newspapers and destroy my career. I grabbed her by the throat to stop her and, before I knew it, she was dead.'

He started crying. Maybe for his career that would be destroyed now anyway, along with his life.

'But why the horses?' Oliver asked, the pain of their loss clearly greater in his voice than his grief for a dead daughter.

'I panicked,' Tony said. 'I didn't mean for them all to die.'

'Just Prince of Troy?' I said.

He nodded. 'The fire took hold so fast.'

*All that shredded paper bedding*, I thought.

The five of us stood there like a silent tableau at the end of a play.

I reached carefully into my breast pocket for my phone.

'Are you still there?' I asked.

'I certainly am,' said DCI Eastwood.

'Did you hear?'

'Every word,' he said. 'Recorded it too. My sergeant's already on his way.'

# 34

Eleven days later I took Kate to the Derby.

With uncharacteristic generosity, ASW had laid on a car and driver for us in spite of the fact that I wasn't actually working.

The news of my success at solving the mystery of the dead horses, to say nothing of the dead human, had spread fast through the company and I was now regularly referred to by Georgina as her very own Hercule Poirot.

Tony had been taken away from Declan's yard in handcuffs by DS Venables, and he was now languishing in Norwich Prison on remand.

Even after Tony's revelations and removal, the remaining Chadwick men had continued to argue among themselves, pointing the blame at each other as well as at Tony.

'You should never have spoken to Simon Varney without discussing it with me first,' Oliver had yelled at Ryan, as if that was what had been the tipping point in making Tony set the place on fire.

But Ryan had clearly had enough of being subservient to his father.

'Don't *you* tell *me* what I should or shouldn't do,' he had shouted back. 'You do nothing but interfere all the time. Why don't you and your bloody floozy piss off and live somewhere else? Let me get on with training the horses how *I* want to.'

Oliver had been visibly hurt by Ryan's attack but, if he'd thought he would receive any solace from his second son, he was much mistaken.

Somewhat irrationally, Declan blamed him fair and square for Arabella's death, maintaining that she would have still been alive if only he had told the authorities years ago that Tony was the father of the aborted foetus.

'I never want to see either of you again in my life,' Declan had declared, before walking out of the stable in tears.

The shameful secret that Oliver had exploited to hold his family together under his close personal control had ended up being the very reason they were torn apart.

Gone were the days when the Derby festival went on for a whole week, with hundreds of thousands of Londoners descending on the Surrey racecourse to drink, gamble and party; when even the sittings of Parliament were suspended so that members could attend the race.

But, on this particular day, the June sunshine had

encouraged another huge crowd to make its way to Epsom Downs by car, train and bus, many intent on enjoying the alcohol-fuelled carnival atmosphere in the centre of the course, where the bars and funfair had been open from early morning, and would remain so until well after dark.

Kate and I, however, were in the posh seats as guests of Sheikh Karim. Hence, we were dressed to the nines, me in a morning suit, complete with fancy waistcoat and top hat, and Kate in what she reliably informed me was called an asymmetric summer dress, a stunning off-one-shoulder creation in light-blue chiffon silk with a pink floral print. To top it off, she wore a blue feathery fascinator and pink high-heeled shoes, and carried a matching pink clutch bag.

'You look absolutely stunning,' I said to her as we had our tickets scanned at the racecourse entrance.

'You're not so bad yourself,' she said. 'Is it hired?'

'Bloody cheek,' I replied with a laugh. 'Of course it's hired. Moss Bros' best.'

Kate had stayed the previous night with me at my flat in Neasden, having caught the train from Cambridge on Friday evening after her day's work at Tattersalls. And I had gone to King's Cross Station to meet her, not wanting to be apart from her for a second longer than was necessary.

I had spent the last week in a far more mundane manner than I had the previous fortnight at Newmarket.

Monday had been idled away at Westminster Magistrates' Court on the Marylebone Road, when I should have been in the office completing my report.

I'd represented a pair of idiotic eighteen-year-old professional footballers who'd been caught sniffing cocaine in the gents' toilet of a West End nightclub late on Saturday night. They had then compounded their difficulty by initially giving the police false names and addresses.

Simpson White had been engaged by their club to keep the incident as low-key as possible, the two boys being members of the youth squad rather than the first team, and it was after the end of the football season.

By using a spurious pretext that one of my clients was unwell, I had managed to persuade the clerk to move their hearing to the end of the day in the hope that any journalists lurking would have given up waiting and gone home.

The case itself had taken precisely four minutes as the pair pleaded guilty to possession of a Class A drug, were each fined a hundred pounds, and warned by the magistrate as to their future conduct.

At first, the two had laughed and joked outside the court about how they had got off so lightly, but that was only until the representative of the club had informed them that their lucrative playing contracts were being cancelled.

I'd initially felt sorry for them, but one's actions always have consequences, and maybe the sooner one learns that, the better. The Chadwicks were a good example of how unacceptable behaviour going unpunished for so long had made them feel invincible. And the fallout had been much heavier as a result.

The rest of my time had been taken up with dealing with

a national hamburger chain, the directors of which had failed simply to put their hands up and apologise when a member of their staff had refused access to a disabled customer. Instead, they had tried to make the excuse that the man had been excluded not because he was in a wheelchair, but because he'd been rude. However, as seemed always the case these days, mobile-phone footage had soon appeared on social media showing that it had actually been the staff member who'd been rude, and the subsequent PR disaster was threatening to bring down the whole business.

Interesting work it may have been, but it was nowhere near as exciting as solving a murder.

Kate and I had arrived at the racecourse good and early, not only to enjoy the build-up to the big race, but also for lunch with our host in a private box on the fifth floor of the Queen's Stand, two levels up even from the Royal Box itself.

The Sheikh had secured use of the box in the expectation of personally witnessing Prince of Troy's sprint to victory, and he had decided to come to the day anyway, not least because he wanted to hear, first-hand, my account of the curious events in Newmarket.

'Harrison, my friend,' the Sheikh said, greeting me warmly with a firm handshake at the box door. 'Come in, come in.'

I introduced him to Kate. He smiled at her and raised his eyebrows in approval at me.

There were several other guests but the Sheikh arranged that I was sitting next to him for lunch.

'Tell me,' he said.

So I did. Quietly. Everything from start to finish, leaving nothing out.

He pursed his lips in disapproval.

'I am sorry, sir,' I said. 'I don't wish to be the bearer of distressing news.'

He asked for my advice concerning his horses, so I told him to move them from Ryan but not to send them to Declan. Not yet, anyway.

'Why not?' he asked.

'Because,' I replied, 'there's an old Arab saying that a camel hit with a stick too often may turn nasty, and strike back.'

He roared with laughter and slapped me on the shoulder.

Kate and I viewed the first three races from the balcony at the front of the Sheikh's box but, for the fourth, we went down to see the horses in the parade ring behind the stands.

The Derby was the fifth race of the day and we could almost taste the tension in the air as start time neared.

The connections of the victorious horse would take home almost a cool million pounds in prize money but, in spite of that, it was far from being the richest race in the world. In fact, it didn't even make the top ten. But the prestige of winning the Epsom Derby was more valuable, to say nothing of the potential future stud value of the horse.

We watched the fourth race on a large-screen TV near the weighing room before walking over towards the saddling boxes on the far side of the paddock.

It was Declan's travelling head lad that I saw first, standing next to the horse in the box second from the end.

'Hi, Joe,' I said.

He did a bit of a double take but then he recognised me under the top hat. He grunted a greeting of sorts. The horse was already saddled and looked ready to go, with a stable lad standing patiently holding his head.

'Where's Declan?' I asked.

'Just had to rush to the khazi,' he said. 'He's that nervous.'

'How's the horse?'

'Never better,' Joe said. 'Raring to go.'

At that point Declan returned but he didn't seem very pleased to see me, almost as if he was embarrassed. As well he might be.

He did a quick final check that everything was in order, then he sent the horse off into the paddock with Joe and the stable lad both leading, but on opposite sides. They were clearly taking no chances.

'I got a letter from Suffolk Police,' Declan said to me.

'Yes, I know,' I said. As his lawyer, I'd received a copy. It had stated that he was no longer 'under investigation' for the murder of Zoe, but that the police were continuing to conduct inquiries into the possible historical sexual abuse of a minor.

'I was only a kid,' Declan said softly but earnestly, pulling me to one side. 'As soon as I was old enough to realise it was wrong, I stopped. Ryan and I fought about it. It was all him. He used to laugh at me and tell me not to be so bloody self-righteous. And then, when Tony became mature enough, it was Ryan who encouraged him to join in. That's why I went to America. To get away from what was happening.'

Perhaps he should have taken his sister with him, I thought, or at least told someone in authority.

'Are you going to win this?' I asked, changing the subject.

'Oh God, I hope so,' he replied, the nervousness clear in his voice.

'Good luck,' I said. I was quite nervous too.

Kate and I went back up.

In the lift, I spotted some familiar faces – Mike and Michelle Morris.

'How's Momentum?' I asked, subconsciously moving a hand up to the scab that still existed on my right ear.

'Oh, hello ...' Michelle said, clearly not remembering my name.

'Harry,' I said. 'And this is Kate.'

Hands were shaken all round.

'Momentum's fine,' Mike said. 'We've moved him to a new trainer but he's as lively as ever. He runs next week at Yarmouth.'

'And he's still got his balls,' Michelle added with a grin.

The lift doors opened at the fourth floor.

'This is us,' Mike said, stepping out with Michelle. 'Bye, Harry.'

'Bye,' I responded as the doors closed.

'Who are they?' Kate asked as the lift again began to move.

'I met them at Newmarket races,' I said. 'They're the owners of that crazy horse I was shut in with at Castleton House Stables.'

Kate was shocked. 'But they seem so nice.'

I laughed. 'It wasn't them that tried to kill me, only their horse.'

'Even so ...'

The lift arrived at the fifth floor and we went into the Sheikh's box and out onto the balcony to watch the race.

The crowd was, by now, almost at fever pitch and was further galvanised by a fanfare from six scarlet-uniformed trumpeters as the eighteen contenders came out onto the track for a parade in front of the stands.

'Isn't it fabulous?' Kate said, gripping my hand tightly.

'Certainly is,' I agreed.

The big screen in front of the stands flashed up the current odds for the race. Orion's Glory was quoted as the sixth favourite at sixteen-to-one. One more time I reached into my pocket to check I still had my slip from Ladbrokes at fifties.

The runners made their way across to the far side of the track, away to our right, to the waiting starting stalls.

'Loading,' announced the race commentator, further cranking up the anticipation. And then a huge cheer greeted his call of 'They're off!'

The Epsom Derby is run over a distance of a mile and a half.

For the first five furlongs the horses climb steadily to the highest point of the course before swinging left-handed and steeply downhill towards Tattenham Corner. As Oliver had said, the most testing stretch of racetrack on the planet.

The horses were well bunched in the early stages, the white cap of Orion's Glory's rider clearly visible about a third of the way back in the field. But as they started down the hill the pace visibly quickened and the leading group of eight managed to break away from the remainder.

On the big screen I could see that Orion's Glory was hugging the inside rail in fifth place and, to my eye, he seemed to be rather boxed in by the other horses. However, as they turned sharply into the finishing straight, the leaders tended to drift wide, allowing Declan's horse a clear run.

Even I could tell that he was moving easily as he swept past two of those ahead of him into third place, and the jockey hadn't yet lifted his whip.

At the two-furlong pole, Orion's Glory was asked for his final supreme effort, and he responded with the same turn of foot that had so excited Declan on the Limekilns gallop at Newmarket four weeks previously.

He quickly caught the two horses in front and hung on, stretching his head out to win by a neck, as Kate and I jumped up and down with excitement.

It may not have been such a convincing success as the record ten-length victory of the legendary Shergar, but a neck was more than enough. Even a short head would have been ample.

A win was a win, irrespective of the margin.

The crowd cheered enthusiastically as Orion's Glory was led triumphantly into the winner's circle right below us, with Declan smiling from ear to ear.

It was the happiest I'd ever seen him.

Eight months later, Kate and I went on a twelve-day *non-honeymoon* to the Maldives, although to a different resort to where she had been previously.

Ladbrokes had happily paid out my two thousand pounds of winnings in the Derby and I had used the money to upgrade our flights to business class. Hence, we sipped chilled champagne at forty thousand feet while I thought back to what had happened since that glorious summer's day at Epsom in June.

And much had indeed happened, especially to the Chadwick family.

Tony had been indicted for both the murder of Zoe Robertson and for attempting to dispose of her body by setting fire to his father's stables. In the face of the police recording of his disclosures to me in Declan's stable, plus the discovery of traces of Zoe's DNA in the boot of his car, he had pleaded guilty to both charges at the earliest opportunity, saving everyone the stress of a trial.

But if he'd been advised that early guilty pleas would keep the sexual abuse element of the story out of the newspapers, he'd been sadly misguided.

Two days after Tony started a life sentence behind bars, a Sunday newspaper had run a four-page detailed exposé of the Chadwick family's big secret, although from where they obtained their information I knew not. It certainly wasn't from me.

Ryan was portrayed as the main villain of the piece and, if his racehorse training business had been in trouble before the revelations, it was in complete free fall afterwards, with owners deserting him in droves. Indeed, two weeks later, the racing authority decided that he was no longer a 'fit and proper person' to hold a training licence. And then, to top off all his problems, Susan walked out on him, taking their children with her, citing the reason as the need to keep their young daughter safe from any potential sexual abuse by her own father.

The reports also depicted Oliver as a manipulative patriarch who had shamelessly tossed Zoe's life aside in order to protect his predatory golden son. Oliver's previous high standing in the racing community had stood for nothing and he was now very much *persona non grata*, even in his home town. And he too had matrimonial problems, with Maria announcing that she was suing him for divorce, and claiming half his assets.

I personally wondered if Maria had been the newspaper's source. It had to have been either her or Yvonne, maybe even both of them, and perhaps with Peter adding his share of malice as well – for a sizable fee of course.

Declan was the only Chadwick male to have emerged relatively unscathed as the reporters had correctly pointed out that he had been away riding in the United States at the time Zoe had become pregnant.

Hence, he had kept his trainer's licence and the majority of his owners, not that he hadn't personally lost perhaps the most of all of them.. In spite of being unable to have children, his marriage had been loving and strong, and Arabella's suicide would forever be a source of huge pain for him.

The Suffolk police had recently informed me officially that Declan would face no charges in relation to historic sexual abuse of a minor. The same must have been true for the other Chadwick men.

I wasn't surprised. The likelihood of a court conviction without the testimony of the victim would have been remote, although that hadn't stopped the newspapers from concluding that Ryan was as guilty as hell.

And some of the scandal had inevitably rubbed off on Declan.

'No smoke without fire,' I overheard someone say.

*Fire,* I thought.

Fire was what had brought me into this sorry saga in the first place. But it wasn't all bad. If ASW hadn't sent me to Newmarket, I would never have met Kate, and my life would have been much the poorer as a result.

Our flight touched down at Malé International Airport and, as we walked from the aircraft to the terminal, we revelled in the tropical heat, having left London in a snowstorm.

Twelve whole days together, and the nights too. How wonderful.

Kate and I had spent as much time as possible with each other over the previous eight months. With her still working full-time at Tattersalls and me still living in Neasden it was not always easy, but somehow we managed. Indeed, I had become such a familiar face at Cambridge Station that I was now greeted warmly by the railway staff.

But we had big plans.

We had just had an offer accepted on a cottage in a small village close to Stansted Airport, from which Kate could drive up the motorway to Newmarket, and I could catch the airport express direct to central London. We had high hopes that we would be moving in before the summer.

But, for now, twelve days together with no work and no travelling was total bliss.

Having cleared immigration and customs we were taken by minibus to a dock from where we climbed aboard a Twin Otter seaplane for the final leg of our journey to Halaveli, one of some twelve hundred separate Indian Ocean islands that make up the state of the Maldives.

Halaveli was the archetypal tiny desert island, rising just a few feet above the turquoise sea and ringed by white sandy beaches. But it was also a five-star boutique hotel with bars, restaurants and luxury villas set among the lines of coconut palm trees. In addition, on the south-western corner of the island, there was a raised wooden walkway stretching several hundred metres out from the shore, with more villas on each side, built on stilts above the water.

Ours was one of those, a palm-thatched oasis of paradise.

Over the next twelve days, we swam and snorkelled, went in search of whales and dolphins, and sailed on sunset cruises. We breakfasted each morning in the sunshine on our private terrace, dined each night on the beach under the stars, and made love in the afternoons.

And, on the last evening of our non-honeymoon, when we were both sure we adored each other far more than even the idyllic place in which we were staying, I put one knee down onto the soft white tropical sand and asked Kate to marry me.

# PULSE

## WITH THE STAKES SO HIGH, RACING CAN BE A DEADLY BUSINESS

Chris Rankin is a specialist in Emergency
Medicine at Cheltenham Hospital, but is a
doctor who also has health problems.

A smartly dressed man has been found unconscious
at the local racecourse and is rushed to the
hospital, where he subsequently dies. But who is
he? Where does he come from? He had no form of
identification on him, and no one claims the body.

Doctor Rankin is intrigued by the nameless dead
man, obsessed even, and starts asking questions.
However, someone doesn't want the questions
answered and will go to any lengths to prevent
it, including attempting murder. But no one else
believes that someone tried to kill Chris, leaving
the doctor no option but to discover who the
nameless man is and why he died, preferably
before following him into an early grave.

SIMON &
SCHUSTER